CONVERSATIONS WITH A PHILOSOPHER FROM ANOTHER PLANET

OTHERWORLDLY WISDOM

CONVERSATIONS WITH A PHILOSOPHER FROM ANOTHER PLANET

JOHN F. BARDI, PH.D.

THREE IN THE MORNING PRESS

Otherworldly Wisdom
CONVERSATIONS WITH A PHILOSOPHER
FROM ANOTHER PLANET
Copyright © 2017 by John Bardi, Ph.D.
THREE IN THE MORNING PRESS
P.O. Box 6556
Woodland Hills, California 91365
www.johnbardi.com

Cover art by Amy Lee Coy
Manufactured in the United States of America
Library of Congress Cataloging-in-Publication Data
Bardi, John F. (John Francis)
Conversations With A Philosopher From Another Planet/
John Bardi
1. Philosophy. 2. Psychology 3. Self-Help
I. Title.
ISBN 978-0-9863246-0-4

A MESSAGE FROM THE AUTHOR

This is a work of fiction and is meant to be entertaining. But it also aims to further advance the liberation of humanity. That is a tall order for a novel, especially one with an alien in it.

In *The Tempest* Shakespeare has Prospero say we are "such stuff as dreams are made on." I fervently hope so. To be 'made on a dream' certainly beats the alternative—being made into a completely conditioned robot.

When we make ourselves 'on a dream' we turn ourselves into a work of art, a fiction. If the dream is good art and not bad fiction, this is a good thing. The key point here is that fiction can be edited and rewritten. Bad stories can be improved. This is especially hopeful news because it means that the two greatest works of fiction in our entire history—self and society—can be edited and extensively rewritten. We can turn ourselves and our society into good art.

Now in practical terms, to say that self and society are works of art simply means that the 'stories' we live can be edited and transformed. It should come as no surprise, therefore, that an alien, who by the nature of the case is not 'made' on the fictions of Earth culture, can see better than Earthlings that our own 'stories' are what is dehumanizing and disempowering us. In this sense you could say that bad art and weak fiction are alien forces that have invaded us. It is time for a rewrite.

Any story can be rewritten. This book touches on why we are having such a hard time doing so. Briefly, it is exceedingly hard to identify our stories let alone rewrite them. We are like video game players in that our game gets more intense when we forget it is a game. But here is the rub: the intensity we gain from forgetting we are the authors of our world comes at the steep cost of *losing our editing rights*. This book is about how the loss of authorial control over the stories we are 'made on' means these often intense stories become our prison. Trapped in a bad script, we thus become unwitting victims of our own powerful, creative imaginations. Plato called this the cave.

Dear reader, the vital thing about this novel is not the arrival to our planet of an imaginary alien. It is what this imaginary alien does when he gets here—namely, to try to help us grasp that our very self and society are made out of stories. And the fact that these stories are mostly bad art and weak fiction only means we should undertake a massive rewrite. Of course, in order to rewrite these stories we first have to become aware of them. We need to re-imagine ourselves and our society in order to make them both more just, more human, and more fun.

Aliens and philosophers notwithstanding, this book is about each of us and the increasingly urgent need to liberate ourselves from the prison-cave of our socially constructed mind/world. This is the way we make the world a better place.

As for the actual writing of this book, there are many people to thank, extending all the way to childhood. Please know I thank you all. However, I do want to single out one special person for thanks, and that is my wife, Amy. She gently pushed me to start this book; once started, she warmly encouraged me to keep going; and when finished, she skillfully prepared the manuscript for publication. But perhaps best of all, she was sweet company when I wasn't working on the book!

You can't see the face of Mount Lu
when you are standing on top of it.
—*ancient Chinese proverb*

CHAPTER 1

ANGEL, ALIEN,
OR ORDINARY GUY?

How to begin this amazing tale? How can I properly describe a series of life-altering conversations I had with Philo, a music-loving philosopher who claimed to be from another planet? How might I do this without making it all seem frivolous, almost like a joke?

Towards the end of our conversations, I mentioned to Philo I was going to write this book. I fully expected him to be pleased but instead he looked troubled. Fixing me with an unsettling stare, he asked me pointedly what my purpose was. I told him I wanted to do something about the environmental and social mess we humans are creating on our planet and I thought sharing our conversations would be helpful in terms of clarifying how the situation got so dire and urgent. "I want to get people to grasp how utterly horrible the situation is," I said.

He searched my face for a moment and then said, "That is a *terrible* idea!"

Now please let me point out that he said this to me *after* I had already completed hundreds of hours of intense discussions with him. In these conversations we not only talked about every possible difficult issue I could think of, but we did so in a particular way. That is, as we talked we took special care to try to 'catch out' any of our own hidden assumptions, issues, or irrational resistances that might be operating beneath the level of our own everyday awareness to *construct* what we then would subsequently see as the spontaneous appearance of the 'real' world. In the process of doing this over many months, Philo had earned my complete and total trust—repeatedly. So when he said my idea was terrible, I did not dismiss him or get defensive. Instead, I was actually eager to hear why he thought so.

He said it was a terrible idea because the people on our planet did not need to learn how bad things are. "The problem now on your planet," he said, "is not that people don't know how bad things are, however much some of them may pretend it isn't so. It is that they don't know what to do about it."

"But there are a lot of people—perhaps a large majority—who are in denial, ignoring if not rejecting the facts," I responded. "Their collective influence is keeping those who are not in denial from taking effective action."

"It certainly *seems* that there are many people in denial," he answered, "but if you look more deeply into the denying ones, you will find that they are full of fear about what might come *after* the problems are admitted. John, the problem here is the generous presence of fear, not the stingy absence of facts. So while it certainly would be interesting to analyze how the situation got so bad, if you really want to help, that is not what is needed now."

I must have looked a bit puzzled, so he clarified. "There is a need here, John, but it is not for more bad news. We have a saying on my planet that expresses what is needed now on your planet— 'wake up and root down.' By *waking up* people on your planet will be able to see for themselves what needs to be done, and when they *root down* they will take these actions naturally, without prodding. It is like touching something that is burning hot—you don't have to be told to move your hand."

"But helping people to wake up is what I want to do," I replied.

"Yes," he said, "but you think people need to 'wake up' to how bad things are. That is decidedly not what humanity needs right now. People *do* need to wake up, but not to the horrors all around. They need to wake up to an awareness of how great humanity is. People need to be able to see how absolutely amazing the human being is. They need to realize that when they condemn others, viewing them as degraded and wretched, they are diminishing themselves and the very idea of human greatness. In doing this, they are expressing a degraded cultural imagination, not the magnificent truths of humanity. That is the reason that humanity's greatest need at this time is to re-imagine the human being."

I was processing what he said and didn't immediately respond, so he continued. "After spending almost a year here on your planet, what stands out to me most is not the environmental and social problems you keep talking about, as massive and intractable as they undeniably are. No. What strikes me most prominently is the way so many of you Earthlings, especially those who are the most informed and caring, are losing trust in your own species. Many of you humans are beginning to think humanity itself is the problem! In a spirit of triage, John, *this* is what requires immediate attention."

He looked at me with raised eyebrows, waiting for me to say something. Somewhat confused, I replied, "I guess, Philo, it seems a bit irresponsible to try to convince people how great they are when they are so misinformed and deluded about what is happening."

He smiled. "That is *exactly* the point on which so many of you progressive humans are stuck on. You act as if there is some easy-to-see objective reality that you are able to observe without distortion, but which those others do not. You think if you could just get them to see what you see, then the bad things would no longer happen."

He was right. That is exactly what I thought. Puzzling over this, I asked, "Are you saying I should not try to do anything relative to people's denial of our greatest problems—pollution, inequality, and expanding state violence? Should I just cheer and applaud all the people who are in denial about what is happening and what needs to be done?"

He looked searchingly at me. "You and I both know there are real problems. Some of them are even at a crisis level. The point is not about *whether* to do anything. It is about *what* to do. I think the best approach would be to try to help more people understand that what they consider to be concrete reality—the very solidity of the things they can touch and see—is actually more a product of their culturally conditioned imagination. In other words, the solid thing people experience as 'reality' is actually a highly malleable psychic construction erected entirely within the shared psychic space of human culture. Trust me, this is something someone from another planet can see clearly. In my time here I have heard it called 'consensus reality.' So if you want to do something to help your planet, teach people to move past consensus reality. To do this, they will have learn to identify the filters and conceptual walls that create consensus reality in the first place. Of course, since these filters and walls operate beneath the level of ordinary awareness, people are often not willing to put in the effort required to discover them. To put it in Earth terms, you humans are suffering from a cultural software problem here, not a biological hardware problem."

He paused a moment to let this sink in, then added, "Of course, as far as the mandate to clean up cultural software is concerned, the place to start is with yourself."

Ouch! That stung me in the way only the truth can sting. It hurt a lot, but I'd realized long ago that if one is serious about loving wisdom and being a philosopher, one has to seek out and embrace this 'sting' of truth. In doing so over the years I discovered that the sting of truth isn't a very deep sting and it only hurts for a few brief moments. I also experienced that if I did not resist the sting, it would rapidly dissolve into a calm of acceptance. I had also discovered that to be calm is to be clear. So I waited a moment for the sting to subside and the clarity to emerge.

When I felt the calm, I asked Philo how he had come to free himself from consensus reality.

"My experience is not particularly instructive in this area, John," he replied, "because I am not from here. That means the internal filters and hidden conceptual walls that generate the consensus script you humans take for reality do not operate in me. So I never had to free myself from human illusion and culturally constructed selective blindness because, not being a native, I never had it in the first place. As a result, it is relatively easy for me to see freshly, observing for myself the truth of how things stand. However, since you are a native, you have had to struggle against your own cultural programming. For that reason, it will be very instructive to your planetmates if you share *your* experience of coming to grasp that what you took as reality was a projected illusion. And I do think sharing our conversations will help with that."

I then asked him if he had any other advice about my book. What he then said, like so many of the zingers he threw into our conversations, struck me as profound even as it made little sense. "John," he said, "the problems *with* the cultural programming of humanity you keep mentioning had their origin *before* the emergence of humanity, so if you start with them you will be jumping *ahead* of yourself. But we'll get to that in time."

"So where might I start?" I asked, still puzzling over what he had just said.

"Begin with an honest confession," he said.

He explained: "People have been so consistently deceived by authorities for so long that they no longer trust anyone, let alone a guitar-playing philosopher with a story to tell about a most improbable visitor from another planet! To get past the increasingly thick wall of emotional and conceptual isolation people are busy building around themselves, you must start your book by being so personally honest, open, and vulnerable that such walled-in readers might be moved to make an exception for you, trusting you enough to let you tell them about our conversations."

Once again, what he was saying made sense. In fact, I resolved right then and there to follow his advice.

So in that spirit, let me begin with a personal confession.

CHAPTER 2

MY CONFESSION:
I WOULDN'T DO WHAT I AM
ASKING YOU TO DO

As Philo suggested, I want to begin with a personal confession. As your guide on this incredible adventure of ideas, I confess that I would be so completely turned off by the title, "*Conversations with a Philosopher from Another Planet*," that I seriously doubt I would read any further than that. I am certain, also, that if Philo had originally introduced himself as a "philosopher from another planet" (rather than let it slip out only after our conversations were well established), I would have avoided him and these conversations would never have happened.

So if you are having a problem with the concept and title, you are not alone. But it isn't just the two of us. Case in point: As soon as I finished the manuscript—and I was feeling very upbeat about it—I sent a few chapters to several literary agents. I was told by people with great experience in this area that I should not expect much response, if any. To my great pleasure, however, most of the agents replied quickly, and each politely requested to see the entire manuscript. With great excitement and high hopes, I sent a complete copy to each one.

I began to hear back within the week, and they all said some version of the same thing: "We want to get your manuscript published—but not in its present form." They said they anticipated the book being a best seller but I would need to make some significant changes, starting with the title.

As one agent put it in his letter to me, "Your manuscript addresses what increasing numbers of readers are most interested in reading about, which is how to live more passionately and meaningfully in the middle of their ordinary daily life." Another agent said, "This heart-centered stuff is really hot in the publishing world right now, and your manuscript is potentially incendiary, detailing in simple and practical steps how to bring passion and meaning into everyday life—into work, play, romance, politics, finances, and health!" Still another said it was possible my manuscript, being original and appearing at exactly the right time in an already established genre, could actually become a trendsetter. "If it becomes a text others will imitate," she said, "its sales potential will remain high over an extended period of time."

Then came the "but" part.

Each agent said the manuscript in its current form is stuck between science fiction and self-help, and they all agreed it "needs to go one way or the other."

But which way? Here the agents disagreed, with some urging me to science fiction and others to self-help.

The science fiction group advised me to write in some space battles and exploding starships, making the story more like *Star Wars* or *Star Trek*. "If you can make the book more appealing to the sci-fi crowd," one said, "we could market it as 'deep' science fiction, perhaps even *creating* a new sub-genre" (which he tentatively identified as 'self-help science fiction'). "Above all," he warned me, "you must cut out the philosophy crap. People just do not want to read that stuff." He said I could keep most of the conversations, which he acknowledged were "surprisingly good," but he said they had to be spiced up with space battles." He suggested I call the book, *Conversations with a Space Warrior about saving our Galaxy while becoming All We Can Be.*

The self-help agents took an opposite approach. They told me I needed to take out the sci-fi references. "No aliens" as one put it! He liked the conversation format but suggested I remake Philo into an enlightened Buddhist from a mysteriously hidden place high in the Himalayas. He suggested I have him come down, reluctantly, from an elevated place of enlightenment to help the planet in its time of greatest need. "People will believe that," he said. He suggested as a title, *Conversations with an Enlightened Master on Heart-Centered Living*.

Another agent from the self-help group asked me to substitute "angel" for "alien" and "heaven" for "another planet," calling the book, *Conversations with a Loving Angel from Heaven*. She said this would enable their marketing team to appeal to the religious readers without necessarily driving away any of the self-help crowd, which, she added, includes a lot of atheists. "Cross-over is where it's at these days," she said.

For all of their interest in the manuscript, however, they dropped me without hesitating when I tried to assure them that the conversations had really happened. I remember one agent, the one who originally seemed the most eager to represent my book, saying to me, "I can work with fiction, but I can't work with an author who cannot tell the difference between what he is making up and what is real!"

Obviously I declined to make the changes they suggested, but why? Why not simply reshape the manuscript, making it either about space battles among the stars or about heart-centered living on Earth, pretending these inspired thoughts and teachings were delivered to me directly, either from a warrior from outer space, an enlightened master from the mystical land of Shambala, or a loving angel from heaven?

I confess that this is not easy to answer. Even though what I write about actually happened, I can't say that I *know* my philosopher friend, Philo, really *is* from another planet. I can't even say that I *know* there are other inhabited planets. I further confess that Philo never took me up in a spaceship, never showed me any futuristic technology, and never revealed to me any advanced scientific secrets. In fact, we spent almost all of our time talking about humanity, society, and Earth, not aliens, spaceships, and outer space. However, what he accomplished in these conversations was to show me a different way of seeing what we were both looking at. As he put it to me, "The way a person sees everything *is* everything!"

But here is what I think is the most important thing in all of this. Even though I was then (and remain now) skeptical of Philo's alien status and intergalactic origins, I noticed that as our conversations continued, I began to feel more energy for living, more appreciation for the opportunity to walk the Earth as a human, and more joy and delight in my daily life. It sounds a bit trite, but my life began to feel less like an imposed burden and more like the gift of an unfolding adventure.

This is why I want to share with you what he shared with me, and to do so as close to the way he shared it with me as possible.

CHAPTER 3

MAKING BEEF STEW OR
WHY THESE CONVERSATIONS
ARE IMPORTANT

Even before I met Philo, I was aware that our sense of reality is filtered and shaped by sordid manipulations in our shared culture space. Individuals in both government and the advertising industry (which are becoming hard to distinguish from each other) now sometimes boast at how effective they are at this, which they call "creating reality." What they mean, of course, is that they are able to engineer our psyches to have the *perception* of reality they want us to have. In politics this is called "controlling the message."

Reflecting on this—again, before I met Philo—I kept thinking about how beef stew is made. It starts by boiling beef bones to make stock. After the bones have been boiling for a while, the scum from them rises to the top, at which point it can be spooned off.

For most of my life I have watched us busily boiling our own bones. The scum has long since risen to the top, and we need to scoop it out to make our stew palatable. But after a lifetime of pointing out the scum and the need to scoop it, the results seem abysmal. I suppose the good news is that the scum is now so prominent that it can hardly be denied any longer. The bad news, however, is that the scum—a puffed up unhealthy ugliness roiling on top of the stock—has become brazen. The scum no longer even attempts to hide itself but instead describes itself in an astounding number of ways including "too big to fail," "indispensable nation," and "American exceptionalism." Meanwhile, our planet and our world just keeps getting worse.

Now let me make an important clarification. When I say the scum has risen to the top in our society, I do not mean simply (or even primarily) that morally lesser people now have the most important jobs, having risen to the top in positions of power and profit. There is that, of course, but I am referring to something much larger and ominous. Beyond the merely personal activities and career trajectories of scumbags, if you will, the horrible, sad fact of our day is that scum ideas, scum songs, scum movies, scum business, scum religion, and scum politics—scum of every sort in every area of human endeavor—has risen to the top.

We have become a scum society.

So after a lifetime of watching the scum rise to the top and naming it as scum, calling out its existence to others, I still do not see any significant scooping. This is deeply discouraging! Indeed, before meeting Philo, I had begun to wonder whether I would ever see significant numbers of people disabusing themselves of the scum ideas and practices that have been cleverly programmed into our shared culture space and which now, increasingly, characterize our nation and our world? Torture, the loss of the very idea of privacy, unjust economics, murder by drones (targeting determined by metadata), environmental devastation, hungry children, suffering families, bad air, depleted soil—I want to scream, "This is a crisis!" It is getting to the point where if we don't start scooping the scum, we will ruin the stock!

Will we ever scoop the scum? That is the question, of course, and it is a multiple choice question with only two choices: (A) *never,* and (B) *starting right now with me.*

I greatly prefer (B). It was the answer I gave entering adulthood. Then and now, I prefer to live as if there is hope for our planet and for us. I want humanity to be a good thing, not a curse on the land.

But as much as I prefer to think that, I am faced with the brutal truth that throughout my time of life, the horrors have continued to mount and expand, with many of the things I identified more than forty years ago as problems needing to be addressed having continued to get worse, and often dramatically so. Watching this unbroken and seemingly accelerating line of social decay, I, like many others who have thought, acted, and struggled for a better world over a long period of time, have been losing hope.

Indeed, as the dark forces register victory after victory and the little resistance there is fades into twilight, it increasingly seems as if a better world will not be arriving any time soon, if at all. The most hopeful thing it seems possible to say—that things work slowly in the area of global mind change and so there may not be any significant improvement in the mid-term immediate future—seems pitifully small and inadequate. Not to put a number on it, but it easily seems as if it could be at least a few hundred more years before wisdom and goodness inspire enough numbers of us genuinely to seek a better way—and this is the hopeful way of looking at it! Of course, by then it will be too late.

Then I met Philo.

I can't say precisely what he said to me during our conversations or what I became clear about while we were having them, but in looking back I can see there was a definite 'before and after.'

Before I met Philo, as I sketched above, I was rapidly losing hope. Again, after a lifetime of struggling in earnest and often at personal expense to alert people to the dangers of what was really happening on our planet, all I could see was things continuing to get worse—and often spectacularly and dramatically so. It seemed the 'system' had learned how to colonize our shared cultural space and so was now able to create from within our psyches a completely illusory simulacrum of reality that served odious purposes. Spiritually, socially, and morally, most people were now living almost entirely within that constructed illusory culture-space. To me it seemed clear that it was simultaneously the elite manipulator's finest hour *and* suffering humanity's poorest moment.

I had lost faith in humanity.

After our conversations, however, I was a different person. In some ways I had returned to my earlier, hopeful self, but it was so much more than that! I had cultivated a working sense of myself as a legitimate being, as a King Lion of my world. I understood that I belong here, *especially* given the way I think! I also had developed a powerfully vibrant sense of the magnificence and majesty of humanity, which I was able both to recognize in myself as well as to accord to all others. I could now view the tragedies and disappointments of our shared world as temporary states, no less tragic and troubled for that, but not ultimate and permanent truths. I had my energy back. My entire outlook was different. Same body, different mind.

What brought this about? Again, I am writing this book to share that with you. In this book I try to recreate the feelings, thoughts, and experiences I had when I was having these conversations. I am inviting you into the process.

I've already confessed that for all I know, Philo may or may not be from another planet. Certainly there is nothing in this book that will prove his true origin to you one way or the other. But I can promise you this: whether or not Philo is actually from another planet, you will discover he is from another world.

Please let me introduce you to that world.

I intend to do so by sharing with you what he shared with me, which is why I am presenting our conversations to you in as close as possible to the exact form in which they occurred. Regarding this, however, I need to make an important qualification.

When I first starting talking to Philo, I had no idea who he was. I didn't even know who he *said* he was! To me he was just some strange guy who seemed to love music, especially music that was creative and improvisatory. He was, in fact, the biggest fan of my solo act, Hippy Jazz. But even so, he was still only some guy—and a strange one at that—who loved music. At first, when I was willing to talk to him so extensively, it was as if I was doing *him* a favor!

As we continued to talk, however, it gradually became clear that something special and unique was happening. There was something about Philo, something incredibly different. At first, even when I started sensing this, I just thought he was a little bit weird. An eccentric. But the things he said stuck with me, and it was the collective impact of his wisdom and insights that kept me involved.

At some point he did tell me he was visiting from another planet. By then our conversations had been well established, however, and the benefit I was deriving from them was well beyond doubt. As I remember, therefore, his revelation of his alien status did not at that time matter much to me. It wasn't that I believed him, but it wasn't that I totally didn't believe him either. It was more that, relative to what we were talking about, it didn't seem to matter.

Later, of course, I began to sense the epic significance of what was happening, so I started taking notes after each of our talks, even recording them when I could.

The problem, of course, is that I don't recall our earlier conversations nearly as well, if at all. This means that I have had to reconstruct the experience. I have tried to do so appropriately, fully attempting to capture the flow, direction, and thrust of our conversations. To do so, however, I had to rearrange the order a bit to make the conversations more coherent. As a result, the book starts out roughly one third in, right after Philo had told me he was a philosopher from another planet.

Still, as far as the core message is concerned, none of this matters because the core and substance of what he had to say is all here.

Friends, Americans, and Planetmates—I give you Philo!

Chapter 4

Love, Wisdom
and Prostitution

Given the great and beneficial impact Philo had on my thinking and on my life, you would think we had first met, philosopher to philosopher, to discuss life's greatest mysteries. You would further assume that in these discussions he had illuminated me with his great—and decidedly otherworldly—wisdom.

Your assumptions would be wrong. In actual fact, it was not anything like that. Surprisingly, neither of us knew the other was a philosopher until we had been speaking for a while—and even then it was not particularly significant. To draw an analogy, it was as if two friends from different parts of the country suddenly discovered that each had experienced a similar difficulty in getting his driver's license. Interesting—but not especially significant.

It was not philosophy but music that first brought us together!

Even though I make a living teaching philosophy at a major research university, I am not by any stretch what would today be considered a *professional* philosopher. Please understand that I do not say this to put myself down. The term "professional" is today commonly used to identify someone who is so highly skilled at something that he or she is able to make money from the practice of that skill. The companion term to "professional" is "amateur." An amateur denotes someone who exercises the same skill as the professional, but on a much lower level of mastery. In accordance with this usage, it *commends* someone to be called a "professional" while it *diminishes* them to be called an "amateur."

In this sense, I suppose I *am* a professional philosopher. That is, even though I am situated on the lower levels of the profession, I do make a living from it. But this is not what I have in mind when I deny I am a professional philosopher. In truth, I am bragging when I make that denial!

Professional philosophy today is very analytical, precise, and rigorous, and the professional philosopher works very hard to achieve advanced conceptual *clarity*. Professional philosophers are very good at this, and I can respect and admire the skill involved. So when I say I am not a professional philosopher, I am not denying or minimizing what professional philosophers do. I am merely recognizing that the clarity-seeking, analytical thing they do, fully granting its validity and usefulness, is not the *whole* of philosophy. And that *other* part of philosophy, the messy, unclear, fuzzy part having to do with wisdom and one's love for it—this other part is what I do, not the professional part.

So what is that *other* part? To love wisdom sounds good, but what does it mean in down-to-Earth terms? As someone said to me recently, when I hear you talk, it is clear that this is where the rubber meets . . . the sky!

Let me use an analogy to clarify. If you think of philosophy as a restaurant, then contemporary professional philosophy, with its emphasis on clarity and rigor, is an effective disinfectant and cleaner. Needless to say, disinfecting and cleaning is very important in a restaurant. It is essential for the restaurant be clean. As philosophers might put it, "cleanliness is a *necessary condition* for a restaurant to be successful."

Still, however *necessary* it is for a restaurant to be clean, its being clean is not in itself *sufficient* to make it a restaurant. To be successful a restaurant would have to be more than clean; it would also have to serve food. Ideally, the restaurant would serve healthy, well-prepared, delicious meals on perfectly clean dishes and linen in sparking clean surroundings. Once again, cleanliness is a *necessary condition* for a restaurant to be successful but not a *sufficient condition.*

The point is that professional philosophy works hard to keep everything clean, clear, and precise, but it does not aspire to serve any meals. And, of course, the 'meal' of philosophy is *wisdom.*

It has been said that the only things that really count in academia are the things that can be counted. Significantly, *wisdom* can't be counted. Wisdom is not clear. Wisdom is not evidence based. Wisdom isn't even conceptual. Indeed, to the analytical mind seeking clarity and precision, wisdom is embarrassingly messy, fluid, slippery, and shape-shifting. Self-awareness is a big part of wisdom, to be sure, but the awareness involved in coming to "know thyself" is more the result of a spiritual discipline than of a method of clear and precise conceptual thinking.

So let me put it this way. When I acknowledge I am not a professional philosopher, I am saying I am a cook and not a dishwasher.

But there is more. Let us return to the contrast between professional and amateur mentioned earlier, where the amateur and the professional are thought to be situated at different ends of a single continuum of skill. There is another way of looking at this contrast, one in which the defining difference between an amateur and a professional is not the *level of skill* but the *source of motivation.*

To explain: philosophy is a lot like love-making.

I mentioned this comparison to a physicist friend recently and he immediately and enthusiastically agreed. "Endless foreplay without penetration" is how he put it. He added, "Wisdom is female, and so while philosophy may be able to get her in the mood, it is only science that can get her pregnant."

When I told him that was not my meaning, and that philosophy can penetrate lovingly where science fears to tread, he called me an "amateur." He was completely correct. Of course, he did not mean it as a compliment. Regardless, I am indeed an amateur, so much so that in telling you about this exchange, I am once again bragging. Let me explain.

The word amateur comes from a root that refers to the heart. In accordance with this, an *amateur* is someone who does the activity in question out of love, unlike the *professional*, who does it for the money. Of course, a person can be paid for doing what he or she loves. This is ideal. But on the deepest level of our core motivation, we tend to do what we do either for the love or for the money. And to do something for love rather than for money is a higher and nobler motivation.

Of course, in our market-dominated society we do not generally think this way. Again, we contrast the professional and the amateur in terms of the greater skill and ability of the former. Compared to the professional, then, we think of the amateur as one with lesser, deficient skills. In accordance with this meaning, we say to the talented amateur, "You could be a professional," and we say to the untalented professional, "You are just an amateur!"

I admit that this way of thinking makes total sense when we are talking about things like plumbing or space ship design. When we need to fix our plumbing or design our spaceship, it makes sense to say, "If you want it done right, get a professional to do it."

But what about lovemaking? Are not romantic lovers by definition amateurs? Coming from the heart, with all its confusion and turbulence, their loving is curvy, spontaneous, inconsistent, frequently unpredictable, often contradictory, and always intensely feeling-based.

There are professional lovers, of course. These are the people who engage in the activities of love making not as a result of the heart's leaning but for the money. Technically speaking, one would assume they are quite skilled. Of course, in love-making, the professionals would be called prostitutes (or, with a gentler connotation, sex workers).

Now to extend this analogy to philosophy, one could say that the professionals of philosophy function as prostitutes of wisdom. As my physicist friend might have put it, they are really good at faking "wisdom orgasms."

This is why it is for me a point of pride that among the professionals of philosophy I am considered an amateur. Indeed, I am pleased to identify myself as one who on the most fundamental level philosophizes for love and not for money (in the form of tenure or career advancement).

Interestingly, the situation is completely reversed among guitar players. Having been gigging on and off since 1961, I am widely recognized by other guitar players as a pro. That is to say, the professionals of guitar, unlike the professionals of philosophy, recognize me as one of their own.

And this leads back to Philo because it was at one of my gigs that I first noticed Philo.

CHAPTER 5

WHAT DOES AN ALIEN
LOOK LIKE?

The first time I remember seeing Philo was one evening when I was playing my weekly solo gig billed as Hippy Jazz. Even though what I play is best described as background music, it is not thereby boring or low energy. I would describe it as spirited, jazz-flavored extended improvisations played at a conversation-friendly volume with a riveting rock/blues guitar sound. In other words, rather than play jazz standards, which increasing numbers of people no longer recognize, I structure my improvisations around familiar melodies from Hippy flavored popular songs from the '60s and '70s. People tend to recognize these tunes, which I then play with a flowing, easy-listening jazz treatment.

For me, the experience is more profound than it may seem. The essential requirement is for people to be able to carry on conversations while I play. Many musicians would chaff at this limitation, but I flourish within it because it lets me play in a way that matches the ebb and flow of the room energy. As a player, I try to feel the peaks and valleys of the collective conversation in order to provide the perfect soundtrack for the particular gathering of people in that room.

This isn't as prestigious, of course, as having people focus exclusively on what one is playing, but it is precisely this lack of focus that opens space for me to explore creative harmonic and melodic ideas, being able to develop them without worrying about people losing interest. In other words, because people do *not* focus exclusively on what I am playing, I am free to play more creatively, less predictably. I can take as much time as I want to develop and explore an idea.

It is much more engaging than one might think. As the various conversations in the room swell, ebb, and fade, often in noticeable synchronicity, people in the room tune in and out of what I am playing. They are constantly transitioning from passively hearing my background soundtrack to actively focusing on what I am playing, gently moving back and forth. So while everyone *hears* everything I play, they do not always *listen* to it—and even when they do, it is an in-and-out sort of listening.

Except for this one guy.

I first noticed him sitting in a far corner, obscured. For all intents and appearances, he was not paying any attention to the music, looking decidedly distracted and preoccupied. But I could tell he was listening intently. Whenever the music would take a particularly interesting turn, I could tell that he could tell. He missed nothing. So when his gaze was directed elsewhere, which it mostly was, I found myself more and more discretely looking at him.

In describing him, the word that immediately comes to mind is "nondescript."

Recently (now that I have spent quite a lot of time with him and know him quite well), he asked me to describe my first recollection of him. I described it to him with this image. If he had committed a horrible crime in the room and had immediately run away and I was asked as an eyewitness to describe him, I would have used the non-specific words "average," "normal," and "ordinary." In other words, it would be very difficult to identify him on the basis of eyewitness descriptions. His clothes, his appearance and his features were all so completely nondescript that even moments after speaking with him face-to-face one would be hard-pressed to describe him accurately.

I remember that he seemed pleased by what I said, vindicated even. Though he would not discuss with me details of how he had arrived here, I got the impression that a lot of effort was put into making his appearance completely forgettable. I later suspected that there might have been some sort of psychic cloaking mechanism at work, making it harder than normal to recall details about him, but that is only my speculation.

I realize it is hard to imagine that this amazing person who had such a positive impact on my life would be so difficult to describe, but such is the case. Even now, after all we went through and all the time we spent together, I have difficulty saying much more than that he was average height, weight, and build without any striking features and with a general demeanor that seemed to disappear into his surroundings.

But of course, it was not how he *looked* that was important. As he often remarked to me, it is most revealing (and not in a good way) how so many humans use physical appearance not only to identify one another, but also to assess and calibrate how to act towards one another. "And I'm not just referring to how Earth males act around a pretty girl," he once said.

Still, him sitting there on that first night, listening with full, devoted attention while appearing to be distracted if not completely disinterested—this is my first memory of this incredible being.

CHAPTER 6

I'M CRAZY—
HOW GREAT IS THAT?

Please know that I have thought long and hard about how to present the insights and perspective that I now have, thanks to Philo. I wish I had complete recordings of every single one of our conversations. Short of that, I wish I had carefully written notes and remembrances for each of the conversations. I have neither. But let me assure you that I retain fully the essence of what Philo had to say, and I promise that I will share all of it with you in this book.

On this topic of not having a complete set of chronological notes, I can only hope you, the reader, understands, as I previously mentioned, that I had been talking to Philo off and on for months before I realized that something special and unique was unfolding. Before then, I thought he was just a quirky music lover—brilliant but weird. As I would have put it then, "Philo may be a bit weird, but he is a whole lot wise!"

But even after I fully realized that Philo had some sort of crazy wisdom quality, I still did not keep notes. In fact, it was not until our conversations were well established in their own right and Philo let it slip out that he was not from this planet that I began to keep notes. It is these notes that form the bulk of this book.

So there is one possibly confusing thing about our conversations that I have to clarify for you as you read this book. Even though our conversations were meaningful enough and, in a wisdom sense, productive enough that they had a life of their own, it was not until our conversations were relatively well advanced that Philo told me he was from another world. Although in recounting these conversations I do my best to be chronological, in my retelling I seem to be aware of his claim to be of alien origin even before he told me. This comes about because I had to partially reconstruct our conversations, not because all along I knew or even suspected. It is just the way the story comes out.

Also, when the alien claim did slip out, it was not particularly significant in our conversations. You might expect his announcement would have been a major event to me, galvanizing me, but it was not like that at all. This is partly because I did not fully believe him at the time, but mostly because I accepted his alien claim as an appropriate metaphor for his impressive agenda-less objectivity. That is, he really did look at things with a calm, measured detachment—just the way I could imagine an alien would. So when he would mention how things were done on his planet or anything alien related, I would receive his point as a metaphor for how things might be done on a more evolved world. I mean, knowing that the actor playing Julius Caesar is not really from ancient Rome does not diminish our appreciation of Shakespeare's play. In the same spirit, I accepted the alien Philo as an imaginative philosopher speaking in terms of a brilliant extended metaphor.

Later, towards the end of our conversations, I did struggle with whether I believed his claim to be alien, but what led to this struggle was my frustration at not being able to tell others about our conversations. I feared that if I did so, the people I told would mock both of us—him for making the claim and me for not calling him out on it.

At some point I realized that I actually believed him, though I was never without crippling doubt. Mostly, though, I just rolled with the conversations.

With that in mind, I want to return to what Philo said about how we Earthlings use physical appearance as a basis for categorizing, understanding, and behaving towards others. After he first made that observation—and this was shortly after he had first told me he was visiting our planet—I found myself puzzling over what was wrong about using physical appearance as a way of identifying a person. I mean, Bill looks like Bill and Barney looks like Barney—pretty much always. I can mistake one for the other if I am limited to a partial view of one of them, but with a full frontal and up close view, there is no mistaking one for the other. To me, then, it almost seemed that Philo was criticizing us humans for relying on our eyesight to recognize each other. I was thinking this was a poorly thought out criticism on Philo's part, and I decided to call him out on it.

The next time I saw him, we chatted for a while and then I posed the question. "So how would you recognize and identify a person if not by looking at them?" I tried to ask cleanly, but I sensed a slight edge in my tone.

"Please, John," Philo replied with great concern, "I hope you do not think I am *criticizing* the use of physical appearance as a means of identifying people. Even I identify people by how they look. I notice when you play a different guitar. How much more would I notice when a different person was playing your guitar!"

"So what was your point in pointing that out," I asked a little defensively?

"No point," Philo responded lightly.

"But your point must have had a point," I insisted. "You did not just make the observation for no reason. There is a subtext. There has to be."

Philo looked at me carefully. "Fair point," he finally responded. "I guess there *is* a subtext in there." I felt immensely pleased to hear him admit that, and it illustrates one of the reasons I had kept talking to Philo even before he told me where he was from. You see, with Philo there is never any falsehood. He is radically honest in conversation, even at his own expense. There are things he would not tell me, but rather than hide them, he would tell me openly he would not (or could not) reveal them.

Of course I asked him what the subtext was. "Nothing special," he immediately responded. I didn't say anything and there was a pause where he seemed to be thinking. He continued, "It is just that I have noticed that you humans rely so exclusively on physical appearance to identify each other that you rarely recognize there are other modes of awareness."

"Like what?" I asked, still a touch defensively.

He responded strangely, which he often did. He didn't say anything at first but instead closed his eyes while looking directly at me. After a moment he opened his eyes and, with just the hint of a smile, said, "Like that."

"Like *what*?" I demanded, feeling confused and thus a little edgy.

"Like what I just did," he answered, smiling even more broadly. "And the fact that I did it means that in principle anyone can do it."

"Do *what*?" I demanded, feeling my frustration beginning to mount to where it started to shade into anger.

Philo was unfazed. "You sense the energy of a person's vibe," he replied calmly. "There is a lot of information to be had from the vibe."

"Now you are getting all mystical on me," I replied, feeling disappointment and a looming loss of interest in the topic.

He cocked his head as he looked at me quizzically. "You say that as if reading vibes is something to be shunned . . . thereby establishing my point."

"*What* is your point?" I pressed, making no attempt to contain my frustration. "You seem to be saying to me that you can just vibe out a person, that you can actually *see* and identify them just as a result of sensing their vibe."

"No," he replied as his smile grew wider. "I'm saying that you and all humans can see way more deeply than you normally do. In fact, most of you *do* sense vibes from time to time. It is just that you don't fully believe you can do so, and so you do not practice it, meaning you tend not to get better at it. Also, when you do get information from reading a vibe, you generally attribute it to something else—a newly recalled memory, a sudden logical connection, or something mystical you call intuition. Some of you humans even attribute the information you get from reading a vibe to the activity of a disincarnate spirit whispering to them. And if this were not enough of a distraction already, the fact that so many humans mask themselves when someone else 'vibes' them, immediately and even fervently denying what someone who *has* read their vibe can see. Of course, this makes the process of reading vibes much more difficult than it otherwise actually is. You see, routine false denials do not help the vibe reader to calibrate his readings and thus get better at it, especially when the most fervent denials are routinely directed at the most accurate readings."

I sat there stunned, feeling challenged and confused, the way one does when something bedrock in one's world is being denied. "Look," he said, noting my response, "you are taking this too deeply. Let me ask you, how can you tell whether it is Jimi Hendrix playing the national anthem and not John Philip Sousa?"

"It is pretty obvious," I said, exasperated. "They *sound* completely different!"

"Indeed," he said with satisfaction. "There is your answer. You do not have to *see* to be able to tell. In fact, if Hendrix was in a perfect Sousa disguise, you would still know it was Hendrix."

"But that is too obvious," I protested.

"Ok, let me deepen it. I happen to know you love Jimi's playing, and I've heard some nice jazzy versions slip into your set. But let me ask you, do you ever try to sound just like him?"

"I do."

"Do people who are listening with their eyes closed ever mistake you for him?"

"They do not."

"Again, John, there is your answer."

I was finding this all deeply frustrating and wildly off the point, so I cut right to the point. "Philo, you are claiming to have just read my vibe. OK, so what did you read?"

Philo seemed perfectly at ease as he replied. "Well, John, you are a complex person and your vibe is of course very rich and complex. Still, I could sense that you were feeling somewhat protective of humanity. You perceived me as attacking humanity, criticizing it for its shallowness and materialism. And like the good human you are, you felt a need to defend your species."

He was right. I would not have put it that way, but he certainly had correctly described the general contours of what I was feeling. I didn't know what to say. There was a long moment of silence. Finally, feeling a need to say something, I reverted back to a familiar academic prejudice: "All this talk about vibes sounds like crazy talk to me."

Philo leaned back looking at me and then smiled in a sort of patronizing amusement. "Here we go," he said, "a classic case of the standard human response to something new and different—that is, to label it as either crazy or evil." He sighed and looked up and away, saying wistfully, "I suppose I should be thankful you are labeling me the one and not the other."

There was a period of focused silence between us as we looked at each other. He seemed relaxed and even slightly amused by what was transpiring while I felt exposed, like a rat on a treadmill being watched by someone in a white coat holding a clipboard. Finally he took a deep breath and broke the increasingly heavy silence.

"John, I came here at great risk and expense, and I did so for one reason only—because humans are so completely and totally amazing. In all of inhabited space, they are the gifted species. I can tell you there is much jealousy among certain elements in outer space regarding the unlimited potential of humanity, a feeling that the great talents and abilities of humans make them dangerous. To make one of your analogies, it is as if you humans discovered that monkeys not only could sing opera far better than the best of humans but could also develop and expand calculus far more extensively than the most brilliant mathematicians. Such a thing would not sit well with the Pavarottis and Newtons of your world."

"But we have made our planet into such a mess," I protested. "How can there be jealousy about us?"

A look of trouble, very deep trouble, flashed on Philo's face. Then, as if he had caught himself, the troubled look passed. "I don't want to talk about that right now," he said, "but let me just say that the state of your planet, which seems to disprove human magnificence and potential, actually reveals it. Earth people are suffering from something deeply unfair and horrible."

"That doesn't make any sense at all," I snapped.

Philo still looked troubled. "You're right," he finally said. "It doesn't. Let me put it this way, and then I do not want to talk about it further. Maybe later I will say more, but for right now this will be the only thing I say. You teach at a university. Imagine that someone had a pill that provided perfect learning overnight. How might educators respond?"

"They would oppose it, certainly," I replied immediately. Such a thing would render the entire educational system obsolete."

"Precisely," he said, as if he had just established something important.

CHAPTER 7

ARE WE ADEQUATE
TO UNDERSTAND REALITY?

It was an entire week before I saw Philo again. I'm sure I did something other than simply puzzle and ponder what he had said about vibes and human potential, but in looking back on that week, the only thing I recall is thinking about those things. This was at a time when I would see him at my gigs or not at all. He didn't always come to my gigs, especially at first, but when he did, he always sat in an obscured spot and never tried to catch my eye. In fact, unless I walked up to him and initiated a conversation, you would have no way of telling that we had spoken before.

I was the one who initiated our conversations, and since it was also usually the case that I had been thinking about our *previous* conversation during the interim, I was the one who set the topic. I would typically initiate our current conversation by referring back to some point or issue having to do with our previous one.

That was certainly the case when, during my last set, I saw Philo sitting by himself in the back corner. As soon as I finished, I hustled over to him. After a brief welcome in which he generously appreciated my playing, I initiated the following exchange.

"Philo, I've been thinking about what we talked about last time and your Jimi Hendrix example, and I think I grasp what you mean about reading vibes. It isn't as 'out there' as I pretended last time. In fact, when I am playing music with others, I am reading vibes constantly. Indeed, to be able to do so is part of what it means to be a musician. Most musicians will tell you that it matters more *who* you are playing with than *what* you are playing."

Philo smiled. "That is good, John."

"No, wait, there is more. I can tell when the person I am playing with is active and present with the music, being at the cutting edge of creativity, or if the person is just sliding automatically on past patterns. Moreover, when musicians are actually present, it is not knowledge or certainty that guides them in the moment but trust and courage. Also, I can usually tell when a musician goes automatic, beginning to coast on what he or she knows rather than engaging and expressing what they are feeling in the moment."

Philo looked pleased in a relaxed sort of way.

"So your Jimi Hendrix point got me thinking about *reality*," I continued. At this Philo suddenly perked up, taking on an aura of increased focus. "Here is what I mean," I said. "Given that we can tell if it is Jimi or not even with our eyes closed, reality has to be such that we *can* do that sort of thing. In other words, this vibes thing is a point about *reality*, not just about Jimi."

Philo nodded his head in assent but didn't say anything. I continued.

"I mean, somebody can tell you that they're not upset but you can tell they are. It's not that you have facts or evidence. It's more that you're seeing with your eyes closed."

Philo arched an eyebrow. "And?" he said, inviting me to continue.

"Ok, so here is my point. If you believe it is not possible to see with your eyes closed then you're not likely to try to do it. In other words, it is not *just* reality that limits what is possible, it's also what we see or fail to see that sets limits. This brings us to how culture shapes our perception of reality. More specifically, culture sets the limits of what people believe and therefore sets limits on their ability to engage reality directly. So, Philo, even though I am saturated with contemporary earth culture and psychologically constructed by it, I want to bypass Earth culture in my psyche. To that end, I want you to tell me about reality because there are a lot of things I'm not seeing that I don't even know I'm not seeing."

He sat there for some long moments, looking increasingly pleased. "Well," he said finally, "look who is getting all mystical now."

Although Philo looked pleased, he also seemed a bit troubled. It seemed to me at the time—and I now know this to be true—that he had some sort of deep and terrible secret that he wanted to share with me but which for some reason he was limited from doing so. So as I watched, Philo seemed to focus internally, almost as if he were having an internal debate.

I remember noting this because retreating into internal focus was not what I was used to with him. More than anyone else I know, Philo always seemed attentive to his surroundings. So this state of heightened inner focus stood in marked contrast to what I was expecting. It not only caught my attention but also highlighted how he normally was and what I was used to with him.

Then, in a flash, he came out of it and placed his full attention back on me. "So you want me to tell you about reality," he said, his subtly amused expression returning. His gaze did get a little distant when he repeated my last thought out loud—"You probably won't get served tea on a world in which people believe it's not possible to boil water." Then he returned to me with full focus, "That is good, John. Really good." He seemed satisfied.

"Moving along here," I said a little impatiently. "I'm asking you to tell me about how the world is such that we can see by means of vibes and feelings." He looked at me intently before replying. He often did that, and I always found it unsettling, and this time more so than ever. But then he relaxed and his enigmatic smile—what I could call his 'Mona Lisa look'—returned. He said, "There is an Earth saying that seems to apply here: In the valley of the blind, the one-eyed person is king. So you are asking me to use my one eye to describe reality to you." His right eyebrow arched up slightly.

"Don't patronize me," I replied sharply.

He seemed amused. "Perish the thought," he said. "I was trying to be self-effacing, not superior." He sat back expansively, "If only my friends could see me now." He gazed up thoughtfully. "You see, John, on my own planet I am not thought to be particularly good at reading vibes. You could say that in the context of the culture of my people, I am a one-eyed person in the valley of those who have Superman's x-ray vision."

He often used popular culture references to clarify his points, making him seem decidedly not of alien origin.

He continued. "Still, in this as with all skills, there is the question of adequacy. A person could not understand advanced math concepts without an adequate math background. So, John, please accept that I am not belittling you but only making a simple observation that you, a teacher, should understand. You would need to be adequate to enter into these areas, but please do not take that as a diminishment of you or of humanity. Once again, let me point out that in this and other related areas, the potential capacity of human beings is off the charts."

"Fair enough," I said, noting stubborn traces of my own defensiveness. "But as a teacher, if someone without an adequate background but with, as you put it, potential capacity—if such a person asked me a question, I would not dismiss them because of their inadequacy. I would guide them to grasp how they might acquire the adequacy."

"And fair enough back to you," he replied good-naturedly. "To clarify, am I correct to conclude that you are asking me to help you become adequate to understanding what I might say about the larger nature of reality? Right?"

"That is entirely correct," I responded. Perhaps it was the way he generally looked at me before speaking, but I had the strongest feeling that he had some special knowledge and understanding beyond the conventional. No, that is too strong. I had the strongest feeling that he *might* have knowledge and understanding beyond the conventional. I was curious to find out. I noticed that he seemed pleased.

"That is quite impressively admirable, John," he said. "You've heard the Zen story about the cup being so full it could not take any more tea. Kudos to you for emptying your cup. In fact, I read one of your essays in which you challenged the common notion that when Socrates would say, as he so frequently did, that he did *not* know, he was being ironic, simply setting up the person for a fall. But as you put it in your clever, thoughtful essay, Socrates was bragging when he claimed not to know! You point out that it is an advanced accomplishment of consciousness to attain a state of not-knowing. Do you remember that?"

"Quite well," I responded. I have to admit that I was both flattered and impressed.

"Do you know what this means?" He looked at me inquisitively.

"I hope it means you are going to stop beating around the bush and tell me how to prepare myself to be adequate to understanding the deeper dimensions of reality."

Philo immediately broke into a rollicking laugh. "Indeed it does. There is no stopping a philosopher who has active curiosity and is on a wisdom hunt."

CHAPTER 8

CASTLES, TENTS,
ANIMALS, AND MINDS

To become adequate to understand the deeper aspects of reality—this was all I could think about for an entire week. I hoped Philo would come to my next gig, of course, but I also kept hoping I would run into him somewhere on the street. I even took more walks than usual hoping to see him. Towards the end of the week I began to worry that he would not come at all, that I might never see him again. As he said, I was a hungry philosopher on a wisdom hunt.

The next gig was a downer. There were fewer people than usual in the wonderfully restored Civil War barn where I played—the Battlefield Brew Works. Normally this would not bother me as it would afford me the opportunity to become even more introspective—and daring—in my playing. I remembered one of my earliest shows. There were only a few people there, and a rock musician acquaintance stopped by. After the set he said to me, "Before I heard your Hippy Jazz, I figured you called it Hippy because you are a peace and love guy, but I had no idea why you called it Jazz. Now I do. You call it Jazz because you don't have to follow anything—not the progression, not the chord, not even good taste."

I have to admit that as a musician who challenges convention and overrides boundaries, I often think that some people simply do not get it. This night was like that. I was perhaps a little more 'out there' in my playing, and the few people there were not listening anyway.

And Philo was not among them. I played well enough—even wonderfully—but I was feeling distraught about his not being there. Then, just before I finished for the night, I saw him. He was hidden in a different corner and, as usual, appearing to anyone who might be watching that he had no interest either in me or in the music I was playing.

As soon as I finished, I rushed to his table. The barn was almost empty and we were safely isolated. He smiled as I approached and once I made my greeting, he said, "Quite experimental tonight. Most engaging. My favorite."

I thanked him and moved immediately to the issue. "Tell me about reality so I can see where I need to boost my adequacy."

"Reality is like music," he said without his usual pause.

"In what way?" I asked, perhaps a little too eagerly. He noted my urgency.

"Hmm," he mused, smiling and looking above, almost as if he was teasing me. Then he summoned a single-pointed focus and said, "When you play music—like you did tonight—and creatively explore harmonic extensions, fitting together elements that don't normally exist together, adding 9ths, 11ths, and 13ths to your melodies, then altering them, flatting and sharping different extended notes, even exploring flat-five substitutes—when you do this and it works, it is still never quite what you are aiming at. You get closer, ever closer, but even as you do, the rim of possibility always just expands into the far horizon. Right?"

I was stunned, not only by the musical accuracy of his remark but also by the exquisite poetry of it. "Quite so," I said, reflecting on how accurately he had said it. "I call what you are referring to as the 'agony of art.' By that I mean that the actual work of art or performance always has *less* luster and impact than it does in the artistic vision of the artist or performer. This gap is agony to the artist. He or she is always trying to close the gap, but the gap always dances a few steps ahead."

"Reality is like that," he said. Absorbing this, I was not sure what to say. My mind was racing with the comparison. He continued. "To put it differently, there is every reason to accept that reality is larger, more complex, more mysterious, and more flat-out amazing than even our most advanced ideas can recognize or accommodate. Agreed?"

"Yes, absolutely," I replied, feeling I completely understood what he was saying. It was my constant beef with my academic colleagues that they often seemed to adopt an attitude of non-wonder, assuming that most of what could be discovered had already been discovered, leaving only details to mop up.

He looked at me with his look and smiled his enigmatic smile. It occurred to me that if this was being filmed, he would be hailed as a most expressive actor. The economy of his facial expressions was astounding. "Well, John, not to quibble, but perhaps the word 'absolutely' is not the ideal word to use in this context. After all, to be absolute and certain cuts off inquiry, and here we are just starting out on our inquiry. Perhaps 'provisionally' or 'probably' would be better terms in this context."

"Absolutely, in a provisional and probable sense," I smiled.

He smiled back. "I love humans," he said with a great feeling of sincerity. "Such—how do you say it on Earth—such smart asses. I love it. Now, John, I mention the perils of the absolute because there are two distinct ways to approach a deeper understanding of reality. The first is to *limit* what one is willing to admit about reality to things that fit or cohere with what one already knows. A helpful image is to think of human conceptual understanding as a brick building, one that is being continually constructed and expanded. That is, one is always adding bricks to the expanding building, expanding the original structure. Conversely, one rarely takes bricks away, and ideally would never do so. This is the normal way on

Earth. Another day at the office and another brick in the wall. This is the way of both religion and science, building up as they do a large and solid wall of thought-created understanding."

"Except for when the building collapses," I added.

"Except for when the building collapses," he repeated approvingly. "While I love the smart-ass quality of that observation, it brings up another topic entirely. Let's just focus on the construction stage for now."

"So what is the other way?" I asked. "Building up a wall of understanding brick by brick sounds pretty solid. Build, build, build, and more build—until there is a partial collapse, which happens every now and then, leading to more building. Is there another way?"

"Yes there is. The other way to approach a deeper understanding of reality is to be looser with what one thinks one already knows, being willing to adjust, modify, and even abandon what one thinks one knows, making it easier to fit with what one is beginning to discover and see. Here the metaphor of building a brick wall of knowledge does not illuminate the process. We have to change the metaphor. The metaphor for this other approach is that knowledge is more like a tent in a campsite than a solid and rooted brick building."

This seemed deeply profound, and I was fully engaged. Philo continued, "A tent *forms* itself to the lay of the land where a brick building *imposes* itself. This is what a good musician does, making a tent out of the melody rather than a brick building. This is what you were doing tonight."

I felt both understood and complimented. Glowing, I replied, "We need more tents and fewer brick buildings on Earth, don't you think?"

"Yes and no. Yes because both science and religion on your planet are brick buildings and so radical inquiry is naturally limited by their solid walls. I might add that from my point of view, it is such an earth thing to see science and religion at war, like two castles. It would be better to re-house each of them in tents."

"Nicely put."

"But also no, John. No because both buildings *and* tents are useful in a journey of inquiry. Sometimes solidity is beneficial, sometimes flexibility. The task at hand is not to aim for one or the other but to learn how to benefit from both, knowing when to hunker down in a castle and when to venture forward in a tent."

I was struck by how profound this was, but I was not entirely at peace with having both castles and tents. "Philo, from my perspective, teaching at a university, I often feel trapped behind brick walls. I feel it is necessary to tear many of them down. This is where Socrates' bragging about 'not-knowing' comes in. To be able *not* to know is to be able to see beyond the limits of what one knows. It is to be able to leave the castle and walk in the meadow, forest, and stream."

Philo looked at me with appreciation and I felt a warm glow inside. Then he chuckled. "There is no doubt, John, that you are a tent guy. I wouldn't be surprised if you have been called an intellectual gypsy, even a vagrant of the mind. Because you leave the windows and doors open, you are being constantly reprimanded."

Philo was right. I have often been called an intellectual gypsy and a conceptual vagrant—and never as a compliment.

Just then I noticed that we were the last people left and the staff was preparing to close. We did not have much time left.

"I am curious, Philo, what this wonderful metaphor has to do with my becoming adequate to understanding some of the larger aspects of reality. Are you saying that as a tent guy I need to build a castle? But in a castle I can't just take a leak, I have to go to a specific room dedicated to that purpose, which I'm feeling an increasing need to do right now."

Philo smiled in warm appreciation. "I can only hope, John, you appreciate the magnificence of your situation, being both an animal and a philosopher. The animal wants to urinate and the philosopher wants to understand. You are wonderfully balancing the two, and that is what is needed with castles and tents. The philosopher/animal combination is eminently enjoyable, and never more so than in the urinal. So before you go, let me give you something to think about."

"Please do—but quickly. The animal is in danger of breaking his strict house training if he waits much longer."

Philo looked happy. "Let me say this quickly. No, John, you do not need to build a castle of understanding. That is not at all what I mean by adequacy. You will always have castles and tents just as you will always have the animal and the mind. Adequacy does not mean having more of one and less of the other. It means *purifying your consciousness* so that you will see more clearly when to stay behind the walls and when to venture forth with a tent. That is how you cultivate adequacy."

I was literally bouncing up and down with the pressing need to relieve myself. "*That,* Philo, is something I can take with me to the urinal. The animal leaves now, but the mind will return." I left for the toilet, feeling excited and fully engaged, thinking about purifying consciousness. How intriguing.

While relieving myself, I thought about where to invite Philo to continue our conversation. I came up with three options and thought I would let him choose. I couldn't wait to hear about how to purify my consciousness! The very concept made total sense to me.

When I came out of the bathroom, Philo was gone.

CHAPTER 9

PURIFYING CONSCIOUSNESS

It was another long and agonizing week of waiting to see Philo again. This time, though, as eager and impatient as I was, I was not worried that I would not see him again. I mean, what sort of philosopher could drop a bomb like *purifying consciousness* and then disappear. Where is the purity in that!

Finally, the day of my gig came, and it seemed to me my playing had an extra spunk to it. It was more energized somehow. I would like to say it was more purified, but that seems a bit much. At any rate, thankfully, just as I started my last set, I saw Philo, looking as unlisteningly detached as ever. I played with intensity, doing my best for him, trying to play in a spaced out way. As soon as I was done I hustled over to his table.

"I think we were talking about purifying consciousness," I said, pulling up a chair.

"Indeed we were, but first let me say that, once again, I particularly enjoyed your playing tonight."

"It was more spacey than usual."

Philo smiled. "It just brings me closer to home."

"Philo, I've been thinking about our conversation last week and I want to say that most of the thinkers and academics I know would deny that we can get beyond our knowledge. In terms of our imagery from last week, they would say we are trapped—even imprisoned—in our castles of understanding. We can open a window occasionally or even stand on the roof, but that is about it. They would firmly assert that we are necessarily limited to the constructs and projections of our knowing."

Philo looked at me impassively. "Your point?" he asked.

"My point is that the best minds I know would deny the very thing you are proposing, namely to venture forth from our castles of understanding, searching about the constructs and projections of our knowing, seeing them but not using them to see."

Philo repeated my last phrase with a spacey look in his eyes. "Seeing them but not using them to see," he said, pondering the words. "Nicely put, yes. *Very* nicely put. But I am asking you what your point is regarding this observation about what your colleagues might think about what I am saying."

"They will flatly deny the possibility of what you propose—that is my point!" I said this pointedly, almost like a slap, feeling ever so slightly defensive of my academic colleagues.

Philo seemed to be enjoying himself. "Well," he said, pretending to seem confused by what I was saying, "let me ask you if these people you know make that point themselves—namely, that we cannot get beyond the constructs and projections of our knowing."

"They do," I replied firmly. "Some of them do so repeatedly and at every opportunity. They are generally targeting those who make religious claims or express belief in things for which there is no hard empirical evidence."

"Indeed," Philo said, fully engaged. "But let me ask you this. Does not their very claim that we cannot get beyond how we see in order to see—doesn't this very claim suffer from what we call on my planet a self-reflexive fallacy? That is to say, isn't the point they are making refuted by the point they are making?"

"I'm not sure I follow you, Philo," I said, feeling overwhelmed.

"OK," he said, "let me put it this way. If one can only see in accordance with the way one is constructed to see, how is it possible for one to have a sense of that? To have a sense of that, one has to be able to step back from the way one sees in order to be able to observe the way one sees. And to step back like that, John, is something decidedly different than simply seeing the way one sees. Otherwise, the point under discussion here would simply be an extension of these very constructs and projections and the claim being made would not have the truth value it pretends to have. It is like wearing red tinted glasses that make everything one looks at take on a red hue. In order to know that, one has to be able to take the glasses off."

"I see what you are getting at, Philo, but I think they would say they are just observing, taking note of how things are."

"Ok," he said, "let me ask it this way. You say they are just observing. Is their observation taken from the castle ramparts, so to speak, or are they standing apart from the castle and observing its battlements?"

"The later, definitely. They are standing apart to observe."

"Then the fact of their observation contradicts the content of it," Philo said with amusement. "That is, if they can stand apart from the castle to observe that they are stuck inside of it, then it becomes possible not to be stuck inside of it."

I was silent. This was such a good point, such a sharp observation, that I was not sure what to say. Philo continued.

"The question then is which we will privilege—what they *say* cannot be done . . . or what they actually *do* in order to be able to say it. There is a saying on my planet I have always liked that applies here: *You can't see the glory of a spaceship flying low in the sky when you are the one flying it.* The point is, John, they can't have it both ways. If they can stand aside to see, then it can't be that what they see when they stand aside is that it is not possible to stand aside."

I continued to ponder what he was saying. It seemed a very large point, one that applies to all sorts of things. For example, when a person says that everything we do is causally determined, is that observation itself causally determined? If so, then it does not have truth value. It is merely a causally determined utterance. To have truth-value, a statement cannot be causally determined. It has to be the result of an ability to stand back and freely observe. In this sense, the ability to recognize strict determinism would seem to be incompatible with the assertion of it.

As my mind was spinning, Philo again spoke. "But, John, you are not stuck on that. You have what I would call the mystical grasp. As Hamlet said to his friend, Horatio," and Philo was smiling when he said this, "'There are more things in heaven and earth than are dreamt of in your philosophy.'"

"Nice allusion, Philo. And very true."

"So let's move past, dare I say it, that silly objection and focus instead on what a purified consciousness would look like."

"Yes, please let's do." I felt a bit humbled, but not in the slightest deterred. This was exciting.

"Ok, so let me direct our shared examination of a purified consciousness by observing that there are two general directions human consciousness can move in, towards the positive or towards the negative."

"This sounds a bit superficial, Philo."

"How so?"

"You know, positive thinking and all that. Be positive. Don't be negative. That sort of thing."

Philo chuckled. "That is indeed superficial, but it is not at all what I am trying to say to you. Try to hold back on your assessment of the superficiality of what I am saying until I say it." He said this without any emotional charge. He could have been telling someone who had asked for directions to stay in the left lane at the light.

"That I will do," I said. Then I added, "I have to say, though, that I really do not want to hear a positive thinking rap."

Philo looked at me with amusement. "John," he said in a theatric voice, "please do your best to be a little more positive here." We both laughed.

"Ok," I spoke up before Philo could resume, "before you develop the idea of everything being either positive or negative, what about the fact that people have different definitions and understandings of what is positive and negative? To one person my music is a cacophonous jumble; to another it is an exquisitely imaginative work of art. Your terrorist is my freedom fighter. The farmer needs rain, the person on vacation prays for a sunny day."

"Point well taken, John, but I am not talking *content* here."

I expressed dismay. "You want to talk about positive and negative without mentioning anything actually positive or negative?" I asked.

"Precisely," Philo replied without hesitation. "I want to direct your attention to the general mental structure of something being perceived as positive, no matter what that may be, and also to the completely different mental structure of something being perceived as negative, no matter what that may be."

"I'm not sure what you are getting at," I said, feeling uncertain of where this was going. "I assumed that since we are talking about purifying consciousness, you would be advocating certain positive thoughts and ideas and attempting to eliminate the negative ones."

"That is a reasonable assumption, John, especially given the current state of American smiley-face consciousness. But that is not my drift at all. I am probing more into the internal psychological structure of the mental apparatus that perceives things as positive and negative."

"Please continue," I said, feeling both confused and intrigued. I noted how focused Philo seemed, and how much of a pleasant state of mind he seemed to be in. He was enjoying this.

"OK," he continued, "when we stand back and do not assess what we think is positive or negative but simply observe how what is perceived as positive and negative functions in our awareness, I think we can make this general observation: The positive direction is usually marked by an internal sense of *idealism*; the negative direction is usually marked by an internal sense of *fear*. I'm not saying people who make a positive observation are idealists or those who make a negative observation are afraid. I am saying that, structurally, the positive perception usually has factored into it more of what can be called an ideal while the negative perception is much closer to what can be called a fear."

"I can see that."

"Can you? Are you sure, John? This is a profound point I am making, not one that is widely grasped among Earth humans. This point is certainly not a given in your world." Philo looked concerned.

"I really do think I grasp it, Philo. Beneath our attitudes, judgments, and endeavors there will be something deeper, usually hidden, that is driving them. At the deepest level—again, which is almost always hidden—there will either be a sort of curiosity or wonder or . . . there will be a sort of fear."000

Philo looked pleased. "Very good! You do have it. Now given this very loose observation, here is what I want to say about it. Generally speaking, there is truth on *both* sides. That is, a positive person driven by an ideal can and often does speak a truth. Not always, but often. Similarly, a negative person driven by fear can and often does also speak a truth—not always, but often."

I must have looked confused because Philo continued. "Now let's ignore for now delusional people fantasizing, whether positive or negative. Let's ignore both 'everything happens for a reason' and 'nothing ever works out.' Let's focus instead on the things, positive and negative, that people say when, in full integrity and honesty, they are trying to put into words what they are seeing. My point is that both the people speaking on the basis of ideals *and* the people speaking on the basis of fear can, and often do, speak truth. They make accurate observations. In other words, reality, from the human point of view, is both positive and negative."

"I think I am getting this, Philo."

"Good. This is important. There is a tendency in your world today to psychologize truth claims. For example, a person full of fear might express concern about something, and the response often is to dismiss their claim as being the result of fear. Certainly it frequently happens that people with deep fear imagine and self-create scenarios based on their projections. But—and this is so important—often a goodly portion of what they fear is rooted in truth."

I was rolling along with what Philo was saying. "That seems especially true today" I said. "Things are looking bad, and often when I give voice to the bad things and trends I see, people dismiss me as being negative. The truth is, however, that I do have fear. I am truly and deeply afraid that if as a nation, a people, and a species we continue on the path we are on, we will eventually get to where it leads. I am afraid of that."

"And right you should be. Standing back as a deep outsider, I would observe that it is most unfortunate that today among those who build their home of understanding on fear will often deny the insights of those who base their home of understanding on hope, trust and ideals. The opposite is true as well. Those who build their home of understanding on hope, trust, and ideals tend to deny that there is any basis for fear and thus reject the accurate observations and correct claims of those who are fear based."

"This all seems correct to me, Philo, but I still don't see what this has to do with purifying consciousness."

"Here is the connection. There is both a positive and a negative aspect to human experience. Given this, purifying consciousness does *not* mean abandoning one for the other, accepting one and denying the other. Purifying consciousness means accepting both, but purifying each, removing from both all delusions, exaggerations, and fantasy projections!"

"I am grasping this, Philo, but through a glass darkly. Please continue to clarify."

"You could say, John, that there is an occupational hazard to both of the poles, the positive and the negative. The occupational hazard of spending most of one's awareness on the positive pole of experience is to be correspondingly ignorant of the negative pole, thereby becoming liable to fall into a posture of denying that bad things are really and truly bad. Conversely, the occupational hazard of spending most of one's awareness on the negative pole of experience is to be correspondingly ignorant of the positive pole, thereby becoming liable to fall into a posture of denying that good things are really and truly good."

"Again, Philo, I can see this, but I am not clear what the point is."

Philo looked pleased. "The point, John, is that a purified consciousness will not be caught in this bi-polar trap, floating between fantasized, unrealistic ideals on the one side, and strong habits of maximizing negativity and generating fear on the other."

Suddenly the wisdom light came on for me. It was like lightning struck in my mind. "I think I get it. Purifying consciousness does not entail believing in good or denying the bad, or the opposite, believing in bad and denying good, or any combination of the two. It involves completely accepting both, though in a purified form."

"Yes, John, and to accept both, one must learn how to refine and perfect one's awareness. That means learning to open to goodness, but it also means learning to work with negativity. Both are necessary, and this balanced dual focus is required from everyone, regardless of whether he or she is primarily positive or negative. Of course, any given person at any given time might have an imbalance and thus would need to work more on one end or the other, but either way, it is the *balance* marks a purified consciousness. This is because—and this is so important—human reality and experience is *both* positive and negative."

I felt illuminated and blurted out without thinking, "What is bad is bad and what is good is good, and Philo wants the twain to meet."

Philo smiled broadly. "You nail it! Of course, once again, this purification needs to be done in a context that is not distorted by illusion, fantasy, or abnormal fear patterns."

"That's the hard part," I said.

"Indeed."

CHAPTER 10

THE RIGHT AND WRONG
OF GOOD AND BAD

W hat Philo had said about purifying consciousness really hit me as significant, and it was for me personally especially clarifying. Even before Philo and I had this talk, I had come to the awareness that, to speak in the broadest of generalizations, there were two types of people in the world—those who were really skilled at detecting the good in a thing, situation, or person, and those who were really skilled at detecting the flaws in the same thing, situation, or person.

Personally, I was always more of the first type, the type who could see the good in things, situations, and people. In fact, I had a special gift at being able to see the potential good in others, an ability that serves me extremely well in my teaching. More so than most, I can somehow see what a student could be good at. This has little to do with the student's scores or grades or the quality of his or her performance in school. I could see through all of that, often with no evidence, to what the student really loved and thus had the capacity to excel at.

But if this capacity to see the potential good served me well in teaching, it did not serve me so well in relationships, both romantic and musical. To use music as an example, I typically would meet another musician and clearly see what he or she was capable of, how he or she could merge with what I was doing, and how the hidden gift of the person would blossom into magnificence if given the opportunity. I was seeing potential, and I think on that level my vision was generally entirely correct.

How things worked out in reality, however, was often quite different. It took me years of frustrating failure to realize that 'potential' and 'actual' are entirely different states, and that the existence of the former does not in itself mean the emergence of the later. Something else was going on, something darker than mere potential, and something that, all things being equal, consistently trumped potential.

For some time, therefore, I had been paying attention to the downside of my habit of noticing potential good. I was slowly coming to grasp that the greatest light also necessarily casts the darkest shadow.

I had noticed that people who were quick and accurate at pointing out flaws would often describe themselves as perfectionists. I remember once working for days at making my efficiency apartment perfect. I painted, decorated, and moved things around until—voila!—the apartment was perfect. I invited some friends over to see the perfection I had achieved. One friend came in and, in a most pleasing manner, immediately picked out a number of tiny flaws—a picture was a little off center, some books on a shelf were unbalanced, there was a chip in the table. I remember being struck by the incredible accuracy of her observations but also at how quickly she noted them. She was really good! It was as if she had a cheat sheet.

But the part that stood out the most was what she said when I asked her if she saw anything she liked. She seemed a bit put off and replied, "Hey, I am a *perfectionist,* so if you don't want me to notice these things, don't tell me they are perfect."

I have thought about that brief exchange for years. Her critical observations were entirely correct, and she had offered them in a helpful way, not in a spirit of criticism. Still, something did not seem quite right about her calling herself a perfectionist. Years later I had a breakthrough of understanding. What she was, I suddenly realized, was an *imperfectionist.* That is, she had an incredible talent at seeing what was not quite right about something. This is a valuable gift. It is not, however, the gift of a perfectionist. A perfectionist, properly so called, would be able to see what was right and good about the thing or situation, however cluttered and disordered it might otherwise seem to be. This is my gift, and it is different, yet equally valuable to the one she had. While both gifts are valuable and important, however, we tend to elevate the one and denigrate the other.

I then realized that most educators struggle to master her gift of identifying imperfection, not mine of identifying perfection. They make the pedagogical assumption that the way to produce something of high quality is to criticize everything that is of low quality about it. The idea is like Michelangelo's method of sculpture—to take a block of marble and chip away everything that does not belong on the finished masterpiece. The idea is that we can *criticize* our way to improvement.

But to do the opposite, identifying merit in the work, however inadequate the work may be in its current state, and to pursue improvement by building on the merit—this approach tends to be at odds with mainstream conventional thinking in education.

In addition, there is the shadow side of positivity. I first came upon this at spiritual gatherings. Generally speaking, the people at these gatherings were very positive. They were peaceful, supportive, and fun. These are the people who would greet you not by saying "hello" or "how's it going," but by saying "Namaste." Being myself an appreciator, I felt at home among them. And at least at first, I wanted to be more like them.

But as I spent more time in these groupings, I discovered two troubling things on the shadowy underside. First, just because a person said "Namaste" did not necessarily mean the person was positive in his or her personal life or respectful towards all others. In fact, it came to seem to me that sometimes the positivity was a psychological cover for the opposite. That is, the positivity was functioning like a deodorant or perfume, smelling clean and fresh but covering something up. There is nothing wrong with the use of perfume, of course. It is just that in terms of personal hygiene, so to speak, a person may have a sweet smelling presence but still need to take a bath.

And the second thing on the shady underside I discovered was that the positive people sometimes had an irrational aversion to hearing anything that sounded negative. Sometimes they would even forbid anything that sounded negative to be said in their presence, and especially when the negative thing being said was true! Thus, any discussion of politics, the environment, or war was forbidden. I remember it often happening that those who were morally troubled by the cruelty and injustice they could see in the world and who wanted to come to a deeper understanding or some sort of resolution—these people would be silenced when they tried to give voice to their trouble. They would be accused of negativity. Invariably, someone would say to them, speaking from on high, "Here we do not choose to surround ourselves with negativity."

End of discussion.

So even though I am myself a positive person, I had come to discover the *shadow* side of positivity. Of course, the negative people have their own shadow side—an opposite but parallel reluctance (if not incapacity) to see anything good in the world.

So while I could see these things, I was not able to make any sense of them until Philo told me about purifying consciousness. Suddenly I could make sense of my own experience, both with myself and with others. As Philo pointed out, positive and negative people each have a core truth and a lurking shadow. The core truth of positivity is that there *is* a lot of good in the world, even a preponderance of it. So when positive people see the good in a situation, they are often entirely correct. We would all do well to listen to them. The shadow, however, is a tendency to deny anything *but* the good, thereby silencing the very discourse that might lead to an improvement of those things that are not good.

The core truth of negativity, conversely, is that there *is* a lot of unnecessary pain and suffering visited upon the people of this planet, much of it heartbreaking in its savagery and maliciousness. So when people give voice to the negative they see, they are often entirely correct! There *is* a lot of negativity in the world, and much of it is completely unnecessary! Of course, the shadow of seeing the negative is a tendency to despair, to lose hope, and to become cynical, ending up incapable of seeing the good things.

After talking to Philo, I felt much clearer about this. Purifying consciousness involved purifying the positive *and* the negative, not just one or the other. And since every person has both the positive and the negative inside, every person, whether predominantly positive or negative, has to purify both. This made perfect sense to me, and I was eager to get started on it.

There was a problem, though. *How* does one purify consciousness? It is one thing to say it must be done, but *how* does one do it? I couldn't wait to see Philo to ask him.

CHAPTER 11

PURIFYING CONSCIOUSNESS—
HOW, NOT WHY

The next time I saw Philo the situation was perfect: we were isolated and able to talk without any interruptions. That meant I got to go directly to the question that was on my mind.

"Philo," I said, "please explain to me *how* one purifies one's consciousness. I fully grasp the value and even necessity of doing so. I just want some guidance about *how*."

Philo had an amused expression on his face. Leaning back, he said, pleasantly, "Well, here we have John in his attack dog mode. I must say, you are attacking this point the same way you attacked that sweet melody you were just riffing on. What is that melody?"

"It is a nice one, for sure," I replied, feeling flattered not only for how I had played it but because I had picked it out. "It is called "Moonglow," I answered.

"It has such a nice change in it," Philo added, with a distant look on his face. "The first chord is a minor, and then it moves up a minor third to another minor chord, only now with a major seventh note in the root. Most unusual . . . and most pleasing."

I was blown away by his knowledge. That change was the *exact* thing I liked about that song and the reason I played it at all. But this wasn't the first time he had knocked me out with his insight—and not just in music but in all sorts of areas. In fact, the more I talked to him, the more impressed I was with his penetrating insight into all things having to do with Earth culture, art, and politics.

At the time, however, I was completely focused on the purifying consciousness thing that I restated the question again: "Please, Philo, talk to me now about just *how* one can go about purifying one's consciousness."

"Gee, John, that is a very deep topic. Could we just drink a beer and chill for a bit." He smiled broadly at me, looking the very picture of radiance.

"I have a better idea," I said. "Let's drink a beer and chill while we talk about this topic."

"Well put. Let's do it." I motioned to the waitress to bring us two strong, dark ales. The place was almost empty, so she brought them right away.

"John," Philo, intoned gravely, "before we get to the how, there is something I want to express to you."

Hearing him say this and sensing the gravity of his tone, I felt a bit knocked back. I couldn't imagine what was concerning him. I had been feeling increasingly appreciative and, yes, respectful towards him. Many of the things he said had struck me so deeply that I was eager for more. And his points were not just theoretical. He often observed things I had not observed, thereby helping me not only to see those things, but also and more importantly, to help me to improve my own seeing. He also made points that, as I considered them, led me to insights of my own, insights of great quality.

The point is, I was feeling very good about him. In some deep way, he was becoming my teacher. You can probably imagine my surprise when, feeling the appreciation and respect I did, I heard what he said next.

"John," Philo said, riveting me with a focused stare, "I am concerned about the attitude towards me that you seem to be adopting."

I was astounded. I could not think more highly of him. I was almost to the point of revering him. He had my total trust. After a moment of stunned silence, I found myself laughing, gushing in relief as I started to explain how I really felt. I don't remember my exact words, but it was something to the effect of how awesome he was, how magnificently he was helping me, how insightful I found him to be . . . ."

"JOHN!" he said sharply, more in tone than volume, interrupting me. It was sufficient to silence me. "*That* is the very thing that concerns me," he said, "the exaggerated respect you accord to me. Admittedly, my extraterrestrial origins lead me to have a certain perspective, enabling me to observe things that only an outsider could see. Clearly, my sharing of my observations is of great benefit to you."

"That is an understatement, Philo," I said.

"Keep in mind that I grew up in a different world, a world that to you is completely alien, a world you know nothing about. There is therefore a tendency to glamorize me and my world. Since you do not know about our problems and failings, there is a danger you will not realize they exist, not to mention how grave and destabilizing they are."

Philo was right. I was forming a fantasy picture of aliens being a bunch of, if you will, enlightened Buddhists.

Philo continued. "Still, given all of that, I think it is safe to say that any disinterested observer would recognize that the cultural mind-space my people inhabit is more evolved—more *humane*, let me say—than the cultural mind space that your people currently inhabit. *You*, John, are an exception. Not that you are better than your planetmates. It is just that most of them do not know they inhabit a cultural mind space and you, even before we met, had begun to grasp that you do. Similarly, coming from where I do, I can see things and offer alternatives that you have not seen or thought of. That is because I am an alien. It does not make me better. You could do the same thing on my planet."

"I didn't say you were better," I interjected, feebly.

"That's right," he replied, adopting a kindlier tone. "You didn't." He paused. "But you are starting to act like it. You must stop. I do not deserve it. But more than that, it creeps me out. On my world, I am what you would call an ordinary guy."

"I thought you were a philosopher on your planet," I said, confused.

"I am. But it does not quite have the meaning you think it does. We do value philosophy on my planet and so we subsidize anyone who applies himself to it."

"How amazingly wonderful," I interjected!

"Don't get so excited," he replied. "I admit it sounds good, but it isn't the way you think it is. The philosophy subsidy functions as a sort of public assistance program. Sort of like welfare. If one of my people is a ne'er-do-well or just flat out lazy, he or she can simply register as a philosopher and thereby receive adequate if not generous support. There *are* some true philosophers among the registered, individuals of brilliance who use the public support to think ever deeper thoughts, always seeking ever higher levels of consciousness development. But generally, among my people to admit one is a philosopher is a lot like one of you here in your country admitting you are on welfare.

"But, you, Philo, are one of the true philosophers. One of the respected ones, surely. Who cares what others do with their subsidy."

"There you are wrong," Philo said flatly. "I'm not at all recognized as what you call a true philosopher and I am not particularly respected."

He looked aside for a moment with what struck me as a strange look on his face. I had this weird impression he was talking to a camera and making a private joke.

"I do have a profession that accords me a measure of notoriety and even public recognition, John," he said. Then looking back at me, he added, "I'm not one of the worst, to be sure, but I'm not one of the best, either. I would put myself in the middle." He paused again and then looked at me slyly. "Sort of like you."

I was too surprised to think of much to say. I asked him, "Does this mean you don't know how to purify consciousness either?"

He looked at me for a second and then . . . broke out laughing. "I guess there is no stopping an attack dog. Good for you and thank you for asking. Let me put it this way. Yes, I do know how. But that is only because this is pretty common knowledge on my planet. Imagine that you were on a planet and someone there asked you if you had ever heard of a hamburger and if you knew how to make one. The answer would be yes, of course. You could show them how to make one, but it wouldn't be because you are some sort of special person. It would be because you are from meat-eating, fast-food America. Even a vegetarian in your country could explain to an alien how to make a hamburger! So it is with me explaining to you how to purify consciousness."

"I think I get it," I said, not sure if I was feeling any better.

"I hope so, John, because the exaggerated respect you have been showing me makes me almost want to stop talking to you. Please treat me like the ordinary person I am. And above all, please never forget that even when I think I am right, I could be wrong."

"Well put, Philo. And now let me get you another beer and you tell me how to purify my consciousness."

Philo smiled. "A tempting offer, but I am afraid I have to leave now." He must have seen my crestfallen expression because he immediately added, "I could meet you this weekend, however. How about Saturday afternoon in the Parrot, say at 3:00?"

"I'll see you there."

It was going to be the first time we did not meet in the barn.

CHAPTER 12

PHILO LANDS
IN THE PARROT?

I won't say I wasn't excited when I walked into the Parrot at 3:00, but my enthusiasm level had definitely dropped from its previous peaked out levels. In the few days since I had last talked to Philo I had been reflecting on the fact that I knew virtually nothing about him. All I had were the things he said, and however outlandish some of them were, I had no way of determining whether they were true. I had begun to wonder if perhaps he was playing a sick, extended joke on me, maybe one that was being secretly filmed. That would explain the seemingly hidden places he carefully chose to sit.

On the other hand, I found his points intriguing, and, speaking as a philosopher, he did seem to be in possession of a deeper insight and more refreshing perspective than what I was used to. I realized that as long as this was the case, then no matter what I might think or resolve in my tortured internal deliberations, our conversations now had a life of their own. In short, I realized there were now three of us with a stake here—me, Philo, and our ongoing conversations. So even if I wanted to end the conversations now, I would be outvoted.

But if I was resigned to the conversations continuing, I was definitely feeling less enthusiastic about them. Such, at any rate, was the flavor of my thoughts as I stepped inside the Blue Parrot at 3:00. Since it was quite bright outside, it seemed unusually dark inside. Reflecting on whether this was an omen or not, I did not see Philo anywhere. I had to walk from front to back twice, checking the hidden corners and darkened spaces before I noticed him. He was cleverly situated in a booth in the middle of the far wall, somehow less noticeable for that.

"There he is, none other than Mr. Ordinary," I said with a feigned brightness as I walked up, trying to be light and elevated even as I referred back to our previous conversation.

"And there *he* is," Philo responded smilingly, "the man who will hound me back to my home planet if I do not answer his questions quickly enough." He beamed acceptance at me.

"And what question would *that* be," I replied in a mock tone, putting my index finger to the side of my mouth and looking off into the distance while pretending to try to recall something. "Oh," I exclaimed in an even more dramatized voice, "maybe it's my question about purifying consciousness, which I seem to have all but forgotten, it having been neglected by you for such an impossibly long time."

Philo seemed to be enjoying himself. "That is quite sophisticated, John. Sarcasm is so very Earth and so deeply human. Thank you for that. And you will be pleased to learn that now is the time to answer your question. But, first, please, indulge me and put your question into words. I have a reason for asking you to do this."

It seemed like a strange request, but I did not quibble. I was feeling much better, more energized. I realized right then that I really liked Philo and very much enjoyed these conversations. It didn't seem too much to ask, so I put my question to him: "We were originally talking about understanding reality. You said in order to truly understand anything, a person had to be *adequate* to the task. When I asked about how one becomes adequate to the task of understanding reality, you mentioned the necessity of purifying consciousness. Since I want to be adequate to cognize reality, I asked you *how* to purify consciousness. That's when we ran into some delays."

Philo was smiling broadly. "You realize, of course," he said, "that the delays were entirely fabrications of your imagination and had no basis in fact."

"Whatever," I replied distantly.

He chuckled. "Another brilliant Earth thing, John! The expressive mileage you natives can get out of that single, ostensibly unrelated word is nothing short of amazing. What a great tool of communication. You express your attitude plainly, and I receive it loud and clear."

"I'm glad you are amused," I answered, noting that my mood was actually quite light and that I did not have a bad feeling about any of this. I smiled.

Philo smiled back, also seeming to be enjoying himself. "Thank you for posing your question. And as I suspected, there is one tiny but, for our purposes, hugely significant detail in the way you phrased your question. I find I must quibble with it. You just said that you understand the value and even necessity of purifying consciousness in order to be adequate to *cognize* reality. But cognize is the wrong word there. We are not trying to *cognize* reality. We are trying to *apprehend* reality."

I didn't quite understand what Philo was getting at. My mind was in a flurry. What is this difference he is focusing on, I thought, and what difference could it possibly make? Perhaps this would qualify for what certain medieval philosophers would have classified as a distinction without a difference?

I even regretted having said 'whatever' earlier because the attitude that that word relays would have been much better applied to this. I didn't say anything, however, and so Philo continued, "I suspected you would not grasp the distinction, which is why I asked you to put the question into words in the first place. Not many Earthlings do. John, this is not a mere terminological point."

"You have lost me on this one," I said.

"I see that," he replied kindly. "Let me try to explain. The fact that you would conflate these two words indicates that you are operating on the basis of a certain deep core assumption. I want to bring that assumption into awareness better to examine and question it."

Philo had talked about the process of identifying and questioning core assumptions. This is a most difficult thing to do, he had previously explained, because core assumptions function at the base level of how we construct our experience. To question one, therefore, generally seems absurd because the assumption also shapes our questioning of it. Understanding and expecting this, I was therefore ready to try to identify one of my core assumptions.

Philo continued, "The significant assumption lurking here is the unexamined expectation that the way to apprehend reality is to cognize it. The reason this matters is that cognition is a function of thought, unlike perception, which is a function of awareness."

"What is the difference?" I asked, still not getting it.

"Quite simply, to *cognize* something is to think about it in terms of categories, concepts, and distinctions. To *perceive* it, however, is simply to become aware of it. Apprehension is the larger category, one that includes cognition but is not limited to it."

"I'm not sure I get the significance here," I interjected.

"It is hugely significant," he answered, oozing patience and calm. "You can apprehend by means of thought, certainly. You can also apprehend by means of sensory perception. You can apprehend by means of feeling. You can even apprehend by means of"—here he looked off into the distance as if searching for the right word—"let's call it, for lack of a better term, mental magic."

"Mental magic," I uttered in a tone of academic disappointment.

"Don't think about that right now," he answered quickly. "We will get to it later, I promise. For now the point is that it is possible to apprehend reality without conceptual thought."

"But how else to understand reality if not by thinking about it?" I asked, grasping his point but also recognizing that most of my academic colleagues would deny it.

"Simple. By being *aware* of it. As your Buddhists so correctly observe, awareness is empty. It has no content. Awareness is not itself a thought, not a perception, not a feeling. It is the *consciousness* of thoughts, perceptions, and feelings."

"Is this important?"

Philo started to say something and then suddenly laughed out loud. After a long sequence of chuckles, he caught himself and looked at me apologetically. "I'm laughing at myself, John," he explained apologetically. "You see, I caught myself almost saying 'absolutely' when you asked if this is important. Oh, the horror of it! Me almost saying 'absolutely,' and not in an ironic sense! A few months on your planet and I am already becoming native!"

I sort of got the joke. It just didn't seem funny. He quickly gathered himself.

"Let me put it this way. I *personally* think this distinction is important, the majority of people on my planet, including the wisest, would say it was important, and many of the wisest among you, especially advanced explorers of consciousness, whether Buddhists or depth psychologists, would say it is important." He paused a moment while looking carefully at me and then added, "We could all be wrong, of course."

"Help me with this, Philo," I asked sincerely. "I don't really grasp the significance of what you are getting at. I see the distinction. I just don't get the importance of it. For example, the different ways of apprehending you mention, don't they all work *together?*"

"Indeed they do, John. But even there, those who correctly make this observation do so in accordance with the unexamined assumption that the different ways of apprehending work together under the rule and mastery of thought. Not to be unsympathetic, but it often happens that Earthlings will see what they think is there, not actually what is there. In this way perception can be projection."

"But perception is famously misleading. Therefore, perception must defer to the corrective power of thought. Right?"

"Yes, this is often the case, perception being, as you put it, famously misleading. Perception does indeed need to be corrected by thought—but not always! What this comes down to is a basic territorial conflict. I am not by any stretch suggesting an abandonment or diminishment of thinking. But are there any limits to its territory? What I see and am trying to point out to you is an overvaluation and overreliance on thinking."

I was taking this in, trying to clarify it for myself. Philo continued, "Again, thinking is wonderful, helpful, and more often than not, essential. I am not putting thinking down. Thinking can take you places. And many of those places are inaccessible except by means of thinking. Indeed, you could safely say that on the journey of truth, thinking is an essential vehicle. But its importance on the journey to truth is at about the same level as the importance of your personal automobile is in the context of your total life. That is to say, your auto is probably extremely important, even essential, but it is not the only thing that is important."

"I get your image, Philo," I said. "But to bring it back to the thinking mind. What else is important other than thinking?"

"Simple," answered Philo, looking poised and confident. "*Awareness, presence,* and what many of you on your plant are now calling *mindfulness*—these things are also important, and arguably even more important. But note carefully, John," and here he looked at me with particular focus, "awareness, presence, and mindfulness are not conceptual. Being mindfully present is not an idea. It is not a concept in the mind, not a spiritual ideology, and decidedly *not* a way of thinking. Mindfulness is simply the presence of awareness here and now."

What he said was making sense to me. "So you are saying that I have to become more mindful, more present with awareness in the moment in order to be able to be adequate to apprehend reality. And the way to do so is to purify my consciousness."

"That is it exactly, John. Excellent."

"Good. So can we now talk about how to do so?"

"Yes, John, now we can."

"Ok, you mentioned that people tend to be positive in their outlook or negative, and that the positive is usually based on a sense of idealism and the negative on a feeling of fear. Generally, these two outlooks are at war. 'Be more positive,' the one says to the other, to which the other's reply is, 'Be more realistic and not so delusional.' Does that get it?"

"Quite brilliantly so, John," Philo replied. "I am impressed. Given this, then, what we need to do is purify the shadow of each— the tendency of idealism to grow out of illusion and for realism to grow out of fear."

"This doesn't sound like it will be easy," I observed.

"To the contrary," Philo replied, "it will be delightfully easy. We just have to keep in mind that we are not talking about two separate groups of people, though it can certainly seem that way because it is so convenient to talk about positive and negative people. In actuality, however, both the positive and negative can be found in each of us. Depending on how these two relate to each other, and usually there is a sort of internal sadomasochistic dominance of one or the other and not a functioning balance, people can then *seem* to be either positive or negative. It is more the case, however, that the so-called positive people have just suppressed their inner negative, so to speak, while the seemingly negative people have suppressed their inner positive."

"This is a lot to absorb," I said, covering my confusion.

"Don't give up on it," Philo said encouragingly. "And there is one important clarification to add. It is also essential constantly to keep in mind that there are both positive and negative things and events in reality."

"I think I understand," I said without confidence. "That clarification helps. In other words, since there is positive and negative in reality, we need to avoid denying one on the basis of the other. Instead, we must attempt to balance both. And as you say, it is a sort of *idealism* that leads people to elevate the positive and diminish the negative. Conversely, it is the presence of *fear* that leads them to do the opposite. What we want in this situation is neither to elevate nor to suppress but just to see. But once again, I say it isn't going to be easy to do this, which is why I want to know *how*."

"Very nicely summarized, John, but with one minor correction. It will be easy to do this because all of you already know how to do this. Think about it. People on either side of the positive/negative divide *already* know what those on the other side need to do. Simply put, negative people *already* see clearly that positive people need to purify their idealism of denial and delusion. Conversely, positive people already see clearly that negative people need to purify their realism of unacknowledged fear."

"And *how* is that done?" I asked with a sly smile.

"Again, it is surprisingly easy. I say it is easy because it isn't as much something you Earthlings need to *do* as much as it is something you just have to *stop* doing."

I must have looked dumfounded so Philo continued to try to explain. "Let me walk you through the process. The key here is mindfulness. With focused awareness we can observe our inner functioning. On the deepest level, beneath the level of the ordinary awareness of daily life, we operate according to certain assumptions or mental protocols which have long since become habits. These habits, over time, become automatic. We are then not even aware of them. Even when they function to shape, filter, and construct our experience, we are not aware of them."

"It sounds bleak," I said gloomily.

"Not at all," Philo replied brightly. "Earthlings are not generally aware of these mental habits as they function—*unless* they cultivate sufficient mindfulness in order to be able to go deep within and look at them directly. Lacking that ability to be mindful on this deep level, the mental habits shaping human experience will seem to be hardcore aspects of brute reality. Being automatic and unconscious, these habits present a constructed picture that appears to be coming from outside of the person."

"So how can an Earthling change these hidden mental habits?"

"Earthlings can't. They shouldn't even try. In fact, trying to change them will not work. What you can do is become *aware* of them. That's it, John. It really is that simple. Awareness is the key. Your awareness, not the exercise of your will—this is how you transform. You use your will to focus your awareness, that's all."

I must have looked unconvinced because Philo, after measuring me up, continued.

"Let's look at this in an operational way. Say I am very idealistic. Good for me. But ever so gradually, I establish an inner protocol that shies away from negative things. This shying away then eventually becomes a deep, inner habit of my mind. Later, I *identify* with the habit of shying away, calling myself a positive person, an idealist. I might think to myself that I am illuminated, but all I have done is become an automatic machine of avoidance. As soon as I can *see* that, the automatism is broken. Quite simply, to *see* my automatic habit of withdrawal puts me in a position where I don't have to withdraw automatically. I can choose not to."

"I follow you." It really did make sense to me even if I still was not clear and confident that I could actually *do* this.

"And, of course," Philo continued, "it is the same with the fear that leads to negativity. Generally, the originating fear is hidden from me. I do not realize that it is driving me, leading me to focus on certain things and to recoil from others. This habitual pattern of selective focus and recoil then becomes automatic. And once it is automatic, seemingly happening independently of me, I no longer realize it is something I am doing. Instead of realizing I am functioning like a machine, I function as if I am actually seeing what is. However, once I can *see* the fear and how, on a deep level, it functions to shape my understanding and self-image, the mechanism is broken. I am now free to choose where before I was not."

"I really think I am getting this, Philo, but what does this have to do with becoming adequate to apprehend reality?"

"That is exactly the point, John. When the mechanism is broken, and you are no longer *automatically* taking an attitude or having a perception, you have then become *adequate* to apprehend reality. Instead of being a machine, automatically being positive or automatically being negative, you can now *apprehend* the negative as negative and the positive as positive. Your mind, no longer functioning on automatic pilot, can see clearly."

Philo looked at me intensely. He must have liked what he saw, because he continued. "You have heard the old saw about how a broken clock is correct twice a day. Similarly, when you are self-programmed to be automatically positive or automatically negative, you will be like that broken clock, only you will *often* be right, not just twice a day. But you will be right the way the clock is right—that is, your broken machine will just happen at various points to correspond to reality. Remember, there are both good and bad things that happen in reality. Given this, when you purify your consciousness so that you no longer function like an automaton, your inner clock, so to speak, will be able to calibrate with reality and tell you the time. You will see the good as good and the bad as bad."

We talked some more, but my mind was so overwhelmed that I don't remember much of it. I do remember that I walked out of the Parrot feeling different than when I walked in. I was involved in something big, something transformational.

CHAPTER 13

A PHILOSOPHER FROM ANOTHER PLANET CAN BE FULL OF CRAP TOO, RIGHT?

Philo and I had agreed to meet again in a few days, but I found myself still feeling slightly skeptical about the things he was telling me. I kept having a duck/rabbit experience. That is, I would be thinking how deep and profound what he told me is—the duck—and then suddenly it would seem crazy and completely unreal—the rabbit. Back and forth, almost as if I was looking through two entirely different windows.

So I appreciated what he was saying, but I was also immensely skeptical. Surprisingly, it wasn't his claim to be from another planet that was nagging at me. That was never a point of focus for me anyway. No, the issue for me now was not so much about whether to believe him about that but about whether to believe him about anything he was saying!

Still, I could not completely ignore the alien thing either. If nothing else, it meant I could not openly discuss our conversations with my academic colleagues. Even so, I want to emphasize that my growing skepticism and sense of alarm had little to do with the alien thing. Instead, my doubts were almost entirely about the main thrust of what he was saying about reality. I mean, a philosopher could be from another planet and still be full of crap, right?

I remember reading an essay by Virginia Wolff, *How to Read a Book,* in which she recommended giving oneself entirely and without criticism to whatever book one was reading. Let the author take you where he or she wants to, she advised, and only pull back and evaluate critically *after* the experience is finished. This became my method for all things. I would give myself over completely to whatever was being said or performed, and I would only later, after the experience was completed, step back and evaluate. As my friends often joked, "You believe everything—for fifteen minutes!"

So I decided it was time to pull back from Philo and look at what he was saying from a distance.

Standing back, I found I fully accepted his observation that I was *assuming* that correctly apprehending reality meant thinking about it, that is, cognizing it. This opened me experientially to consider that there may be other ways of apprehending reality, as for instance ways having to do with what we call vibes. So as I kept thinking about this purification of consciousness thing, I found that the basic notion that there are actually multiple modes of reality apprehension made raw, animal sense to me.

Of course, since my academic qualities had kicked in, I was now probing for ways to disprove his claims, to distance myself from them. The academic practice, which I am schooled in and fully support, is to criticize without restraint any and all claims to knowledge and understanding. The idea is that if a claim can *resist* open and earnest attempts to discredit it, its credibility goes up correspondingly. The highest credibility goes to something that has successfully resisted all attempts to discredit it. Having done so, it is then recognized as a "theory."

In academia, being recognized as a theory is an accomplishment of status. It means that all the learned attempts to discredit or minimize this explanation have so far failed. Future attempts may well do so, and in fact can reasonably be expected to do so at some point as our knowledge and understanding continues to grow and expand.

In this sense I suppose you could say there is no final truth in academia, only what has not yet been minimized, corrected, or disproven. This makes sense because, as Philo so often remarked, truth is a living, growing, organic and vital thing. Religion often acts as if truth is a frozen, dead thing, something that is given in final form by God. Your job as a believer is to accept it, for which you will get rewarded in the sky. If you do not accept it, however, you get punished in the underworld. Either way, the truth is thought to be a frozen given. Take it or leave it.

So the academic approach has always been my approach. I often put it this way. I am not against religion. I am against *any* attempt to freeze truth. Indeed, I lament to see truth frozen anywhere, whether in religion, business, politics, or even—horrors!—in academia. I am, if you will, an equal opportunity opponent of freeze-dried truth.

Still, when I began to think about Philo's ideas critically, it straight away struck me that his whole project of purifying consciousness is itself based on a rather large assumption—namely, that there is, objectively speaking, good and evil in the world. Is this an acceptable assumption? After all, denying the notion that there is actual metaphysical evil in the world has always had a well-established, if minority position in human culture and thought, even in religion. Indeed, from the depths of religion, science, and philosophy there have always been those who would downgrade the ontological status of evil. The idea is that what we call evil only seems evil from a certain limited, self-interested human perspective. If we could take a wider, more cosmic view, we would see, as Shakespeare so famously put it, "nothing is good or bad except as thinking makes it so."

Certainly the doubting of the objective reality of evil dates back to the birth of philosophy. Socrates himself sported the idea that the people who commit evil acts do so because they are *ignorant*, not because they are *evil*.

Religion, of course, offers its own denial. No less an authority than St. Augustine tells us that evil, far from being a power or intelligence in its own right, is merely the privation of good. Carrying the religious denial forward, at times of despair, when there seems no possible reason or moral explanation for whatever painful, tragic thing has happened, one often hears it asserted that "everything happens for a reason." In other words, this tragic event one is suffering from *does* have a reason and a moral explanation; it is just that one does not know what it is.

But perhaps the most powerful denial of the objective (i.e. scientific) existence of evil today is the one offered by evolutionary science. Evolutionists explain that nature operating in accordance with the survival of the fittest mechanism of natural selection is not merely a good thing—it is, in fact, the only thing. So when a smaller animal screams because it is being eaten by a larger animal, his agonizing death screams do not indicate that an evil is happening. It is only from the smaller animal's unscientific point of view that an evil can be said to be occurring. Indeed, naturally occurring things and events only seem to be cruel and evil from a provincial point of view—in our case, that means from a human point of view. Looked at objectively, each species is simply doing whatever it takes to survive.

Of course, this blanket acceptance of 'whatever it takes to survive' is extended to human social activity, meaning that the game-rigging, predatory, and decidedly unjust behavior of the oligarchical ruling class is, when properly understood, an entirely *natural* matter of the fittest surviving. Given this, the heartfelt lament of the weak, downtrodden, and poor that something is not fair has no more truth-value or ethical import than do the screams of a mouse being eaten by a hawk. In fact, people shaped by these ideas say, "You would do the same thing if you had the chance." According to them, complaints based on notions of justice and fairness simply expresses the resentment and envy felt by whiners and moochers. Those who are not whining and mooching are out there making money!

Hmmm.

Standing back, one can see a number of options regarding how to understand what we see happening in society and nature. Of course, there is certainly the *appearance* of bad things happening, not to mention the actual *experience of badness* when those things are happening to one, as when one is being beaten or is hungry, homeless, and broke. The question is how are we to understand all of this? There are, it seems to me, three basic alternatives.

The first is to see good and evil as enemies involved in a war that only one can win. Good and evil are therefore locked in a cosmic struggle for dominance and victory. They are nearly equal powers, and one will ultimately win and the other will be vanquished—but which? This view is sometimes called Manicheism, referring back to Mani, its original progenitor, but more generally it is called dualism. It can be found in all thought systems, whether it is God vs. Satan or sustainable living vs. continuing resource depletion and unchecked pollution.

The second is to deny ontological status to good and evil. Good and evil are just *attitudes* we take towards reality; they are not themselves independent realities. For the farmer rain is good, but for the person who had planned a picnic, rain is bad.

And the third alternative is to see good and evil as real. Unlike the first, however, it does not see good and evil as independently existing realities at war with each other. As the great writer and Soviet dissident, Solzhenitsyn, once said, the line between good and evil runs through every human heart. In other words, in the third alternative, good and evil are real, but there is much more relativism to what we identify as good and evil than those people who accept the real existence of good and evil are generally prepared to accept.

Now Philo's whole purification of consciousness thing is based entirely on the third alternative—namely, that both good things and bad things really do happen in the world, and while neither the good nor the bad is an illusion, the designation of which is which is to a striking degree *relative* to many other concerns in a most complex way. That is to say, there is good and evil in the world, but not in an objective sense. One person's treat often really is another person's poison.

In standing back and reviewing all of this, I found I could accept Philo's assumptions here. Unlike the first alternative, he does not have an absolutist understanding in which some things are objectively good and others objectively evil. Instead, he is a relativist, recognizing that good and evil are relative, but not in the way the second alternative is, denying the reality of good and evil. For Philo, good and evil are both relative *and* real. That is, there really is good and evil, but they are elastic and relative, not fixed and absolute.

I felt better about Philo after stepping back and reviewing everything. I was ready to resume our conversations. And beneath it all, I felt my gusto had rekindled!

CHAPTER 14

DEEP INSIDE,
IT IS AN EARTH THING

I don't know what you are experiencing as you read these recollections of mine, but for me, when Philo and I talked it was mostly after my gigs, so it seemed like every time we really got going in our talking, it would be time to stop. I was finding this increasingly frustrating!

I mentioned this to Philo and he nodded in approval. I wasn't sure what he was approving, so I asked him, "Are you pleased I am expressing disapproval of the way we meet . . . or are you pleased with the way we meet?"

"Oh, fully the later," Philo whipped back without hesitation. "In any area touching on personal growth, it is best always to go in small, sequenced steps, much like we are doing. In our case, it is circumstances that lead us to tread the appropriate path, not our collective wisdom."

"If it were up to me," I replied, ignoring his subtle jibe about the wisdom we had together as a team, "I would let the conversation go all night. What could be more important than what we are talking about? It is agonizing to have to keep stopping—and more often than not, stopping right at the moment of delivery."

I said this passionately, almost confrontationally. To my surprise, Philo burst out laughing. "Oh, so well put, John. The Earth approach, indeed. It is almost perfectly the opposite of the serially truncated way we do things on my planet—which, by the way, I think is an entirely superior practice."

Philo rarely talked about or even mentioned the way things were done on his planet, and I don't recall him ever comparing the two in this way before. I must have looked hurt because he immediately smiled warmly and said, "Please let me take that back. It is not that the way of my planet is superior to yours. It is that what we are aiming for is superficially similar but actually quite significantly different than what you are aiming for. Therein lays the difference. We are aiming at different things, so it is not a matter of one planet having better aim than the other."

Feeling confused and uncertain about what he was getting at, I said, "Well, Philo, I can't speak for what the people on your planet are aiming for, but I thought we were talking about purifying consciousness. So if there is a *better* way of doing so, even if that better way comes straight from a race of gooey aliens in need of a bath, I want to know about it. That is what I thought we were aiming at!"

Again, I was surprised to see Philo burst into spontaneous laughter. Moreover, it was the laughter of pure merriment. He was enjoying himself. "You are *so* Earth. You can't fake that depth of authenticity. 'Impressive to the max,' as an Earthling might put it today."

This was bothering me. Usually I felt very close to Philo—and I certainly did not have anything like an experience of being with a member of another *species*. But this felt different. His reaction, his delight, and the joy he was taking from what I was saying—it all seemed so alien! I did not feel Philo and I were on the same page, let alone in the same room. And it definitely did not feel like we were similar species!

Whether or not Philo noticed my reaction, he immediately apologized. "Forgive me, John. I am amusing myself. I love Earth and the Earthlings. You must know I came here at great expense and an even greater risk as a result of that love. Nothing I have experienced here has diminished that love. It has only grown."

"So what is your point," I asked, feeling confused about what he was getting at?

"It is just that when you act in such an archetypical Earth way, doing or saying something that a non-Earthling would never do or say, it totally delights me. I sometimes even burst into well-meaning laughter I am so delighted. However, I realize it is not that way for you, and you might think I am laughing at you. I apologize for my insensitivity."

This is a small thing, but his apology, while eloquent and seemingly fully heartfelt, seemed to be more of a statement being delivered to a different audience. It was a weird sensation and I pushed past it.

"Apology accepted, Philo," I said, "but I still don't know what you are getting at. What archetypical Earth thing did I do or say?"

"Well, this won't be easy to explain, but let me try. When you accept the possibility and desirability of purifying your consciousness and seek to do so, you do so in accordance with a deeply structured Earth understanding. That is what I mean." I must have had a look of revulsion hearing this explanation, so in an even softer tone, Philo continued. "I realize that this does not make a lot of sense, but that is precisely *because* it is a deeply structured Earth thing we are talking about."

"Ok, I get that," I replied, thoughtfully. "That is, I can grasp the *type* of thing you are talking about without actually grasping the thing."

"Nicely put," Philo responded kindly. "Again, that is exactly what makes this difference so hard to explain—namely the fact that it is so different." Smiling, he added, "It would be so much easier for you to grasp if you were an alien like me."

Hearing Philo say this, I had an intuitive flash. "Philo, you have a saying on your planet about how it is impossible to see how glorious a spaceship looks flying low in the sky among the clouds when you are the one flying it. That seems to apply here." Philo's eyes widened, indicating he was impressed, so I continued. "So how about if *you* describe to me the thing it is hard for me to see because it is so deeply structured into my whole way of seeing. How about describing it from the perspective of *your* planet and let's see if I can get that?"

"A wonderful idea, John. Let me try that."

This was another one of the things I really liked about Philo. Even though he seemed to be teaching me, he was always very open and interactive. He did not have to monopolize all the good points or suggestions. I was very much a partner in the conversation, not just a recipient.

After sitting thoughtfully for a few moments, Philo took a breath and said, "This will still be difficult, but I think it will help. Please forgive me, John, if in attempting to describe this from the perspective of my planet, I come off as patronizing."

"Not a concern."

"Ok. Here is the thing. On my planet, we recognize that changing one's mind is a deep structural thing. It is a deeper, more complex process than simply making a different choice. There are all sorts of connected, peripheral features that alter and change as well. You could say we understand that one's knowledge of the world functions like a hammock, with all the parts connected, though not directly. The weight of the body, so to speak, is distributed throughout the entire web, so that any shifting of the body will impact the entire hammock."

"I see that, Philo, but how does that apply here?"

"That's exactly the point, John. That *doesn't* apply here—on your planet that is. You Earthlings think differently. You are much more individualistic in your overall, general approach. You tend to think of a body of knowledge as being made up of individual items.

And in your deeply structured outlook, these items do not make a web but a collection."

I was following. Often when Philo was explaining something, I felt like someone learning to ride a bicycle. That is, I am following, following, getting it—then, boom! I fall. That was happening now. I was getting it and then I fell from the bike. Philo must have noticed, because he changed tack.

"So what does it mean in practical terms to think of a body of knowledge as a collection of discrete items and not a web of fully interrelated components? Here is what it means. If knowledge is a collection of items, like the packages and cans in a supermarket cart then you can simply put in and take out items. Your body of knowledge is your shopping cart, and you can alter it easily by putting things in and taking them out. But if knowledge is a web, anything you touch or move will affect everything else. The entire web will be different, not always significantly different, but always different. To take an item out or put one in changes everything!"

"I can see this, Philo, but I'm still not getting the point."

"Think about the difference between the way you would fill a shopping cart and the way you might strengthen and extend a web. With the shopping cart, you can be fast. Put these things in and take those things out—simple, fast, done! But with the web, you have to be more careful, more measured, constantly checking the results of the changing distribution of forces."

"So what does this have to do with my wanting to stay up all night continuing our conversations and you finding that so funny it makes you laugh?"

"It is the eagerness to do it all at once, as if it could all be done at once. With a shopping cart it could be done at once, but not with a web. So we would never rush something like what we are going through. I am coming to understand you Earthlings so much better, and you are coming to understand yourself as an Earthling so much better as well. But this is a slow, gentle process that involves the entire web. That is why taking it in small, discrete steps is best. Put one item in the web, see how the entire web responds, how it adjusts and accommodates, then, once stabilized, perhaps gently place in another item, always giving the entire web the time to adjust."

I really could see the point. I wanted to make change quickly—out with the old, in with the new. It was like I had filled my shopping cart before I discovered the organic section. More to the point, when I sensed Philo had a better, more comprehensive understanding, I would want to get that understanding for myself immediately or at least as quickly as possible. If it meant overturning my entire cart, I was willing to do that. The fact that our conversations were always limited struck me as a big problem.

For Philo, conversely, limiting our conversations to bite sized chunks that could be thoroughly chewed, digested, and assimilated *before* the next bit—this was essential and much to be desired. Therefore, slotting our conversations into these bite sized chunks, rarely having more than fifteen or twenty minutes at a time, was an entirely good thing. Slow down. Digest. Assimilate. Take a few days.

Philo was smiling in appreciation. "So you can see, John, you and your planetmates are aiming for a quick change in the contents of your shopping cart. I and my planetmates are aiming for a gentle transition in the distribution of forces throughout the entire web, understanding that we are creating a completely different web and allowing ourselves plenty of time to do so. Not to brag, but on my planet we generally end up with a different web where you Earthlings mostly end up with the same cart. Since we are working together to change your cart, so to speak, we have to be sure to take enough time to do so."

"I guess that means we won't be up late tonight."

CHAPTER 15

BACK IN THE SADDLE
WITH PHILO

A s I looked forward to the next time we might talk, I noticed that I was feeling significantly more interest and enthusiasm than I had been recently. I also had less reluctance to dare to open up and get deep with Philo, having more trust in him. But even more than that, I noticed that the texture and feel of our conversations had somehow changed. They had always been deeply engaging, but now it felt more like a shift was happening. Philo was *instructing* me—not theoretically but practically.

A musical example works here. Though I know quite a bit about music theory, I am completely self-taught. My knowledge is very playing oriented—knowing what to try in certain playing situations. It is similar to what Aristotle says about finding things to say in a speech. He says there are certain fishing holes, if you will, where points can be found. The point is an experienced fisherman will cast there first. There is no guarantee he or she will catch a fish, but the odds go up significantly in those special spots.

Similarly, in various playing situations, I have a few things to try, a few, as it were, fishing holes to cast my strings into. There is no guarantee I will catch anything, but those are the best places to try.

But let's say I met a musical master and was studying with her. Even though I know a lot already and am fully functioning, it is not likely that my master teacher would just fill in the gaps in my understanding. Instead, she would likely start at the very beginning and overlay my already extensive knowledge, which had gaps in it, with a complete framework. There would be lots of covering what I already know, but the point would not be to explain what I already know to me but to help me place that knowledge in a larger framework, situating my pre-existing knowledge in the context of a master frame.

This is what Philo seemed to be doing relative to philosophy and my personal understanding of and attempts to master life. That is, I already knew a lot about these things, but what Philo was doing was not filling in the gaps as much as helping me to put all that I knew into a larger, more comprehensive framework.

So the following week when I saw Philo at my gig, I took the very first opportunity to join him. "My wise friend," I said warmly as I approached him.

"And my *strange* friend, John," he replied warmly as I pulled out a chair. I sat thinking that was an odd greeting.

"Strange is not the word I would pick to describe me, and though I have heard it used on occasion when referring to me, I have not heard it in this context of seeking wisdom about life," I replied, still feeling warm and fuzzy and not at all defensive. He looked at me blankly, so I continued. "But given how little of me you have witnessed, I find your use of this word to describe me in this somewhat limited context of our togetherness somewhat . . . *strange*!"

Philo chuckled good naturedly. "Perhaps I should explain why I used that word and why it seems to me to be fully appropriate even in this, as you say, limited context."

"Oh, you must explain," I replied, enjoying myself, "you *absolutely* must." We were both in a light and pleasant state.

"Well, if I *absolutely* must," he responded, "then so be it," subtly acknowledging my violation of our tacit understanding that we did not deal in absolutes. As he had often pointed out, many Earthlings, both scientific and religious, are habituated to using absolutist claims and assumptions. On his planet, he had said, thoughtful thinkers characteristically deal with admittedly fallible explanations and 'good enough' claims, not absolutes.

"Absolutely, you must," I replied with a sense of self-aware irony. The word 'absolutely' had an almost naughty feel as it rolled off my lips. The way we humorously bandied it back and forth reminded me of two lovers saying "fuck" to each other as they made love.

"Ok, John, if I *absolutely* must, then please prepare yourself," he said as he ever so slightly sat straighter, seeming to shift physically into a more serious mode. I matched him, sitting a bit more stiffly myself. There was a moment of calm silence as we looked at each other. I must have raised my eyebrows ever so slightly because, almost as if on my cue, he nodded and began.

"Here you are, a most highly accomplished individual, totally flourishing in life, expressing yourself creatively, expanding yourself philosophically, informing yourself politically, all the while taking care not to be burdened with illusions and delusions. Fair enough?"

"More than fair," I answered. "Quite flattering, actually. So whence cometh the *strange*?"

"Whence cometh the strange," he repeated, seeming to enjoy my phrasing. "Well, let's consider that this accomplished, flourishing, creative, expanding person who aspires, quite successfully, not to be burdened with any delusions or illusions—this magnificent being wants to know what it all means—this seems strange to me!"

"But hold up here," I replied perhaps a tad too quickly and definitely a dose too defensively, "you are perhaps forgetting what we talked about early on in our conversations when I clarified that I was not so much seeking an intellectual *explanation* of what life means and is about as a fuller *experience* of being fully alive."

"Ah, yes," he said, "the Joseph Campbell thing. Quite wonderful. But now the strangeness gets even stranger."

"How do you mean?" I asked, feeling genuinely confused and perhaps even diminished.

"So now you want not just an intellectual explanation of what life means. No, you want actually to *feel* fully alive. Not to mock you, but have you tried taking a cold shower recently? I've always found that works wonders in directing my attention to what I am experiencing in the moment. It is cold and it is unpleasant, but it definitely reminds me that I am alive!"

"Now you *are* mocking me," I said with a bit of an edge. "We are philosophizing here, and mockery does not fit."

"But what is the point of philosophy?" he shot back. "What is the practical concern it attempts to address?" I could tell he wasn't asking me for a response. I didn't say anything, so he continued. "Doesn't this willingness to philosophize with no practical point, with no awareness of what one wants or is seeking—isn't this the very thing that gives philosophy a bad name on your planet?"

"I see," I replied, feeling myself regain some of my presence and humor. My mind was bubbling with argumentative responses having to do with the assertion of the ultimately practical importance of pure theory. I recalled a favorite anecdote about the great Hegel giving a lecture and being interrupted by a radical student committed to actual social change, not theory. 'Talk, talk, talk,' the student reportedly said. 'All the talk in the world won't move the chair from one side of the stage you are talking from to the other!' Hegel reportedly considered the student's point, and then replied majestically, 'But my dear young man, it is not the function of philosophy to move chairs.'

I also thought of another favorite comeback of mine—the notion that a medical researcher does not have to be suffering from a headache in order to study them.

But instead of recounting this anecdote or making the medical research point or giving voice to any of the clustering points and responses buzzing through my mind, I felt something opening inside of me. I then responded from a deeper level than my clustering thoughts.

"You are right, Philo, to observe that I have a full and even blessed life, one rich with opportunities to discover, create, and explore. But I often do not experience it that way. I rarely feel the joy, value, and meaning of what I do. I am usually aware of it in an abstract, conceptual sort of way, but I don't actually *feel* it very prominently or very often. I am like a rich person who mostly feels poor."

There, I had said it. I had admitted it to myself. Philo did not say anything but just looked at me with deep, consuming interest. I continued. "Tonight is an example. My playing this evening, and especially my transporting and setting up my equipment—all of this felt more like a chore than a privilege, more like a burden than a blessing. I *know* it is a privilege and a blessing, but I didn't *feel* that. I felt burdened."

He had been looking at me pointedly, but now seemed to be staring with fierce intent. "Bingo," he finally said! I remember he said it most pleasantly, as if the most amazing thing had just been found. "Now we have identified a problem. That means we can now know what we are looking for, what we are addressing. So let's take a deeper look together."

"Absolutely. Let's take that deeper look," I said eagerly.

Philo smiled slyly, "Indeed, John, but for that we will have to wait for the next time." And so, once again, I found myself forced to have to wait to hear Philo's illumination.

CHAPTER 16

SO HOW AM I REALLY DOING?

Even though our last conversation had ended with Philo putting me off, I had actually been feeling better about our truncated conversations... sort of. It still bothered me the way the conversations would end just as they felt like they were beginning, usually with Philo slinking off suddenly. Present, involved, gone—that was the rhythm. He would be there, fully present; we would get involved, fully engaged; and then suddenly he would be gone, fully gone. I was used to it, but it still struck me as strange. Also, he would just sit there until I came up. If I didn't say anything, he wouldn't say anything. He always engaged, but I always had to initiate. And when he left, it would usually be surreptitiously. More often than not I didn't even see him leave. He would just suddenly be gone. "Who was that masked man," I would want to ask?

Still, I did feel better having heard his take on this—that we had to pace such deep inner work. We weren't going for "aha" moments—quick, sudden, and complete—but were attempting to construct an entirely different way of seeing, one based on restructured defaults and different assumptions. And even if I still valued and sought those "aha" moments, I at least knew where he was coming from.

There was no question I had been through a period of doubting him, but after our last conversation, the one in which he called me "strange," I found myself anticipating our talks with an even greater eagerness. I really felt he was helping me to see myself clearly—and to do so with gentleness and acceptance. I certainly felt calmer and more self-accepting than I ever had before.

To the entire world (as well as to myself) I have always been a happy person. I am rarely depressed, highly functional, and living a full and rich life, one to be envied, both as a philosopher and as a musician. Observing this about me, people were often stunned to discover that in both the academic and music worlds, I was at the bottom of the career pool. In academia I held the lowest possible rank of instructor, being retained on a year-by-year contract, a ranking even lower than the entry level of assistant professor. And not only did I not have tenure, I had never been on tenure track. And in the music world, even though I was looked up to as a master musician, I mostly played for free. Few people came to my gigs, and more than once I had been fired from a gig I was not being paid for. In both music and academia, therefore, I was, certainly at my age, the very model and definition of a failure.

Yet I *felt* successful. Moreover, I was seen by many as such. My musician friends envied the great day gig I had. "Teaching philosophy by day and playing creative music at night—what a dream life," one of my friends had said recently. And my friends in academia respected and even envied my musical activities, often commenting on how satisfying it must be to have such a powerful creative outlet.

I agreed with them.

But that was my outside life, my life as it appeared. On the inside, however, it was a different story. It wasn't, as the pop song trope would have it, that I was laughing on the outside but crying on the inside. I wasn't crying on the inside at all. As I mentioned, I wasn't particularly sad, didn't feel bitterness, was rarely depressed, and seldom troubled— except by the state of the world. But as it bubbled out to Philo in our last conversation, I was often flat inside. The sparkling joy and rich meaning of my outside life, which was authentic and not a pose, just did not percolate in the same way on the inside. Inside I was more flat than sad, more regular than thrilled, and more routine than excited.

Strange as it may sound, I was truly happy on the outside but not thereby truly sad on the inside. It was more like the inside and outside were disconnected or only weakly connected. I would describe it this way: I was having wonderful experiences but I was not fully experiencing the meaning of them. Typically I would do something and get positive feedback and a friend would observe, "You must feel great! Way to go." I would say the right thing in response about how great it did feel, but until my friend had pointed it out to me, I was not feeling the impact. I had not realized how great it was.

The last conversation with Philo had brought all of this into clarity. I kept thinking about how totally right he was. This inside-outside disparity is indeed incredibly "strange." Deep strange. Totally weird *cowabunga* strange!

So after deeply doubting Philo, I now found myself appreciating him more than ever. Our conversations had reached a point where I had begun to trust that he really did have a wisdom that was, if you will, 'out of this world.' I felt he had a wisdom that could feed and nurture me. I was, in fact, starving for it.

In the early twelfth century, the philosopher Abelard wrote a book he called *Sic et Non,* which is Latin for 'yes and no.' In the book he took a number of ethical and theological problems and lined up quotations from the Bible and church authorities on both sides of the issue, some indicating a 'yes' answer and others a 'no.' In the introduction he acknowledged that doing this would lead a person to doubt the Faith. But, he pointed out, it is by doubting that we are led to question, and it is by questioning that we come to understand. In other words, rational doubt serves faith.

This is exactly what had happened to me with Philo. I had come to doubt him. By doubting, I had come to question the things he said. And by questioning the things he said, I came to understand them more fully.

I felt sad when he did not turn up at my next gig.

CHAPTER 17

PHILO CAN BE WEIRD
(AND UPSET) TOO

Three weeks went by before I saw Philo again. The time was agonizing, but I can't say it was time wasted. Having come to recognize, admit, and accept that an abundance of goodness on the outside did not necessarily translate to a feeling and experience of goodness on the inside, I had spent the time apart cultivating deep inner awareness.

Philo had helped me to understand that in order to cultivate deep inner awareness, one has to be in a clean mode of observation. He once described clean observation as being something like finding oneself bedridden with a terminal illness in a tenth floor hospital room overlooking a park across the street. The window is sealed, but two children can be seen playing in a sandbox in the park. One can watch the children but has no way of contacting them. One just watches—with no opinion about how they should play and whether they should share. This is watching in a clean way.

Philo emphasized that one needs to watch oneself in the same way—hands off and from a distance.

This was actually a powerful suggestion because, when I did watch myself, I had an internal commentary constantly going on that was evaluating and making critical comments about the 'me' being watched. It was anything but clean.

Philo did not advise me to try to shut this voice up but rather to learn not to pay primary attention to it. "Let it prattle on in the background," he suggested. "You can always tune into it if you wish.

Think of yourself as the King and this voice as one of your advisors. Even when your advisors are accurate and strong, as King you must never forget that *you* are the King, the decision maker. This advisor is your servant. The advisor advises, but it is you, the King, who commands and decides."

Trying to apply Philo's advice and thus paying closer attention to the prattling voice in my head, I was somewhat shocked to discover how aggressively judgmental, harsh, and negative this inner advisor was. It wasn't easy, but I finally got to where I could not pay primary attention to it.

It never did stop prattling, however.

Anyway, having learned not to focus on the inner prattling, I then could see for myself the details and mechanisms of how this great disconnect functioned. The 'great disconnect' was Philo's term for how internally vacant we Earthlings so often are, running almost completely on automatic pilot.

I was able to note my own vacancy and automaticity. The awareness came in flashes. It was as if I was sliding down a slippery slope to vacancy, and I could make a quick observation of the vacancy before I became vacant myself. One simply cannot take note of one's vacancy from within the vacancy, but one can catch glimpses going in and out.

Once I caught enough glimpses of vacancy, I found that the flashes of awareness gradually became longer. From flashes they became moments, and the moments gradually got longer. In these long moments I could observe what was shocking to me—namely, the lack of a correlation between the beneficent presence of goodness and joy on the outside and the free floating vacancy on the inside. In other words, the vacancy seemed to be a response to the world, a comment on it, but actually it was completely disconnected from the world.

This was the great disconnect, and it was difficult to see, but I did see it, and much to my benefit. Seeing the great disconnect led me to anticipate it, sensing when and in what situations it was likely to kick in. Anticipating it then led me to see it all the more clearly. I rarely got caught by surprise anymore. And best of all, seeing it clearly put me in a position where, if I wanted, I could connect rather than disconnect. That is, I could allow myself to feel deeply the happiness and goodness I often actually experienced.

But I did miss Philo. In fact, as the days wore on, I became increasingly worried that I would not see him again. I 'watched' myself worry. I could see my mind working as a machine. Something would remind me of him and I would begin to feel a bit sad. It was an appropriate sadness. But then different possibilities would branch off from this sad feeling. I could actually see them doing so! For example, one branch led into a 'woe is me' cycle. On this branch my mind would bring up chains of memories of experiences of loss and disappointment in my life. Another branch would shade into anger at Philo. I would feel increasingly angry at Philo as my mind dutifully brought up links to memories of having been misused, taken advantage of, or let down by others. I could recall the sharpest things Philo had said to me while enhancing and amplifying the sharpness.

Once I saw these mental paths and where they invariably led to—the first to depressed despair and the second to boiling anger—I could choose whether or not to take them.

Still, I did deeply and honestly miss Philo. I could see that as well. In looking at that, I could see that we had reached a point in our conversations where he was about to reveal a step-by-step procedure by which I might grow and blossom internally. I wanted that procedure. I felt I needed it.

And then something strange would happen which, thanks to the power of self-awareness, I was able to watch. My desire for illumination, which of course is a Very Good Thing, would ever so slyly shade into righteous anger at Philo for raising my expectations and then leaving me completely flat and alone. Abandoned even! Grrr!!!!

How quickly elevated thoughts of enlightenment turned into petty anger!

I won't say that I always caught myself from going down the anger path or even that I mostly caught myself. But I *could* catch myself and, increasingly, I was able to do so. It wasn't that I did not miss Philo or even that I did not feel a touch of anger. It was that my interrelated feelings of missing him and then of feeling angry with him—it was that I could acknowledge these feelings, fully validating them without having to allow them to shape the texture and flavor of my inner disposition. I could feel sad without becoming depressed; I could wish things were other than they were without becoming angry. As long as I maintained inner awareness, I was free.

Then, gradually, even though the anger path was an open and inviting possibility, I began to be aware behind my disappointment at not seeing Philo, I was way better off now than when we had first started talking. Instead of feeling anger, I would reflect on what he taught me about purifying consciousness—about how the process of doing so involved two different tracks, one involved in healing the fears which close one off, and the other involved in pacifying the illusions which replace reality with fantasized projections.

Mostly, though, I just missed him. It wasn't just that he had become my teacher. We were also friends.

And then I saw him!

I was walking through town 'watching' my mind as Philo had encouraged me when—kabamm!—there he was, sitting by himself on the front porch of the Ragged Edge Coffee House. I hustled over and walked up to him, bubbling with excitement. "There he is," I said, "the man of mystery and, no less for that, the man of the hour." I was feeling joyful, both on the outside and the inside. "Do you mind if I have a seat?" I said, pulling out a chair.

Then it hit me. He was different. I even had a quick, panicked thought that this was not Philo, just another non-descript loner. But he smiled weakly at me and I knew it was him. He seemed weary, beaten down even. "Greetings to my musical marvel, guitar-ace philosophical friend," he said. His greeting seemed sincere—but sad.

"So," I said, jumping right in, perhaps a little insensitively, "we were talking about a process to cultivate meaning in life, that is, the *experience* and *feeling* of meaning."

"That we were," he replied with a weak smile.

"So let's continue," I said brightly. "A good place to start would be with the first step."

"I'm not entirely sure we should be having these conversations," he said distantly. There was sadness clinging to his words but not much conviction. I didn't need advanced training in reading vibes to sense that there was something going on with Philo.

"Speak for yourself," I quickly replied. "I don't think I've ever been more energized to hear what someone has to say."

He smiled a weak smile suggesting gratitude. "That is nice of you to say, John, but it may be that I am unable to talk to you about this."

"But you have already been talking to me about this. A lot! You can't stop now. I beg you to continue. It is like you played a complex suspended chord. It is just hanging there, unresolved. All of everything is waiting for it to resolve. You can't leave a suspended chord just sitting there. It must resolve."

He seemed to appreciate my image. "But what if my instrument has lost its tuning," he answered sadly? "If I try to resolve this 11th chord, I will just produce an even more unsettling cacophony."

"Then we tune your instrument!"

He got that far away look. "Hmmm. Nicely put," he said weakly.

He had the look of someone distracted and disengaged by distant events, but whose mind is hyperactive and racing. He was accessing internally with lowered eyes. I watched in silence.

Then he seemed to resolve something. He looked up sharply, meeting me in the eye. "*Very* nicely put, John," he said with new conviction. "What do you say we talk after your gig tomorrow? Same time and same place, Ok?"

"Yes, *absolutely,*" I answered, putting special emphasis on absolutely. He missed the bait . . . or at least ignored it.

Standing, he said, "See you then."

It was the first time he had ever left this way. Every other time he just seemed to disappear. He would go to the restroom and not return, or I would go and he would not be there when I returned. I once called him the Lone Ranger, as in, 'Who was that masked man?'

After taking a few steps, he turned and smiled in his old way. "I appreciate your energy and enthusiasm, John. I really do. And while there are few absolutes or certainties in the external world, it is different when talking about one's intentions. With regard to one's intentions, to be absolutely certain is a function of one's capacity to choose. Let me say, therefore, that I *absolutely* intend to see you tomorrow.

Then he was gone, leaving me thinking, "That was weird." Was Philo concerned there might be an interference to our meeting tomorrow?

CHAPTER 18

PHILO WAS GOING
TO BREAK UP WITH ME

It is strange about gigs. There are all sorts of external factors that indicate and shape the experience of them—the number and type of people in the audience, why they are there, their current attitude and mood, the acoustics of the room, one's own attitude and quality of motivation, the reliability of the instruments and amplification, the time and venue of the gig, and so on.

All of these factors matter in determining the quality of the musical experience, some of them critically so. For example, if the P.A. system does not sound right, the music will sound bad no matter how well it is played.

But the most important factor is what I might call the "wild joker X factor." That is, even when all the indicators are positive, the gig is sometimes (not always) a letdown. Conversely, even when some of the indicators signal catastrophe, the gig sometimes (not always) turns out to be spectacular! Although there are causal factors in this equation, the result—spectacular or catastrophic—often feels more like the result of serendipity than of causality. I have often thought that uncertainty supports hope. Uncertainty is what makes it impossible to know how the gig will turn out. This means that no matter how poor or weak the gig was the last time out, there is always hope that this time will be better.

At any rate, the stars were aligned at my next Hippy Jazz gig and the music was fantastic! I was on fire. My grooves were infectious, my tonal textures fresh and intriguing, and the emotional impact strong.

Towards the end, during the last set, I noticed Philo, sitting discreetly as usual but in a new spot. Even though I had been looking for him all night, I did not know how long he had been there when I did finally see him. I felt great excitement to see him, and as soon as my set ended, I hustled over to his nicely hidden spot. As I walked up, he broke our pattern to speak first.

"Rocking out tonight, eh? You reached a new level."

"Thanks," I replied, feeling good to be recognized. Then I added, thoughtfully, "It is interesting, Philo, but I am always trying to take things up to that next level. It just doesn't always come together like tonight. It's a mystery."

"Just like our own lives," Philo added, even more ponderously thoughtful.

"Which," I said while taking a seat, "leads us right back to our ongoing conversation in which you, Philo, share with me, John, a step-by-step procedure for dual-track growth—*healing* the fears that limit, thereby *opening* me to the meaning that expands awareness."

"Rather nicely put," Philo answered, seeming a bit flat. Later I would reflect on the significance of his pointed remark 'just like our own lives.' Though I didn't take it so at the time, this statement can indicate an awareness of forces out of our immediate conscious control that nevertheless shape our lives. At the time I was so focused on getting instruction from Philo that I missed this meaning.

I did notice as I took my seat, however, that he seemed to be undergoing an inner struggle. An image popped into my mind. He looked like someone who was on the way to an urgent appointment to which he could not be late when his beloved mother calls with an urgent request he could not refuse. It was as if he knew he had to help his mother, but the dire consequences of the fact he would now miss the meeting were just then percolating through his awareness.

Looking back on this conversation, I am now certain that Philo came that night to 'break up,' so to speak. He was going to terminate our conversations, maybe even go back to where he came from. I am speculating here, but looking back on this night, especially in the light of Philo's claim to be from another planet, I would speculate that visiting Earth is highly illegal in his world and that perhaps there were some looming legal consequences he was facing. But of course, I didn't know this at the time.

Whenever someone is acting in a way that seems radically different from what I might expect, I have a method I have been using for years to illuminate what is going on. It has served me well. I pretend I am a movie director some hundreds of years in the future directing an historical movie about the very event that is happening now in my experience. The actor playing the part of the person acting strange then says to me that his lines don't make sense. "How do I play this part?" he asks me. "What is going on inside of me that is leading me to act this way?"

I then answer him in a way that makes his behavior explicable to him. In this instance, the actor playing Philo would ask me, "How do I play this part? Here we have this growing relationship between the two philosophers, John and Philo. Their relationship has been developing, and Philo has been wonderfully patient, calm, and wise throughout. John went through a difficult period of doubting Philo, but worked through it and is now fully committed to their conversations. But now Philo is suddenly acting weird. What is going on? How do I play this?"

How do I, the Director, reply? What *would* make sense of Philo's distance here? Again, perhaps he was facing legal complications for being here in the first place. That would certainly explain it. Perhaps he had escaped from jail or had run away from probation and was now a fugitive. That would explain his extreme secretiveness. That would also explain why Philo might suddenly have to run, leaving John without any explanation. His running would impact John but would have nothing to do with him.

My imaginary actor accepts my explanation, and it lets him play the part perfectly. Of course, the real Philo in real time was playing the part perfectly already. Whether this is what was going on with him or not, I did not know, but my imagined explanation is not limited to what I think I know. Philo aside, I have found again and again that this method leads to great, intuitive insights.

So while I didn't know at the time what was going on with Philo, I am now relatively certain that he did want to terminate our conversations at that time. I could readily imagine that his problem was that he had too much class to just disappear, but that he also was facing too much legal hazard to just tell me. Given this, he came that night to fudge his way through it.

Strangely, the situation was a lot like what I said earlier about gigs. If you think of our conversation as a long-running gig, then suddenly all the indicators were showing bad gig! In fact, the indicators were so negative that the 'wild joker X factor' rose up and entered the situation. And tonight anyway, I was the wild joker X factor.

Our conversations had all been profound, at least for me, but as far as he was concerned, they had not been particularly personal. It somehow did not feel quite right to ask Philo direct personal questions. For example, I never asked him to locate where he was from or to tell me in detail what it was like there. Did he have a girlfriend? Was he married? Was his mother alive? What did he do for a living?

As you might imagine, I was increasingly curious about all these personal things. Yet in spite of my sometimes all-consuming curiosity, it just did not feel right to ask. And this was not a wispy feeling of faint reluctance. It was a strong and clear feeling—do not go there!

In fact, so strong was this feeling that I even had the notion that my *not* asking about these personal things was a condition of our continuing to talk. Certainly Philo never did anything to welcome personal questions.

Maybe it was something to do with my magical evening of wonderful playing and music, but seemingly out of nowhere, acting on a sudden flash of intuition without any filtering on my part, I asked Philo a highly personal reverse question. With great focus and intensity, I suddenly blurted out in a seemingly random matter, "Please ask me a question."

It was a weird thing to do, but I noticed it somehow struck something in him. His face seemed to register deeply conflicting thoughts, as if two powerful, contradictory things were going on with him. He seemed for a moment to be struggling internally and then, quite suddenly, reached a resolution. From my perspective, even though I had no idea what it was, it seemed palpable.

He smiled warmly, relaxed, brought forward his customary concentration, fixed me with one of his burning stares, and said to me, "Here is my question to you. If you met someone from another planet, what would you ask him?"

He stared at me expectantly. Looking back, I think it was probably a test of some sort. At the time, however, I did not feel any pressure. In fact, I answered immediately without thinking. I *knew* exactly what I would ask. In a rush of words, I said, "I would ask if there was a right and wrong way to live and, if so, upon what is it based. I would ask him what he thought we should devote ourselves to as we live our lives. I would ask him about his religion, whether he had any and, if so, what it was like. I would ask him if he thought our individual life predated this incarnation and continued after it. I would ask how his people organize themselves collectively, that is, their politics."

He seemed pleased, mightily pleased. "You wouldn't ask about how his spaceship works," he queried, a smile playing with his expression?

"No," I replied without hesitation, "any more than I would ask about how his refrigerator works. I would be more interested in his culture, his religion, his art, his politics, his understanding of death. I might be interested in how his refrigerator works and all that, but that would be much lower on the list of things I would ask him about."

He just sat looking pleased. At the time I felt I had passed some sort of test. Certainly he seemed changed. It almost seemed as if he had made some deep and significant decision.

"Well, John," he said with a completely different energy from when we began, "let's continue with our conversations at the next available opportunity."

And with that, he got up and left.

CHAPTER 19

PHILO FINALLY CONFESSES

It turned out that I had another gig the very next night, and Philo came to that one as well. I was feeling good about the previous night. Not only had I sounded really good, which is always satisfying, but I thought Philo and I had worked out whatever was bothering him.

How little I knew.

The gig was good. It can't be that every night is as magical as the previous night, but this night was quite good in itself. Over my years of gigging I'd come to accept each gig for what it is. After all, if every gig was magical, then there would be no such thing as a magical gig.

In fact, regarding the nights of magic, I had come to understand that as one continues to play regularly, eventually becoming a master of the instrument, the magical nights do not necessarily come more frequently. It seems that the magic follows its own inclination and cannot always be manipulated or controlled. What does happen, though, is that the worst nights, the worst moments, the uninspired stretches—these get better. As a musical elder said to me once many years ago, "Your best playing is a gift given to you from time to time. You cannot demand it or control it. All you can do is be *available* for it. But your worst playing—*that* you can do something about! There is no upper limit on how great the gift of your best can be, but you can lift up the lowest level of your worst so that, no matter what, it never falls below a certain standard."

I think most touring musicians understand this. Even when what they give you is not their best, it is always at a pretty high standard.

So on this night after some inspired playing, I joined Philo as soon as I could. He seemed calm enough, sitting back with his hands folded in front of him, the right hand lightly resting on the left. He said, directly alluding back to the conversation we had been having about meaning, "We were talking about how it is often the case that a person will *not* experience the meaning and joy of his own life, *even when that life is going wonderfully well.* When you first told me you were precisely such a person, I thought, perhaps insensitively, how totally *strange* that is."

I sat thinking what a treat this was. Philo was exactly correct, and he had zeroed in on exactly what we were talking about. Normally I would be the one who brought up the topic and context of what we would talk about. But here Philo had nailed it. "Yes," I said brightly, "exactly that! You recognized and understood the troubling propensity we humans seem to possess of having the experience while missing the meaning of it. You were going to help me with my own version of it. Take for example this very evening," I said. "My playing involved some things I have been working on and so . . ."

"John," Philo said somewhat sharply, interrupting me. I must have been so startled as to have a look of shock on my face. Philo normally never interrupted me, especially when I was on a roll, as I clearly was. There was a moment of confused silence between us. We stared at each other and I noticed for the first time that he still seemed troubled. To me it looked as if he was wrestling with some issue of great magnitude.

After a few more strained moments, his expression softened and he said, "Please excuse my interruption. I do not intend to be rude." I didn't say anything but just kept looking at him, feeling more alarmed. "Something has come up," he finally said, looking forlorn. "It is a problem."

"I am sorry to hear that," I answered, though without feeling any sorrow. I noted, ruefully, that even here I was saying one thing and feeling something else. As he looked at me, I felt he could see this and that, whatever was going on internally with him, he was calculating into the mix my hurt reaction. I even wondered if this was some Zen-like ruse, specifically designed to put me in a situation where what I might say and do on the outside was not congruent with what I felt on the inside.

He didn't say anything, so I blurted out, "Not a problem," adding yet another falsehood to the one I had already offered. I actually was feeling that this was a HUGE problem. I meet very few people who strike me as powerfully as Philo did, seeming to me to have something important to teach me about life.

My colleagues sometimes jokingly accuse me of confusing philosophy with pop psychology. The accusation never stings, however, because I have always thought that the core, essence, and value of philosophy is the hope and promise that it can help us to lead a better life, a good life as Plato and Aristotle called it.

In my daily round of activities I meet and interact with many people who possess advanced knowledge and exquisite skills. But people with deep wisdom about the good life—this is not a regular feature of my existence. Lots of people say very wise sounding things, to be sure, but as an ex-girlfriend once said to me regarding my own behavior, verbalization is not actualization. Philo seemed different. I think that ex-girlfriend of mine would have appreciated him according to her standard. He certainly seemed wise, but as wise as he spoke, his words often seemed like a tease. It is as if his actualized wisdom was a pinhead sitting atop a vast reservoir of wisdom. I wanted access to that reservoir.

But now this!

Philo was looking at me intently as these thoughts flitted through my mind. "What has come up," he finally said, "may not be a problem for you, but I am definitely having a problem myself." He left it hanging at that.

As I looked at him, he seemed so sad, so troubled, that I began to feel compassion for him. My own disappointment and hurt feelings that perhaps he was thinking I was not *capable* of understanding or that I was not *worth* it—all of this melted away. Suddenly as I looked at Philo, I saw a very troubled person. I felt my heart soften and then crack open. "I am so sorry to hear this," I said, feeling the sweet warmth of compassion.

Now I may be imagining this, but at the time I felt certain he could sense this change. My words were suddenly aligned with my depths, *expressing* what I was feeling (compassionate concern) and not *covering* what I had been feeling (insecure rejection and its erstwhile companion, bubbling resentment). "Is this something you can talk about?" I asked with tender concern.

"Thank you," he said with depth, seeming to be moved by my concern. "By the nature of the case, it is not possible for me to talk about this with you at this time," he answered sorrowfully.

"That's all you have to say?" feeling understandably put off but responding kindly. He seemed to be struggling, even suffering. "C'mon," I said brightly, trying to encourage him, "you can tell me a little bit. I can be a good listener."

"I appreciate your offer, John," he answered, smiling wanly. "But there is a paradox here. You see, if I told you everything you would then understand why I can't tell you anything."

I reflected on that clever response later. At the time, it just passed me by. Having passed me by, I pleaded warmly, "Just a little?"

"Ok," he answered, looking worse than ever. "It is something about where I am from."

CHAPTER 20

HE TELLS ME...
AND I LAUGH

I laughed heartily. It wasn't a chuckle or a gentle sound of amusement. It was a full-bore belly laugh. I knew a Buddhist teacher once who used to say that such a laugh, fully spontaneous, not calculated, and seemingly bursting with its own exploding energy is the closest natural experience to the feeling of enlightenment.

"I'm pleased you take my plight with such good humor," Philo responded, smiling. My infectious outburst had lightened the mood.

"So where are you from?" I asked, still chuckling. It is hard to explain humor and what makes something so funny, but hearing this strange person, obviously a loner and an outsider, say in great sadness that he was not from Gettysburg, which is where our conversations were taking place, as if that were some revelation of high order—well, it just struck me as hilarious. I had no idea at the time where he was from, but if I had been forced to guess, I would have said some small town in Indiana.

"From far, far away," he answered. We both laughed at this. The mood was entirely different.

"Far, far away from another galaxy, no doubt," I said, still bubbling with laughter. The notion of this obvious stranger being a stranger still struck me somehow as hilariously funny. He didn't say anything but seemed to have a distant look on his face. "I know what you mean," I continued. I live so far from this barn that I have to drive home, especially if I have my guitar and amp with me. It would take me too long to walk, but I don't get sad about it." It was a bit of a jab at Philo.

Looking entirely serious, Philo asked, "What if leaving your home and driving here was highly illegal?"

"Well that could present a problem," I conceded. "I would have to be quite sneaky, I suppose." I wondered if perhaps Philo had a DUI conviction and had lost his license.

"Quite," he said, looking sad again. It was as if I was reminding him of some grave risk he was taking by driving.

"So you're from out of state?" I asked, trying to be helpful. His look let me know I was not even close. "From another country," I added, wondering about his generic American accent.

"You are getting ever so slightly warmer," he said, "but you are still on the sub-zero part of the guessing scale." He was not chuckling, but he said it kindly enough.

"Ooohhh, that is extreme," I answered, joining into the charade-like guessing game. "Well," I reasoned, "if you being from another country is still sub-zero on the scale of accuracy, then it follows that you must be from another planet." I drew this conclusion breezily, enjoying myself. I was thinking that he did seem a little like an alien. It was the first time I had thought of him as an alien.

At the time I was struck by the expression on his face—more precisely, it was the *lack* of expression that struck me. I was joking, of course, but he wasn't responding. "In fact," I continued, "you must be from a galaxy far, far away," I continued, mocking him slightly. "I could see the words 'from a galaxy far, far away' scrolling up and away at an angle, remembering the first, magical time I saw *Star Wars.*

"Farther than you can imagine," he said in full seriousness.

The mood had changed again. No longer light, but not with the somber heaviness of slightly earlier, now it was charged with a sense of confused expectancy. He seemed not quite sad now, but very definitely heavy. Deeply solemn.

Trying to lighten things up, I asked, "Are you telling me that you are an illegal alien?"

He smiled ever so slightly at my faint stab at humor. "That is a technically correct way of putting it," he said in the manner of a professor, "though in order to understand what you are saying in full context, you would have to put the emphasis on the illegal part."

I was too stunned to be stunned! I stared at him for I don't know how long. My mind was racing, trying its best to see humor in what he was saying. I kept expecting him to burst into merriment and say to me something like, "Hey, I'm just pulling your leg here. You don't *really* think I'm an alien, do you?" But he didn't, and the seconds just ticked by in agonizing slowness.

Finally, I heard words coming from my own mouth. "Are you telling me you are a philosopher from another planet and that you are here illegally?" I asked. Actually, it was more of a statement than a question. His expression did not waver.

"No," he replied firmly, "*you* are saying that."

"Well, I am only trying to make sense of what *you* are telling me, Philo," I answered, a bit argumentatively. "I'm not saying I believe it, either," I added.

"Please do *not* believe it," he replied with rock solid certainty. "But above all," he continued in unnerving earnestness, "please, please, and pretty please do *not* tell anyone else about this. Whatever you do, do *not* tell anyone. No matter how nice they are, no matter how much they pump you, no matter how much they claim to know about these sorts of things, you must say *nothing!*" He seemed so troubled.

I had another one of my flashes of intuition. In an instant I felt a sense of clarity about what was being said here. He was from another planet and was here illegally and probably in great danger as a result. He could not admit that to me, however, because doing so would probably compound his crime . . . and his danger. Strangely,

I felt this to be true even though he had not actually said so. Even more, I felt he would not admit it, but realized, too, that his not admitting it did not make it false. I also realized that I would not get much more out of him, and that I should not try. The personal benefits I was getting from our conversations, with the rich promise of so much more to come, was itself sufficient to keep me going.

"Well," I replied deliberately, in effect making a strong policy statement regarding the entire question of his origin, "can we return to the point of *feeling* the meaning and joy of life internally and not just understanding it intellectually? I mean, given where you might be from, this means your wisdom quite literally qualifies as that of a transcendental sort, and I've always been told that is the best type of all.

He smiled broadly. "You take my meaning," he replied with satisfaction.

Suddenly the alien thing didn't seem as important as it had when this conversation started. What did seem important, however, was getting further access to Philo's unique perspective and wisdom.

Chapter 21

I Am Not Concerned
Philo Is An Alien

Not surprisingly, things changed between us after that revelation. What is surprising, though, is that I find it difficult to recall that moment in any detail. It isn't that I can't remember what happened or what was said. It is more that I put it all together in a strange way, one that left the revelation as less significant than it was. Put differently, it was like I didn't put it together at all.

It was as if I was hungry and broke on the street and a banker walked up and told me I had a fortune in a hidden account in his bank and handed me the account number. Imagine if I then stuck the number in my pocket and continued scrounging for food. Something would need to be explained. Did I not believe the banker? Did I have some principal against having money? Did I fail to understand? In other words, why do I not immediately go to the bank and retrieve the money I need?

Looking back does not clear this up. I mentioned earlier that he had begun teaching me. That is not quite correct. Yes, he taught me much—more so now than ever—but he was never a teacher to me, if by teacher is meant someone with lessons and an agenda. Instead, all he did was answer some of my questions, and not without resistance. Indeed, he did not seem to be here in order to teach me anything. So why was he here? And why was he spending so much time with me?

As crazy as it sounds, he seemed to be here to listen to music. For some reason, he loved the music I played. He often said it was because of the total improvisatory approach I took. He said that even though my playing wasn't always at its peak, it was always interesting and significant, full of daring, courage, and a fully embraced freedom to explore. "You remind me of our early space travelers," he once said. "They flew to planets and galaxies without having an exit strategy or even a route home. Instead, they made it up as they went along."

I mention this because his limited willingness to answer my questions seemed to be a *quid pro quo* for my unlimited willingness to talk about my approach to music.

But more than the fact that he was a most reluctant teacher, there is something else as well. Even though the planet he was from seemed to be considerably advanced ethically, intellectually, and culturally, he never acted as if he or his people knew better or were wiser than me and my people. His counsel never took the form of his being right and my being wrong, or that what I thought was primitive compared to what he thought. It was always a matter of him saying that on his planet such and such a thing was generally accepted as being true. Even when what was generally accepted as true on his planet directly contradicted what was held to be true on Earth, he would never assume or infer that his people were right and we Earthlings were wrong. He seemed completely comfortable with the contradiction.

But the main thing that stood out was that he did not seem to think that Earthlings were dumb, savage, primitive, or unworthy. An inviting image would be that he was like a most tolerant anthropologist living temporarily with a remote aboriginal tribe, but even that image is not quite true. Unlike such a tolerant anthropologist, who would be constantly aware that he was visiting a *primitive* people, Philo in no way seemed to think that we Earthlings were unevolved, primitive, or inferior. Even though I gleaned from his limited remarks that his planet had produced a significantly more highly evolved civilization, he did not in any way compare it to ours.

Indeed, in our talks it would usually be me pointing out what I perceived as human stupidity, greed, and wickedness, especially from high places. He would then defend humanity from my accusations and disappointments, but his defense never took the form of embracing the things I pointed out, calling the 'bad' things I pointed to as really being 'good' things when properly understood. He accepted the genuine badness of the things I pointed out, but he would contextualize them differently, not seeing them as good in themselves but rather as small things. With all things fully and rightly considered, he would say these things are fully understandable, though 'small.'

He also often would remark in these contexts that in spite of all the talk on this planet about evolution, there were very few people who understood the implications and details of an evolving world.

One particular pattern of exchange between us that often repeated would involve my pointing out a wicked behavior, like for example the murder of people from the sky with drones, the targets chosen by a metadata analysis of their behavior. In other words, if a person did a certain number of things (visit a store, take a drive at a certain time, etc.) that certain authorities had decided are the types of things a known 'terrorist' might do, we would kill that person on the basis of that similarity. There would be no charges, no trial, and no opportunity to clear up mistakes or recognize mere coincidences. Instead, there would just be sudden death dealt from the sky.

And if anything could be worse than that, the way we programmed the murdering drones to stick around and murder the first responders to the original murder—that was even more shockingly horrific! Typically, I would angrily point out that this policy of murder was supported by large numbers of American Earthlings who clearly and obviously were operating under a number of delusions!

His response would always be some version of pointing out back to me that these people—often the majority in my country—were in fact *operating under a number of delusions!* "You should take your own observation more seriously," he would say.

Another of his points he would often bring up in this context would be to ask me how I would assess the ethical quality of a friend who did not know I was a vegetarian but instead was operating under the *delusion* that I was a big meat eater. If this friend went through considerable difficulty to serve me steak when I was hungry, doing his best to feed me what in his *delusion* he thought I wanted, does this make him a bad person?

This was his attitude to the people of this planet. Often deluded, yes, and even often *deeply* deluded. But he would add, acts done in delusion are not always revelations or even valid indicators of personal ethics and merit. One of his favorite examples in this context was to pose a question based on some version of this scenario: I need immediate medical care and a friend is urgently driving me to the hospital. This friend turns right when he should have turned left, honestly but mistakenly thinking the hospital is to the right. This delays our arrival, which is unfortunate and, depending on how long it takes to correct the mistake, perhaps might even be catastrophic, leading to my death. But would it be fair to conclude that this friend did not want me to get the medical treatment I needed or that he wanted me to die? If I died in transit, would my friend be guilty of murdering me?

As strange as it must seem for me to say this, we actually did not talk about these things very much. What we talked about was philosophy—and specifically, about how best to live, think, act, and be.

Which brings me back to my original question to Philo about *feeling* the meaning of our lives.

CHAPTER 22

PHILO FINALLY
COMES AROUND

The next time I saw Philo I immediately referenced our previous talk about feeling meaning. Without any introduction or banter, I walked up and said, "You were going to explain to me how I might begin to feel the meaning of things more fully."

Philo looked at me with an amused expression. "Oh, John," he demurred, "I don't think I can explain much of anything to you, let alone something like that."

I was certainly disappointed and even a little shocked by his reluctance. "How can you refuse?" I protested. "To do so is cruel."

"Cruel," he said, mouthing the word as if it were a specimen in a laboratory jar. He pondered my use of the word and then, more in humor than defense, said, "Is it cruel to respect—no, more than respect, fully to appreciate—your being and way of life? Would it be cruel for an alien artist to refuse to correct the enigmatic expression created by the mouth angle on Leonardo's *Mona Lisa,* making her either to smile or to frown without the delicious ambiguity of expression she is known for?"

What he said made sense, but it also seemed to be a cover to mask his reluctance to speak. I was certain that he possessed a specific wisdom in this area, and I was even more certain that I wanted this wisdom. I was like a kid asking an adult for ice cream on a hot, summer day. A simple refusal was not enough to make my desire for the ice cream go away, and my asking for it the first time was only the beginning of my endeavor to get it. I was going to keep asking, though in endlessly new and creative ways.

In that spirit, I changed strategies. "Ok," I said, "tell me about how it is on your planet. Do people on your planet ever fail to feel things as richly and fully as they might? Do they ever, as I so often do, have an experience but miss out on the satisfaction of feeling the deep and rich meaning of it?"

Philo sat back, looking a bit startled, but in a good way. My impression at the time was that asking about how it was on his planet both engaged him and alarmed him at the same time. Again, I am imagining this, but it seemed as if he could bypass some prohibition about giving me advice by simply talking about what the wiser ones on his world might do. Again, my impression was that while he might also be prohibited from doing that, the prohibition was not nearly as strict as the one prohibiting him from giving me direct, personal advice.

Now I should add here—and I am well aware of how unsettling and confusing this is—that my personal attitude towards this 'alien thing' was very confused and unsettled. It was the romantic poet, Coleridge, who talked about the need for what he called a "teleological suspension of disbelief" in discussing poetry. That is, the best poetry sketches out a truth, but it is not an empirical truth about the phenomenal world, something we can see for ourselves and validate with our own senses. It is a poetic truth, what Aristotle would call a larger truth, being more of a vision than a fact. So in order better to grasp that truth, Coleridge recognized we must suspend our ordinary empirical attitude of not believing unless we can see with our own eyes. Because we are suspending our ordinary and rational attitude of disbelief in the interest of finding a higher truth, our suspension is teleological.

This is what I had done with Philo the philosopher from another planet. It wasn't so much at the time that I *believed* he really was from another planet. It was that I had cultivated a teleological suspension of my extreme *disbelief* in such a thing. For all practical purposes, therefore, I accepted him as an alien visitor, but not because I believed him. If you had challenged me at the time, asking me why I did not demand proof from him and was instead playing along, I would have said I was playing along in a poetic sense. I had suspended my disbelief.

Doing so is not as strange or as difficult as you might think. In fact, we do so all the time with each other. When a person is acting strangely, not according to what we expect, we might say, "What planet is that guy from?" In saying that, we are not intending to raise an empirical question about the person's planetary origins but only to observe that the person is acting differently than expected. Similarly, I was able to relate to Philo's claim to be from another planet in a poetic sense. And as I have mentioned, whether or not he came from another planet, he was clearly and definitely from a different world!

Now my impression was that Philo was somehow legally prohibited from making corrections to me or to any of the other people I saw him relating to. And this made sense. I remember in *Star Trek* the prime directive of the United Federation of Planets was never to interfere in the internal development of a planet. To do so was strictly forbidden, and of course, Commander Kirk's great gift was the ability to skirt around the directive, interfering without interfering.

Philo was not Kirk, but the prohibition against speaking about his own practices, leaving it entirely up to me if I was influenced by what I heard—this seemed to be a much lesser prohibition. Later I learned that I was entirely correct about this, but at the time it was only an intuitive inspiration in the form of an enjoyable thought experiment.

I remember that my train of thought at the time was suddenly interrupted when I noticed Philo staring at me. He had a look of utter amazement on his face, as if he had just heard a monkey quoting Shakespeare.

"Well, John," he said kindly, leaning ever so slightly forward, "that is quite a question you are asking."

"I am asking in the simplest possible sense, Philo," I pleaded. "I am just looking for a step by step procedure by which I might begin to experience more of the meaning I already have in my life." Philo looked thoughtful. "It isn't that I want to change the world to make it more to my liking, though of course I would love to do that. I am decidedly not happy with the way things are on Earth. I am not asking you for help in that regard, as much as I would like to. I do think that if things were more to my liking, I would experience more meaning and satisfaction."

"So what you are asking me for, John, is not a way to make your world better?" Philo queried in a razor focused way, clarifying what seemed to be an important point for him.

"Again, Philo," I answered, smiling slightly at the sudden and uncharacteristic obtuseness he was showing, "I want to feel more passionately the meaning and joy that is already in my life *now*. I recognize it. I can identify it. I can even talk about it and describe it. I can convince others of its existence. But I don't always *feel* it. And even when I do, it is usually a weak feeling.

Philo leaned back, looking pleased as punch. "*That* is a topic we can explore, John," he said.

CHAPTER 23

WE TALK RELIGION

After sitting calmly for a few moments collecting his thoughts, Philo leaned forward again. "Your question is somewhat complex even though I know you don't intend it to be. So let me try to respond to it as methodically as I can."

"You could start with step one," I interjected, smiling.

"Oh, John, if only it were that simple. There is a first step, but it involves what you humans would call religion."

"Just give me the secular version," I shot back.

"Again," he said, smiling and seeming to be enjoying himself, "it isn't that simple. This *is* the secular version, you see."

"But you mentioned religion," I said, not understanding what Philo was getting at.

He smiled good-naturedly. "I warned you this was not simple. Let me give it a go. I have noticed it is quite common in your culture to separate the sacred and the secular. In this way, you think of the secular as one thing entirely distinct from the sacred, which you think of as something entirely different."

Philo's point seemed acceptable but not particularly complicated. I thought I knew what he was getting at. To clarify, I asked, "Are you saying that we tend to think of the secular and the sacred as two completely different things but that actually they are more intimately related and connected than we realize. For example, ice and steam are decidedly different, but you are countering that while ice and steam are completely different in our experience, they are in their underlying nature simply two different expressions of essentially the same thing?"

Philo laughed. "No, I am not saying that at all. But you, John, are making this already complicated issue even more complicated." I must have had an uncomprehending look on my face, because Philo, after looking at me carefully for a moment, continued to try to explain. "You see, your ice/steam example is inadequate because it assumes that the sacred and the secular *are* two different things, as steam and ice decidedly are.

"But," I interrupted, they are not. They are both manifestations of the same chemical mixture of two parts hydrogen and one part oxygen."

Philo burst into laughter, as if I had just cracked a hilarious joke. I looked at him in horror as, bubbling with dying chuckles, he gradually returned to ordinary speech. "Sorry," he said. "I guess I just take unlimited delight in your Earth tendencies."

"How is making an unassailable point about the similar chemical composition of water and ice funny," I demanded?

"It isn't, John. Not funny in the slightest. What I took delight in was your willingness to completely downgrade, even abandon your sensory experience, substituting an abstract intellectual explanation for your actual embodied, phenomenal experience. It is such an Earth thing."

"But steam and ice are both water. That is a fact."

"Call it what you will, but steam and ice are totally different things in the phenomenal world. In this context, the fact that they share an underlying similarity is a detail—and a detail of abstract thought, not of phenomenal experience. After all, one would never make a drink steaming to cool it down or stand over a bowl of ice and breathe in deeply to soothe the throat. Right?"

"Ok," I said, "I'm lost. Help me out."

"I told you this is complicated." Philo did not seem frustrated at all. "Think about it this way. There is the secular. We are in it right now. The wonderful beer we are drinking, the seats we are sitting on, the guitar you play, this magnificent nineteenth century barn with its complex timber framing—all of this is secular."

"Granted. Your point?"

"John, the sacred is not some *other* world where the beer is even more tasteful and the guitars are even more tuneful."

"Many of my colleagues would agree with you. They would say the exact thing you are saying as a way of *denying* the existence of a separate realm, the sacred."

"But they stop there, you see? They mistakenly think that in denying a separate realm of the sacred, which they do in a very specific way, making the point that there is no material evidence in the phenomenal world of the existence of a separate, non-material sacred realm—in doing this they mistakenly think this means they have established there is no realm of the sacred."

"But, Philo," I pleaded, speaking as if he did not see the most obvious thing, "if there is not a separate realm from the secular, then there is only the secular."

"Correct! It is called the universe. The word 'universe' means one world."

"So you are an atheist."

"Again, John, "the very concept of atheism involves accepting the bi-polar division between the sacred pole and the secular pole and then, in a very specific way, denying the sacred pole. I am trying to show you how on my planet these terms 'atheist,' 'believer,' 'sacred,' and 'profane' do not apply because we do not make the bi-polar separation between the two in the first place."

"But, Philo," I said, "that leaves you with the secular only. Call it the universe all you want, it is still atheism. I know lots of Earth atheists, but not a single one who denies the existence of the universe! In fact, that is their point. They say there is only the universe, parts of which we experience here on this planet. It is like waves in the ocean. We may only experience a limited number of actual waves on our beach, but in that experience we can grasp the entirety of what a wave is and thus can know in principle what waves are like everywhere."

Philo looked at me in appreciation. "I told you this was complicated," he said.

"But I'm being simple!" I protested.

"Not quite. It seems to you that you are being simple only because you are thinking entirely in terms of this bi-polar split. Where I come from we do not make this split, so for us everything is different. You see, it is not simple to think in terms of this bi-polar split. It takes a lot of cultural support, training, and individual practice in order to be able to do so. Your minds have to be carefully culturally constructed in order to do this."

Listening to Philo, my mind starting alternating between a sense of total confusion based on the absolute nuttiness of what Philo was saying and a hint that I was about to grasp some amazing, huge insight. Back and forth, crazy talk/major insight. Then my mind got calm and went blank. It was not as much as I was confused mentally as that I was empty mentally. I felt a sort of total mental cancellation. In that state I noticed Philo looking at me with great intensity.

"To put it in words," Philo said gently, "we think of the sacred as more of what you Earthlings would call an attitude. That is, the sacred is an attitude towards the secular, not a separate realm from it. Anything in the universe, and in fact the entire universe, becomes sacred when looked at a certain way. To see the sacred is not to be transported to some other place; it is to be aware wherever you are. Your own Earth poet, William Blake, said it as good as anyone ever has—it is to see eternity in a grain of sand."

"Any atheist would agree with that," I said condescendingly. "Your planet is atheist."

Philo laughed merrily, seeming to enjoy himself. "You just can't get away from that bi-polar foundation, can you?"

"So your planet is atheist?"

"We do not distinguish between atheism and belief, between the secular and the sacred the way you do. We are not bipolar ontologists or, as an Earthling might put it, metaphysical dualists. To us it is not that one has to be an atheist or a believer, one or the other."

I went blank again. "Philo, I'm confused. I don't even know what we are talking about anymore."

"We are getting to step one of the 'method of meaning' you asked me for. But this bi-polar separation of the universe into two different realms prevents that—no matter which of the two poles you plump down on."

"So the first step is seeing the secular as sacred?" I asked, trying to understand.

Philo moved his head back and forth, indicating a 'no.' "Not quite, John. But there is a bit of warmth in that."

"In what way am I getting warm?" I asked, still not sure what he was getting at.

"You are warm in that you do need to see the secular differently than you do now," he answered with conviction.

"So where am I cold?"

"You are cold in that you are still looking at things in terms of the bi-polar division between the secular and the sacred. This is why you ask if you should try to see the secular as sacred. The answer is no. You should try to stop seeing the world in terms of a division between sacred and secular."

With that, our conversation ended.

CHAPTER 24

DANG, THIS IS HARD!

It was two entire weeks before I saw Philo again. He had missed the gig the following week. Granted, I was not particularly worried that I would not see him again, but the extra week of waiting was still difficult to bear. I kept reminding myself of what Philo had said earlier, about how this time apart gave me the opportunity to review, observe, consider, and eventually *implement* the things he was telling me. None of it was easy.

I thought I could grasp well enough what he said regarding the structure of how I looked at what were considered religious questions—that is, in terms of a way of seeing based on a radical bi-polar division between the sacred and the secular. But while I could grasp and even accept the *idea* that this is the case, I could not move beyond it. Of course, as Philo later pointed out, the very nature of being structured to see in a certain way meant that I could not see things in any other way. And strangely enough, it was the very fact that I could not see things in any other way—not even imagine them as being different—that convinced me that I was locked into seeing them this way.

I kept thinking that I already *could* think of the sacred as being more of an attitude towards the secular than a separately existing reality. "I got this," I would say to myself. But then I would realize that Philo was saying something more than that. As he so often put it, one does not move beyond a bi-polar structured way of seeing by simply denying one of the poles. Philo agreed this is what many Earthlings are trying to do these days, with the more scientific humans tending to deny the sacred and the more religious humans denying or at least significantly downgrading the findings of science. But either way and despite the negations coming from either pole, the way of seeing of both scientific atheists and religious fundamentalists is still structured in terms of a bipolar mode.

But how do you change the very way you see things? It's not something you simply just do! It would be like changing the prescription of your glasses while you are wearing them! The best you could do is wear bifocals, enabling you now you see it this way and then to see it that way. But of course, mastering the duck/rabbit thing is not the point. It isn't a matter of learning to switch back and forth between the two poles; it is a matter of not having poles in the first place.

And how do you do that!

I really tried to grasp this, and sometimes I thought I had. Then it would melt and I would realize I was still in bi-polar awareness, just negating one of the poles from within that awareness. Still, I had the feeling that something really significant was involved here. In the end, it was something Philo said that helped me. He said that since one could not simply change the structure of the way one was seeing the way one can change the channel on a TV, it was a waste to try to do so. What one needed to try to do, he said, is to take care to notice the way one is seeing.

I remember expressing disappointment when he said that. "That's *all* I have to do?" I asked flabbergasted.

I remember well his reply. "John, he said without any trace of recrimination, "if you can manage to do that, you will enter the lists of champions."

So it was a long two weeks of working at seeing how I see. Every now and then I would think I might have caught a glimpse, but mostly I felt I was being stupid and wasting my time. As my students might have said, "I am not learning anything!"

I noticed Philo looking at me with interest as I walked up. This was different. He usually acted like he didn't know me. "I missed you last week," I said as I arrived at his table, pulling out a chair.

"Some things came up that required my attention," he answered, his tone suggesting finality. "How did your first step go?"

Even though he was focused on me, I felt I could sense a change in his 'vibe' when he said some things had come up. He seemed to be remembering something troubling. I had no way of knowing, of course, but I would guess he was facing some sort of trouble in intergalactic law. Perhaps he was being searched. Whatever it was, I could tell it was troubling. No, more than troubling, it was acutely dangerous.

But there was another angle to the fact I could sense his feelings so well, one that absorbed me more than my speculations and guesses about what might be troubling him. In fact, I'd been thinking a lot about this, especially the past two weeks. It was how, more so than with anyone I knew, I could sense the ebb and flow of his feelings.

Now the fact I was more empathic with him than with anyone I knew was totally counter-intuitive. You would expect me to have a natural simpatico with other Earthlings, if anyone, not with an alleged alien. If anything, this simpatico counted as evidence *against* his alien origin.

Even stranger, it seemed—and this was so subtle that I might be imagining it—that each time I was able to sense his internal state to a high level, my ability to sense the internal state of the people I knew got better. In short, I was becoming amazingly sensitive to other humans, but always starting with Philo.

I had resolved to bring that up with him, but for now I ignored it and responded to his question instead. "It was quite thoroughly frustrating," I answered, opening up to my feelings of being blocked and/or incapable of being able to see the secular and the sacred as aspects of the same thing.

"They are not the same thing, John," Philo replied definitively. "What I am talking about, the *consciousness* I am trying to describe, is recognized in your more esoteric spiritual traditions where it is called 'non-dual' awareness."

"Are we talking about monism and dualism here?" I asked, referencing a train of thought I had been travelling for much of the past two weeks.

"Not quite," he answered, seeming to sense my frustration. "What I am talking about, the way of seeing I am referring to here, is indeed 'non-dual,' but what you call monism is not. There is a joke about this. How does it go?" Here he looked up, thinking, "Ah, yes, here it is. What is matter? Never mind. Well what is mind then? Never matter."

It wasn't the sort of joke that makes you laugh, but it got the point across. Monism is generally the bi-polar awareness with one of the poles either cancelled out or reduced to the other. Thus, materialism is simply dualism with the spirit pole either denied or reduced to being an epiphenomenon of the material pole. Similarly, what you Earthlings often refer to as 'spiritualism' is the same dualism, only now with the matter pole denied."

"So why is this so hard to grasp?" I asked, feeling two weeks of pent up frustration.

"It isn't hard to grasp," Philo answered brightly. "It is impossible!"

CHAPTER 25

TREES AND TEMPLES

I was still reeling from what Philo said. Impossible! He said what I had just spent the past two weeks trying to do, obsessing on it and working on it throughout the day, was impossible! I must have look horrified because Philo jumped right in. "But you are doing a bang up great job, John. You have not wasted your time, I assure you. Just realizing, as you are doing, that the world you see as being 'out there' is literally being constructed by an implant—that is, your culturally constructed way of seeing—this is significant. It leads to a sort of humbled awareness."

"A humble awareness," I interrupted. "That could stand as a literal description of me."

Philo laughed. "Now you are boasting," he muttered between fading chuckles. "John," he continued, "we are touching upon the architecture of your awareness. This is significant, not just for you personally but also for your species, for your entire planet, even for the entire universe. Your aspiration in this must not be to *change* the architecture but to become aware of it as architecture, as a constructed thing. Once you have done that, movement begins."

"I'm doing my best," I said a bit weakly.

"Better than that," Philo said with emphasis! You have already done it!"

"I have?"

Philo looked at me directly, his vision seeming to drill right into the very architecture he is telling me to become aware of. "You are familiar with the primal distinction the ancient Greeks made between nature and art."

"Yes," I said, "everything is one or the other. It has to do with origin and causality. Nature is comprised of everything that happens without human agency, like the growth of a plant from a seed or the falling of the rain. Art, on the other hand, consists of everything that happens only because a human agent made it happen, like building a bridge or carving a statue."

"Precisely," Philo said, looking pleased. "Now let's imagine there was a tribe that came across a beautifully crafted temple and they marveled at it, wondering where it had come from. Let's further imagine that their elders told them it had come into existence the way an oak tree appears, that is, from having grown naturally from a 'temple seed.' This notion of temples growing naturally from temple seeds then becomes part of the architecture of their awareness, of their way of constructing/seeing the world.

"Not hard to imagine at all. There are frightening numbers of people in my country today who think that is how our increasingly unregulated economy in all its irrationality and injustice came about. Because a free market is entirely 'natural,' they say, they implement a policy of deregulation. 'Let the market police itself,' they say, 'and all will be well.' They totally fail to acknowledge that the economy is a cultural artifact."

"Again, John, precisely as you say. Now let's take our tribe believing that the temple is a naturally occurring thing, growing from a rare seed, sort of like a dragon's egg. Now let's say one member of that tribe was told by an outsider that the temple was fashioned and built by human hands. It was the shape and size it was because it was built that way. It could have been built differently. This new awareness would be HUGE! It would change the person and eventually the tribe. And even if this person continued to refer to the temple as having grown from the soil, still, everything would now be different in that tribe because of this new awareness. Core cultural assumptions would be in ferment, and even when the language remains the same, the understanding and consciousness are changing deeply."

"I see that, Philo, but isn't this dualism again—you know nature and art, one or the other."

Philo lifted his eyebrows looking impressed. "Nicely questioned," he said while nodding in affirmation. "Here is the answer to your point. A denial of identity is not a denial of difference. To deny the essential *identity* of a tree and a temple is not to deny the *difference* between them. There is still a difference between a tree and a temple whether we are seeing with the eyes of dualism, monism, or enlightened non-dual awareness."

I was assimilating what he said. Normally he would allow my turmoil of thoughts some moments to work their way out, but this time he interrupted me. "But, John, we can move on from this. This is not step one, however important it may be for you to dwell on it to prepare yourself for step one. So if I may borrow one of your lines, 'Let us just skip forward here and go straight to step one.'"

"I don't feel prepared, Philo."

Philo laughed. "This is a new one. I would have expected you to suggest moving straight to the final step before admitting you were not quite ready for the first one."

"It is how I feel, Philo. I don't feel ready. In fact, this whole discussion is not only difficult, it also feels somewhat pointless."

"Acknowledged, but I can assure you we are on track and you are prepared regardless of how you might feel about it. So let's roll along to what you are calling the first step."

"Ok, fine with me," I said, noting a touch of an edge in my voice. "But please let me give voice to one concern first." I took a moment to gather myself and connect with what was bothering me about this. "You are always telling me to clarify my intention, to become aware of what I want. My intention is to feel more meaning, purpose, and joy in my life. And it isn't just to create these things. I have them already. It is to *feel* more deeply that with which I am already blessed."

"Indeed."

"But Philo," I snapped, "this isn't helping. It isn't helping me feel more meaning, more joy."

"Nor will it," Philo snapped back. I sat back in shock. He continued. "As great, wonderful, and essential as philosophy is, philosophical understanding and insight is not what provides a sense of meaning and purpose."

"What does?" I asked, wondering if I should feel offended.

Philo looked at me in mock shock. "An earnest question," he said, raising his eyebrows.

"Earnest," I mused. "Is that another word for impatient?"

Philo smiled. "That's the spirit, John."

"Is that spirit in a non-dual sense?" I replied. We both laughed.

"That's a brilliant rejoinder, John. It isn't just funny, which of course it is. More than that, it also illustrates the very point at issue here."

"How so?" I asked, not seeing it at all.

"The illustration is not your words. It is not the point you are making. It is the spirit of your response. You see, when I refer to the 'spirit' of your response, I am not referring to some otherworldly thing, to something transcendental. But, again, let's move on because this is all preparatory."

"I'm sorry, Philo, but I just don't get the point at all."

"No need to worry. Step one is opening to and becoming aware of a larger perspective. Let's call it an eternal perspective, a mental stance above and beyond the rushing turbulence of the moment."

"I can't believe it," I said, feeling a complex mixture of unease, confusion, and concern. "You are going all religious on me."

"How so?" Philo asked, not seeming disingenuous.

"By adopting an eternal perspective! Philo, that is God talk. You are talking about adopting God's point of view!"

Philo smiled good naturedly. "Oh boy, that word 'God' is so heavy with and burdened by assumptions and baggage that using the word does more to get in the way than to illuminate things, doesn't it?"

"Exactly."

"So let's change the word. Let's not say God or even eternal perspective. Let's say," and here Philo looked up pretending to be thinking, "that instead of the term God we use cosmic force." He paused for effect. "No, that won't do either. Let's call it the red energy. Hmm. That won't do either. Red isn't everyone's favorite color, after all, and the poetry of red, indicating force, will, and passion, may or may not be effective here. Hmm. How about the blue force? Different poetry, but is it better? No."

"What's your point, Philo?"

"I'm not making a point as much as illustrating the problem. One of your philosophers—I think it was Heidegger—once brilliantly observed that we do not speak language as much as that language speaks us. That is, there are deep cultural assumptions, judgments, and predispositions built into language. A language is not just a bunch of symbols. It is a life form. In this sense, there is no 'clean' language.

"Math?" I suggested.

"The filthiest of all!" Philo exclaimed.

"I have a lot of mathematician friends who would strenuously disagree. They love the clarity and cleanliness of math."

The dirtiness of math does not come from the clarity of what it assumes or says. In that sense it is pristine, sparkling clean. The dirtiness comes from what it leaves out." I must have had the stupid look on my face because Philo continued with an explanation. "Let's say you needed immediate medical attention and the physician you went to refused, saying you were an unworthy sort and that you deserved to suffer."

"Totally filthy."

"Exactly. But let's say the person you asked replied, 'Would you like cream and sugar with that?' It is still filthy in the sense that you are not getting the medical care you need. The person you ask tells you he only serves coffee and the only thing he can do is add cream and sugar. The filthiness of his response is a matter of the possible scope of answers he could give. Not being a physician, none of his possible responses are adequate. He can only give you cream and sugar or not."

"What does this have to do with math?"

"Math deals with *quantities.* It does not address *qualities.* 'How should I live?' is not a math question. The answer is not a number. It is in that sense that math is dirty. It is because of what it does not do, does not address, does not see—this is why the turn to math is dirty."

"Just like asking a coffee vendor to perform an advanced medical procedure," I chimed in. "It is the wrong person to ask."

"Yes, John. So when I talk about adopting an eternal perspective, I am not making a dirty claim about a floating divinity. I am talking about a posture of consciousness, a mental orientation, not an object of awareness. That is why the name is not so important."

I really started to grasp what he was talking about but before we could continue, he was gone.

CHAPTER 26

THE VIDEO GAME OF LIFE

As by now you can imagine, I spent the week before seeing Philo again puzzling and wondering about what we talked about. I was hoping he would be there the next week, and when it finally rolled around, I was ready. Interestingly, even given that I had no idea of whether he would be there, I managed to convince myself numerous times during the week both that he absolutely would be there and that he absolutely would not. There was no new evidence, but my mind, working over what I knew, was able to draw the firm conclusion that he would definitely be there—until my mind, still with no new evidence, drew the equally firm conclusion that I definitely would never see him again.

Of course, the difference was how I was feeling. It was therefore most illuminating (and humbling) to note for myself how my mood of the moment shaped my 'rational' thinking.

Still, I was expecting him to be there. And he was! But there was one thing. He seemed even more circumspect than normal with his appearance and location, somehow finding a place to sit that was obscured from general view even more so than before. Maybe I was imagining this, but it seemed like he was taking extra precautions after having told me where he was from.

But he was there and I had just spent an entire week thinking about what he was telling me, so I launched into my questions without any introduction. "So, Philo," I said as soon as I was in earshot, "when you say step one is taking a larger perspective, the eternal perspective as you put it, am I correct in these two points?"

Philo had been looking a bit paranoid when I walked up, but he smiled now with a calming radiance. "So we are jumping right in, are we? Good. What are your two questions?"

"Thanks. They are qualifications, really. The first is this: When you say to take the eternal perspective, you are not affirming a God or a particular God. You are not affirming theism or pantheism or anything like that, right?"

"Correct." Philo remarked. "But at the risk of being a pedant, I am not denying them either. Properly understood, since I am not referring to the *object* of awareness but rather to what I might call the orientation of awareness, any claim about the existence or non-existence of God is beyond the purview of my point. It is like two high school kids facing expulsion and the one says to the other, 'We will remember this at our twenty year reunion and laugh.' In saying that, the student is accessing the psychic orientation of what I am calling the eternal perspective. He is not making a claim about what the school authorities may or may not do or about what will happen to the two of them in the intervening years. It is an orientation of awareness in *that* moment."

"Got it." I said. "And the second qualification is that when you talk about opening to this larger perspective in the moment, you are not in any way denigrating or denying what is happening in the moment. You are not saying that the two high school kids you mention do not recognize they are in trouble or that terrible consequences for them may well be imminent. You are not denying the world in any way."

"Exactly that, John," Philo said, looking pleased. "Let's say you are playing a video game and you are deeply involved in the action."

"I'm not much of a video gamer, Philo."

"This is just an illustration. Follow along. I'm connecting this to what you insist on calling 'step one,' and which you've got me calling it as well."

"What's the connection? That I'm playing the game and loving it?"

"Precisely. You are involved. Deeply involved. But now, ever so gradually, a new danger arises, one not *from* the game. You get so involved that you stop enjoying yourself. You become intense, concerned, angry with your performance and results. You begin to suffer."

I tilted my head in thought, "It happens all the time. In fact, the more fully it happens, the better the game. I've always been struck at how video games, as they become better, become more like everyday life. It makes me wonder if what we call real life isn't just a video game that has been perfected."

"Careful, John, you don't want to jump ahead of yourself here. So back to the game. You are so intense with it, so involved, that you have begun to suffer. Now if the person playing and now suffering was wise, what would he or she do at this point?"

"Quit playing. I mean, if you are playing for fun and it stops being fun, you stop playing. Simple."

"That is certainly an option, though hardly a simple one, and not one we see taken very often, even by the wise. That is because it defeats the purpose to quit. Our fun is in playing the game, mastering it, succeeding within it, not *quitting* it. We could quit, but we would be retreating from our suffering, not mastering it."

"Fair point."

"So what other options do we have?"

"I guess there are two. We could quit . . . or we could continue to play."

"And suffer?"

"Yes, and suffer." I mused. "Is there another option?"

"There is, John. And interestingly, it is just the way it is in life. When things are wrong in our lives, it often seems that our only choices are to continue to suffer or to commit suicide. We have a third option. We can continue to play, but without suffering. We could experience more joy, fun, and meaning while we play. This is what you want. It is what *all* Earthlings want."

"It is, but how to get that? Believe me, I have tried. Since the suffering comes from caring so much, I have tried to play the game, so to speak, without caring about the result so much. If I don't care whether I win or lose or how I play the game, I can just sit back and enjoy the process."

"And how has that worked out for you?"

"It hasn't worked out very well. I either manage not to care, in which case the game just isn't as much fun anymore, or I do care, in which case I begin to get frustrated and angry and begin to suffer again. Just like life! Either way it sucks. You get to choose the cool agony of not caring or the hot agony of caring and frustration, anger, and defeat."

Philo seemed amused. "Yes, just like life—only life without a third option, which, interestingly enough, is what we might call the first step."

"I'm ready for that Philo, but I'm just not seeing it."

"Ok, let's go back to our video game. You love it. You are thoroughly involved in it. You are fully enjoying yourself playing it. But then it starts to go bad. You get frustrated, show flashes of anger, and begin to suffer. What do you do then?"

"I could quit."

"Yes, but now you are not having any of the joy of playing. You just quit. Any other options?

"Well," I said, "I could do what the Buddhists suggest. I could realize my suffering comes entirely from my desire to win. By giving up my desire, I give up the ground of suffering."

"Indeed you do, but the game is about winning. You play to win. The joy is in the winning or at least to be on the path to victory. So giving up the desire to win is a lot like quitting, only you don't stop. You quit inside, so to speak, but continue to play on the outside, only now without passion or caring. Suddenly it doesn't *mean* anything when you win or lose. In other words, if you succeed in not caring, your suffering goes down, but at the cost of enjoyment, meaning, and satisfaction. You no longer suffer from the game, but you also no longer experience joy, fulfillment, and meaning from it either."

"That seems about to cover the situation, Philo. Certainly life is like that. To open myself for fulfillment simultaneously opens me to the possibility of suffering. The greater the possible fulfillment, the greater the possible suffering. This is why players who lose the championship generally feel much worse than players who did not even qualify for the playoffs. Again, this is life."

"But it isn't, John. This is where step one applies."

"Please explain, using the game as an example."

"Certainly. To recount. You feel frustrated in the game and are suffering. What to do? You could just keep playing and suffering, playing what your Thoreau called a game of 'quiet desperation.' Or you could quit, ending the suffering but also ending the joy. Or you could continue playing, but not care about the result. You don't suffer now, but you don't feel exultation at success or pain at failure. You have no passion because the game no longer has meaning to you."

"I got this, Philo. What is the other option? What is step one?"

Philo laughed good naturedly. "There is the old John back again."

"Give it to me. The first step applied to the game."

"It is to flash into the awareness that this is just a game—that is the eternal perspective—while continuing to play the game *and* to continue to feel passion about the outcome. It is *just* a game, but it also *is* a game! So you continue to play passionately having allowed your awareness to touch into the fact it is just a game."

I somehow felt illuminated by this. "Ok, Philo, I think I get the non-dual thing as applied to the game. I touch into a sort of transcendental awareness, seeing myself playing a game which exists in a smaller perspective from the one that sees it is a game. I keep playing *and* I keep caring. I do not leave the smaller awareness but rather frame it in the context of the larger awareness. And I don't avoid the frustration and pain of losing. I embrace it. Having touched into the larger awareness, I exult in the experience of it."

"That is exactly it, John," Philo said, looking mightily pleased. "The hook is to stop trying to avoid the frustration and suffering but to embrace it. You still have a bi-polar dualistic awareness *in* the game, but now it is framed in the eternal perspective. There is a tension between these two, to be sure, but you never let one dissolve into the other."

"So that is step one," I asked, "to access a larger perspective— that it is just a game—without thereby denying the game, minimizing my passion, or unplugging the screen?"

"Yes. Even when you lose, the experience is still passionate, meaningful, and even fun. Losing is not failure. It is merely the shape of your experience in the game at this time. Accessing the larger frame let's you experience this for yourself."

"And life itself is just such a game," I mused, feeling wonder.

"Bingo," Philo said excitedly.

"So what is step two?" I asked.

CHAPTER 27

WHY IS IT SO HARD
TO START THE CAR?

A ll along I had been trying, earnestly and devotedly, to do the things Philo was suggesting to me. They were working. It wasn't like magic where there was a clear before and after. It was more like learning to play the piano where one was practicing earnestly and sufficiently. Even though, day by day, there would not seem to be much improvement and sometimes even a falling off, there were various markers—a friend hearing you after two weeks and commenting on how much better you have gotten or how easy a tune you could not play two weeks earlier was this time—that indicated steady improvement. It was that way with my perception of my own life.

Needless to say, I was eager to clarify with Philo what we had spoken about regarding step one. I understood the *idea* of it, that I needed to touch into a larger 'framing' perspective, what he called a 'transcendental awareness,' without thereby leaving the many 'games' of life or diminishing my passion for them. I fully understood the idea but was not too clear on how to implement it.

I felt the normal surge of excitement when I saw Philo, sitting especially carefully hidden. It seemed like the more time he spent among us, the more paranoid he got. He never said specifically what worried him, but I imagined it being some crack intergalactic force that, having learned about his transgression, would swoop in and kidnap him. Whether or not that is true, he certainly acted suspicious in a way that suggested something like that was true, or at least that he was convinced it was true.

Anyway, when I greeted him, I mentioned my desire for 'how-to' instructions. "There he is," I said in a jocular manner as I approached, "the man of wisdom dispensing advice about the steps needing to be taken in words of wisdom but not in actions of impact."

"An interesting welcome," Philo replied, seemingly unfazed by my implicitly critical comment. He did fix a look on me as if he was staring at a medical X-ray. I always felt uneasy when he did this. It felt like he was looking at me beneath my presenting surface. As over the weeks I was myself managing to see myself beneath my presenting surfaces, it felt less creepy and more like an actual X-ray, but it still unsettled me somewhat.

After a long moment, he released the single-pointed intensity of his gaze. "A little bit uncharitable in our remarks it would seem," he said pleasantly enough. He often did this, saying something that might otherwise be considered confrontational, but saying it in such a tender way that it did not come across that way.

"Not uncharitable, Philo," I answered lightly, "just eager. I've been thinking a lot about step one since we talked last."

"And?"

This was another thing Philo did often, which I had come to appreciate. That is, he never assumed he knew what I meant but always asked me to clarify, asking as many times as was necessary. This regular practice of forcing me to clarify served to help me be much clearer myself. I noticed I had begun to ask for clarification with my Earth friends, to great, productive benefit.

"Well," I replied, "I love what you explained about step one. It seems really useful. I agree with it without any hesitation whatsoever. I am determined to do it . . . ."

"And?"

"It is more of a 'but,' Philo."

Philo smiled indulgently. "Then please continue. You were saying you 'liked' the idea of step one, of touching into a transcendental frame, *but . . . ."*

"Yes, exactly," I interrupted, feeling intensely pleased to be understood. This was another thing Philo did that I really appreciated. He would often ask for clarification from me, and he often corrected me, but he rarely if ever argued with me. It was never a matter of me being told I was wrong. He seemed to respect the integrity of the thought process that had led me to whatever understanding I had and instead of rejecting it he would add to it.

I continued. "The *but* part, Philo, is that I don't know how to implement step one. It is like I am seeking advice about a long and potentially hazardous journey I am about to take, and you tell me the first step is to start my vehicle, an alien flyer you have given me. I certainly understand that I need to start my vehicle and I am eager to do so, but how? *How* do I start an alien flyer? Does it have a key? Do I just push a button? Which button? I'm not questioning whether the vehicle can fly or whether it will take me to my destination. I am asking how to start it."

I had spoken with feeling and passion and as I finished I noted Philo had a strange look on his face as he peered intently at me. I couldn't tell whether he was pleased, frustrated, or disappointed. Finally one of his signature half smiles flashed across his face and he said, radiating understanding and kindness, "I see your point."

"Can you help me with this?" I said, sounding to myself like I was pleading.

"Hmm," he mused. "I could say this is what you Earthlings would call a 'you can lead a horse to water but you can't make him drink' type of situation, but that wouldn't be fair." He then seemed to lose himself in thought. I always found it disconcerting when he introspected, as he was now doing. He really seemed to go somewhere else when he did this. It was as if all outer systems were on minimum watch while something significant and hidden was being developed inside. In my more paranoid moments, I even wondered if he was entering into some sort of communication with someone or something far, far away. The longer it lasted, the more unsettled I got. This one was mercifully short, however.

"You know, John," he said suddenly, looking up and coming back fully into operating mode again, "you make me wish I was a proper teacher. Your request is a fair one, one I should have anticipated. It is, however, one that is most difficult to satisfy."

"You're a great teacher," I rushed to exclaim. "So just help me here. What do I need to do to get that transcendental overview?" Philo looked pained, as if I was asking him to reveal a deep family secret.

"If only it were that simply done," he replied, looking a touch frustrated.

"Give it a go, please. You could do what one of my favorite blues song describes—to let your mind go on vacation while keeping your mouth working overtime."

Philo smiled. "Moses Allison," he said. "It is an apt allusion, John." He appeared to get distant. Perhaps he was accessing the song. I watched as there were some long moments of intense silence. Paradoxically, even though his mouth was on vacation, his mind seemed to be working overtime. "It is so complex," he finally said, expressing a sort of exasperated weariness.

"What is the problem," I asked in full earnestness?

Sighing, he answered, "It goes back to religion." His voice seemed tired.

CHAPTER 28

WHAT IS IN THE RED BOX?

It seemed that Philo had somehow reached an impasse and the block was religion. It was strange to me that this would be the case. I am not particularly religious myself. I am, however, what would today be called 'spiritual.' In fact, I fit the template, 'spiritual but not religious.'

Philo did not seem even slightly religious. He clearly was deeply spiritual, however, and I was under the distinct impression that we had connected on a spiritual level. I had trouble understanding or even anticipating what the block could possibly be.

There was no doubt, however, that there *was* a block of some sort, and it often manifested, this being just the latest expression of it. I would ask a question, seemingly no different than any of the questions I was asking constantly, and Philo would (on these rare occasions) get a pained look on his face. He clearly was operating under some sort of restraint, though its particular nature was unknown to me.

I had this thought picture. In it, Philo desperately wanted to talk to me, to tell me things, to answer my questions, to share with me everything he knew. Some higher authority, secular rather than religious but entirely unknown to me, had given him permission to tell me anything—except, if you will, what was in the red box. "If you mention what is in the red box," the authority warns him, "some dire, catastrophic consequence will ensue. You must never to that!" the authority sternly warns him.

Of course, this was just a picture in my mind. Still, if the situation *was* like my thought picture indicated, then this would explain

Philo's reaction. It was as if I asked him, brightly and cheerfully, "Philo, what is in that red box?" That would explain his pained look, his mumbling about how complicated it all was, and—for me, the worst part—his complete failure to respond. In this thought picture of mine, he *wants* to respond, to tell me what I want to know. It is that he is prevented from doing so somehow.

Since Philo was looking more pained than usual and since he still had not volunteered anything, I told him my thought picture. His reaction was the most puzzling thing yet. I expected him to laugh, to gently chide me for my fevered imagination, or at least to flash his enigmatic smile. That did not happen. Instead, he looked stunned. It was as if he had been busted, as if I had revealed that I knew his secret. He was catatonic. He reacted as if, joking, I said I could read his mind and then went ahead and did!

Stunned, shocked, silent!

Gradually—or so it seemed at the time—his reaction seemed to morph from one of stunned, shocked silence to one of maximally impressed amazement. As I sat there, not understanding, he seemed to begin to look at me with newfound respect, awe even. I felt his gaze on me more deeply than usual, as if he was checking something. Then he got that far away look again and said something incredibly strange.

"I can see why they consider you Earthlings to be such a threat," he said plainly, without affect.

That was stunning—not only completely out of context, but chilling in its implications. Before I could process, however, he abruptly changed. Whatever was going on in his mind seemed to reach some sort of resolution, and he took a breath of resolve. Focusing on me and becoming once again completely present, he said, "So you want to know what is in the red box."

"Absolutely," I replied, without thinking. "Only now we can begin with who 'they' are and why 'they' see humanity as a threat."

Philo smiled pleasantly. "I suppose it is in the nature of an attack dog to attack." I must have had an uncomprehending look on my face because he immediately added, speaking in a most calming, soothing tone, "Don't worry. We will get to all that. Right now, however, let's focus on step one."

"That would be fine with me," I answered, not entirely feeling it. This often happened with Philo where, in talking, our positions would reverse. Even though I had been bugging him about step one and he seemed slightly withholding, now that he was ready to go, I wanted to focus on 'them' and the threat they perceive.

Philo seemed to be inside of me. "So you say," he said gently. I didn't say anything, but my mind was racing. After a moment, he added, enigmatically, "I suppose we will soon find out."

Then he said something that was both puzzling and troubling. Something had affected him and he was different than I was used to. Normally he is smooth and on top of things, very artful. This was different. It was not that he was mean or cutting. It was more that he was freaked out. "Anyway," he continued, "Many of you Earthlings look at your planet and see a fine property. Some of you even recognize the property is being trashed, dirtied and denigrated and so, increasingly, you want to clean it up. Some of these look at the way it is dirtied and think they are seeing the depths of human nature being revealed. The real dirty thing, they think, is humanity. I have even heard Earthlings say that what is called the 'environmental problem' is really a human problem."

"Aren't these people correct?" I asked, feeling confused about what Philo was getting at here. "You don't see it this way?"

"Hardly," he answered, but it did not feel like he was talking to me as much as with himself. "Earth is not a property. It is a prison! You Earthlings see jail behavior and think you are witnessing the revelation of human nature. I see jail behavior and I weep. This magnificent being, the blossom of evolution, is in jail. Humanity is in prison."

"I don't get what you are getting at, Philo," I said, feeling concern. He continued, almost as if I was not there.

"The magnificent human is in jail. I weep and gnash my teeth, tearing at my clothes. This is why I might seem indifferent to the things you hate—the prejudice, injustice, suffering, greed, selfishness, and corruption. You want to punish the evil doers. I want to liberate the jail. I do not see human nature revealed but the sociology of prison exposed."

Suddenly he got up, turned and said, "Forget that rant. I am not myself tonight. I will see you next week."

With that he was gone. I just sat for a minute, stunned. I kept thinking, "That was really weird."

CHAPTER 29

SEX AND THE SINGLE ALIEN

O ur conversations changed (again) from that point. No, that is not quite right. It is more the case that our relationship changed from that point. How? I could say that he seemed to respect me more, but that is not quite it. As strange as it sounds, it is more that he had come to have a new and deeper respect for humanity. This new respect applied to me, of course, but I don't think it was primarily about me. I just received the glow of it.

Let me use an example here to clarify my meaning. Imagine that you were working with monkeys and that, further, you respected the species and thought they had great potential, especially in the mental/intelligence areas. Among those who study monkeys, in fact, you are known as having significantly *more* appreciation for the potential mental capacity of monkeys than most of your colleagues think is warranted.

Imagine, further, that you are working with a uniquely talented monkey and you hope to get some data from him that would show your colleagues just how high the bar is as far as the mental capacity of monkeys is concerned. You want to prove that monkeys are capable of significantly more than they are given credit for in the research community. Things are going well in your research.

And then!

Imagine one day this monkey started to talk to you, holding a normal conversation, even making philosophical observations, but most impressively, using his mind in higher-order, intuitive ways that you thought was the defining characteristic of your own species.

Try to imagine the impact of that!

You already had a high opinion of the species—the highest among all of your colleagues by far—and you already had a high opinion of this individual you are studying. But now! Things are off the charts. Not only are monkeys smart, they are potentially smarter and more gifted than your own species!

In that moment your appreciation of the individual monkey would go up, but mostly, your already high appreciation of the species would soar. This is what it seemed had happened to Philo regarding humanity.

In fact, let me take a break from recounting conversations with Philo about step one, which I will return to shortly. This is a good time to recount a completely separate conversation, quite brief, that occurred later and thus is out of sequence but which illustrates this expanded, even excessive appreciation of humanity that Philo had come to possess.

The conversation was about sex. Now Philo did not strike me as the sexiest person around. I have mentioned how difficult it is to describe his physical appearance, how nondescript he appeared. Even so, he was not repulsive or disgusting in any way. He was withdrawn, to be sure, but not creepy. You could bring him home and he would not embarrass you. It is just that nobody would remember much about him the next day.

Anyway, my point is that he was certainly *eligible* for a date. So this one day I asked him whether he had dated or had any interest in dating an Earth girl. His response surprised me and I want to share it with you now in the context of establishing his huge appreciation of humanity, a valuation larger even than my own or that of any human I know.

Now keep in mind that when I asked him this I did not know what his core physical nature was. I knew what he looked like to me, of course, but I did not know what was behind that appearance. I didn't know if the Philo I saw was what he actually looked like or if he was wearing a high-tech disguise. And if he was wearing a disguise, I didn't know if the disguise was a physical covering or shell over his actual material body or perhaps even some sort of advanced psychic alteration device designed to shape my perception so that I would 'see' a non-descript human before me when actually sitting before me was, say, someone who looked like a lizard.

In other words, I did not know if it was physically possible for him to have sex with an Earthling.

His response, even before he said anything, caught my attention, however. To wit: he acted stunned, as if he had been hit. But it wasn't the question that stunned him; it was the subject. I could tell immediately that sex was as charged and significant a concern for his species as it is for us.

People who say sex is *just* a natural function, like eating and going to the toilet, have always seemed to me to miss not only the magic of sex but the cosmic significance of it. As someone so wisely and insightfully put it, sex is more mental than physical. There is the physical aspect, of course—the raw, physical urge and the often sweaty, grunting fulfillment. But so much *more* than that is the culturally coded, mental aspect. Indeed, to be sexy is a lot like being rich in that it creates a social presence, an appealing identity. In fact, so strong is this tendency that I recall Marx once opined that one of the main appeals of a money system is that it enables the wealthy person to get women he would not normally be able to attract in nature.

So even before Philo said anything, I could tell that among his species sex had a similar function. Once again, that was so much *more* than a mere natural function.

But what he then said surprised me so much that I am sharing it with you now.

He looked crestfallen when I asked him about dating an Earth girl. He looked down for a moment and then gathered himself.

"John," he said, "imagine that you were a poor and unwashed peasant visiting the capitol of the realm, surrounded by beautiful princesses from luxurious palaces, all dressed resplendently and smelling sweet. What would you do, being a lowly and poor peasant? Would you just walk up and ask for a date? Compared to them, remember, you are unwashed, boorish and vulgar. Would you break into one of the palaces and introduce yourself?

"Philo!" I replied in shock. I'd never heard him express any level of insecurity, let alone this pathetic, demeaning, self-wallowing image of total repulsiveness. "What a poor image. How about this one? You are a Prince of the realm, a pure aristocrat. You are walking through the slums, surrounded by working peasants. Many of them could be a potential Cinderella, and you are a definite Prince Charming. You pretty much have your pick of the liter. Given that, I'm asking if you have an interest. Have you tried dating any of them? What is your level of interest?"

I still remember the look of shock and horror on Philo's face. It was as if I had said the most completely inappropriate thing possible. "You just don't get it, do you," he said. I felt he was judging what I just said. I was not used to from him, not even in a milder, lesser form.

I was stunned. I said that to be nice to him, to support him. Feeling so massively judged and rejected, I got defensive. I tried to explain: "I was just asking a simple question and when you put yourself down . . ."

"I did not put myself down," he said emphatically, interrupting.

"But you described yourself as an unclean peasant among shining Princesses," I countered.

"No, not that. I described myself as a peasant *in comparison to* the Princesses of the realm. I was elevating the Princesses, not putting myself down. If I could jump higher than anyone on my planet and I visited a land where everyone could jump at least six feet higher than me and if someone on that planet asked me if I had any interest in jumping along with them, I might reply by saying something like, 'Compared to them, I can't even jump.' I would not say that to put myself down. I am a champion on my planet! I would say that in acknowledgement of the magnificence of the people I am visiting!"

This was said with great passion. He looked at me with disappointment, saying again, "You just don't get it."

"Get what?" I asked, not trying to be difficult.

"Get how magnificent and elevated the human being is."

Philo was right. I did not see the magnificence and elevation that he did.

I mention this episode to provide context for our continuing conversation about purifying consciousness. And now, let me return to that conversation.

CHAPTER 30

BACK TO STEP ONE

I was mentioning how it seemed that Philo had an exalted, even excessive appreciation for humanity. What puzzled me about this was that he was not unaware of any of the horrors that I mentioned, our human wars, manipulations, cruelties, and actions based on greed and fear. He knew all of this, more than I did even. Yet he still elevated humanity to the peaks. But back to our conversation which occurred one week after he had described Earth as a prison rather than an intergalactic property, dripping with emotion as he did so.

"So," Philo said, seeming almost eager, "you indicated that you understood step one but were having trouble knowing how to implement it. You said you knew well the value of establishing a larger perspective but were not clear precisely *how* to do so. You asked me for clear 'how-to' instructions."

He looked at me for validation and I nodded eagerly in assent. It always feels good to be completely understood, and all the more so by an alleged alien. "That's exactly right, Philo," I said. "But in our last conversation you said this was all too complicated and that it went back to religion."

"Precisely," Philo intoned.

"Well, let's start there," I said decisively.

"Ok," Philo replied, "the first step *is* complicated, but the complication is not in the first step."

"Keep it simple, remember," I interrupted.

"Given a chance I just might," he responded, smiling. "Again, the complication is not in the first step itself but in the terms one must use to express and understand the step." He paused, looking at me. I must have looked confused. Certainly I felt confused. "Don't worry," he said, "I'll clear this up. Trust me."

"Thanks," I replied, actually feeling the trust he was asking for. Something felt really special about this conversation, and I was fully attentive. "I'm all ears."

Philo smiled in appreciation and then looked wistful. "If only," he said, lightly. Then gathering his wits and looking directly at me, he continued, "Here is how to do the first step. Get into a meditative posture, whatever makes you feel maximally comfortable and relaxed. It could be sitting, lying down, whatever. The point is to feel relaxed. Try to find a place that is calm, quiet, and undisturbed. Then relax yourself. You might use a technique where you start by relaxing parts of your head, your scalp, ears, nose—all the way down, bit by bit, to your toes."

"I know how to do this," I said.

"Good. Can I assume you also know what to do with your thinking, which tends to get louder and more intrusive as you progressively relax?"

"I think I do," I replied. "The idea is not to engage it, not to try to force it into silence. Instead, just stop paying attention to it, directing one's attention to the various body parts one is relaxing. The thinking continues, but like when you walk past a carnival barker, the voice doesn't stop but becomes distant, sliding into the background from the foreground."

Philo looked impressed. "And when your thinking is jabbering like a carnival barker, intruding on your relaxed awareness, as it certainly will, taking your attention off your meditative state and right into its ongoing chatter, what then?" Philo looked at me expectantly.

I smiled, knowing exactly what to do. "Gently and without blame or recrimination, I redirect my attention back to my body, once again being careful not to engage my thinking. Here, for me, it helps when I focus my attention on my breath, sensing the breath coming in and the gentle turn when it starts going out. I could also use a chosen visualization to focus on or even a mantra, a simple saying repeated, but mostly I use the breath."

"Quite that," Philo exclaimed, pleased. "So now we are in a relaxed meditative state. There will be repeated, rude interruptions by our thinking, but we know what to do. We gently direct our awareness to our body or to our visualization or mantra. It doesn't matter which, just the one that seems the most effective."

"You make it sound easy," I said. We both laughed.

"As do you," Philo said, still chuckling. "Now once we reach this state, and it is just a mild state of calm, relatively easy to attain, you use your imagination to take your awareness and lift it above your body so you can look down on yourself relaxing."

"I've done that," I said proudly.

"Good," said Philo. "Now rise even further above your body, above the ceiling, above your neighborhood, above your planet. Go to the stars. Keep going all the way to God."

I am sure I looked disappointed, even horrified. Philo was looking at me expectantly. "To God?" I sputtered. "Why not to Zeus, or Krishna, or Superman's grandfather?" I protested.

"Why not, indeed," Philo replied calmly. How do you say it here, 'whatever works.' Zeus, Krishna, Great Father Spirit—these are all artifacts of imagination. You can use any of them, but they are not all equally effective. What determines their efficacy is a function of cultural conditioning and self-awareness."

"But . . ."

Philo interrupted my interruption. "But, but, but, but! A whole roomful of buts. A huge public toilet full of them, all spewing foul smelling objections. I told you, John, that this was complicated."

"Yes," I said, feeling testy. "But you also said the complication was not in the step itself but in the terms used to express and understand the step."

"I did, indeed."

"So explain."

"What's to explain?" Philo replied evenly. "Is there a more confusing and contested concept than God?"

"Then why use it?"

"No need, really. You can use Superman's grandfather instead. Or Zeus. Or the wisdom and force of your own unconscious mind. No matter what terms and concepts you use, and the available terms are legion, you will be using your imagination."

"But what about *truth*," I protested. "What if God is the real one of the bunch. Or even worse, what if there is no God!"

"There isn't," Philo replied firmly.

"But you just suggested that I imagine myself rising above my body, up and up, all the way to God! Why?"

"Because God is real."

"Now you are talking in circles," I said, feeling a mixture of disgust and anger.

"No, John, now you are *thinking* in circles."

"But how can I use my imagination so carelessly?"

"Oh, my," Philo exclaimed in mock horror, "now we have the second most confusing concept, that of imagination."

"This is a big problem, Philo," I said, feeling completely frustrated.

"Indeed," he said patiently, "but like good engineers, let us not just describe the problem but try to find the source of it." He pretended to be searching. "Aha," he announced dramatically, "I found it. The source of the problem is *your* understanding of the terms 'God' and 'imagination.'

"Give me a break, Philo," I moaned.

"I'm doing better than that, John. I'm giving you an excuse. After all, you have often said, in both writing and speech, that the most important question in religion is not whether or not God exists. It is about what we mean when we use the word God. And of course, the same is true of imagination. You, along with all Earthlings, understand and accept that there is such a thing as imagination. The question is not whether it exists but what it *is* that exists. What can it do? What is it good for? What are its limits?"

I just sat there. I understood what Philo was saying, but I was completely confused. I understood his sentences, but his meaning was eluding me.

After a few moments, Philo spoke gently. "Fortunately, John, we can bypass all of this. Try this for me. Do the meditation as I described. When you rise up in your imagination to the source, what I am calling 'God,' try not to think or define what is happening. Imagine there is a completely natural cosmic energy bathing you in a special light that is energizing you. Try to have that experience, sort of a cosmic version of standing under a heat lamp after taking a shower. Try to feel it physically, not just conceptualizing it."

"I'll try it, Philo, but this God talk has me disturbed."

Philo smiled. "You and so many others. Please try to grasp that you are disturbed, not that any "thing" is disturbing you. Avoid the term if you want. Think of the completely natural, entirely secular energy of the cosmos bathing you."

"But there is not an ultimate cosmic energy. It isn't in physics."

Philo laughed. "Gee, John, why would you use your imagination *that* way? Still, let it be. Just try to have this energizing experience."

"But I don't believe . . . ."

Philo interrupted. "Belief is a function of thought. In bypassing thought, you bypass belief. You are aiming for an *experience* here, not an *understanding.*" Then, smiling, he asked me in the sweetest voice, "Do you understand?"

CHAPTER 31

IT WORKED,
BUT WHAT'S UP WITH PHILO?

I tried what Philo had suggested. I relaxed into a meditative state and imagined my spirit or awareness or *whatever I wanted to call it* rising up into the cosmos where it met God or the cosmic green force or *whatever I wanted to call it.* There I was being bathed in love and acceptance while being replenished with life force or energy or *whatever I wanted to call it.*

It worked. In fact, it worked so well it freaked me out. The feeling of being energized and replenished was surprisingly strong and even pleasant. Granted that the pleasure was faint, it still felt deep and nourishing. It was a spiritual pleasure. It felt that my soul or my psyche or *whatever I wanted to call it* was experiencing the pleasure, and while it did seep through the body, it did not have a body sense to it. That is, it seemed more than a physical pleasure, even though I could definitely feel it physically. I would describe it as expansive rather than focused, glowing rather than tingling.

It was, as the song says, more than a feeling. And it was not just a matter of feeling good. It rocked my world!

Of course, as soon as I finished this exercise, my active critical mind began to doubt, question, and diminish the experience. Instead of either arguing with my mind or conforming to it, I was able to stand back, amused, and simply 'watch' as my machine mind tried to assimilate the powerful experience into my established assumptions.

But I got the same pleasant, energizing result each time I

repeated the experience, which at that time I was doing two or three times a day. After a few days of this I noticed that the 'cosmic glow,' if you will, was sticking with me throughout the day, albeit in a gentle, subtle way. When something stressful happened, it was not that I now had a pleasant bubble of calm I could escape into. It was more that I now had a pleasant bubble of calm from which I could effectively deal with whatever problem ordinary life was presenting.

It was really quite remarkable and I couldn't wait to see Philo again.

The next time I saw him was during the last set of my regular Thursday night gig. As the night went on and I did not see him, I began to worry that I would not, even though he generally didn't appear until the last set. Finally, I did see him, though I had not seen him enter. This was unusual because I had been scanning for him more than I normally do. Once again, he somehow slipped in the way he slipped out—quietly and secretly.

As soon as I finished, I rushed up in more eagerness than usual, pulling out a chair while excitedly exclaiming, "It worked!" It was only then, having expressed my peaking enthusiasm and excitement, that I noticed him—that is, his state of being and not just his physical presence. It was not that he seemed upset, but there was . . . something. Of course, I didn't know anything about his life except for the crazy science fiction claim he had made that he was from another planet which, as you know, I did not take seriously, accepting the claim more in a poetic, symbolic sense. If you had asked me at that time what he was getting at in claiming to be from another planet, I would have said something like he was indicating to us that he hailed from an entirely different cultural constellation. For all I knew, he was from some Hippy commune in New Mexico. I even wondered if perhaps he was a contemporary gypsy.

Anyway, Philo looked up—he seemed to move slowly—and said, "It worked, but as opposed to what?"

I replied in a forceful way. "This is a really big thing, Philo. It is as if there is energy for free in the universe. It is like magic. It works. It really works!"

Philo smiled indulgently. "I am very pleased to note your enthusiasm, but keep in mind that for me, this is an ordinary feature of our existence. It is sort of like gravity. It is as if I told you about gravity, about how if you jump up as high as you can, you will come back to where you jumped from without doing anything. You try it and it works, so you come back excited about your new discovery. But for me, of course, you are just jumping up and down."

"Then why am I so excited to discover this?" I asked, feeling genuinely confused by Philo's attitude.

He looked at me indulgently. I felt loved at that moment. "You Earthlings, all of you, have been systematically misled about the fundamental aspects of existence, what you might call the 'ordinary.' To you this seems like a major revelation and discovery only because your culture is contaminated and functions in many ways to disorient and alienate you. This can be seen in your politics especially. It is significant that those who are the most fervent, even fanatical about their political ideas are more often than not also the most deluded. As Yeats, one of your great poets, puts it, 'The best lack all conviction while the worst are full of passionate intensity.' Very apt."

"This is spiritually significant, Philo, intensely so!"

Philo brightened with a smile. "Aha," he said, as if tasting some gourmet delight, "here is that dualism again. I would observe, being an outsider, that you and your planetmates live in culturally desiccated, decidedly unspiritual fantasy of what existence is like. You call it reality but it is really just the material pole of your dualism. Some of you, feeling confined by being limited to the merely material, invent non-material fantasies that you then believe. This is usually called religion. Of course, others then deny the fantasies, endeavoring to yoke culture back to the purely material pole of your matter/spirit dualism. Either way, materialism or spiritualism, you are living in an imagined fantasy of what the world is like."

I was stunned. He was thundering and raining on my sunny experience. I did what he suggested, it worked, and now he was denigrating the experience. Noting my reaction, he said more kindly, "I do not mean to denigrate the experience, John. I do entirely agree that this experience, which is accessible and ordinary and decidedly pleasing, cuts right through the dualism."

That helped a bit. Still, Philo seemed to have an uncharacteristic edge this evening. I didn't say anything and after a brief moment of silence, Philo continued. "Please forgive me, John," he said with completely convincing sincerity. "I have been troubled lately and I have brought my troubles to this table. Give me a moment to touch into what you experienced."

I watched in mounting amazement as he took a breath, lowered his eyes, and ever so gradually began to vibrate differently. The edges softened. It wasn't that he changed physically, at least not in any way I could detect. It was more like the sun had come out and the quality of light had changed. Where his visage seemed clouded before, now it was appearing luminous. His 'vibe' also seemed different, more calm but also more intense. The whole transformation only took seconds, but there was a definite before and after. He smiled as he opened his eyes. "There," he said, "that is better."

"Did you just do the same thing I have been trying?" I asked, most impressed by the subtle yet massive transformation I just witnessed.

"Precisely," he replied pleasantly.

All of a sudden my mind was full of doubts. It was like an army of doubting just launched a surprise attack. Noticing my converse transformation, he smiled gently. "I see you have some doubts and questions. These are important, and I want you to be able to share them with me. Something has come up in my orbit of existence, however, and it was only with difficulty that I was able to be here at all tonight. Not only did I feel it was important to check on your 'experience' of step one, but there is also your sublime musical creativity which, with all your improvising, delights and soothes me in my depths. How about if we agree to meet tomorrow to discuss all of this?"

It was only the second time we had scheduled a meeting. Having done so, he excused himself and slipped out. It was also only the second time I had actually seen him leave.

Something was different. I felt stimulated, excited, and wary, all at the same time.

CHAPTER 32

PHILO HIDES IN PLAIN SIGHT

We had agreed to meet the next afternoon in Garryowen, an Irish pub in town. I had suggested it because the building, while certainly nice to be in, had some real 'old world' hiding places. In fact, in the side room hidden under the stairs is just such a spot, and I was certain Philo would find it. It was one of those 'see and not be seen' spots.

I entered on time and headed right for the spot. Empty. I walked back to the bar room where there were also some nicely hidden corners. Empty. Back to the side room. Still empty. On my third time back to the side room, feeling a mixture of worry, frustration, and aggravation, there he was, sitting right in front of the window! It was the most open seat, yet it was somehow the most hidden. "How long have you been here," I asked, sitting down.

Philo flashed a large smile, "Let's just say I watched you walk back and forth three times with increasing desperation." We both laughed.

"How did I miss you?" I asked, genuinely puzzled. "I was looking specifically for you. I even thought I knew where you would be, the most hidden table in the entire place which, by the way, is still empty if you want to move there."

Philo laughed out loud. "Aha," he said between chuckles, "there we touch on trade secrets. But in the spirit of our discussions, let me say this. You missed me because of what you thought you knew."

"That doesn't make any sense, Philo. I did think you would take the best table, which is still available. But that is just one table in a relatively small place. I looked everywhere, not just at that table."

Philo was smiling, a big change from yesterday evening. "I think this is worth explaining to you, John, because it connects so nicely with what we have been talking about."

"How so? I don't see any connection."

"And there, John, we have precisely the point," he said, his words almost jabbing me, the way a long stick with a point would jab me. He continued, more softly, "You see, most of the connections our minds make and most of the inner cognitive protocols they use to filter and shape our experience are made and implemented *beneath* the level of our ordinary awareness. They happen automatically. Within the flow of our ordinary experience, it seems like we are seeing directly what is really there."

"I get that, Philo," I responded with a slight edge, "I just don't see how that applies here."

"Fair enough," he answered. "Let me explain. You were looking for me and you anticipated that I would choose a discreet seat, one hidden from view. Correct?"

"Exactly correct."

"Now you may not have specifically thought this, but you were putting yourself in my shoes and noting what I might do. Fair point?"

"Yes. I didn't have that specific thought, but I felt relatively certain that if the table under the stairs was available—which it still is—then you would take it. I wasn't thinking that *I* wanted to sit there. I was thinking that *you* would choose to do so."

"Right. Now what was my objective?"

"To keep from being seen."

"Really?" he asked, seemingly bewildered. "If you think about it, it couldn't be that. If I couldn't be seen, you would not be able to find me. It therefore wasn't to keep from being seen that was my objective."

"Your parsing my words pretty finely, Philo. Ok, more precisely put, you wanted to avoid being noticed. You could be seen, but you didn't want to stick out."

"Very good, John. That is exactly right. Now, let me ask you to do this. From the intent of not being noticed, walk through these two rooms again and pick out the table that most recommends itself."

It was a weird thing to ask, but Philo had a great track record on asking me to do things that seemed weird. So I did it. And speaking of weird, the results were totally different from what I might have expected. Certainly anyone *looking* for someone trying to stay out of the public eye would look first at the dark and hidden corners, not focusing on the exact table Philo was sitting at—the brightest and most exposed table in the entire place. It was a great paradox, but somehow the most exposed table was the most discreet.

I sat back down and looked at Philo. He had a look of quiet satisfaction. "Not to be pompous here, John, but it always helps to fine tune your objective to get the nuances right. That is true, too, of anticipating the objective of another. But enough of that. I was a little distracted last night, but you were indicating to me that the 'floating up to God' exercise went well."

"Actually it was floating up to the cosmic red force, but yes, it went marvelously well. It is a little hard to show the appropriate enthusiasm right now . . ."

"No it isn't," he interrupted. "Oh listen to me," he immediately added, sounding like a fussy old schoolmarm. "Back to the step. Have you tried it more than once?"

"Yes I have," I replied confidently. In fact, I've done it a couple of times since we talked last night!" He looked pleased but didn't say anything so I continued. "It feels really good to do this, Philo, but what does it mean? I mean, it doesn't prove anything. I could just be imagining the whole thing."

"Oh, John, it is so much *more* than you say." He seemed

amused and enjoying himself, a far cry from last night. "You say you *could* be imagining it. Let me assure you: you *were* imagining it! There is no question. You put images to it, right?"

"Well, yes."

"Let me guess," he continued. "You imagined your soul essence, the core of your psyche, rising up to some divine spiritual presence, perhaps a warm, glowing light." He said this slowly, word by word, staring at me the whole time as if he was reading something in me. "No," he said, still gazing intently at me, "perhaps the light was bright, even commanding. Yes, bright and overpowering." I had the distinct impression he was reading my mind. He continued, "But it was also loving, soft, and supportive. Right?"

"How do you know that?" I demanded, feeling surprise and a little violated.

Philo laughed merrily. "You humans are all so . . . human. I love it! You always want to fence off your own experience, to make it special, unrepeatable, unique to you. To think that a spiritual experience like the one you had is generic, a lot like popping open a cold beer on a hot day—this is not appealing to the human. The human wants his experience to be unique and special." He seemed genuinely happy, excited even. "But enough of this blathering. You seem to have some concerns. I would be pleased if you would share them with me." His intense gaze was gone. Now he just looked at me expectantly, waiting for me to respond.

CHAPTER 33

PHILO, IMAGINATION
AND MEANING

It took me a moment to gather myself after Philo seemed to make light of what was to me an intense spiritual experience. It seemed to me that I had communicated with a divine presence. When I asked him whether it was real or whether I had imagined it, he said I definitely imagined it. So I felt, again, as if he had knocked me off my seat. My mind felt more jumbled than when I walked in. He was looking at me expectantly, however, waiting for an answer. I said, "I came here impressed mightily by my experience but also wondering whether it was real or whether I had perhaps just imagined it. You said I had imagined it, pointing out, much to my surprise, the exact images I had used."

"Yes, a bit of an interruption, that," he said with the air of an apology.

"But, Philo," I protested, sounding ever so slightly whiny to myself, "that isn't what I meant when I wondered whether I imagined the whole thing. I know I used images to picture it. I wanted to know if I made the whole thing up. I mean, I can make up images in my mind that have me dunking on Kobe in the NBA. But as spectacular as the dunk is, it won't make SportsCenter because it didn't happen! That is what I was wondering."

"A good image, John, dunking on Kobe. Much easier to pretend it happened than actually to do so."

"But what does my experience mean, Philo? What does it prove? What does it tell me about reality?

"Perhaps nothing," he replied. "Perhaps the answer to all three questions is nothing."

"Philo," I responded sharply, "you are making me confused. I'm not even sure what we are talking about any more. I had a reality-bending, mind-alerting experience—three of them actually—as a direct result of your guidance and you are telling me they might not mean anything!"

"Guilty as charged," Philo responded good-naturedly. "What's your point?"

"That is the point," I almost shouted, "the fact that you are suggesting there is no point. What is the point of pointlessness! Why did you tell me about this? This is step one of what?" I could feel my heart pounding and I was almost panting.

"Fair enough, John," Philo replied, "and it certainly is a bit upsetting, especially since you took to the experience so well, even repeating it."

"Yes," I said, "I had the experience last night, first thing this morning, and again right before coming here."

"How exquisite. Once you get more established in it, you will be able to touch into it when you feel unsettled—like right now, for example. You look like you could use a bit of that calm right now."

"Philo, I'm lost here. Now you are suggesting it *means* something, that it is something I could do now because I feel agitated." Just then our waitress showed up with our order. She seemed a bit wary, as if she was afraid she was interrupting an argument. However, Philo smiled at her in the most engaging way and put her at ease commenting on her very artfully designed blouse, which I hadn't even noticed.

We took a few moments preparing to eat and Philo said, "Let me help you here."

"Thank you," I replied, feeling relief.

"You were talking about the meaning of life, understanding the

Joseph Campbell point that what you really want is not an intellectual explanation of what life means but the actual lived experience of feeling fully alive. You mentioned that you often do not experience the meaning of your own wonderful life and that even the accomplishments in the musical area often slip by you. For example, people sometimes say how much they would love to be able to play the way you do, and while you appreciate their appreciation, you reflect on how you do not feel the same hit of delight while playing that they would if they could suddenly begin to play as well themselves. As you put it, you often have the experience but miss the meaning of the experience."

I felt relief and growing focus. That was exactly what we talked about.

Philo continued, though now in a more serious tone. "The exercise I gave you, which we are calling step one, is a technique designed to increase your own personal sense of the meaning of your own life. The idea is to touch into and experience this seemingly transcendental realm from time to time to gain a larger perspective on your life while you are living it. You do not aspire to escape. Rather, you touch into this realm while continuing to live your life. If you do this regularly, being especially careful to *feel* the warmth, love, and support of the light, the 'flavor' of your experience will begin to change. Gradually, a palpable sense of meaning will begin to cover all your activities, like snow falling in the forest."

"But what if I'm just *imagining* more meaning?" I asked.

"Well then it would be 'hoorah' for your imagination! More power to it!"

"No, Philo, what if there is no transcendental realm I am touching into? What if I am only pretending there is? What if it isn't real?"

"Oh," said Philo, adopting a mock attitude, still amused, "what if this transcendent realm you have already experienced is not material. What if the entire experience is not the sort of thing physics either studies or recognizes? What if it is only a product of wishful thinking?"

"Exactly!" I said, like a hammer striking the table.

"But that is precisely the way it is, John," Philo said without expression.

"So it isn't true; I am imagining it."

"True, truth, truly," Philo said, doing his best Pontius Pilate imitation. John, I didn't realize we were talking about truth as in 'the truth of physics.' I thought we were talking about meaning and an expanded sense of purpose."

"We were."

"Then why this obsession with truth? When we are trying to describe the way the world is, then truth becomes a reigning idea, a ruler of possibilities. But when we are talking about meaning and purpose and one's own sense of appreciation, then what matters is *what works* in helping us to feel more meaning and appreciation. We are going for a certain feeling, not an understanding or conceptual explanation. If you continue to touch into this idea each day, always being sure to *feel* the nurturing and acceptance of the light, then you will notice that your experience of your own daily life, the ordinary round of your activities—all of this will begin to seem more meaningful. You will feel value in what you do, even when you are goofing off! You will sense more purpose in all your activities."

"This is what I want, Philo."

"This is what you already have abundantly," he answered with conviction. "You are starting to practice noticing it and thereby learning to allow yourself more spontaneously to *feel* it."

"This is definitely what I want."

"It is what *everyone* wants, John."

CHAPTER 34

IMPRISONED ON EARTH

There is simply no other way to put it: what Philo showed me, the touching into a transcendental realm, was working. And not only did the exercise give me a sensation of being bathed in energizing love, but I noticed that my otherwise mundane everyday experience began ever so gradually to improve. The improvement was not dramatic, but it was clearly noticeable. I was continuing on my round of activities as before, but now when I was running on auto-pilot, running on a grim motor, so to speak, I could feel a gentle mindfulness emerge, a calm and sweet presence.

I was naturally eager to see Philo. As hard as it may be for you to grasp, I really did not think much about his claim to be from another planet. That was made all the easier by the fact that he didn't look or act alien. He looked and acted like a brilliant philosophy graduate student from a small town in the mid-west.

When I thought about this, I would reflect that the whole thing with Philo and his alien status was similar to falling in love with a person in spite of the so-called 'red flags.' It is not that a person falling in love accepts those red flag warnings; it is that he finds them easy to ignore. Those warnings may or may not become issues later in the relationship, but in the giddy falling in love days, they are functionally irrelevant. It was this way with me. Even though Philo was dropping more hints about the way things were in his world, I did not make as issue of any of it or put a focus on it. It was like he was telling me what things were like back in the small town in Indiana he grew up in.

The time back in the barn when he was so distracted did concern me, but he was so rollicking and present the last time we talked, I assumed the problem, whatever it was, had passed. It stood out, therefore, when I noticed him back at the barn during my last set. Where he used to seem innocuous, so much so as to appear invisible, he now looked wary, worried even. He kept glancing around, seeming to be worried about being seen by the wrong person. It was back to the paranoid Philo . . . or was it? Was I imagining this?

I finished playing with an energetic flourish and, putting my guitar down, I immediately approached his table. In spite of what seemed to be his distraction and worry, what he had shared with me so far was working so noticeably in my life that it felt very natural and appropriate to approach him in genuine joy. I mean, I could have been imagining things. So I said as I walked up, feeling mounting excitement, "There he is, a visionary among the far-seeing, a giant among the tall, a man claiming to hail from another planet."

He turned towards me, a look of terror on his face. It quite stopped me. He looked around nervously and then said through tight lips, "Sit." I pulled out a chair.

"Do *not* speak like that," he commanded, eyes still darting around the room. He was acting like someone on the lam, someone running from the authorities and afraid of being identified.

"Gee, Philo, I didn't mean anything," I apologized, feeling shaken.

"Don't do it again," he said in a low, menacing tone. Feeling disturbed, I didn't say anything and my silence opened up as a space between us. Each second was excruciating.

"In fact," he said a little more calmly after waiting for maximum effect, "I only stopped by to tell you that I will not be able to talk to you anymore."

It was crushing news. I felt like a person head over heels in love being told by his lover that she did not want to see him again. It hurt in a shocking sort of way. I heard myself mumble, "You can't," knowing full well, of course, that he could.

"Shh," he hushed me, eyes again darting nervously. His manner was so dramatic that I began to feel frightened—not just at the prospect of him leaving, but for some unnamed menace that might be lurking nearby.

"I should not have come here," he said as much to himself as to me. I must have looked panic-stricken, because he immediately softened and, looking directly at me, added, "Meeting and speaking with you, John, has been more meaningful for me than you can imagine. It is just that the risks are too catastrophically high." He looked at me expectantly. I thought to myself he was like someone breaking up who wanted the jilted partner to accept the breakup.

"Philo, this is incredibly upsetting."

"I must ask you not to tell anyone about me. Above all, never mention I am from another planet." I didn't say anything, feeling too stunned to speak. He looked down and then said, more to himself than to me, "I should never have even mentioned it. I guess I was just feeling too excited to be here, to be fitting in so nicely. I blundered."

"Oh, Philo," I said, trying to be light, "you don't have to worry because no one would believe me anyway."

"Do not say that," he hissed, a look of panic crossing his face. It was really upsetting to see him this way. I would say he was threatening me if he did not look so afraid himself. I felt fear, but not from him but from what *he* was afraid of. Something had spooked him, and I doubted it was the ghost that was alleged to haunt the old barn we were sitting in. He sighed and continued.

"There are things here, John, that you do not understand, dangers you do not realize. I was wrong to talk to you and tell you what I have, but now I must terminate." He looked at me with anguish, "I have come to be very fond of you and of what you do. I am not withdrawing willingly."

"Philo," I pleaded in lowered tones, "please reconsider. I have not said anything and I promise I won't. As it is, people already think of me as being 'spacey.' They often describe me as being 'out there.' The last thing I need is to say I've been talking to an alien." There was a moment of heavy silence. Trying to add a touch of lightness, I added, "In fact, if I told anyone, someone would be certain to respond, 'So you've been talking to the mirror again, have you?'"

Philo looked like I had punched him. His face narrowed in focus and, with fear percolating under his features, he looked at me with unsettling intensity. "Have you mentioned me to anyone, anyone at all, perhaps just in passing?"

"I have not," I replied firmly. "And I am not likely to, either. And even if I did, I would not be believed."

"Why is that?" he asked pointedly.

"I had a TV show here for ten years on the local cable access channel here."

"The John Show," he interjected.

"That's right," I said, so surprised as to be wary. "How would you know that, being from where you say you come from?" I asked, feeling suspicious.

Philo suddenly adopted a professorial air. "Your show, which ran from 1998 until right before the 2008 election, was broadcast live each week on Wednesdays from 8 to 9 PM. In the ten years of broadcast, you missed very few weeks. Each week you pretended to have travelled to planets in various regions of inhabited outer space, the places you called the civilized parts. Once there you would give speeches supporting the 'Leave Earth to Earthlings' movement. You were opposed by an intergalactic consortium of corporations that wanted to purchase the planet Earth in order to rape the land and enslave the people, claiming that they would only be doing what the

Earthlings themselves are doing, only more efficiently. Each week on your show you would read letters from aliens purporting to have heard your speech and were now asking questions to clarify what you had said in your speech. Each week you would read these letters on your show and discuss the points raised."

"Yes," I said, feeling both stunned and flattered, "it was a way of creating an alternative sci-fi scenario within the frame of which people who called in to my show could discuss philosophical and political concepts without the mud and distractions of propaganda and ideology. It seemed to me that otherwise intelligent, caring people were being mind-controlled or mind-locked or something, and this was a way of bypassing the control and locks."

"More effectively and brilliantly than you imagined," Philo added.

That felt good. I was truly proud of my show, even though people would often laugh when they saw me saying, 'There is the alien guy.'

Philo continued. "You also pretended that your show was a big hit in the intergalactic media—the highest rated show on the Holographic Cable Network you claimed—and that you yourself were a well-known intergalactic star, a top celebrity. You even claimed to have been the recipient of the coveted 'Philosophical Entertainer of the Year' award for eight years running."

My jaw dropped. A person could know about my show, even watch a replay or two. But to know this they would have had to watch it for much of the entire ten years. The only person I knew who did this was me!

"John, you were closer to the truth than you can imagine. You might explode if I told you everything."

"Philo," I begged, "tell me more. Please. Anything."

He stared at me, love, confusion, and uncertainty flashing across his face. It looked to me that he was undergoing a surprising change of heart given his just manifested paranoia, "I'll say two things," he said suddenly. "First, I'll meet you tomorrow, but not here." Then in hushed, conspiratorial tones, he told me where. It was a most surprising location. He then got up to leave.

"And the second thing?" I asked.

"Oh, yes," he said flippantly. "You were wrong about the intergalactic corporations wanting to buy your planet. Earth is a prison, not a property."

And with that thought bomb, he was gone.

Chapter 35

Talking In A Dead Zone

The bench at the corner of Breckenridge and South Hamilton Street was a most unusual place to meet. There is a nice bench there. Cut at an angle to the intersection, it faces southwest and thus receives the full force of the afternoon sun. It also overlooks the park.

My mind was still spinning—so much so I had trouble doing my calming meditation. I didn't know what to make of Philo's panic, his extensive knowledge of my show, or his bombshell comment about Earth being a prison and not a property. What I did know with certainty, however, is that the things I was doing under his guidance in terms of purifying my consciousness were working. They were making a difference.

But this bench, nice as it is, is open, exposed, and completely unhidden. It didn't seem at all like the exposed window table in the Garryowen pub. Here anyone sitting on the bench would draw immediate attention. Maybe the people who were looking for Philo would not think to look here. I don't know. It just didn't add up.

I was wondering about this—no, worrying would be a better word here—when I sensed Philo. And sure enough, there he was sitting next to me. I was spooked! "How did you do that?" I asked, somewhat ungraciously.

"Do what?" Philo responded pleasantly enough. I could tell he was not spooked like he was last night.

"Sneak up on me like that!"

"You mean," he answered with his characteristic half smile, "how

I walked up the street while you were facing the sun with your eyes closed, absorbed in your thoughts, and so did not see me? It was quite easy, really. I didn't even need any alien devices."

I noted that I felt anger, which seemed inappropriate in this context. So I just sat, with eyes closed, letting the sun warm me. It *was* possible he had just walked up as he said. Still, the whole situation seemed off somehow, including even my own rough and hard-edged attitude.

"I must say," Philo said gently, interrupting my silence, "that for someone who wants to talk me into staying longer on your planet in order to continue our conversations, which you claim to find helpful, I find your attitude more than a little suspect."

"Why did you come here?" I blurted out, asking my question as if I were delivering a physical blow.

"Simple, John," Philo replied smiling, "we agreed last night, mostly as a result of your urgency, to meet here today. And true to form, it seems obvious that we both kept to our agreement."

I looked at Philo with dissatisfaction. "That is not what I mean," I said, feeling exasperated. "Why did you come to my planet?"

Philo looked at me with particular interest. It was one of those moments where I felt he was studying me. This time I interrupted *his* silence. "So, tell me."

Philo broke off his studying look and smiled. "The big one, eh? Why did I come to this wonderful planet to be with these wonderful people, especially including you?" He seemed to ponder the question. Then he said, "John, I didn't realize you actually believed me."

"I still am not sure," I snapped back.

"Fair enough," he replied evenly. "How about this. Let's agree that whenever I mention the planet I am from or how it differs from here, we both understand that I am talking about a different level of consciousness, not necessarily another actual place."

I must have looked at him with anger-tinged exasperation because he added, "Not good enough, I see."

"Philo," I said, reaching out to him with an appeal, "just be straight with me. This whole alien thing is very upsetting. I don't know what to think. You're right that I don't fully believe you. Mostly, though, I don't think about it. I don't make an issue about it. I would have left it at that, but it seems to me *you* have forced the issue."

I sat stewing in my words. Philo just watched, radiating calm, patience, and acceptance. I continued. "For all I know, Philo, you are taping all of this to make me seem like a fool." I noticed Philo's eyebrows lift slightly when I mentioned the taping. That freaked me out. I glanced nervously around. "There must be a dozen places around here where a camera can be hidden."

Philo looked impressed. "Not bad, not bad at all. You continue to amaze. As usual, you are closer to the truth than you can imagine."

"So you are taping to mock me?" I stammered, feeling lost.

Philo smiled. "Yes and no. Yes, taping, but no, not to make you look like a fool."

"You *are* taping me?" I asked.

"Well not me personally. John, *everything* is taped. I'm not the one taping you, but taping is occurring. Lots of it."

I must have looked alarmed and freaked out. Philo continued in a studiously calm tone, "I assume you know about the interference pattern of superimposed waves. At certain spots, the waves will cancel each other out. The spots where this occurs would be what you call 'dead zones.'"

"Yes," I said, feeling mildly distracted by what he was saying, "there are spots on a guitar where an interference pattern can occur creating a dead spot on the neck. No matter what you do with such a guitar, you can't get it to sound right."

"You certainly don't have any dead spots on your guitars, John," Philo said with a warm, embracing smile.

"Don't distract me with compliments, Philo."

"Compliment? That was merely an observation, John. It's what you *do* with the guitar—there is where the compliment would be. But to return to your concern. This bench just happens to sit at the node of the intersection of cancelling patterns. That means as far as taping is concerned, it is a dead zone."

"And the barn?"

"Well it would hardly seem fitting to call the place where I listen to exciting improvised music while sipping on artfully brewed fresh beer a dead zone, but, yes, it is what we call a modulating zone." He looked at me, reading my look of incomprehension, and added, "This bench is dead. No taping can occur here. The barn, however, is only mostly dead. In other words, usually, no taping can occur, but when the zone modulates, like it did last night, taping becomes possible."

It was a cogent explanation and I certainly understood it. However, something inside me was screaming, "He is lying to you. He isn't telling you the whole story. "Philo," I said abruptly, "why are you here?"

He smiled. I had the image of a sophisticated criminal in a cross examination in which he knew the authorities did not have enough evidence to keep him detained. Philo had that sort of sneaky confidence. What he said did not dispel the image. "John, my friend, I came to visit your wonderful planet, to spend time with your interesting planetmates, but mostly to speak with you, a most interesting but, as it turns out, pretty typical Earthling."

Was that last remark a putdown, I wondered?

CHAPTER 36

EARTH IS SICK

The setting sun was now low enough in the sky that it was becoming difficult to stare straight ahead, which I had been doing a lot of during this conversation. What a strange turnaround. I came here worried about Philo and eager to do what I could to help him and now I was worried about myself. He even admitted I was being taped!

The sun was warm and pleasant on my face, however. I sat with eyes closed, bathing in its warmth. I was thinking that even if he was lying earlier—and of course I had no way of knowing if he was, just that strong, sudden feeling—I have had a wonderful and productive time with him. I was starting to recall the many warm moments we shared, gradually feeling my disposition warm up.

"Let me ask you," I said, turning to Philo so the sun was not as strongly in my eyes, "about my planet. You say you are visiting my 'wonderful' planet. But what is so wonderful about it? Surely you have noticed how abysmally clueless so many of my planetmates are? Special interest politics, state-sanctioned murder from the sky, evisceration of the very notion of privacy, idiot religion working to justify God-less injustice, an increasingly poisoned environment, an ongoing capture and corruption of culture, increasing inequality—the list goes on and on." I noticed Philo seemed to be enjoying my rant. "Maybe I am missing it, Philo, but where is the wonderful part, a part so wonderful that it would entice you to risk I know not what, but probably some steep punishment, just to come here? I'm not buying it."

Philo laughed in merriment. "How utterly appropriate. Spoken exactly like a moderately informed Earthling of the early 21ˢᵗ century."

"Insults aren't going to work here, Philo. I'm serious. Am I wrong?"

"Oh, utterly wrong, John. Indeed, dare I say *absolutely* wrong. Completely, utterly, and *absolutely* wrong!"

I was confused by his response. I felt like a valued and underpaid employee who had gone into his boss to ask for a raise and was fired instead. "Which part am I wrong about, Philo?" I asked with a nasty tone. "The murder from the sky part? The part about the ongoing destruction of the environment? The part about the gutting of democracy? You tell me."

"Oh, John, you are certainly right about all of those things. In fact, there is horribleness at work here that you don't even know about. There is indeed much to lament on that level, and I certainly am with you, *on that level*, lamenting them. You have the facts down."

"Once again, Philo, I am confused."

"Unfortunately, John, you are not. You are certain. Righteously certain. Your frothing outrage comes directly from your certainty."

"But you said my facts are right."

"As indeed they are, John. It is not the facts that are wrong. It is the picture that frames them. It is the meaning of what is going on— that is what you are wrong about. It is on that level, the level of the larger meaning of it all, that you are, may I say, somewhat off in your understanding.

I was feeling confused. It was almost as if he was messing with me. I noted that I was now the one freaking out. I was a mess.

"John," Philo said gently after a few moments, "remember how you shared that in your life you had many wonderful things happen but that you didn't always feel a parallel sense of meaning and wonder. You put it so wonderfully, how was it? Yes, that you had

198

the experience but missed the meaning. Remember?"

"You hardly need to remind me, Philo. That is what you have been helping me with."

"Well, the situation is the same here, John, only it is on a much grander scale. On the one hand, there are the troubling facts you list so thoroughly, the injustice, greed, cruelty, and deception."

"There is another hand to those facts," I exclaimed.

"With aliens there is always another hand, John," he replied with a coy smile. Then smiling even more broadly he added, "In fact, among us aliens there are sometimes quite a few other hands."

It was not a hilarious remark and I did not laugh. But it was humorous. It did have a sort of appealing, ironic tilt. And it did serve to lighten the mood a bit. Philo continued.

"Let me put it this way. Let's say you have a beloved child, a much loved daughter, a toddler. She is funny, intelligent, curious, constantly learning, loving—a complete delight."

"I have just such a daughter," I added, "though she is grown up now."

"And continues to be completely wonderful," he affirmed.

"Absolutely!" I remarked.

"Ok, so let's imagine back to her toddlerhood. Did she ever get sick and feverish?"

"I can't remember a specific incident, but I'm sure it happened. Actually, I just remembered an incident where she was completely covered, from scalp to the bottom of her feet, with vicious poison ivy. She was in agony and could not sleep the entire night. The hospital did not open until 9:00 the next morning, so I stayed up all night smothering her in Calamine lotion and giving her a cool bath, one after the other, all night long. She was in agony the whole time. My heart was breaking. I wanted to help her so badly."

"Let's add to her malady," Philo said. "We are only imagining this, of course, but let's say she was also vomiting, had diarrhea, and was coughing uncontrollably, alternating all night between screaming, vomiting, and crying."

"It was pretty bad as it was, about as bad as it gets, so I don't think those other things would have added much to the misery."

"Ok, so now let me ask you this, John. Would you conclude she is bad, damaged, broken, not worthy of being treated, needing to be disowned?"

"Perish the thought," I said. "The poor baby was suffering, and I, seeing her suffer, was suffering along with her. How I wished I could have taken on her pain to myself to relieve her a bit. So what is your point with this?"

"It is simple, John. Beloved humanity is sick. It is suffering from a cultural virus, the cultural version of extremely potent poison ivy. And it has infected the entire social body, from the scalp to the soles of the feet. Everything is red, inflamed, spotty, and painful. Religion, government, business, education—everything is suffering. Even music is infected, though your own music is a notable exception. But even there, John, I can't help but note that musically speaking, you are a complete nobody. People like what you play, but they don't really appreciate it."

"What are you getting at, Philo? Forget the part about my music, isn't this what I am saying, that our entire society is sick?"

"I suppose that is what you are saying. But I am saying something different. I am not pointing to the beloved daughter but to the loving father. John, your society is sick. It is deeply troubled. It even looks like it might die. You are right to list the medical symptoms, the torture, state murder, deception, greed—on and on the symptoms go. But the society is your child. You do not have the attitude of a loving father. *That*, John, is the point I am making."

I was silent. He was entirely right. I had the attitude of a disgruntled consumer. Looking at the sickness in my society, I felt cheated. It made me angry. I did not have the attitude of a loving father. This was such a large insight, so comprehensive that I could not assimilate it right away. My mind felt like a pack of cards being shuffled and reshuffled.

Philo was looking at me. After some time, he continued. "So, John, your facts are for the most part correct. In fact, I think I can safely say that the situation on your planet is far, far worse than you imagine in your darkest fears. Where you go wrong is not in your facts. It is the hateful conclusions you draw from those facts. It is in what you think those facts reveal. Humanity is your beloved daughter. She does not need to be condemned for her suffering. She needs help, healing, love, understanding, support. Her symptoms, as horrible as they are, tell you about her sickness, not about her.

"I'm not sure I understand, Philo."

"Oh, you understand. You absolutely understand. You are just not ready to accept the responsibility. But look on the bright side, John."

"What's that?"

"This goes to show that we have a lot more talking to do," he said with a sly grin.

I have to admit, in hearing him say this I felt a warmth in me that was greater than the heat of the sun shining on my face.

CHAPTER 37

IF THIS IS A ZOO
WHO IS THE ZOOKEEPER?

In the few days that passed before I saw Philo again, I thought a lot about what had been happening and, frankly, I was not sure what to think. On the one hand, I really liked Philo. Even more than that, however, I was benefitting from our discussions. The exercises he showed me were working wonders, and the things we talked about were stimulating my mind, opening me to new possibilities.

On the other hand, I was starting to worry about this alien thing. Up until now I had not really thought about it, so I suppose you could say I was in denial. I did not think of it as denial but more as politeness, sort of the way one would be with a close relative who, say, supported fracking and nuclear power and was against any sort of privacy rights. In order to keep the family peace, I probably would only talk to him about sports at holiday gatherings, pointedly ignoring those other things in the interest of harmony.

At any rate, that was my approach to Philo. In other words, I was just ignoring the alien issue. I did worry about it from time to time, but my worry was more that I was the gullible dupe of a complex practical joke intended to mock me and make me look ridiculous.

But now my worry was more toxic. My feelings of worry were more intense, and I had begun worrying less about being ridiculed and more about being caught up in something dangerous. I kept thinking that if Philo really is an alien and really is here illegally, then there might be some serious danger for me in seeing him. Also, what if he is a dangerous person, the intergalactic equivalent of a master thief, someone who fits into the society and is not generally suspected. Then again, maybe the authorities from where he came from are themselves dangerous, sort of like American Special Forces on intergalactic steroids. For all I knew, they could be looking for him to wipe him out and I could end up being collateral damage if, say, some high tech version of an intergalactic drone got us while talking. I even worried they could actually target me and kill me on the basis of a meta-data analysis, the way we do with our drones, taking some similarity between my habits and those of known intergalactic criminals as evidence that I was myself an intergalactic criminal. In other words, I could be eliminated because I liked the same sort of music and walked in the same neighborhood as some notorious criminal.

Above all, I was realizing that if indeed Philo is an alien, then I am out of my league. I had begun to feel fear, and lots of it.

Then I would catch myself and remember how much I liked Philo, how gentle he was, how insightful he could be, how he was clearly helping me. Back and forth it would go, alternating between worrying about seeing him and the dangers that he might be exposing me to, and then worrying about not seeing him and the benefits I would be missing.

His meditation worked, but even there I was having my doubts. I mean, there was nothing alien about it. Heck, there wasn't even anything new about it. I can think of dozens of Buddhists and New Age spiritual teachers I know about, some on a personal level, who could have recommended essentially the same thing.

These thoughts were jostling in my mind when I saw Philo next, and while I did feel a surge of excitement to see him, I also contained it more than I would have done so just a few days previously. Philo looked up and spoke first, which was not what he usually did.

"You look a bit worried, John," he said, searching my face.

"Maybe I picked it up from you," I replied, pulling out a chair. It was ever so slightly a hostile thing to say, and truly, I did feel a bit edgy. I still was not completely sure that this was not some elaborate hoax and that he spent the time we were apart laughing with his friends at my open-ended gullibility. Even worse, what if he was secretly filming our exchanges in order to be able to mock me to a wider audience?

As these fears were flashing through my mind, Philo continued to look intently at me. I could not see any expression on his face, and that made me feel my fear was justified, its foundation proven. "Yes," he said abruptly, interrupting my worrying, "I have been quite perturbed myself recently. Perhaps I have influenced you with my worries."

It was not the response I was expecting, and it did nothing to calm me or assure me. "What has been upsetting you?" I asked, feeling upset myself. I noted I was wary and on alert but also not without a deep and genuine feeling of concern for him. It was deeply confusing to be worried *for* him at the same time I was worried *about* him.

He again stared at me intently. I had the feeling he was trying to decide whether to tell me something, something that would freak me out probably. Then, abruptly, he blurted out, "I have been feeling fearful that my highly illegal visit to your planet would lead to my being tracked down and captured."

My immediate reaction struck me as strange! On the one hand, this was the worst possible news, confirming that there was indeed danger here, and perhaps even for me personally. It served to confirm some of my worst suspicions, thereby validating my strongest fears. On the other hand, I felt a sense of relief to know the truth of the situation, that Philo really was freaked out and I was not imagining it.

"Ok," I said with resolve, "let me ask you some questions about this."

"Please ask away," he answered, not hesitating. His quick answer took me a little by surprise, and I felt some of my agitation subside. I sat for a few moments staring at him Philo-style, gathering my thoughts. My mind had actually gone blank. He looked back impassively—sort of how I might imagine an alien in his position might do. And as I sat, something popped loudly into my mind. I had often voiced concern to him about how things were going on my planet, about how the growing inequality and the increasing damage to the environment were leading to big trouble down the line, which more and more did not seem very far down that line. In all those times he had never seemed particularly concerned, and almost always he defended Earthlings from my scathing comments.

I gathered my thoughts, which was not easy as they were both crowded and confusing. "Well," I said finally, "you have been on this planet for some months now. At least that is as long as I have known you, and I never had the impression you were here for long before that."

"Correct," he added cooperatively.

"In addition to our talks, you have had a lot of time to look around, to talk to others, to get a real feel for us humans and for our life on this planet in the early 21st century. You will have had abundant opportunities, therefore, to see for yourself how totally screwed up everything is. It is terrible and getting worse. Today's unacceptable outrage almost overnight becomes tomorrow's new normal, nothing to get worked up about. You will have noticed, too, how dumb and sheep-like so many Americans are, believing all sorts of nonsense." I paused. I seemed to be almost panting.

He sat patiently while I frothed in silence, gathering more thoughts. "You had a question?" he asked gently after a few moments.

"Yes," I blustered, "why are Americans so willing to believe lies, so eager to support what they would prosecute as war crimes if anyone else did them, so accepting of the ongoing murder of innocents, so accepting of the destruction of privacy, so willing to let the super-wealthy continue to game the system to the detriment of everyone else?" I paused, now noticeably panting. "I could go on, but you get the drift. That is my question."

Philo looked very thoughtful. He seemed to be thinking not just of what to say in response but about what I had just said. After just a short while, he smiled kindly. "That is a clear question, John, and here is my answer."

I felt relief. We were communicating. He was listening to me. He was taking what I was saying seriously.

"You are right, John, that I have been able to look around, to take things in. And here is what I say. Americans are simply not the way you describe them."

His answer shocked me. "What do you do all day," I shot back, "sleep in a hole?"

He smiled indulgently. "John, I see a population that is like a bunch of fine, noble animals confined in a cheap zoo. The cages are small, the sun does not shine, and the food is wrong. But," and here he smiled and lifted his glass, "the beer is exquisite and worth travelling light years for."

"Don't make fun of this, Philo," I said in as menacing a tone as I could muster. "Going along with what you said, who is the zookeeper? And why don't we just jump over the walls of these flimsy cages we are penned in?"

"John," Philo said, riveting me with one of his trademark looks, "the zookeeper is in your mind."

CHAPTER 38

HUMANITY
AS PSYCHIC PRISONER

I don't know what it was about Philo that made the outrageous things he said seem reasonable at the time he said them. Was it that what he said was actually true, and thus his words had, as it were, truth-power to them? Or was it, as our advertisers know so well, that the *attitude* he characteristically displayed while saying these outrageous things made them seem unassailable? He would say them with an attitude of calm confidence. But whichever it was, attitude or truth, either separately or in combination, the result was that it was generally not until hours after our conversation was finished before I had that strong 'now wait a minute' response so beloved of critical thinkers. Again and again he would say the most outrageous things, making the ludicrous seem obvious or at least sensible, and it would not be until much later that I could step back and question what he had said.

Such was the case when I thought about his claim, which he had delivered in a relaxed, almost monotone voice, that humanity was not flawed or fallen but operating under restraint, like a wild animal in a zoo, and that a powerfully effective zookeeper had been psychically engineered into the human mind.

I resisted this claim from the start. My resistance did not seem to bother Philo. If anything, he seemed to anticipate it. He just smiled at my objections and his manner got even more sweetly reasonable. He pointed out that incarceration and leg-irons are rarely self-administered. If a person is either chained or incarcerated or both, he often said, then almost certainly the chains would have been put on against the person's will, either as punishment, as cruelty, or, as is increasingly on earth, as both.

Now *that* last point of Philo's indicates the really maddening thing about talking to him about these things. Even I, in all my doom and negativity, had not charged the criminal justice system with cruelty. Yet here Philo, in arguing with my contention that humanity is flawed and perhaps even broken, upped the ante on my accusation, adding cruelty to my charge against humanity! He did that a lot—namely, adding even more horrible facts to my already gruesome list, but drawing a completely different picture from them.

Anyway, he said since leg chains are not put on voluntarily, a person's dislike of them and preference not to be encumbered by them does not prove or even count as evidence that the person is not in fact currently chained at the legs. "Look more carefully, John, and you will see that those who suffer the most from situations are often the most vocal in denying that the situation affects them or applies to them. So a person's loud and passionate proclamation of the value and importance of freedom is not evidence that the person is not chained at the legs. And this is even more the case when the chains are in the mind. The truly free do not go on and on about freedom."

This is an excellent point. But after days of pondering, I was not so sure it was a true point or a helpful point. I mean, if humanity was in fact imprisoned by some sort of psychic implant, which is what he was suggesting, that would be hugely and ultimately significant, not the sort of thing we would mention in a calm manner. Such a thing would mean that all politics lacked legitimacy. It would mean that all social programs were false, including both the conservatism that would endeavor to hold the masses back and the liberalism that would endeavor to lift them up. And it would mean that philosophy, and especially social and political philosophy, was both impotent and irrelevant, sort of like talking to prisoners serving multiple life sentences about the value of liberty.

The next time I saw Philo I immediately besieged him with these points. He was unfazed. "It means all that and more," he said, once again upping the ante on my claims while drawing an entirely different meaning or framework of understanding from them.

He continued. "But here is where the analogy between the current predicament of humanity and that of someone in leg chains breaks down," he said. He said this with such a manner of calm objectivity that he could have been talking about the flight patterns of a certain species of bird. "A person in leg chains *knows* he is in chains. Even if he forgets, his slightest movement will remind him. Every step is hindered. But a person with mind chains is rarely aware of the psychic imprisonment. This is an extremely significant point, John. A person can be mentally imprisoned and not know it. The limited ability to move mentally will then not be recognized as such. It will be described as a free choice, as a matter of having 'values,' as a simple aspect of the nature of things. Anything but what it is—mental imprisonment!

"I don't get your point, Philo. You seem to be agreeing with me. Americans *are* in chains and they are too *stupid* to realize it."

Philo laughed. "Not at all, John. I am making the opposite point. Since mental imprisonment is difficult to notice, it is not evidence of stupidity to fail to do so."

"Ok, let's say you are correct on this, what is the point?"

"Pretty obviously, John, if a people—a majority of them at least—are mentally imprisoned in such a way that they don't know it, it hardly seems fitting to blame *them* not knowing this. This is what you are doing. You are blaming the sick child for her sickness, the unjustly incarcerated prisoner for his imprisonment."

"Well someone should get the blame."

"Perhaps. But it would be the unjust judge and warden, not the unjustly imprisoned prisoner."

My mind was reeling. Again, what he said made sense. "But let me back up a bit. I'm accepting what you are saying for the purposes of argument. But let me now question that. If what you are saying is true, if much of humanity is in a sort of mental prison, then that would mean politics has no legitimacy and that social theory is pointless."

"Your point?" Philo asked.

"I am thinking that if politics is still possible, if it still is a legitimate possibility, then this shows you are wrong."

"Fair enough," Philo replied. "In fact, I would agree. If politics was still possible in your country, then of course what I am saying would be discredited. Americans are not in psychic prison. They are just voting for the wrong person, supporting the wrong person. Get the right person elected, and things change, right?"

"Exactly."

"John, I am not talking you into anything here. You *already know* politics is dead. The system is so gamed, so governed and run by special interests, that politics in the sense of working through the system to get the right person elected is dead. Again, I'm not trying to convince you of anything. You already know this! In fact, what is your line . . . that now that politics is dead we are left with art. That our task today is to nurture our imagination, our vision."

He was right about that. That was my (oft-repeated) line. I would often say that to other musicians, gently chiding them for repeating old covers rather than writing new songs. And for the ones who wrote songs, I would gently chide them for writing without an idealistic sense of vision and possibility. Philo must have noted that I had been struck silent by the force of his points so, gently, he continued.

"John, let's go back to the point about the difference between leg chains and psychic imprisonment—namely, that the person in leg chains cannot fail to notice that he is in chains whereas the person in mental chains does not know this."

"How can this be, Philo?" I demanded. "How can a person in mental chains not realize he is in mental chains?"

"Simple, John. Because the moment he *realizes* he is in mental chains, he no longer is. And when the chains are gone, he is just left with a nasty habit of bondage which, if he wishes, he can now change."

"So you recognize that not all humans are in chains."

"Of course. Many are not. You are not. Most of your friends are not."

"So why don't those of us who are not chained just tell the others? We can have a liberation party."

Philo started laughing. "Such an idealist. Such a noble thought. You have tried this no doubt?"

"Repeatedly!"

"And?"

"It obviously didn't work."

"Obviously. We both see that, but I don't think you see why."

"Philo, I am mentioning this to disprove you."

"Let me understand you here, John. You point out to people— maybe not in these words, but you know what I'm getting at—that they are in chains. And their result, let me guess, is not just to fail to see it, not just to disagree, but often, to get hostile and angry towards *you* for suggesting such a thing. Right?"

"You nail that one."

"So *why?* Why do they respond to your message of liberation with anger?"

"Because they are stupid."

Philo laughed again, only more so. "No, John. Not even close. Think about this. You are telling them something really important, something ultimately significant."

"Pointing out they are in mental prison is pretty significant, right?" I wasn't sure what Philo was getting at.

"You are not taking what you are saying seriously enough, John. Let me ask you how would you feel if someone came up to you after you had just taken a shower and used mouthwash to inform you that because you had extreme olfactory deficiencies and that even though you did not smell it, you had such a repulsive body odor that you were ruining the world as a result. And behind the ruination of the world was your own inability to smell. You could not even smell your own toxic odor."

I got the point. It would piss me off mightily. Not only would I not believe the person telling me that my smell was so bad it was ruining the world, but I would almost certainly feel angry at the person telling me this. My mind was racing in confusion. As is normally the case in such instances of befuddlement, I defaulted to my earlier view. "So assuming you are correct, Philo," I said, "it establishes that humanity is craven and weak, a bunch of slaves really."

"How so?" Philo asked sweetly. "If I fed poison food to people and made them sick, would their vomiting prove that they are craven and weak. Would it be correct to say this proves they are slaves?"

"I guess not," I conceded, feeling I might be admitting more than would be required by reason. Once again, Philo seemed to be making the most outlandish claims seem reasonable.

Philo then fixed me with another one of his stares. "So, John, other than an internally generated feeling of horror and revulsion at the notion that much of humanity is in psychic bondage, a feeling that is an understandable last line of defense against the unappealing, what leads you to think that humanity is *not* in bondage?"

He had me. That's all I had, my internally generated feeling of horror and revulsion. I suddenly felt like an arrow in flight, heading straight for the center circle of a target, Philo's target! As my resistance to what he was saying weakened, I began to feel a new openness, even calm.

"John, Philo said, "I commend you. But, truly, none of this is the bottom line important thing. Properly understood, there is only one vital concern here."

"Which is?"

"We are talking about psychic imprisonment. The vital concern therefore is liberation. And if liberation is our concern, then what we need is a key."

CHAPTER 39

PHILO FINDS FAULT WITH ME!

Although I was delighted Philo agreed to see me the next day, I was still full of conflicted, mixed feelings regarding him and what he was telling me. On the one hand, he had the demeanor of someone who knew what he was talking about. It wasn't that he shared classified information or amazing facts. It was more like we were talking about Paris and he had been there.

On the other hand, when I was alone and thought about what he had said, I often had a feeling of impatient exasperation. It was his attitude and not his actual words or revelations that gave rise to this feeling. The very same attitude that suggested he had been to Paris also often left me feeling patronized, as if he was not telling me everything. There is more to Paris than the Eiffel Tower.

I was having a back-and-forth emotional struggle, from eagerly anticipating seeing him (and worrying I might not see him) . . . to feeling angry with him for toying with me. In that struggle the two of us, Philo and me, felt like a troubled couple, spending increasing amounts of time talking about how we talk and analyzing endlessly why we didn't talk the way we used to when we first met.

And to add another layer of complexity to the situation, I was still doing the meditation and it was clearly and definitely working. It wasn't as much that I did some specific technique as that, a couple of times a day or more, I would step aside from the rushing flow of my life and, in a deeply relaxed state of mind, mentally project myself to the 'source.' It was very calming and helped provide focus throughout the day—until I got agitated about how Philo was not telling me everything and was perhaps even leading me on.

That was certainly how it was when I saw him the very next day. We had agreed to meet in the barn, and even though I was not playing, he still sat in the back, obscured, looking to all the spies in all the galaxies as someone so ensconced in his own space that he would be best ignored.

"You're not telling me everything," I asserted bluntly as I approached his table. He looked up languidly and stared at me the way he did, observing and interpreting.

"Not the most profound revelation to be heard in this historic building," he replied, looking up at the barn's high ceiling with its carefully placed, cleverly interlocking timber frame beams.

"See," I said, jumping on the informational emptiness of his response. "You are doing it even now. Given what I just said, you don't agree or disagree. You just pass it over." I finished sitting as I said this.

"Well, John, let me help you with this one," he answered with a fully believable tone. "You are right to observe that I do not tell you everything. Of course, that is not surprising. After all, when two intelligent beings converse, they can only give voice to a tiny portion of what each knows and thinks at any given moment."

"That is quite true and even obvious," I said, settling into our now familiar mode of conversing, with me challenging Philo. "But that sweetly reasonable point you are making does not address what I said to you, that you don't tell me everything. Instead, you are speaking to deflect, to redirect, and to avoid."

He looked directly at me for what seemed like an unreasonably long time. He did not seem pleased. I wondered if he was deciding whether to tell me something more, like a seasoned fisherman putting a little more worm on the hook. Finally, by ever so lightly shaking his head 'no' while making a bit of a face and taking a deep breath, he seemed to come to some sort of resolution.

"My own feeling, John," he replied evenly, without a trace of defensiveness I could detect, "is not that I should tell you more but that I have already said way too much!" He paused, not looking at me this time but seeming to access the depths of his own awareness. Having reached what seemed like some sort of resolution or conviction, he then focused on me, riveting me with the concentration of his gaze. "You do not ask me very good questions," he said bluntly. It felt more like a slap than a point. He continued to glare at me.

I did not say anything. My mind was racing, however. What he said seemed to have the sting of truth to it. Considering I was talking to someone who claimed to be a philosopher from another planet, my questions to him were probably pretty pathetic. Instead of picking his brain, it seemed more like I was playing with it. He was learning about me and my planet, but what was I learning about him and his planet?

He continued. "Yesterday we were talking about freedom—or more precisely, about the lack of it among humanity. I mentioned to you that humanity is in psychic bondage and that your culture is functioning as a sort of prison of the mind."

"That's right," I said with passion, "and I wanted to ask you about the 'key' to liberation."

He smiled. "Yes. A fair request. But not an especially deep one."

"How so?" I asked, not grasping his point. Like so many of the things he said, it struck me at first as outrageous—but not entirely. It also hinted at a truth, at something I was not seeing but which could in principle be seen, even by me. Something I sensed but could not quite recognize.

"Look at it this way," he explained. "Let's say poor and struggling and a fat-cat banker walks up to you and informs you that you have an active account in his bank in the amount of 50 million dollars. He says you can draw on it anytime you want."

"Sounds pretty fantastic."

"A shallow response, John. Try to add some verisimilitude to this scenario."

"How? I'm feeling excited about my money. Isn't that real enough?"

"No, it isn't. Let's try to be real. He tells you he is a banker and that you have 50 million in his bank. Of course, you would not automatically believe he is a banker, and you definitely would not immediately believe that you have an active account worth millions and start to buy things on credit. Right?"

"Yea, that makes sense. So what do I do?"

"You would investigate, of course. You obviously would like to have the money but you just don't automatically believe the alleged banker when he tells you it is there for you. So you ask him real questions. Almost certainly you would immediately try to make a withdrawal just to find out."

"Sounds reasonable."

Philo exploded. "Sounds reasonable! John, we are talking about your being told by someone who looks, talks, and acts like a banker that you have a fortune in his bank, and you say it would sound reasonable to question him about this! That is exactly what I mean when I say you are not responding deeply, that you ask bad questions. You show no existential urgency in your response, no feeling of amazement, no sense of the magnitude of the claim under discussion. It is as if you said to the banker who is telling you that you have a fortune, sneering while you said it, 'Oh, yea, Mr. Big City Banker, which branch of your bank is my money in?' It is a question, to be sure, but it lacks vitality. It isn't serious. You are not actually trying to determine if he really is a banker. Instead, you are debating with him as if you both were in a seminar. John, given the circumstances, this is pathetic."

"I see your point about the banker. It would be pathetic if I responded that way to someone telling me I had a fortune in his bank. But how does that point apply here, to us now?"

"John," he responded with passion and deep feeling, "humanity is in bondage and I hint I have the key to liberation, and how do you respond? You respond by saying, punk fashion, "Oh yeah, well what's the key?"

I felt exposed, naked. He was right. I didn't act as if humanity really *was* in bondage, and I didn't seek the key with anything even remotely close to the urgency the situation required. I was guilty as charged.

Philo continued. "Don't feel too bad, John. This flat attitude on your part is not just something about you personally. I noticed that almost all of contemporary philosophy is this way. Someone will write a book or an essay with a scintillating title referring to the crisis of life on the planet involving the loss of humane values in culture and the ongoing evisceration of learning in schools. Really troubling things, catastrophic even. But when you read it, the author talks about these disasters as if he or she were talking about how the petunias in the garden were not as pretty this year as they were last year. The trifling quality of the discussion is not congruent with the dramatic scale of the problem.

I knew what he was referring to, having often noted and commented on the same thing myself. Again, he was right. Though I was not the only one by far, I was indeed an academic punk, lacking essential seriousness.

And I still did not have the key!

CHAPTER 40

PHILO IS SAD

Our last conversation was upsetting, with Philo seeming to take aim at me and my attitude. Perhaps it was in compensation, but Philo had agreed to meet me the very next day in the Battlefield Brew Works. That didn't leave much time for me to mull over the details of our upsetting conversation, but it certainly didn't stop me from devoting myself to the task. In fact, I mulled so intensely and in such a troubled state of mind that I had difficulty calming myself sufficiently to do my meditation.

Philo had correctly charged me—and by extension, not only the entire profession of philosophy but all of the humanities—with an essential lack of seriousness. We academic humanists take life and death issues involving global crises in which the very continuance of life itself is under threat, and proceed to discuss them as if they were puzzles in a Glass Bead Game.

Now I didn't want to make a childlike 'it takes one to know one' response, but what Philo was saying to me seemed to apply even more to him. Indeed, one of the things that stood out prominently to me about Philo was his seeming lack of an emotional life. So was this a case of the pot calling the kettle black? Even more, was Philo calling out my own lack of seriousness so forcefully because it paralleled his own? Then again, he was clearly risking great danger of some sort by being here. Or was he? Where was he *really* from?

Round and round my analytical mind would go, hour after hour, never really getting anywhere.

I kept thinking about how in our culture we express that we care and show that things matter to us by getting emotional and freaking out. This means that if you do not freak out about a certain situation, people will read your reaction as if you do not care. People then often exaggerate their emotions for rhetorical purposes, doing so to send you the message that they do indeed care, and care deeply.

I thought a lot about this phenomenon of the rhetoric of emotional expression and the confusions it invariably creates. After all, some people are more emotionally expressive than others. Two people can be sad, but one of them will minimize the expression of their feelings, even hiding them, where the other will express their feelings openly, even amplifying them.

Of course, it is even more complicated than that. The person who expresses sadness may not be nearly as sad as that person's expression would indicate. And the opposite could be true as well. That is, that same person's level of expression, even at its most dramatic, might be a lesser expression than the actual depth of feeling the person is experiencing.

Conversely, the person who does not express sadness might be the saddest person of all, even sadder than the person who expresses sadness so dramatically. Also, the person who does not express sadness might actually not feel particularly sad, not expressing much sadness because he or she is not feeling much sadness. Perhaps this is because the person is wise, or perhaps it is because the person is deficient in the affective areas.

And to further complicate the picture, sadness (or any feeling) can be sublimated. A person who feels sad, say, about his family situation might sublimate that feeling and begin to exercise with a manic energy. Alternatively, a person who is sad about his family situation and who is not expressing it in an open, healthy way might suddenly begin to get extremely angry about lights being left on overnight.

The point is, I think, that the expression of emotions, which is much encouraged these days, is not an especially 'clean' affair. That is to say, in the area of emotional expression, things are not always what they seem. The available data, so to speak, can mislead as readily as it can illuminate. This is because the object, intensity, and form of emotional expression can be 'dirty,' which is to say that they can all be different than what they seem on the surface to be.

Now my impression of Philo was that his emotional expression was profoundly understated but nevertheless mostly clean. That is, you could tell what he was feeling, but the feeling was never particularly strong. That was his nature, I would say.

Given this nature, there are, according to my analysis, two potential communication problems that could ensue. First, with him not having particularly strong emotional expressions, one could falsely conclude that he simply did not care. And second, by him generally not having strong emotional expressions, one could falsely conclude about an occasional *stronger* expression on his part indicated that he cared way more intensely than actually he did.

My best guess was that his recent emotional explosion—that is, what was *for him* an emotional explosion as compared with his normal low intensity mode of expression—fell under the second category of seeming to care more than he actually did. In other words, he actually was not all that upset. In fact, I had come to think that the reason he so readily agreed to see me the very next day was to take the opportunity to calibrate with me the correct measure and depth of his feelings and correct any misinterpretation on my part.

So when I entered the Barn I felt I understood what had happened the previous day, which is that it was not particularly significant. Given that, I was finally able to feel excited to be seeing him and—the most important thing here—to be getting the key to freedom.

Imagine my surprise when I saw Philo and he appeared to be

deeply conflicted and sad. So much for my analysis!

I had bounded up to his table with eagerness but quickly turned down my energy when I noted his depressed emotional state. "What's up?" I asked, feeling concern.

"Well, John," he said wearily, lifting his eyes slowly to take in my face, but without the studious attentiveness I was used to, "things seem down on your planet these days."

"These *days*!" I exclaimed, not thinking about what I was saying. "Why is today 'down' as opposed to any other recent day?" To me it seemed as if Philo had just observed that we Americans are not riding our horses to work very much this week. This *week*?

Philo just looked at me without reacting. Trying to take back a little bit of the explosion of my response, I said more gently, "Things are down, yes, but let's look on the bright side. All is not down. There is still beer, music, and you."

Philo smiled a tortured, pained smile. "I'm afraid you might have to take me out of that happy picture, John," he replied morosely. I suddenly felt a great sense of concern and alarm for Philo. I was worried about him.

"You were going to give me the 'key' to freedom and liberation," I babbled, immediately regretting my words because they did not express the concern I was feeling for *him*. Even so, my words seemed to galvanize him and he slowly lifted his head to fix his gaze on me. This is more of what I was used to. I felt him reading me, but this time it felt reassuring.

"Your eagerness is quite charming," he said somewhat languidly after a brief moment of studying my face. "Not to mention," he continued a little more brightly, that I not only indicated I would give you the magical key, but I called into question your lack of seriousness regarding its existence."

I felt a surge of relief. I often talk about philosophy as a journey and not a destination. The philosopher *loves* wisdom, as Socrates clarified, but he or she does not necessarily possess it. Indeed, the claim of philosophers is to love wisdom and to be willing to go through no end of difficulties to pursue it. And that loving search for wisdom is undertaken, presumably, with oodles of patience. After all, the prospect of taking up thoughts, questions, and concerns that have been pondered by the greatest minds for thousands of years without resolution—this daunting prospect does not daunt the philosopher. This is because it is the journey and not the destination that arouses one to philosophize. And on this interminable journey of philosophy, one philosophizes in hope, not in expectation. It may be that the journey itself never ends, but the philosopher never stops, philosophers being in this sense a most patient group.

But looking at myself at that moment, I could sense my eagerness to get the key. Is this eagerness unphilosophical? If so, then why did Philo criticize me the day before for having an abundance of it? Or did I misunderstand? Was he criticizing me for not having enough of it?

Either way, I was feeling considerable excitement today to know someone who said he possessed the key to liberation and that he was willing to share it. Of course, this someone also claimed to be from another planet, but even that alien connection was itself an exciting scenario—even if it turned out not to be true!

So did I lack philosophic patience? And if I did, was that a good thing? And if it was, then was philosophical patience, which is largely promoted as a virtue, really more of a rationalization for what would almost certainly turn out once again to be wasted effort? And my worry and concern about seeing Philo, my source, sad? Was that worry 'dirty,' being really more of a muffled expression of concern about seeing my source compromised? Or was that worry 'clean,' an honest expression of my love and compassion for this strange friend of mine, Philo, who seemed troubled?

My rumination and concern here was like a burgeoning cloud of smoke that was starting to obscure my sight and interrupt my breathing.

Suddenly Philo dispelled it, however. In an instant it was gone. I could immediately see clearly and breathe deeply.

What brought this clearing about? It was Philo saying, "Let's look at that key."

CHAPTER 41

PHILO SAYS EARTHLINGS
ARE SICK

As we continued to talk, Philo gradually came back to what I had come to think of as normal for him—sitting in a centered awareness registering what is appearing both externally in the environment and internally in the psyche, all from a seat of awareness that is infused with love, compassionate support, and wise acceptance.

I suppose at any other time I would have been more focused on his seemingly troubled emotional state. I probably would have tried to talk to him about it. But he had brought up something that engaged me from the depths. My entire adult life I have wondered why, given the possibilities of life on this planet, it is so grim? Why are some people hungry? Why do some people steal? Why is there so much violence? Why war? Why inequality? Why cheating? Why?

It was ironic to hear Philo's criticism of me—that I didn't ask good questions, that my questions sounded more like they were coming from a smart-ass punk than from some freedom-loving person in bondage being offered the key to his chains. Let me clarify for you that his criticism really stung me. It hurt—a lot! But I could recognize the sting of truth in that hurt. His criticism was valid.

But how did it get to be that way? I was always in trouble for being too critical, especially in the lower levels of school. It wasn't until college, which I assumed was simply another stupid waste of time, albeit on a higher level than high school, that I discovered that

I was not the only person who was critical. Few of my classmates were and most of the faculty was not, but *some* students and faculty were. That changed everything for me. I stopped being a cynical idiot and started being a committed intellectual.

Since then I have had people from three generations telling me to lighten up, that things are not so bad, that there is something wrong with *me* for wanting the world to be more normal and people-friendly. It was always difficult and it was often really painful. I think, however, that over the years I got beaten down. Bit-by-bit I lost a lot of my edge, a good part of my fire, and a whole lot of hope and passion. Even so, I hung in there, beaten but not entirely yet broken.

This is what Philo saw and criticized, and he was right. I suddenly remembered this weird fantasy story I'd heard years ago. In it, God is going to put something in the water and make everyone crazy. He first goes to this one guy and tells him what he is planning to do. He tells the guy that everyone is going to go completely bonkers nuts. He advises the guy to set aside a lifetime supply of his own water, which the guy dutifully does, storing it in the depths of a huge cave high up and overlooking the valley below.

The guy moves into the cave with his water and, in complete sanity, watches the world below go nuts, completely bonkers nuts. For his part, he sips his water and continues to watch, staying completely sane. He starts to get lonely, and the loneliness only grows. Being the only one, after all, makes such extreme loneliness completely sane.

Eventually the loneliness grows so intense that the guy walks down from the cave and drinks the local water, whereupon he is welcomed back into the crazy world with great merriment.

I was that guy. And Philo rightly criticized me for it.

But in fairness to me and to that guy, it is really, really hard work watching your world get increasingly crazy from the distance of sanity. It hurts.

But so does it hurt to abandon the quest for that better world. That also hurts, though it is a different sort of hurt.

So that is why when Philo held out the promise of a key to liberation—and not just a key fitted for a small, personal liberation but one designed for the largest possible liberation of the entire society—I was completely galvanized. I was a hungry dog and this key was fresh, raw meat!

So when Philo seemed his old self again, I could easily just roll with that. We had been talking our way into the problem and I had just finished a long lament about the sorry state of my country, my planet, and my species.

It was at this point that Philo said I was wrong. I exploded! "How could I be wrong? Look around. You can see for yourself the horrors. So many people, especially the ones at the top, are selfish and even mean. They hurt those below and call it 'free market' or 'nature' or 'God's will' or even 'evolution.' They act as if their untold wealth 'just happened' or, even worse, that they somehow 'earned' it."

Philo started chuckling. "What is funny about that?" I asked.

"Nothing at all funny about it," Philo responded lightly. "I was just thinking about one of the things you used to say on your show. How did it go? Yes. You used to say, 'We Americans deserve a better class of people to be our upper class.' Remember that?"

"Of course. It was a good line, wasn't it? But you just said I was wrong."

"Not about that. Your facts aren't wrong, John. Things clearly *are* in a sorry state in your country and on your planet. Your country is responsible for much of it, of course, but not all of it. Your country loves monopolies, but even your country does not have a monopoly on the urge to monopolize in the special interest."

"But how am I wrong, then?" I questioned.

"In that you are not wrong. It is in the picture you draw from this, in the blame you rubbish your species with—that is where you are wrong."

"I'm not sure I get your point, Philo," I said, feeling genuinely confused.

Philo beamed a large smile. "I'm making my 'don't blame the person vomiting from the flu for vomiting' point. That simple."

"Sure, don't blame the person vomiting from the flu for vomiting. By all means. But does that mean don't blame the person damaging the environment and degrading the society for doing so? And why would that be? Is it because the person has the 'destroy both nature and society' flu and is just vomiting?"

Philo laughed with genuine delight. "Good one, John. I have to say, it is really fun speaking with you. But to answer your point, no, that is not what I am saying. I am saying that most of the people on your planet, and not just Americans, though Americans are some of the worst, are suffering from what on my planet we would call a 'cultural virus.' You see, from my point of view humans are not weak, stupid, evil, fallen, selfish, greedy, or weak. They are sick. They are suffering from a particularly toxic virus."

I was stunned into silence. That was a heavy thing he was saying. I didn't even have any questions. I just wanted to hear more about what Philo was calling a cultural virus.

CHAPTER 42

THE KEY
FOR A SICK CULTURE'S ZOO CAGE

As we talked further, Philo also used quite a few images to clarify his point, including likening the human being to top of the line hardware and our culture to degraded software. But the image he used that worked the best with me was the one of a cultural zoo.

He used the image of a fine and noble animal caged in an inappropriate and cruelly confining zoo cage. The confined noble beast was a sad and tragic shadow of his potential magnificence, never getting to run and leap in the wild but instead confined to pacing back and forth in a cramped enclosure.

This image struck me somehow. I could even feel that I was a Lion in a cage. Philo ended his powerful description by saying that however much the noble beast adopted positive thinking and spiritual rationalization to soften his experience in the cage, being confined in this way is tragic and inappropriate. "If you care about noble beasts, it helps to make the food more appropriate and the cage a little roomier, but there is only one real solution to the suffering—to release the animal from the cage. And fortunately," he added, "there is a key to do just that."

I felt wildly emotional hearing about the key. I gushed to Philo how excited I was to know there is a key and that he would share it with me.

"Not so fast, John," Philo responded. "There is a way out, and I do think I can help you to see it, and I am fully committed to revealing it to you."

I interrupted brightly, feeling a surging excitement, "That is what I want to hear."

Philo looked ever so slightly discouraging. "Not to rain on your sunny parade, John, but I must point out that walking out of the cage is never easy. In fact, walking out of the cage is way more difficult than walking in—even when you are in possession of the key I will provide."

That sounded bad but I didn't feel bad. I mean, it is a great downer to learn one is confined in a zoo and lacking essential freedom. So how much of a downer could it be to add to that there is in fact a key that will release one from the zoo cage, and that the person who possesses the key is going to let one use it? To be told that walking out of the cage 'will be difficult' hardly seems serious. How difficult can it be to walk to one's freedom?

Still feeling mounting excitement, I said, "That is a sober thought." I tried to sound sad but I was feeling nothing but exhilaration swirling inside of me. I sipped my beer. It was fantastically tasteful.

"So you want to walk out of the zoo and be free?" Philo asked.

How could that be a question? I thought he sounded like a favorite uncle saying, 'So you want to go to the playoff game?' If your uncle is preparing to mysteriously produce the tickets, then it is less a question than it is a set-up for a trip to the ballpark. I expected Philo to produce the key in the same way.

"Absolutely!" I replied.

"You want out of the cage?"

"Absolutely!"I said again.

"You want to use the key?"

"Yes! Right away!" I replied once more.

Philo sat back slightly, looking pleased. He got a distant look, signaling he was about to make some sort of overview, big-picture observation. I sat in eagerness, like a kid waiting to go to the ballgame.

"Well, John, there is something really significant about you Earthlings, something really endearing. Being an outsider, I think I see it more clearly than you do. I certainly take better note of it. We have a saying on my planet that illuminates this. It is, 'The soul reveals itself more fully in its aspirations than in its dwellings.'"

"That's a good one, Philo," I said, appreciating the wise saying.

"Not so fast, John. Let's not paper over this caged up thing. You look at Earthlings and see weak souls that let themselves be caged up. I see strong souls who, as much as they try, cannot really embrace the cages and, even when the cage is nicely decorated, still yearn to be free of them. Where you see something craven, I see something both noble and tragic."

"So why don't they just step out? That would be both noble and heroic."

Philo smiled. "You make it sound so easy, so natural, but because of this difference in attitude between us, your call for them to 'just step out' is more judgmental than liberatory."

"I don't see that at all, Philo," I protested. "I am feeling excitement for everyone, for all Earthlings. All we need is that key!"

"You're not seeing it, John. But, hey, that's to be expected. Cages do not always provide the best window on the world."

I felt put down by this, patronized even. Philo didn't look like he was trying to put me down. Still, my enthusiasm dropped a few registers. "I don't see how I am being judgmental, Philo," I said, not at all understanding what he was getting at here.

"Let me try to help. I say I have a key to the cages, but I warn that even with a key, stepping out of them will not be easy. You express dismay, wondering why people wouldn't just walk out of their now unlocked cages."

"Exactly! I mean, if someone is locked in a cage, gets a key, unlocks the door, and then still does not walk to freedom—well, yes, I think I would judge them, and harshly at that."

"Beautifully honest, John. But let me ask you. Are you free of your cage? Have you walked out? Aren't you just the person who sits in your cage complaining a bit more than most, turning on the other inmates for not complaining enough? You accuse them from the confines of your cage of accepting their zoo status. That is judgment."

I felt stung by that. The sting was too sharp and too fresh for me to determine if this was the sting of truth, but there was no doubt it stung, and with some force. "That is why I want—why I *need*—the key, Philo. If I stay in my cage after I have the key, then I will accept what you are saying. But right now, all I want is the key."

Philo chuckled good-naturedly. "And you shall have it," he announced with finality. "But again, I am just trying to point out to you that walking out is a whole lot harder than walking in, and none of you walked in lightly or easily."

"What are you saying, Philo?" I demanded, feeling a bit agitated. "I want the damn key. Why make an issue about it?"

Philo looked thoughtful. "Hmm. What *am* I saying here?" He looked away briefly, seeming to think the situation anew. "I guess I am saying two things to you," he began to clarify, coming back to focus. "The first is that, once again, the key is not a magic wand. Walking out of a cage is not a Disney event surrounded by angelic sparkles. There is indeed a key, but using it will almost certainly be significantly more challenging and difficult than you are anticipating."

We looked at each other. It was perhaps the most intense moment between us we had yet had. It wasn't verbal or even conceptual. It seemed really soul deep somehow, as if a lot of pre-conceptual data was streaming back and forth between us. "And the second thing . . . ?" I asked finally.

"Simple," Philo responded, releasing the tension. "The second thing is this. Where there is a zoo cage and a noble creature caged up in it, there is always a key to the cage."

"That's the second thing you want to tell me?" I exclaimed, disappointed. "I already knew that. It is what we are talking about."

"No, that is not the second thing. The second thing is that where there is a zoo cage and a noble creature caged up in, there is also always a key. But that is not all. There is also always a zookeeper!"

"A zookeeper," I said, puzzled.

"Yes, a talented and skilled zookeeper whose job, profession, and pride is to keep the noble beast in the cage!"

"I see," I said, feeling a bit let down.

Philo smiled a smile without humor, a rhetorical smile. "Actually, John, you do not."

CHAPTER 43

I HAVE DOUBTS ABOUT PHILO

O ur conversation had ended without me having the key. That was deeply frustrating. It even made me feel more than a tiny bit angry. Philo was starting to remind me of those snappy promotional offers that promise to reveal some important new secret in order to keep you listening to more marketing than you would ever ordinarily countenance. I kept thinking, with increasing aggravation, "Just give me the key already!"

But also, we had ended our latest conversation with Philo telling me that I didn't understand something about the fact that in addition to there being a key to the zoo cage there is also a zookeeper. Now I admit that when he mentioned the existence of a zookeeper, I felt disappointed. Right away I could see how the presence of a zookeeper would indeed make leaving the cages trickier and more difficult. But certainly I, someone who is very wary of all government claims and who is skeptical if not actively cynical regarding authorities—certainly I of all people could understand and accept that there would be a zookeeper in a system of human zoos. So why did Philo say I did not understand? I kept thinking, 'Just give me the key and I will show you I understand.'

This was the tenor of my thinking during the four agonizing days I had to wait until I saw Philo again. I kept going over and over in my mind that he was stringing me along and feeling mounting frustration about it. This is why, I thought, the time I spend talking with him, as wonderfully valuable and worthwhile as it continues to seem to be, is also frustrating to the max. Again and again in our conversations it felt that just as I was at the point of receiving some significant revelation, the delivery of it would get delayed. The revelation package was always being re-routed, re-packaged, and re-authenticated—anything but a timely delivery. It felt like the closer I got, the further away I became.

Then there was the whole alien thing and the periods of paranoia and worry Philo would enter into. I have to admit, his worries about being apprehended by some sort of intergalactic police force mostly struck me as hokum. But that did not seem like the problem here. He was dangling, delaying, distracting, and what did intergalactic police have to do with that? If anything, *that* is what they would want him to do. In fact, the more I thought about this, the more it seemed clear that if Philo did want to reveal some things to me and if—however implausible it sounds—there was an intergalactic police force, then he would be motivated to tell me as quickly as possible what he had to share before the supposed authorities could apprehend him and prevent him from saying anything further. If there really *was* danger, then he should be *more* giving of information, and there should be *more* urgency on his part.

Maybe I am too gullible? Maybe I need to get tougher with him? He probably thinks of me as a patsy. He already mentioned that many of the people on his own planet think of Earthlings as delightfully intelligent monkeys, sort of like the pictures one sometimes sees of monkeys dressed up in tuxedos, sitting at a luxuriously appointed dinner table, throwing food at each other. Nothing more than a bunch of smirking chimps.

It was really bothering me.

On the other hand, Philo was certainly likeable enough, though in a sort of flat, uninspired way. I reflected that while I did genuinely and truly like him and care about him, it was not the sort of liking and caring that is likely to inspire great deeds. I reflected that it was more like a flat relationship in which one continued to be involved in without there being any particularly strong or passionate reason for being so. It also reminded me of the way attending church is for many people—that is, they attend, but not because the joy or benefit of doing so. It is more a well-established habit that is difficult to break. For such a person, it is easier to stuff one's doubts and experiences than to quit going.

Oh horrible thought! Is that how my ongoing relationship with Philo is? It certainly seemed so. By the third day I had resolved to take a different approach with Philo, one more demanding and less conciliatory. If that ended our conversations, then so be it! I could continue to do the meditations if I wanted. They were still working, though less dramatically now.

Finally the day of the gig came, the day I would see Philo. My mind was set. I will no longer be passive. I will demand answers. If he is not going to provide them, at least that will be revealed. Let the chips fall where they may. No more Mr. Nice Guy!

I played with flourish that night, playing all my best bits. I did some really fast scale things and pushed things more than I normally do. And, as I expected, during my last set I suddenly noticed Philo sitting in a back corner. He was sitting as he normally did, obscured, sullen, and lonely.

When I walked up after putting my guitar away, I felt firm, committed, even reckless. I was going to demand some results! If this brought about a termination of our conversations, then so be it! I was not holding on to anything. I was ready to let it all go, if it came to that.

As I approached I noted that Philo was taking note of *me!* This was not typical. Normally he would pointedly ignore me until I was right there, being especially careful not even to glance in my direction until I either said something or pulled out a chair. And even then, he always reacted as if I was interrupting something, not that he was expecting me.

"May I offer you a seat?" he asked warmly as soon as I got into earshot.

That was mighty strange for him, but I kept my cool. "Why thank you, Philo," I said, noticing my syrupy tone. "I think I will take you up on that." I pulled out a chair a bit more aggressively than I normally would. Philo noticed and seemed to startle a bit. I even thought I could detect a flash of alarm cross his face.

"A most hearty and warm welcome to *you,* John," Philo replied in completely believable warm, friendly, and engaging way. He seemed different. Not fake. It was more that he seemed resolved. He certainly did not seem on edge. Reading vibes, as he had encouraged me to do, I felt a sense that our talking together was important for *him.* I felt a gush of warmth towards him, but I sternly reminded myself that things were different now. No more patsy.

"We've got to talk," I said as nicely and gently as I could.

"Obviously," he replied evenly.

"Ok," I said, rushing right into it, "I think this talk is not only urgent but potentially apocalyptic."

"Obviously," he replied evenly again. This bothered me somehow. Why would he say that? He doesn't even know what I've been thinking.

"So, Philo," I replied, being pushier than I am normally, "if you monitor your own vibe meters, as you encouraged me to do with myself and which you constantly do with yourself, what do you detect that indicates to you that this talk right here now is both urgent and potentially apocalyptic?"

He smiled lightly and said "let's see." He then took a deep breath, lowered his eyelids, and seemed to settle down. He sat breathing deeply and focused within. It was impressive.

"Well," he said, raising his eyelids just as the silence of his introspection was getting too loud, as it were. "This is quite interesting and, well, it is as it should be."

"Oracular doesn't work for me, Philo," I said with a slight edge.

"You are going to have to spell it out for me."

"Yes, of course," he answered good-naturedly. I said that this was 'interesting.' Now as you well know, John, 'interesting' is a word one uses when one is not yet comfortable or ready to share one's thoughts with another. If a warm friend asks you what you think of her poem, which you did not like at all, you are likely to say it was 'interesting.' And if you then add, as I did, that 'this is as it should be,' you are signaling that you anticipate and accept your warm friend will not be pleased with your thought, your friend's reaction therefore being fully predictable."

I had been speaking with Philo for many months at this point and I could tell that for Philo this was as clear and unadorned an answer as I could hope to get, especially in an area that touched upon my own psyche. All along he had been scrupulously gentle, did not push, and allowed me to take things at my own pace. This was good and thoughtful of him, but there was one problem: the pace was too slow! It was not *my* pace but just the pace he seemed to think was mine.

Still, I felt I could work with this response. It seemed clear and direct. In fact, I found myself becoming intensely curious about what he might now say. The fact he had discreetly let me know it was going to be at my expense did not worry me. At least we would be getting somewhere, not just this endless circling.

CHAPTER 44

I AM MY OWN ZOOKEEPER

I settled back and nodded to Philo to continue. I definitely felt myself to be in a more assertive, less passive mode. No more Mr. Nice Guy! Philo had indicated that this reaction of mine was predictable and that I would not like what he said when he explained what he saw. 'Bring it on' I thought.

"I have had a bit of a change of spirit," I said to Philo.

"Obviously," he replied, smiling kindly. "But, John, this change of spirit of yours is entirely natural and, as such, not particularly interesting." I must have looked horrified because on that note Philo ever so slightly pulled back.

"What?" I protested. "There must be *something* interesting here. You are not going to be able to squirm out of this, Philo!"

"I might squirm," Philo replied, "but you are not going to let me squirm out. But why would I want to when so clearly there is something interesting here?"

"Well if it is not the 'new spirit' of my reaction that is interesting, then what is it?" I was feeling frustrated again and I felt aggression surging through me.

"It isn't the *fact* of your 'new spirit of reaction' that is interesting, John. It is the *timing* of it."

That stumped me. I didn't know what to think. I didn't sense any sting behind his words, just the words themselves. "I don't understand, Philo."

Philo smiled. "I won't say 'obviously' you do not understand me, but I am not surprised in the slightest. Let's try to figure it out together."

"Let's do so."

"We have been talking about humanity. In particular, you were quite critical of humanity, excepting yourself and a few others of course. You were holding humanity accountable for all sorts of horrible things, mostly having to do with the corruption, degradation, and even possible destruction of both your natural environment and your social order."

"Yes, that is quite right. And I recall you countered by defending humanity. You agreed with my facts but said people were suffering from what you called a 'cultural virus.' You said humans were not uncaring, immoral, and selfish as much as they were sick. They had been made sick by this virus."

"Indeed. The cultural virus is a metaphor, but in this instance it is a particularly apt one. Just as we would not reject a baby with a cold, and certainly not judge the baby's human worth and potential on that basis, so should we not judge sick and suffering humanity's worth and potential on the basis of the cultural virus it is suffering from."

"That is exactly the way you put it," I said. "Then you further clarified by saying it was like humanity is a noble beast cruelly confined to a tiny cage in a for-profit zoo. When we look at the beast languishing in the cage, therefore, we should not make the mistake of thinking we are seeing the nature of the noble creature."

"Precisely," said Philo, beaming. "But don't forget the next part, the really important part, the part that brings the metaphor back to everyday life, making it practical and useful."

"I'm drawing a blank," I said.

"How interesting," Philo exclaimed with an engaging smile. "And how understandable and even predictable that you would draw a blank."

Hearing him say this with such joy, I felt a surge of angry resistance. "I'm trying to remember, Philo," I protested. "I mean, it's not like you don't go on and on with your words. It isn't always easy to remember an exact point. No need to become my shrink here. Just give me a clue. Help me remember." I was breathing faster.

Philo laughed out loud. "By all means, John, let me give you a hint." Even though his eyes seemed to be sparkling, I was feeling anger surge through me. "Humanity is a noble creature in a cramped, cruel, and entirely inappropriate cage. Suffering. A prisoner in a Zoo. Which leads to a concern of . . . "

At that exact moment I felt an extreme surge of anger. I interrupted, blurting out in frustration, "Which obviously leads to a concern of why we are in that stupid cage."

"No," Philo replied with gentleness. "Why humanity is still in the cage is not the concern. Quite simply, humanity is still in the cage because the door is still locked. Nothing complicated there."

My anger was not abating. "Nothing complicated there, indeed," I protested. "That only leads to THE question—the question of where the damn key to the stupid cage is. I want to find that key, but you, Mr. Philosopher from another planet, keep dangling it in front of me without letting me grab it!"

Philo laughed again and then gave me one of his long 'I'm reading you' looks, only this time he did so with a pleasant smile on his face. As much anger as I was feeling and as short a fuse as I was operating on, I did not feel mocked by Philo and his smile. Just the opposite. I felt him appreciating, accepting, and even loving me. Then Philo said, "It isn't the key—or more precisely, the lack of it—that is interesting here and which is stoking your understandable anger."

"What is it then?" I demanded petulantly.

Philo kept smiling. "Let's figure it out," he said, leaning ever so slightly forward. "Would you say you are in a different spirit tonight?" I felt busted and exposed. I was very much in a different spirit. No more Mr. Nice Guy!

"You're right," I said weakly.

"I could hear it in your music," Philo explained. I looked puzzled and Philo continued. "Normally when you add complex harmonies to your chords, flatting and augmenting the 9ths, 11ths, and 13ths, you don't always know which of these altered notes will appear in your melodies. That is the exciting part for me, namely, listening to you *discover* them. You find them, and then repeat what you found in the joy of discovery. Tonight, however, you *imposed* them. You willed them onto the melodies."

"I thought I sounded good tonight," I replied.

"Certainly you did," Philo replied convincingly. "This is not a good/bad thing. It is a matter of the disposition of your spirit. You were in a different spirit tonight. It is the difference between what you might call the 'spirit of discovery' and the 'spirit of control.' Tonight you were in control. You exercised authority over the notes. Instead of discovering new harmonies and combinations, you imposed them. Am I right?"

Philo wasn't just right, he was revelatory! I felt exposed. "So that is the *interesting* part, the fact I was—and am—in a different spirit?" I asked, somewhat dismayed.

"Not at all," Philo answered pleasantly. "Once again, it is the timing of this change that is interesting, not the fact of it. But let's look at that difference in spirit for a second. You have been in jams where there is little or no arranging or pre-planning. Doesn't it often start well but then begin to degrade as the players stop listening to each other and playing off each other. They then begin to play more mechanically and less artistically. Gradually, as band leader, you undergo a 'change of spirit' regarding the jam, flowing less and controlling more."

"Exactly that," I said, impressed.

"Or, to change the example, you are in a most wonderful class discussion. The students engage, interact, and flow in the most amazing way while you sit back observing and appreciating. But gradually, as certain individuals begin to repeat themselves, badgering the quieter students, the discussion begins to get wooden and predictable. As teacher, you feel a change of spirit. You stand back less and begin to enter more to frame, focus, and shape."

"Exactly that," I said, even more impressed. "So what is the interesting part?"

"Let's review and see if we can pick it out. I had said there is a magnificent being in a cage. The cage is restrictive, more suitable for a dangerous beast than for an intelligent *human* being. The cage is in a cultural zoo. What am I missing?" He ticked off on his fingers, "Magnificent being, zoo, and cage. What is this picture lacking?"

Suddenly it hit me with a flash, just like the fabled "aha" of enlightenment. "The key, which the zookeeper has," I burst out. "Why would I not remember that? You find the zookeeper and you find the key, not to mention an explanation of why there is a human in a cage in the first place." I looked at Philo. He was smiling in satisfaction.

"The zookeeper who has the key to the cage is deeply and truly interesting. But that is not the *most* interesting part. The most interesting part is that you forgot about the key. And it is the timing of this forgetting that makes it so interesting."

"How so?"

"Before you got into this new spirit, you were all fired up about the key. 'The key, give me the key, give it to me.' You were unrelenting. But then you get in this new spirit and you forget about the key. What does that tell you?"

"That I have a bad memory?"

Philo cracked up. "No, John," he said as his laughter died down. "It tells us that you are avoiding this. You are avoiding finding the identity of the zookeeper and the location of the key. You blanked it out. You went unconscious regarding it. You ostracized it from your conscious mind."

I was shocked. What he said stung as only the truth could. It wasn't that my feelings were rocked, though they were. It was more that I was sick to the stomach with the feeling of the truth of what he was saying. In fact, if it were not for my ability, brought about and enhanced by these conversations, to recognize the 'sting' of the sting of truth, I think I would have punched him. I definitely would have walked out. I was in full defensive mode.

"I don't know what to say," I mumbled, chastened.

"How about asking me for the identity of the zookeeper, who of course holds the key?"

"Yes. Thank you. So who is the zookeeper?"

"I think we have just determined that," Philo replied gently.

I didn't say anything. Philo let that remark sit there for a moment, and then added, "That is why it is so interesting that you forgot about this and covered over your forgetting with a new spirit. Truly, John, this looks a lot like avoidance."

"Why would I do that?"

"It is what zookeepers do to keep the cages locked."

CHAPTER 45

THE PHENOMENOLOGY
OF BRAIN FOG

I don't know if it was because he was concerned for me or whether he felt we were really close to a major breakthrough, but Philo suggested we meet the very next day. I accepted the offer without much of a feeling, but I woke up the next morning fully thankful for it.

The thought that I somehow got so righteous and angry with Philo ('no more Mr. Nice Guy!') as a way of avoiding discovering and presumably using the key to my cage in the cultural zoo—this completely freaked me out! It meant (perish the thought!) that in spite of what I might say about yearning to be free, I was actually keeping the incarceration in place. How utterly devastating!

We were not going to meet until late afternoon, so I found myself spending the day dwelling in personal shock and horror over the discovery that I had blanked out in order to avoid identifying the zookeeper and finding the key. This went against everything I thought I stood for. To blank out and sabotage self-examination—this is deeply un-Socratic.

Not to be excessively harsh on myself, but this was not a simple case of forgetting. I forget all the time. It was that I experienced for myself a sort of blank mental fog that, just like real fog, covered up and obscured what I was seeing. It shocked me to discover there was something in me that was blanking out my quest for liberation, and doing so effectively. Indeed, if it had not been for Philo's input, it would have been a perfect implementation of the principle, 'seek and do not find.' What better place to hide than in the middle of the search party!

It also freaked me out that if Philo had not been smiling the whole time, sort of anchoring me in the storm, knowing full well both *that* I was blanking out and *what* I was blanking out to avoid, I would not have recovered myself. I probably would have walked proudly away from Philo, righteously accusing him of falsehood while thrusting my shoulders back as evidence that I am no longer a gullible, adaptable Mr. Nice Guy but have become a tough, hard-nosed detective of my own psyche!

So what was freaking me out was not just that I forgot. I forget things all the time. This was not simple forgetting, however. It was a very sophisticated internal program of avoidance, a psychological version of the classic false flag operation. To think, I was actually feeling hot anger towards Philo for toying with me, for withholding!

And the actual mechanics of forgetting—that was freaky as well. I say it was like a complex mental fog, but that is just a metaphor. In an actual fog, the driver knows his vision is impaired. If your passenger asks why you are driving slowly, you reply that the fog is so thick that it makes it difficult to see the road. You have to drive slowly in order to stay on the road. You *know* the fog is thick and making it difficult to see.

This was different. I didn't know my mind was in a fog. That is such a basic and important fact about mental fog. When one's mind is fogged up and one can no longer see, one does not necessarily grasp this. I didn't say to Philo, "My mind is full of fog and I seem to be blanking out on what you are telling me." Instead, I felt anger towards him. My anger towards him was what I was aware of, not my inability to see past that anger. In fact, the mental fog, which actually did not seem like fog at all, was invisible. Even in the midst of not seeing, everything seemed clear, even clearer than usual. I felt I was seeing things—and especially Philo—better than ever. In other words, it wasn't just that I could not see; it was also that I could not 'see' that I was not seeing.

This fact is so important—and so devastating. Again, if it were not for Philo, I would not have been able to see this. The fog felt so clear, unremarkable, and natural. It was a mental illusion, of course, but that is freaky!

Before I get to my meeting with Philo that next afternoon, let me interject here a conversation Philo and I had some weeks later when we were looking back on this blanking out fog experience. I was expressing horror that it had happened, that it *could* have happened, and that (horror of horrors!) it *could* happen again. Philo tried to console me by telling me that this blanking out fog experience of mine was a major blessing to me. I was astounded! "A blessing!" I exclaimed. How can a complete violation of personal integrity, a complete and totally blind expression of falsehood—how can this be a blessing?"

Philo smiled reassuringly. "Of course, the experience itself is a monster," he said. "It is not only destructive, it is the very foundation of all things destructive. Your horror at the experience is well founded."

"But a blessing?"

"Oh, absolutely. A consummation devoutly to be wished!" Philo often spoke like that, cribbing lines from classics of Earth literature, in this case Hamlet.

"Illuminate me please. As I see it, this experience is horrible, dangerous, shameful, and a consummation devoutly to be *avoided*!"

Philo laughed, "As indeed you should, John. But let me ask you, please, to describe the actual *feeling* of what it was like to be fogged in like that. Describe the phenomenology of the fog."

I introspected and surprisingly easily pulled back the experience. I could then readily see, from the inside so to speak, that 'fog' is not the best describer of this, and for the reason I mentioned above—namely, that while I was in the fog state, I was not aware I was in the fog state.

I told Philo this and he said, "But you can see the fog now."

"Yes, I can. But the experience is different."

"How so?"

"Before I was just seeing. I didn't see the fog. I just didn't see much of anything beyond my anger."

"And now?"

"Now I am not in my mind, I am above it. I can see the fog from above."

"That is wonderful, John. There is your blessing!"

"What blessing? That I can now see how unseeing I was then and how unseeing I could at any time become?"

"Yes and no," he replied with a pleasant, patient smile. "Yes, you could become unseeing, fogged up in the sense that your mind will continue to function mechanically, defending you from change. This is an automatic function and, in full context, is quite an amazing ability. Indeed, the ability to fog out and disconnect, both cognitively and emotionally, is actually a survival tool. It is a *valuable* survival tool."

"But it was keeping me from finding the key of liberation by effectively obscuring from me that I was even looking for the key, that I wanted it."

"That is the dysfunction of this valuable tool. It is like using a hammer to smash your thumb. The hammer does a great job, but that is not what it is designed for."

"But I am afraid it will happen again, Philo. Maybe even with you. I mean, I still don't have the key."

Philo laughed. "The key, the key, the key. Always the key. Don't forget that the key is a metaphor. It isn't a key you want but liberation. But to address your point, John, you can figure that this fog will happen again—and again, and again, and again. Only now it will be different because of your blessing."

"Which is?"

"Your ability to recognize and to sit above the fog, recognizing it *before* it can spread over your awareness and blank you out. Now you not only know that it can happen and how it can happen, but more importantly, what it feels like when it does happen. You have experienced it."

"I don't see how that is a good thing, Philo."

"Let me use an image to help you. Let's say you live in a primitive time of great danger. You live in a jungle, say, and there is a particular wild animal that hides along the jungle path in order to suddenly and viciously attack any unwary passerby. Let's say one day you are attacked. Right before the attack you get a robust whiff of this animal's strong and distinct odor. You survive the attack, but now you are worrying that the animal might sneak up unawares and attack again. Your worry is well grounded. The animal will certainly do its best to attack again. Only now you can smell it before you get close enough for it to attack. You can recognize its distinctive smell."

"What if I ignore the smell? Better yet, what if I am lost in thought and don't even notice the smell?" I was thinking about how often I'm lost in my thoughts and not in touch with my senses.

"Then you get savaged, John. Remember, mindfulness is always the key of keys. It isn't enough to possess a key. You have to use it. And to use it you have to be mindful. You have to be aware."

"Great," I said mournfully.

"No," Philo said back, smiling broadly. It is GREAT! This is your blessing. You can smell this fog, feel it on your skin, recognize it by its characteristic. Therein lies your liberation."

I mention this because I found what Philo said to be entirely correct. I won't say I never fogged out, but I did learn to recognize the early warning signs. I was like a drinker at a party who had the awareness to know when to stop drinking. I thought if I could keep my awareness up I wouldn't have to worry about getting a DUI . . . or slipping into a fog.

CHAPTER 46

BLAMING THE VICTIM
FOR THE CRIME

One of the things my conversations with Philo helped me with was philosophy. Speaking with Philo, I could see that most of my philosophical discussions with people up to that point were unsatisfactory. It is not an intellectual thing. It is not that the people I had discussions with were uniformed or lacking in any way. It was more that the philosophical conversation was a sort of contest. It had, or at least aimed to have, a winner and a loser.

There is nothing wrong with this. Our legal system and the notion of a trial by jury are both based on a similar understanding that staging a contest before a judge and jury is the best way to discover truth. So when someone is accused of a crime, a jury is selected to determine innocence or guilt and two sets of attorneys-- one prosecuting the defendant and the other defending—argue in front of the jury. They make their case, have it picked apart by their opponent and in turn pick apart the opponent's objections. They complete their arguments. The jury then decides who wins, the prosecution or the defense. Yes, they are deciding whether the defendant is innocent or guilty, but that decision takes the form of deciding whether the prosecutor or the defender 'win' the case.

Again, there is nothing wrong with this 'someone-wins-and-someone-loses' competitive approach to philosophy. It is often exciting and sometimes fun. But it is not exhaustive. There is more to philosophy than competing arguments, even granting the arguments are an essential part of it.

Philo and I disagreed a lot, but we were rarely, if ever, competing. There was not a winner and a loser in our discussions. And even though it was the case that he was instructing me more than I was instructing him, we were essentially equals in our philosophizing. As philosophers we were partners who had joined to seek the truth together.

Now there is another important wrinkle here. There is a lot of talk today about the major importance of critical thinking. People frequently lament that schools no longer teach critical thinking. Perhaps the greatest charge against high stakes testing is that it leaves out and passes over critical thinking, which of course is hard to grade. Indeed, testing is destroying learning by subtly redefining learning in terms of remembering rather than in terms of understanding. If you *remember* the answer you get it right on the test. You don't have to *understand* the answer.

But, really, critical thinking is not something that can be taught. Some of the tools of critical thinking can be taught, but critical thinking is something above and beyond the tools. Indeed, critical thinking in education is a lot like creativity in music. There are tools and elements of creativity that can be taught—the different scales and chords and modes. But actual creativity? Again, that is something above and beyond the tools.

So what is the essential component of critical thinking if not the tools of logic, the rules of inference, and the habits of data collection? I learned from Philo it is honesty. In order to think critically one has to cultivate *honesty* with oneself.

And this is why Philo always encouraged me to be fully frank and totally honest about whatever I might be feeling. We could not philosophize effectively if for social reasons I could not say how I was feeling. If I felt Philo was being obstreperous, for example, I had to be able to say so without him getting defensive. Of course, my saying so did not make it the case. So in giving voice to my feelings, I was also opening the possibility that they were based on a faulty reading of things and did not accurately indicate anything beyond themselves.

Either way, if an idea bothered me in some niggling way, I had to be able to enter into and expand that niggle, bringing it into the full light of awareness. Not to be able to do this for whatever reason is to kill philosophy. Indeed, the only real sin in philosophy is less than perfect honesty.

So as I was on my way to meet Philo, I was aware that something was really bothering me about the suggestion that humanity's zookeeper was none other than humanity itself. In fact, I was feeling some anger towards Philo for even suggesting this. Of course, I was fully chastened for my fog of the evening before. This anger was not like that. It had a different quality. It was not at all like last night's *projected* anger, functioning to deflect and obscure. It was more of a *nestled* anger. The anger was not *over* everything, obscuring my vision; it was rather *under* everything, like a splinter in the heel. It didn't keep me from walking, but I could certainly feel it.

So as I approached my meeting with Philo, I had no thought of hesitating to bring this anger out and share it with him. That is what real philosophers do, after all.

So what was the anger about? Actually, it was a complex mix of anger and disappointment having to do with Philo's suggestion that the zookeeper of humanity, the dark entity that keeps the masses of humanity in its current state of suffering and woe, is none other than humanity itself.

This really bothered me. To me it amounted to nothing less than blaming victims for their victimized state. It sounded a lot like telling a homeless person to get a room at the Ritz.

At the same time, of course, I was feeling chastened by my experience the night before of using anger as a means of avoidance. But as a philosopher, I also knew that I had to give voice to this current anger of a different quality. And significantly, I wasn't *just* angry. I wasn't seething. I was aware that something was bothering me. The bother bubbled up as anger, but it was the bother that was the thing, not the anger it was expressing itself as.

Dwelling on this, I reached the square. The weather was nice and Philo had suggested we meet in the square. I was learning how he thought about discretion. Sometimes the best place to hide is in the middle of a lot of people and action. So I looked for him, not immediately noticing him. I smiled. This had become sort of a game. Where is he this time? And there, sitting in the northwest corner on a bench in front of the Gettysburg Hotel receiving the full warmth of the late winter sun, was Philo, smiling at me.

I walked up and sat next to him. We chatted briefly and then I said, "Philo, I am deeply humbled by my experience last night and I want to learn from it. But I also think it would be profoundly mistaken for me to now begin to mistrust myself and to doubt my feelings and instincts. I can become aware of them and examine them, maybe even diminish or reframe them as a result, but I should not programmatically doubt my feelings from here on out."

"Wonderfully well put, John," Philo said effusively. "You save me the trouble of articulating this most essential point." Then he fixed me with the classic Philo gaze and then ever so slightly nodding his head up and down as if he was noting something. "And I suspect, John, there is some aspect of last night, completely separate from your shut down fog that you want to give voice to now, something that is bothering you perhaps."

Philo was like that. At first I thought he was actually reading my mind, but I learned (and he taught me to do so myself) that we can see so much more than we realize. He used to say, smiling, "You can really see a lot when you take the time to look." His explanation is that all humans are somehow deeply connected and that we are always communicating what we really feel. Of course what complicates the situation is that we also often unconsciously adopt attitudes and postures meant to disguise what we are really feeling. I guess with Philo you could say he was a more careful reader of body language than we generally think is possible.

"Yes, Philo," I said, "something is bothering me about what you said last night, wholly separate from my blocking it out. And that is that saying humanity is the zookeeper sounds too much like blaming the victim."

"How so?" Philo asked, seemingly genuinely interested in my thought.

"Ok, a lot of people are suffering." Just then a couple walked in front of us looking distinctly upset. We both fell silent. As they passed, I said, "Exhibit number one."

"Oh, John, you hardly need an exhibit. The sadness and misery in your country and on your planet is overwhelming, especially to someone not used to this level of misery. And, being here, what surprises me about all of this is that it isn't simply the poor and destitute who are miserable. More often than not it is the well off." He glanced in the direction of the unhappy couple who were unlocking the door of their limited edition, top of the line, luxury car. "In fact, I would even go so far as to say that, generally speaking, poor people have more fun."

I groaned. "That is part of the thing that is bothering me, Philo. Here you are romanticizing poverty."

Philo chuckled. "Perish the thought. I think of myself here as describing, not prescribing. I am not recommending poverty for its delight. I am just acknowledging that quite often well-off people are even more miserable than the destitute. And there is a reason for this. The destitute are well aware of why they are miserable. They are hungry. They are cold. They have nowhere to sleep. They can't feed their children. But the well-off? They have everything. They do not know why they are sad or feeling so miserable. Therefore, they suppress the feeling. They detach from it, living an emotionally flat life as a result, which of course only makes things worse. By detaching emotionally from their own feelings, they lose the capacity to feel gratitude, to feel thankful for their material well-being. Instead, they tend to fall into the even smaller zoo cage of struggling for more—more money, more power, more sex, more cars, more gadgets, more houses. It is a lonely and vicious cycle."

"Back to the poor," I said, redirecting Philo's focus. "Saying humanity is its own zookeeper makes it sound like the poor are not poor because a rapacious elite have taken over the government and now write the laws in their interest, robbing the poor of whatever little opportunity they might have had, leaving millions without work or adequate work, poorly fed, housed, and clothed, not to mention without access to quality education. But you seem to be saying that it is humanity to blame, not the greedy rich. In fact, you say that even the greedy rich are sad. So must we now try to have a little more compassion for the suffering rich?"

I noticed Philo smiling. "What's so funny?" I demanded.

"Very nice rant, John. Exceedingly nice, in fact. Strong feeling, a witty sharpness, and cutting allusions to current attitudes."

"Don't patronize me," I said menacingly, scowling.

Philo laughed merrily. "Ok, John. Let me rephrase my point. What an irrelevant explosion of emotion, based of course on a deep misunderstanding, made possible by a highly developed human capacity to look at each dot without connecting them."

I was silent. Even though I was angry at the way the world was, my experience was not anything like the fog of last night. And in the suburbs of my current state, I could tell that Philo was not entirely wrong. There *was* something unhinged about my response: I was ranting, which is not the most purely philosophical of postures. I noticed Philo looking at me intently. As strange as it sounds, it was as if he was aware of this deeper calm and, while completely ignoring my frothing anger, was connecting and communicating with the deeper calm.

"How would you say that this anger you are feeling now connects to the fog of unawareness that you experienced last night?" Philo asked.

It was a fair question. In fact, what struck me about it was that it was genuine. Philo was not arguing with me. He wasn't countering my angry assertions. He was seeking *with* me, helping me to explore the architecture of my outlook.

And how *did* the two relate, if at all? I hadn't thought about how the two related, and while the answer was not obvious, it did seem somehow that the two must have some sort of connection, perhaps both being opposing aspects of something similar. My mind was racing. Philo was still looking at me with calm, loving, safe-feeling acceptance.

"I don't know, Philo," I said humbly. "It sort of feels more like I am being spoken than that I am speaking. I feel more like a dupe of ideas than a doer of deeds."

Philo laughed merrily. "How wonderfully put. John, we have to talk about this."

CHAPTER 47

MINDFUL AWARENESS
AND SUCCESS

We continued to talk for some time in the square, but that is a bit of a misnomer. We did continue to talk about this issue of blaming the victim, of course, but most of the time we sat silently while I thought over the things he was saying, observing my somewhat automatic reactions. It was a very intense session wherein I confronted some of the programs of my own deep ideas.

I think it was because I had been doing that distancing meditation Philo had shown me once or twice a day for almost six months that made it possible for me to rise above my mental state even as I was experiencing it. My awareness could now have a double focus. On the one hand, I could focus on my actual internal state. When it was emotionally extreme, as it now was, it functioned like a seductively swirling whirlpool of emotion and thought that tended to suck me right into it.

On the other hand, there was also my mindful awareness that could float above the swirling turbulence, noting details of it. In other words, I could be feeling anger and at the same time be aware that I was feeling anger. This ability may seem like a given, but it is not. Have you ever seen a person who is hopping mad asked gently why they are so mad? It is not unusual for such a person to reply angrily that they are not angry!

This ability to rise above may not seem all that significant, but for someone doing inner work, it is essential. For example, I was able to rise above my anger at 'blaming the victim' and see that my reaction of anger at such a thing, which seemed to be so nobly rooted in justice and powered by feelings of care, was actually a clever distraction masking a deeper response on my part. This does not mean that victims are not routinely blamed for their plight or that anger at such a thing is not warranted. It only means that in the depths of my psyche, anger over *that* is not what was moving me at that time. Instead, it was *masking* what was moving me.

By rising above—even as I was feeling anger—I could grasp what Philo was telling me. To say that humanity is functioning as its own zookeeper and actually holds the key to the very cage that imprisons humanity is not to blame the victim or excuse the oppressor. It is to provide the secret to (and hope for) liberation. It means the cage can be unlocked, the walls of the zoo leapt over, and caged up humanity liberated. We don't need to beg a key from anyone else or plead or cajole someone to turn the key in our own lock. We can turn the key to our own cage ourselves. This is good news.

It was scary to see for myself how I blocked that insight—first with a fog in my own mind—a dark night, as Hegel once put it, in which all the cows are black. But then, as the fog lifted, I continued to block, only now with hot, fiery anger. Because it was a security buffer between me and the world, the anger was misplaced and inappropriate, functioning merely to redirect my attention away from the world and what I might see there and towards my own internal state, which I was projecting on the world. This buffer protected me from what Philo was saying. It functioned to keep me caged up.

Because I could now float above what I was experiencing even as I experienced it, I could see this for myself.

Philo helped, of course. As quickly as I might flash into that floating awareness, I also as quickly flashed out, being sucked into the whirlpool of my inner turbulence. Philo could tell. And when I was 'out' he did not argue with me or engage me on a content level.

Instead, with great sensitivity and patience, he helped me back into my higher awareness. In that way, by nurturing that sliver of higher awareness, I was able to *see* me being me and not just *be* me being me. I protested every step of the way and was even mean to Philo on occasion. But like an experienced nurse with a vomiting patient, Philo not only knew what to do to clean up the mess, but he did not take the vomiting personally.

We sat in the square for a longer time than we normally spent together in our sessions, though much of that time, as I mentioned, was taken up by silence. If you had seen me sitting silently at that time, you likely would not have noticed that my mind was not sitting silently. It was racing, scrolling desperately through its bag of tricks to accomplish a more perfect fade out. I couldn't stop it from doing this, but I could watch it. And that made all the difference.

We finally ended up our session that afternoon and we both felt a sense of success over what was a most satisfying and productive meeting. With effusive good feelings, we agreed to meet the very next day.

That time came quickly, and I set out, once again, to meet Philo in the square. Things were going so incredibly well and I walked into the square with the highest of hopes and no small expectations.

As I approached the square the next day, I could not help but reflect on what a completely different mental space I was in than just the day previously. Calmer, more aware of my mind's tricks, and more capable of 'rising above,' I looked for Philo.

I felt a surge of anticipation when I saw Philo. He did not seem to have noticed me yet but as different as I felt, he looked different too. And he was different in a most surprising way.

CHAPTER 48

PHILO TELLS ME
HE IS A CRIMINAL

I saw him right away this time. "Good morning to the man above the fray, the guide who trembles not at the cliff's edge," I said as I approached. It was not a spontaneous greeting. I had been thinking what to say the whole time I was walking to the square, and I had decided to greet him in a most positive, appreciative way. I had even rehearsed these words in my mind.

But something was off. Here was Philo, my guide and teacher, so supportive, so ready to smile at my foibles, always eager to discuss the state of humanity, such a hopeful presence—this Philo did not look up to respond. The Philo who did look up said something fitting, matching what I had just said. But it seemed forced, even fake.

"And here is John," Philo said blandly, "a hero of consciousness, dedicated to seeing 'what is' without distortion, being especially careful to discern the mechanisms and tricks of his own mind." He gave me a half smile.

"Nice words, Philo," I said, "but something is wrong." It was the contrast between the high energy I expected and how I remembered the high energy from the previous day that stood out and alerted me.

"You are right," Philo replied, looking crestfallen and not making any attempt to hide it. "Something is not quite right, and that something is me."

"A bit of a bad mood, perhaps," I suggested, a little too brightly. I

269

didn't say it, but my implication was that this was nothing serious and that it would soon pass. I noted, too, that his sadness was leading me to feel increasingly alarmed and unhinged.

"If only this was a passing mood," Philo sighed. "No, it is worse than that. This is a time for a confession, one that I would have avoided—*planned* on avoiding!" I must have looked horror stricken, because he immediately added, "This has nothing to do with you."

"But it's entirely to do with me, Philo," I protested. "You have helped me immeasurably. You've been my wise and patient mentor, a guide to a whole better way of being. And yesterday I had a breakthrough experience, a real turning point in my life. And it is all thanks to you, Philo. You are a true philosopher."

I wasn't panting when I finished, but if a mind could pant, mine would have been panting.

Philo smiled, flashing a pained look. "Such nice words. Such beautiful thoughts. Too bad they are false."

I protested, "Not false, Philo. True! Things are different for me now, and it is all thanks to you."

Philo took a weary breath. "How nice of you to say that," he said, looking totally defeated. "You call me a philosopher. I know coming from you that is a compliment. But, really, all I am is criminal. Don't worry, however. I didn't come here to steal from you." There was a pause. I didn't know what to say. Then he added, "Of course, I could be a liar and maybe I did come to steal."

I looked at him for some long moments then said, "Philo, I'm confused. Help me out here."

"Ok," he said after taking a deep and bracing breath. "You call me a philosopher, but on my own planet I am what you would call a 'rich kid.'"

"So you are able to pay your bills," I protested. "You know so much. You have access to such deep wisdom. I know this because you have helped me so much!" As I pleaded on his behalf I noticed sadness welling in his eyes. It was as if I was attacking him with truth rather than defending him from attack.

He sighed. "I suppose from your point of view I do appear that way. You have improved. I can see that. But you did that. The things I have said are around. You could have picked them up anywhere."

"I could and I have," I protested, "but they never worked the way they have with you telling me about them."

Again he sighed, even more deeply this time. "It isn't quite that way, John. Imagine you travelled back in time a couple of thousand years. Even though you are not a scientist, you would know a lot of science, especially as compared to those living thousands of years ago. You would be the proverbial one-eyed man in the valley of the blind or, as your remarkable Mark Twain put it, a Connecticut Yankee in King Arthur's Court. The point is that it wouldn't be that you were so brilliant or could see so well yourself. It would be that *compared* to the people of the day, you would seem brilliant."

"So are you saying that I and my planetmates are blind and dumb?" I asked lightly.

"Pretty obviously that is the case," he replied flatly. "You were yourself just the other day making that very point, though with much additional emotional baggage. I'm not adding anything to what you have already said."

"But, Philo," I exclaimed at once, beginning to feel troubled, "we determined that my words and thoughts in that regard were a screen. They were a deflection."

"Clearly they were a screen meant to deflect. But that is a psychological point, John. Your words functioned in the context of your psyche's defenses as a screen, but that doesn't make them false. Surely you have noticed that the best wall of defense against the truth is made up out of bits and pieces of truth!"

"So why did you come here, Philo?" I asked, marking an abrupt change of focus for our conversation.

"Because yesterday, feeling good as we both were, we agreed to."

"Not that. Not why you came to the square today. Why did you come to my planet?"

Philo got bug-eyed and stared at me for what seemed like a long while. Far from looking as if he had found my question inappropriate or rude, I had the distinct feeling that he was staring at me in awe. My stock was going up in his eyes. Finally he muttered, "The perfect question." Then he just slumped back in his seat.

"Well," I said after a few more moments of silence, "I'm still waiting for a response. Why did you come to my planet?"

Philo sighed his deepest sigh yet. It seemed like it was full of regret, concern, and fear and even tinged with guilt. "This isn't easy, John," he mumbled, thereby confirming some of my worst suspicions. He glanced around nervously, as if checking for something. I was feeling increasingly uneasy myself.

"Like I said," he continued haltingly, "I am a rich kid on my planet. I have the means to indulge my interests, and one of them is primitive Earth music."

"Primitive," I repeated, almost as a question. I was feeling hurt.

Philo looked at me without expression. "From my point of view, absolutely primitive! A backwards sort of primitive. Neanderthal, as it were."

I was sort of stunned, almost as if I had been slapped. Instead of saying anything, however, I just sat. My defensive reaction quickly passed and I noted I felt a little scared, almost as if I had been busted for something. I still did not say anything. Finally, Philo spoke again.

"One thing most Earthlings do not understand, John, is that being more technically advanced does not thereby mean being more morally developed. Just because an alien civilization can build a spaceship to fly immense distances to visit this treasure of a planet does not mean that the visit is wise or even well-intentioned. Think about Columbus representing the technically advanced European civilization to the Arawak Indians of the new world. Clearly, technical advance does not entail moral advance or even moral comprehension."

"But you are no Columbus," I said warily, wanting it to be true but suddenly fearing things I did not understand. "I mean, why would an alien want to talk to me? I play some nice guitar, to be sure, but not *that* nice."

"No, I am not a Columbus. But I did break a lot of laws to come here. And you play a lot nicer guitar than you give yourself credit for."

"Why, Philo, why? Why did you break those laws to come here?"

"Simple," he said, "to talk to you."

CHAPTER 49

AN EXPLANATION OF SORTS

Being with Philo could be a little strange at times, but this was more than strange. It was a high weirdness sort of strange I had not previously experienced with him. Indeed, Philo was now different than what I had gotten used to. Where he was secretive before, he now was completely open. Where he seemed confident before, even arrogant, he now seemed insecure and uncertain. And where before he knew so much, even to the point of being able to make predictions, he now seemed out of sorts and lost.

"So let me get this straight," I said, noting a hint of exasperated command in my tone and posture that was not in any way characteristic of our conversations. "You are telling me that you are a rich kid on your planet who loves primitive music. So being born to privilege no doubt, you broke some serious laws to come to this planet to hear the most appealing primitive music in all the galaxies, what we call 'rock.' And not only that, but you also befriended me, someone who probably ranks among the most primitive of the primitives, I'm sure."

That very last bit about me being a 'primitive of primitives' was unnecessary, of course, but it did express the upset I was feeling. All along I thought Philo and I were friends, and now it seemed like I was merely a tourist giggle, someone local to take a selfie with to show the friends back home.

Philo looked pained. "Something like that," he said, "but your emphasis is not quite right."

"Then perhaps you can help me get the emphasis right," I

replied with a demanding edge to my voice.

Philo looked beaten down. "Perhaps it was a mistake," he mused, though not to me, thus adding to my sense of being excluded, even used. "My visit hasn't been quite what I expected it to be."

"Sorry to disappoint," I said without any sorrow. "If I had known you had come all this way to experience chic primitive, I would have made an effort to find some bellbottoms to wear. I could easily have spent less time tuning my guitar, adding to the ambience of the primitive, I'm sure." I finished speaking, but I felt belittled by Philo and hurt.

Philo lifted his head and looked at me with more focus. "John, there is no reason for you to be upset," he said almost apologetically. "The highlight of my trip has been our conversations. Knowing you has . . . I'd say it has . . . well, it has changed my views on many things, many *important* things."

This last note about 'important things' hung in there between us like a secret that was keeping us apart. "Please explain," I said.

"You are not going to like this, John," Philo replied solemnly. "But as you yourself have wisely said, it is never the truth that hurts. What hurts is our resistance to the truth, the fact that it so often does not line up with our preferences."

"Let's have it," I said with resolve but not a lot of warmth. I was feeling used somehow, violated perhaps, even betrayed.

"I'll get right to the point. You know me as a philosopher from another planet."

"I only know what you have told me, which, sketchy as it is, I accepted, but now I am not so sure." I noted the blaming, petulant flavor my words had. It was subtle, but my hurt reaction seemed to be hurting Philo, and I was not thereby correcting my attitude to be more Philo-friendly. It was the opposite. I was digging in a bit. This was petty on my part, even if it was expressing the hurt I was feeling.

"I am from another planet, that is true," Philo said sadly, as if he were confessing. "But it is only part of the truth. The larger truth is that there are many inhabited planets, an entire federated civilization of them. Mine is small and relatively powerless. It is also what you would call extremely liberal. By 'liberal' I mean *more* than the fact we are accepting of diversity." He paused and grinned, "This is significantly more of a challenge for us than it is for you on this planet, where diversity is really just a matter of accepting alternative versions of essentially the same thing."

Even though my mind was racing, I just nodded and said nothing.

"More so than any other planet, we do not like the hierarchical system of control and privilege the larger planets possess and exercise over us. This political fact—namely, that we are weak and small and chaffing under the imposed control from above—is why Earth music is so popular on my planet, more so than on any other planet out there. I hear that its popularity is exploding throughout inhabited space, but my planet is still the leader by far. Of course, this is all underground and, on the books at least, strictly forbidden."

"So what is the big deal?" I asked, starting to be intrigued. "I don't have an intergalactic perspective and so I don't have the context to compare, but I can accept that there is some pretty good music here, even on an intergalactic scale."

"Oh, it is so much more than that, John," Philo said with a sudden burst of intensity! Musically it is primitive, almost childlike. Harmonically, melodically, and conceptually your music is more like a bunch of unruly children shouting and clapping their hands than it is like the refined compositions a civilized intergalactic citizen would recognize as music. True, the rhythms are complex and intriguing, but that can be attributed to differences in biology."

"Ouch," I said, mocking pain. "And here I was all along thinking you liked my playing." I did not feel insulted in the slightest. It would be as if I was talking to an intelligent eagle and the eagle said to me that most birds found human music to be a bit cacophonous. That may well be true, but we don't play our music for birds!

Philo answered quickly and with an uptick of passion. "I love your music. Love it! You thrill me, excite me, enrapture me."

"Not bad for a primitive without a civilized grasp of harmony and melody."

"John," Philo almost shouted with intense focus, "it isn't the notes. It is the attitude! Earth music, and especially your own improvisations, gives us hope! You are free where we are controlled. You create and invent where we copy and imitate. You have the courage to try new combinations, expressing spontaneous delight in discovery, where we have the capacity to identify and classify all possible combinations yet are unwilling to try anything new. But most of all, where we try to be fully compliant, you use creativity to challenge, mock, and diminish authority. In short, your music liberates while ours merely provides the soundtrack to our imprisonment."

"This all sounds good, quite complimentary in fact. So why is Earth music illegal?"

"Obvious," Philo said with finality. "The rebel attitude, the posture of defiant distance—this goes against the entire cultural direction of intergalactic civilization. It appeals to the rebels among us, to be sure, but it alarms and repels the establishment."

"Why not import some commercial Earth music, some early Brittany or Taylor Swift perhaps. Not a lot of rebellion there."

Philo exploded into laughter, the most I had seen him laugh in a long while. He was often amused and he frequently smirked. His normal range of expression seemed to range from a smirk to a smile, on the one end, to a polite chuckle at the other. But this was a belly laugh. It was so infectious it got me chuckling a bit. "That is good, John, really good," he managed to gasp between spots of uncontrolled laughing.

It changed the vibe between us. As Philo calmed down, tears were running from his eyes and his entire vibe had shifted. "There is so much I have to tell you," he said.

CHAPTER 50

PHILO GETS TO IT
AND IT IS REALLY BAD

The next time I saw Philo he was ready to tell it all. For my part, I was ready to hear it. No matter what he might say about Earth backwardness and primitive simplicity, I was convinced he was deeply and properly appreciative. I felt I could trust him. I was therefore full of aching curiosity, so when I saw Philo, the first thing I said was, "Let's get to it."

"Right to it," Philo quickly replied, smiling warmly. "There is so much I have to say, and I've been thinking about where to start. I keep confusing myself with the complexity of it all, however, so I can only imagine how incoherent it will sound to you. So after a lot of trying to come up with something coherent, I decided the best thing to do would be just to let you ask questions."

I laughed. "Taking the good old Earth approach, are you? You know, winging it, stumbling forward and adjusting on the fly. It works for me. So let me start." I tried to look thoughtful.

"A real question uses you to ask itself," Philo said. "Why are you pretending to think of a question?"

"Nicely put, Philo. Here we go then. "Why are there no trade representatives from your civilization, no cultural ambassadors, and no political representatives? Why is the only contact between a rich kid with a taste for primitive music and an Earth nobody who likes to jam? This is pretty low on the scale for intergalactic contact."

"Quite good, John. Very good, in fact. You would do well in my world, though perhaps not so well among the higher ups in my world. But let me expand the picture for you. Yes, the commercial elements in my world look at your planet and lick their chops. Yes, as many of you Earthlings realize, your planet is incredibly beautiful. Some would say it is perfect. But can you imagine it as a commercial property! Its value in hard money? The fortune in raw materials? The capacity of Earthlings to be workers in our industries? They see this and lick their greedy chops."

"So that is the situation?" I asked, feeling a bit like a potential pork chop.

"That's part of it. There is more. We also have laws designed to protect intergalactic diversity, which is to say, primitive planets. So politically it is a big contest right now between the strengthening commercial forces that want to buy the planet Earth and open it up to commercial exploitation and the environmentalists who want to preserve the integrity of both your natural cultural development and the pristine perfection of your natural environment."

"So that's it," I asked, "a struggle between the greedy and the caring, just like here on Earth?"

Philo stammered, "Well, yes, it is that. It is that, but it is more complicated. You see, the greedy, as you call them, can point to your own mismanagement of your environment and your own degradation of your social order. This enables them to make the case that *they* are the true environmentalists, that they are not simply greedy to exploit the planet but actually want to care for it, to manage the commercialization and extraction of your planet's resources more efficiently, more in line with what they call 'established practices.'"

This was not good news. "Sounds like 'as below, so above' I remarked cynically."

Philo laughed again. "Nicely put," he said, "though we would say it differently—namely, 'as above, so below.' In other words, we like to tell ourselves that the way we are, especially in our least noble and unethical manifestations, is simply us being natural. Hence, what is true of us, we say, is true of every possible manifestation, including especially the most primitive. Thus we say that we are not essentially different than you primitives, just better. In other words, we both run, it is just that we do so longer and faster."

"So again, why not cultural contact, treaties, and trade?"

"Believe me, John, there are powerful forces that want to buy your planet right away and begin to exploit it. There is a growing movement to do just that, in fact."

"Philo, you've mentioned a couple times the notion of 'buying the planet.' Who on this planet has the authority to make such a sale?"

Philo shook his head while looking at me, seeming disappointed. "This is a detail, John. How did the European settlers 'buy' the new land that is your country? It is a formality, a nice way of saying that we simply take over your planet. The 'purchase' gives the conquest an appearance of legitimacy."

"So why hasn't it happened already?"

"It is not for a lack of desire or effort, I can assure you. Right now there is an uneasy standoff out there, not between commercial interests and the environmentalists but between the different commercial interests. Earth is the prize, the treasure. It represents a fortune. Your planet stands untouched at this point only because each of the vulture planets wants Earth for themselves. So the thinking is, 'Better nobody gets it than them!' So the uneasy truce is that nobody gets it—just yet!"

"So this is good news, right?"

"Unfortunately, no. You see, we have this law called the "Civilized Directive." It used to state that commercial entities from any of the civilized planets had to follow intergalactic law in their dealings with primitive planets. With extreme lobbying and active politicking, the commercial interests got the Civilized Directive redefined. It now states that in dealing with a primitive planet, a commercial entity is fully entitled to do to the planet and the people what the people on that planet already do. Since you Earthlings are steadily raping your land and exploiting and impoverishing masses of your own species, this means the intergalactic corporations will be legally allowed to do the same. It is all so 'civilized' you see."

"This sounds bad, Philo. But not every Earthling favors pollution and inequality. In fact, there is growing disaffection and resistance to our governments and corporations. How does that factor in?"

"That's a key point, John. Take health care. In many countries on your planet there is the thought that government exists to serve the people and that, to use a single example, health care is a human right. In other countries—for example, most prominently your own—there is the idea that health care is a for-profit commercial product. Low income humans are thought to have no more right to health care than they do to luxury automobiles or sprawling mansions."

"But that is just a manipulation from above," I countered. "Many of us see health care as a moral and political right, and the notion of health care being a for-profit commercial product a wicked and distorted falsehood."

"Indeed, and that is exactly what I am trying to get across. Earthlings are divided on this. Therefore, any planet or commercial interest that purchases your planet will have to respect this division. They will be able to deny coverage in your country and pollute without conscience because that is what Americans do. But in certain European countries, for example, healthcare for everyone and support for the weak and needy is provided as a matter of right. So that is another factor that contributes to the uneasy truce, leaving the planet Earth quarantined, so to speak. They are waiting for things to improve on your planet."

"By 'improve' I assume you mean 'get worse.'

"Exactly. You see it clearly but few do. Things are changing on your planet, much in the direction the commercial forces want. They love your country. Take for example the newly established precedent that your government can assassinate anyone in the world, even a US citizen, without a trial or an opportunity for the targeted to defend themselves from what could be false and bogus charges. In fact, if anything could be worse than this licensing of extra-legal murder, it is that the victims are now chosen on the basis of a meta-data analysis of their behavior and habits. That is, if a person acts in some way like someone who is threatening would act—going to the same restaurant, reading the same book, knowing the same person, that sort of thing—they can be killed on that basis."

"This is horrible."

"Truly so, but the commercial people love it. It gives them license they don't usually get. So their thinking is that it only helps by letting things go on as they are. They don't even have to break the law and send agents to corrupt your institutions and degrade your humanity and your culture. You are doing it yourselves! They can just sit back and, once you've completed the dehumanization of your world, swoop in and take it all for themselves."

"This is repulsive, utterly and totally repulsive," I stammered in disgust.

"So you say, and I'm inclined to agree with you. But to them, this is the mother of all blessings. Having the legal right to assassinate anyone they deem a threat to their profit-generating ownership guarantees that their ownership of your planet will be an even greater cash cow than it otherwise might be. I've even spoken to trade representatives who expressed dismay over what is happening in your country, which, of course, is opening the doors for them. As one put it to me when I tried to shame him for what his company aspired to do, 'Hey, if those dancing monkeys are going to treat each other that way, denying food to children and killing people at will, then they deserve what my company has in store for them.' It outrages me, but he has a point."

"Philo, this is completely awful."

"John, you don't know the worst of it, believe me."

CHAPTER 51

AN EVEN GREATER SURPRISE!

My talks with Philo were never very long. At first we would talk at my gigs, slipping in a quick conversation between sets or after my last set. The normal pattern would be that we would talk for a while and then Philo would disappear. When I say he would disappear, I don't mean he would dematerialize. He would just excuse himself and go. At first, before we had much of a relationship established, he would just suddenly walk away. As we gradually got to know each other a bit, he normally would say that he was leaving but, again, our talks were never for long. I never knew what he did when we were not together or who he talked to, but I can say that in the whole time I knew him and spent time talking to him, there never was another person who recognized him, at least not anyone I saw.

This time Philo did something unusual and out of the pattern. I was really feeling upset about his revelation of a looming planetary commercial takeover. And, at the very same moment I was expressing my angst and beginning to explore the deeper nuances of my reaction, like how the outrage I was feeling was sitting on top of raw animal fear, he announced he had to leave. Even before I could protest, expressing my desire that we continue to talk about this, he said that what he had to do would take two hours, and that he could meet me again then.

I jumped on the opportunity. The last thing I wanted, other than an alien takeover of our planet, was to be left stewing with his recent revelation. But two hours is not enough time to do something different and get into it, so it ended up I was left stewing with his recent revelation—for two painfully long hours. It was agony. I was completely stumped. What does one do upon hearing such a thing? Prepare resistance? How? With weapons? Try to reason with the 'civilized' entrepreneurs? What? Does this mean resistance is futile? I kept imagining I was a Native American and hearing about the arrival of the Europeans. What would I do? What *could* I do?

It was a horrible two hours.

Then Philo showed up—at the exact time he said he would. He seemed bright and peppy as I, sitting in anticipation, watched him enter, sight me, and approach. I reflected that usually I was the one approaching and he was the one sitting. That made me realize that while sitting, one could discern *a lot* about the state of a person approaching. As Philo was usually the one sitting, I realized that even though he seemed to not be aware of me on those many occasions when I approached him, he was most certainly tracking me then the way I was tracking him now.

Anyway, Philo seemed entirely too peppy and happy as he approached. We were talking about an imminent mass funeral only two hours earlier—the funeral of my planet. Grief and despair were in order, not the somewhat energized step that Philo seemed to have. I felt an irrational flash of anger towards him even as I was aware that this was an unjust projection on my part. I wanted to shout out to him, "Don't you realize what a terrible, terrible thing this is you told me!" Instead, I waited patiently for him to take a seat. However, as soon as he did so, I began to question his attitude.

"Philo," I said, barely even taking the time to look at him, "what you told me is terrible. No, terrible is too weak a word. What you told me is horrible. Gross. Immoral. Disgusting. Repulsive. Entirely unacceptable. But above all, it is decidedly not civilized. I thought you were supposed to be from 'civilized' outer space!"

"It is disappointing, to be sure," he said diplomatically, perhaps intending to foil my burning anger.

"Disappointing!" I exclaimed angrily. "It is disappointing to lose your wallet. It is disappointing to have your car break down. It is disappointing to lose your job. This is not disappointing, Philo. It is wicked. Evil. Horrible. Unacceptable."

Philo looked at me warily. "Indeed it is. But remember, we are only allowed to do what you are already doing."

"But if we *are* primitives," I exploded, "then you are supposed to be the civilized ones. So how can a people who call themselves civilized even countenance such a thing, not to mention do it!" I said this, not as much asking as demanding.

Philo smiled gently. I wouldn't advise you to begin referring to yourself as primitive. That is our classification, and it is not made with human interests in mind."

"But would a civilized people do such a thing?"

"Not only would they do it, and have many times in the past, they are eager to do it. They are panting for the chance. But they can't right now. They are prevented by the disposition of the situation. But things on your planet are changing rapidly for the worse, a change led, sponsored, and prosecuted by your own country, I might add."

I looked at him and felt such a surge of anger I wanted to punch him! But he wasn't badgering me or saying we Earth humans actually deserve this. He was only articulating the situation in all its horribleness.

He saw me contain myself and then continued.

"Take for example the new precedent your country has established using the law to the fullest extent against others when it serves your purpose to do so, but blandly ignoring the law when it does not. They love this. And the new American idea of being able to assassinate anyone who is deemed a threat, even to the point of defining 'threat' in commercial terms. They totally love this. But these are not things *they* are doing, at least not yet.

How utterly and unequivocally repulsive," I declared. "Utterly, utterly, utterly! This is what I mean, Philo, when I say Americans are deluded. Idiots. Idiots. Idiots!" I had a sudden image of me foaming at the mouth. I took a breath and tried to calm down. I was on fire.

"I have a different take on that, John. But what we can agree on is that the potential buyers of your planet love the 21st century here. In fact, the decline and corruption of your institutions, from government and business through church and school and all the way to art and sports, is so dramatic and unprecedented that some of the more progressive politicians are calling for an investigation. They express doubt that even primitives could decay, corrupt, and decline so quickly. They suspect manipulation from these very commercial forces."

"Has there been?"

"I don't know. I doubt it, I really do. But I don't actually know, John. Don't forget, I'm a nobody in outer space."

I put my hand to my forehead and shook my head in despair.

"But what we do know," Philo continued, "is that these forces love the idea of being able to assassinate anyone they deem a threat, and to do so without any judicial review or even possibility of a subsequent legal challenge. That means they only need to think about profit, and do whatever they want—anything, really—to boost the bottom line. Remember, if your government can do it, so can they, only more so."

"How utterly, totally, completely repulsive," I said with even more of a feeling of disgust. Philo looked at me with a blank expression, reading me no doubt. "I have a lot of hate and disgust for your people, Philo," I said, "but right now I am feeling the hate and disgust for my own. I have spent my life trying to warn people of this. Well, not of the alien takeover thing, but of the horribleness that lies at the end of the road we are speeding down. They not only ignored me, they mocked me. And now it has come to this. I am really hating Earthlings right now, Philo. I'll get to your people later, but right now I am busy hating humanity."

I wasn't trying to be funny.

Philo just looked at me. He didn't seem shocked by my reaction. In fact, it was more the opposite. As strange as it sounds, I had the distinct feeling that he was proud of me. He sat there looking at me for long moments, appreciation seeming to grow on his face.

"Well, John," he finally said, "it would seem that we have a major disagreement here."

"How so?" I demanded. "Please don't tell me you favor buying entire planets to exploit the resources and rape the inhabitants. Are you saying you favor assassination by commercial interests for commercial reasons?"

"Just the opposite," he said quietly and calmly. "There is only one question here, and that is how to stop it. How to civilize the universe—no, how to *humanize* the universe. That is the question? To borrow the words of your President Lincoln, who I gather once spoke in this very town, the question is how we might all align with the angels of our better nature?"

"So what's the disagreement?" I asked, feeling confused.

"Simple. You see humanity as a big problem, as THE problem."

"And you don't?" I asked, flabbergasted.

"Not at all. I see humanity as the last best hope of the entire universe. Humanity may have some dirty hands, to be sure, but it can also be the agent and mechanism of a better universe. Far from being THE problem, *humanity is the solution.*"

CHAPTER 52

RUMINATIONS ABOUT PHILO

O ur conversation ended soon after that and we agreed to meet after my next gig, which was in four days. Given the gravity of the situation, I urged an earlier meeting. I was in crisis mode, but Philo was calmly unyielding. In addition, we had long since established the normal pattern of our meetings, and this was entirely within that pattern.

Even so, the situation had gotten really strange. Pretty clearly, the strangeness started with Philo.

Philo is a strange creature.

Until this most recent revelation about the probable future purchase of Earth by greedy corporate aliens, I had stopped thinking so much about Philo's claim to be from another planet. This may seem ludicrous, but keep in mind these factors. First, we were holding our conversations in Gettysburg, which is also where I live. Now Gettysburg is not just the site of the nation's largest and most bloody battle, but it is also the living capitol of the re-enactor's world. On any day of the year in Gettysburg you could have a conversation with an aristocratic Confederate General or a grand Victorian Lady visiting from an Eastern city or any of a number of personages from in and around the mid-nineteenth century. There are also occasional members of Revolutionary War Militias as well as soldiers and nurses from World Wars I and II.

As one re-enactor put it to me to explain why she loved Gettysburg so much, "This is the one place in the universe where you can dress up in historical dress as someone else every single day of the year and not only be accepted as normal but also to be accepted as that person!"

So given my experience in talking almost daily to historical personages, talking to someone who claimed to be from another planet does not stand out as much as you might think it would.

Second, there is my own personality. It isn't just that I am tolerant and supportive and, I suppose, occasionally gullible. It is that I have a high appreciation of fiction. I am a complete romantic in that regard. It always comes down to words and numbers, qualities and quantities, things you can count and things that count. The perfect use and expression of numbers is found in math and science. The perfect use and expression of words is found in poetry. Poetry is fiction, and fiction is not falsehood. It is truth, but a different sort of truth. It is the truth of experience, the 'terrible beauty' of life distilled into a song. As Aristotle said, poetry reveals a deeper truth than even history because where history gathers together the particular, poetry enters into the universal.

So given this, it was easy for Philo to come across to me as a creature of imagination, much like the genteel re-enactors of the aristocracy of the South. I would be the last person to attempt to pop the bubble of the illusion. Instead, I would encourage everyone to imaginatively re-create themselves, to begin to re-enact a more fulfilling and fun (and thus more authentic) self. As I said at the beginning of this account of our conversations, whether or not Philo was from another planet, he definitely was from another world!

So not calling Philo out on his claim totally harmonized with my general way of operating.

But the most important reason why I did not make much of the alien thing was that it was, until this most recent revelation, irrelevant. My relationship with Philo was thrilling, fulfilling, and productive. I had gained in self-awareness as a result of talking with him. The world was different for me now that I was seeing so much more of it, both in terms of what was happening around me but also in terms of a growing, real-time awareness of what was happening inside of me. That is, whenever I was becoming 'automatic,' there was always a sliver of an opportunity to notice the transition before I became fully automatic in my functioning, a state most of us spend most of our time in. I had begun more consistently to take advantage of that sliver of an opportunity. So I was becoming more truly the captain of my own ship.

Then there was that brief meditation he taught me. I had come to really appreciate that there was not a lot of instruction or procedure with it. Just simply take a brief time out to internally access the largest possible context for what is happening in life. It is, as Spinoza suggested, to view things *sub species aeternitatis,* that is, from the standpoint of eternity. I'd been doing that two, three, or more times a day consistently now for over six months. I would step aside and physically relax, using my imagination to travel high above—so high that the universe itself began to fade into distant oblivion.

I now had the ability to instantly flash to the context of a larger perspective during an intensely rooted moment in the midst of the bustle of life. For example, someone could be giving me difficulty, and just as I was morphing into a conditioned response—say an angry assertion of how generous I had heretofore been, thereby unveiling an implied threat not to continue to be so—I could flash to a larger perspective and regain my sense of humor, taking a measure of delight in the situation. Since it is a scene in the movie of my life, I could play my character more authentically. I was certainly more flexible in how I could respond, and my response would often be tinged with humor. And even when I did not get my way and was thoroughly taken advantage of, I was not left trembling in anger and shaking in frustration.

Philo also made really sharp and penetrating observations about all sorts of things regarding my daily life, helping me be more aware in the middle of it and thus to experience more of the deeper delight of my ordinary round of activities. He would comment on my guitar playing, on how I talked to our waitress, the attitude I would automatically take when I heard a certain type of news. The point was never to criticize or to evaluate. It was always to help me to become more aware in real time of the habits, mechanisms, and patterns that happened within me automatically as conditioned responses.

Interestingly, even as I was acquiring this self-knowledge and thus could access a command capacity to override my conditioned responses, I rarely exercised it. For the most part, my automatic responses were quite functional. Philo said this was true of most people and that the problem generally only came when there was a mismatch between the external situation and one's automatic personal response strategy. It was then that one needed to be able to override. It isn't that automaticity is bad; it is that it is blind. You can fly blind most of the time, he would say, but there are certain times when someone has to be looking.

But if I had not made an issue out of Philo's claim to be from another planet, which I had not done until very recently, his recent revelation that Earth was likely to be purchased at some imminent future point made it something I could no longer ignore.

So in the days until I saw him next, I alternated between a 'crisis consciousness' in which I suffered in panic thinking about our collective future, and a 'paranoid consciousness' in which I suffered the gnawing fear that he was playing me for a fool. After all, other than what he had said, I had nothing to prove the existence of other planets and aliens.

Now to return to my observation about Philo's strangeness, even given his strangeness, he had been acting extra strange recently. High weird strange. Standing back, I would say that in the time I have known Philo, his strangeness has passed through three stages.

The first stage extended from the time I first met him until relatively recently. This is what I would call the 'happy alien' phase. He seemed happy to be here. He was like a child. Everything delighted him. He was fun to be around for that reason. Even when we were talking about difficult, troubling things, he had a light touch. He was not overburdened.

The second stage started relatively recently. I can't place it exactly, but if our last conversation is any indication, he just now seems to be coming out of it. This is what I would call the 'troubled alien' phase. In short, Philo seemed deeply disturbed by something. It is as if he was sorry to have come here. Maybe the legal risks and possible negative consequences had begun to outweigh the benefits. After all, it is really only *background* music I play. At times recently he seemed more than troubled; he seemed scared.

But now the third stage, which I would call the 'revolutionary alien' phase, seems to be starting. It isn't that he returned to the first stage and is once again glad to be here. It seems more than that, almost as if he has made some sort of epic decision. It is almost as if he had joined a revolutionary movement, thereby taking a decisive step.

At any rate, I was really ready to see him when I approached him in the Garryowen pub. I was not freaking out quite as much about the feared upcoming hostile buyout, but I was still upset and concerned. My upset, of course, was flavored by my fear that Philo was making up the whole alien thing. So for me my entire experience of this was like the old style mechanical metronome, where the ticking stylus rocks back and forth between these two fears, alien takeover and being made a fool of, back and forth, tick and tock, tick and tock. I was ready to end the clicking.

He was sitting in the darkened corner under the stairs I had mentioned the last time we were there. I was still half a room away when I could sense his vibrancy, however. It was obvious that it was not just me who was ready for this talk. He was also. In fact, even before I could reach out for a chair, he was pushing the chair out himself while beaming a big, warm welcome at me.

It was like seeing the sun suddenly shine on a cloudy day.

CHAPTER 53

THE CASE AGAINST HUMANITY

Looking into Philo's beaming face was a bittersweet experience for me. On the one hand I was excited to see him, and to see him so ebullient. He had become my friend and I cared for him and how he was. On the other hand, I had just learned that my planet was in mortal danger and I wanted to do something to defend my home, my momma Earth. To be smiling and happy right now did not seem quite right.

And since we are talking about what aliens might do to our planet, let me add a third hand. On the third hand, I was not entirely convinced that Philo was an alien and I was worried that I was being gamed. My two strongest bits of evidence were, first, the general unlikelihood of an alien existing in the first place, let alone one coming to Earth and befriending me. And, second, the fact that Philo seems to be unbothered—even happy—in the face of this mortal threat to Earth.

So in the pleasant glow of the sunshine of Philo's warm smile, I jumped right into it. "Philo," I said, "I am afraid I cannot share in the joy of the moment knowing, as I now know, the doom that faces my planet. I can't believe you told me this and then made me wait four entire days to talk again! But now that we meet, I demand you address the problem."

Philo seemed unfazed by my outburst. "John," he said in a tone oozing with patience, "what I told you is not hot off the press news. It was the case long before I came here. In fact, it being the case was a major part of why I came here."

"You wanted to come here while the planet was still raw and unowned, is that it?" I asked with an edge. "How noble. Excuse me if I don't share your tourist's delight and take some time apart to lament the fate of my planet."

Philo laughed. He often did this when I was being my most difficult and argumentative. He simply refused to take the tainted bait and fight. "I fully support your response, John. I respect you for it. 'That's the spirit' and all that. But the purchase, as horrible and nasty as it will be, is not something that is immediately imminent. Your planet is not going anywhere. Well, technically it is, but so is everything else right along with it."

"Cut the crap, Philo. This is serious. We have to do something."

"Let's do so," Philo said, not smiling this time. That stopped me. He did seem serious, deadly serious even. "And let me say to you," he continued, fixing me with one of his stares, "that I acknowledge and accept that you are a true son of Earth, ready to defend her. Defending Earth is also why I am here. It may not be my primary reason for visiting, but it is an essential part of what brought me here. Our interests line up on this one."

"That's good to know."

"Yes, so you don't have to act all extreme and unhinged to show me how alarmed you are. I get it. Let's move right to saving the planet."

"Can we fight them?"

"Wrong approach," Philo interrupted. "As we say on my planet, 'If they fly to you when you can't fly to them, then they possess the means to conquer you.' We need a different approach."

It made sense. I was also chastened. I've always been a peace loving person, pretty close to a pacifist. There is a line in the *Tao Te Ching* that I always thought was the wisest and most sensible statement on war and military violence I had ever seen. It so impressed me I memorized it. I had a sudden urge to quote it to Philo. "Philo, listen to this great passage from Lao Tzu:

Weapons are the tools of violence; all decent men detest them. Weapons are the tools of fear; a decent man will avoid them except in the direst of necessity and, if compelled, will use them only with the utmost restraint . . . . His enemies are not demons, but human beings like himself. He doesn't wish them personal harm. Nor does he rejoice in victory. How could he rejoice in victory and delight in the slaughter of men? He enters a battle gravely, with sorrow and with great compassion, as if he were attending a funeral.

"Nice passage," Philo said, almost patronizingly. He got one of his half smiles and looked off into the distance, turning suddenly to me to ask, "So, John, given all the great things your earth wise elders have said, what do *you* want to say about the imminent purchase of your planet?"

I was a little taken aback, but I responded as if we were talking about ordinary things. "When we were talking last time," I replied, "you observed that I see humanity, its attitudes, delusions, and blindnesses, as a big problem, even the core problem. In response, you said something that, frankly, strikes me as flat out wrong. You said you saw humanity as the last, best chance for a better universe! Far from being victim, you saw humanity as potential liberator. You actually said—and this is your exact thought—that humanity is both the agent and mechanism of a better, more humane universe."

Philo brightened, which once again bothered me slightly, and replied, "Nicely remembered, John. I am impressed. Let's explore that."

"Yes, let's do so indeed," I readily assented. "In fact," I added, "let's start by exploring how you could be so wrong about humanity. To me you sound like someone in a hospital commenting on how healthy all the sick patients are."

Philo got a sudden sharp look, as if I slapped him. He bug-eyed me for a second then brought his smile back. "The exploration has indeed begun," he said cheerily. "So just for the record, you are accusing humanity of, in effect, crimes against humanity."

"Don't try to get the case thrown out of court on a technicality," I growled, picking up on his imagery.

"To the contrary," Philo responded in full seriousness. "Crimes against humanity is a most serious charge, one not to be tinkered with or thrown about lightly. It is a charge that is not lightly to be dismissed. I must say, however, that I am indeed trying to get the case thrown out of court, but not on the basis of a technicality. I want the case dismissed because humanity is completely innocent of the charges."

I was shocked to hear him say this, even more shocked than when he told me he was from another planet. I exploded. "Humanity as innocent?" "How can you even suggest such a thing? Humanity is guilty! That is a given."

"Well, John," Philo responded gently and with the hint of a sly smile, "I don't think we just assert guilt in a judicial procedure. We establish it. We prove it. We validate and support the charge so that the likelihood of guilt is 'beyond any reasonable doubt.' So I ask you regarding this most serious charge: Do you have any evidence you want to present to the court of common opinion?"

Philo was still smiling but I am sure I was not. This felt deadly serious, no matter the somewhat sharpened joviality of the exchange. I took my time replying, gathering my thoughts. "It is interesting you mention evidence," I said, flashing in my mind to all the courtroom dramas I had seen in the movies over the years. I felt like an attorney with a full dossier of evidence moving in for the judicial kill. "As you must know, the government of my own country has made it legal for it to apprehend, detain, torture, and even kill anyone it deems a threat to public safety and well-being, including citizens. Even more, it is now empowered to do this without needing to make a formal charge, without needing to present evidence, without any requirement for a judicial review or securing a warrant, and without needing to inform anyone of its actions, including family members. Those the government decides to kill, it can just kill, informing no one and admitting to nothing."

"Certainly a grave development," Philo observed seriously.

"Then there is the ongoing pollution of our land and our planet, including the pollution of our air, water, soil, and food supply." I took a breath intending to continue to list the charges against humanity when Philo interrupted me.

"Don't forget the triplets of evil mentioned by Martin Luther King—militarism, materialism, and racism," Philo added, speaking gravely.

"Don't mock me!" I snapped back.

"Please, John," Philo replied in his most conciliatory tone, "this is no mocking matter. The charges you bring up are grave and consequential. If I am to defend humanity successfully, it is against the most serious charges that my defense must stand, which is why I am bolstering the charges."

"But how can you—or anyone, for that matter—see these charges and defend them? How do you defend murder, torture, and the systematic impoverishment of millions?"

"I can't and I don't," Philo replied definitively. "Murder and torture are not defensible. I am not defending them. I am defending humanity."

"But humanity is doing these things."

"That is what we are examining here, John. It is a little too loose simply to assert humanity does these things."

"Fair point," I conceded. "Let me try to be a little tighter in my charges. Please consider this. You are horrified by these deeds, as well you should be. I am horrified by them, as well I should be. But as I look around, I see a majority that is unaware of these horrors. And if they are aware, then their understanding is distorted by propaganda filters and falsehoods. The result is that a large majority either openly supports these things or is willing not to think about them, not to connect them to their own values and character. The end result of this unholy combination of openly voiced support, cowardly silence, or ludicrous delusion is support. That means the American people are complicit in evil and, therefore, guilty. That is my charge, and it is such a grave and horrible charge that I don't think I need you to bolster it. Case closed. What do say to that, Mr. Defense Attorney for Humanity?"

Philo looked thoughtful. It had not been difficult, but I felt I had destroyed his defense. In a way I was sad to win. Here was a situation where the planet and everyone on it was in mortal danger, but also many of those on the planet were themselves guilty of similar mortal crimes. Truly, I did not want humanity to die. I wanted it to get better. I wanted it to be more compassionate, caring, idealistic, and loving. I did want to secure a conviction, however. I might be willing to suspend the sentence in most cases, but I wanted it clarified who was to blame. At the end of the day it was humanity!

Just then our waitress came with our food, which looked delicious. I had ordered Shepherd's Pie, which came with a garnish of fresh tomato on the top, and Philo had ordered the Pastrami sandwich, which looked toasted to perfection.

Philo chatted with the waitress in a way I had not seen him do before. That was a little strange to see. She seemed pleased by his attention. Then he abruptly turned to me to say, "Let's allow the court to recess while we apply ourselves to our belly-filling lunch. We will reconvene our session when we are done."

I agreed. Actually, I thought he was just buying time.

CHAPTER 54

PHILO SUCCESSFULLY DEFENDS HUMANITY

O ur lunch was delicious and surprisingly enjoyable. I really did feel a bit like a high-powered attorney having lunch with his rival. Being cutthroat in court is no reason not to be witty and civil at lunch.

When the waitress, amidst much Philo-inspired jollity, cleared our table, we both looked at each other. "Shall we return to Court?" I suggested brightly.

"By all means," Philo responded, also brightly. "I think you had just made a summation of your case against humanity."

"That I had," I said, feeling somewhat triumphant.

"Then help me with one detail, please," Philo asked humbly.

"Anything," I answered expansively.

"Thank you. What are you saying Humanity is guilty of?"

I exhaled loudly in exasperation. "You are being difficult. Humanity is guilty of the charges on a rap sheet you helped to fill out. I can't imagine you want me to repeat them, but I will." I then angrily spat out, "Guilty of polluting the land, corrupting the culture, agreeing to shifting the economy to create sick inequality, destroying both well-being and opportunity for the masses in the process and, thanks to your helpful suggestion, guilty of militarism, materialism, and racism as well as all the attendant evils that that monstrous triplet brings."

"But guilty in what sense, John?"

I felt completely exasperated. Maybe this is an alien thing, but Philo was being really thick about this. "Guilty of all of the above," I stammered.

"You are missing my point, John. Please allow me to try to qualify my meaning. Let me take the murder of John Lennon as an example. A horrible crime. The shooter and anyone who may have helped the shooter are guilty. But also anyone who knew full well what the shooter intended to do and did nothing—such people would be complicit and thus morally and legally guilty, even if they worked for a government agency. Agreed?

"Absolutely!"

"What about someone who knew nothing about the murder or its planning, but who hated rock music and the ideals of peace and love and was glad to see John Lennon murdered. Is that person guilty?

"Guilty of extreme bad taste and moral insensitivity."

"Granted. But guilty of John Lennon's murder?"

"No."

"What if he went around saying the world was so much better with John Lennon murdered?"

"Again, a tasteless and troubling opinion, to be sure, but not an actual crime."

"Well, John, I rest my case." Philo folded his hands on the table in front of me and looked at me.

"Huh!" I exclaimed. "A bit too clever for me. Where is the defense?"

"It is so simple, John. The great majority of humans, including especially your own citizens, have not actually *done* anything illegal. Their understanding is distorted, to be sure, and their views are often delusional. Their so-called moral compass is inoperative or, even worse, calibrated falsely. This is all grave and lamentable, but it is not criminal. In terms of what they have actually done—the triggers they have personally pulled, the bombs they have personally dropped or thrown, the hungry children they have personally denied food to from their full stocked pantry—they are clean."

My mind was wobbling. The implications of what Philo was saying was simply too large for me to process efficiently. What he was saying touched so many of the threads of the complex spiderweb of my understanding, that other than a feeling of my understanding being vigorously shaken, I could not formulate a thought. Philo waited, watching me closely, and then continued.

"And even those few who did pull a trigger, drop a bomb, or deny food to the hungry—even those surprisingly few individuals, when you look into the completely distorted way they are looking at the world, their guilt becomes harder to prosecute. However delusional and wicked they seem to you and others like you, *they* generally think they are doing the right and moral thing."

"But they should have looked into what they were doing more carefully."

"Oh, yes, John, yes! They should have! How devoutly to be wished that they had done so. But now we are entering into the area of 'thought crimes.' We both know and can agree that you would have looked into the matter more carefully. Indeed, you have *been* looking and continue to *be* looking—even now. But however much we might lament that they did not, the fact is they did not. That means the question now is why they did not. One answer is that they, unlike you, are too cowardly. So let me ask you if you really want to prosecute them on the grounds that they are not you?"

"They made a lot of people suffer, Philo."

"Yes, they did. And it is most lamentable. Something must be done about it. But even there, if you look more carefully, you will see that the majority of humans do indeed suffer. In fact, their suffering is all the greater *because* of their delusions. The very delusions that led to them to commit horrible acts also prevent them from seeing the horribleness of those very acts. As a result, they suffer the consequences of what they have done in an even more terrible manner. Being unable to name the evil, they can't own it, atone for it, and move on from it. They are suffering. According to Socrates, it is the worst sort of suffering, worse even than the suffering of those they hurt and the family members of those they killed."

I felt suddenly weary. "I don't understand, Philo. Really bad things are happening. We can see that. But more and more, these bad things are being *done* by good people, *tolerated* by good people, and even *defended* by good people. If we let them off the hook because they're deluded, then who will be left to prosecute?"

Philo smiled a most gentle smile. "You are making my point. I am defending humanity, remember? But, hey, don't give up on prosecution just yet. But do note that our legal question is evolving. It is changing from 'Who is guilty?' to 'What is distorting the minds of otherwise good people so that they commit and support actions that often express the opposite of who they are?'"

"Alright, Philo, answer *that* question for me and I will drop my case against humanity."

Philo looked pleased. "I will try my best, John, but I have to warn you that the answer is not a simple word, phrase, or point. There will be no sound-bites here. It will be a complex, involved answer."

"Involved?" I asked, not fully understanding."

"Yes. Involved with philosophy for one thing. I love that line from Thomas Aquinas you quote in some of your writings, the one where he says that we do not study philosophy in order to learn the opinions of philosophers. We study philosophy, he says, in order to learn the truth of how things stand."

"It is a great line," I agreed, "but how does it apply here?"

"John, many if not most humans today can no longer see the truth of how things stand."

"Exactly my point," I interrupted. "They are deluded."

"But you don't take your own point seriously enough. They ARE deluded. At the bottom of this is the way your magnificent human minds with their amazing ability to grasp, using concepts and imaginative extensions, the truth of how things stand—at the bottom is how this amazing and magnificent ability is being distorted. John, the ongoing pollution of your American landscape must be of great concern. But the ongoing pollution of your American *mindscape*—this is of even greater concern."

My spirits were lifting. I could grasp what Philo was saying. He really seemed to be onto something. Much of what people are told today—in the constant flow of advertisements, from politicians, from business and religious leaders, even from teachers in school—is misleading and distorted, if not an actual lie. The cumulative effect has to be to denigrate people's complex, deeply nuanced ability to grasp the truth of how things stand."

"Are you up for it?" Philo asked, looking at me carefully.

"If being 'up for it' means the same as being 'down with it,' then, yes, I am up for it," I answered, smiling.

Philo laughed. "That's the spirit, John. But make sure you hold on tight. It is going to be quite the ride."

CHAPTER 55

PHILO IS A HUMANIST

As I walked up to Philo sitting at his table I was recalling that the past few days of waiting to continue our conversation had not been too bad. I had calmed down considerably about the possible upcoming alien buyout and no longer felt the urgency to begin to prepare to resist. Philo had convinced me that the danger, though dramatic, ominous, and real, was not imminent, at least not in terms of weeks and months. But there was a deeper reason I was no longer freaking out about the alien buyout. Philo presented a different analysis to me, one in which the best protection was not opposing the aliens but helping humanity—and specifically, helping humanity emerge from its long sleep.

This was Philo's idea. Philo consistently thought differently. Either he really was an alien or he had a remarkable knack at providing a different perspective. Either way, he often provided a completely different perspective on things, one that was so different it was sometimes hard to grasp. I would argue and make objections, but not to disprove him. It was to join with him to explore together the truth of how things stand. He would always say that everything, even our latest and most valuable insights and breakthroughs, is open to question, revision, and even rejection. Once he added, smiling, that absolutely *everything* is open to question and revision except the assertion that everything is open to question and revision.

When he would take a point of view that was radically different than my own, instead of automatically defending my own point of view, I would pay close attention to my own automatic reactions and strategies of defense. I would also try to get a glimpse of what idea or thought I was automatically defending. Once I could glimpse it, I would try to note where that view had come from, what supported it, why I identified with it. Often, what was behind my identification with a particular view or rhetorical posture was not considerations of logic and evidence but rather the continuity of habit, prejudice, laziness, and wishful thinking.

Of course, looking at one's own ideas and point of view in this way brings one into the spooky realm of core assumptions. Core assumptions is a loose name for the area of mental 'fixes' and automatic cognitive protocols that operate like mental machines. They function to shape, filter, set-up and constitute what one then 'sees' as immediately present.

Since these internal mental operations create one's experience, which is to say that it creates what one is seeing. Normally one does not see these operations because they are what creates what one is seeing. They are like the movie projector when you are sitting in a theatre watching a movie. You watch the movie, not the projector.

As we had talked over the months, but especially recently, I began to grasp ever so gradually how crippled and fractured my understanding and vision is. This was not true only of me, of course, but of all of us. However, as Philo encouraged me to admit, my vision and understanding was slightly less damaged than it was with many others. Even so, Philo was saying all of us are at least somewhat crippled and fractured in our ability to see how the truth of things stand.

I had been especially shocked to discover how much I denigrated my own mental skills and capacities, not to mention those of others. I tended to see humanity as a flawed creature, a species that created so many problems that I had begun to consider that humanity was the problem! To think of humanity as Philo did as the gifted, darling child of Earth and Sky, the very quintessence and destination of evolution—not only did I not think this, but I was also set up to *resist* thinking it. I found that being able to identify my resistance and then staying non-reactive enough to watch it implement itself—this was an education in liberation.

It seemed like just recently our talks had taken on a completely different character. I think I remember the exact moment when they did so, the precise point between 'before and after,' when this change occurred. It was right after Philo had convinced me that helping humanity emerge from its long, fear-driven sleep was the way to protect the planet from an Alien buyout. Based on my recent experience of my own deeply rooted resistance to adopting a radically different point of view, I was ranting about how difficult this was going to be. Referring to how most people are deeply structured to resist the very changes that are now needed, I was going on about how so many Americans are delusional, being open and prone to reality-shaping manipulation by the 'unholy trinity' of government, media, and advertising.

And so, as I was finishing up describing the sorry state of the American mind, I said ominously, "Horrible, nasty, ugly, repulsive, sickening, foul, and tasteless!"

Philo smiled and said in an even voice, "Yes and no."

"Yes and no what?" I demanded, feeling anger surge up in me as he seemed at least partially to be denying the clear and obvious truth of what I was saying. I could sense lurking behind and energizing this anger was the fear that we humans would not be able to resist the alien buyout. At that point I said, pointedly, "The fact that Americans are so prone to delusion and thus are easy to manipulate disgusts and repulses me!"

Philo bug-eyed me. I had experienced such a dramatic growth in real-time inner awareness recently that sitting there I knew with certainty that the sudden rage I felt surge up in me was an automatic defense. Instead of aligning with this surge and defending, I held back, watching. I knew that anger surges like that didn't just happen.

They were mechanisms, protocols of inner functioning. And they were tied to core assumptions which, under the level of ordinary awareness, set-up and constituted our perceptions and awareness.

I had learned to be very suspicious of sudden, strong emotional reactions, especially ones that are triggered by something that is said. These reactions often were defenses against inner awareness, functioning to deflect awareness *away* from the core assumption it was protecting. So I became hyper-vigilant, watching my own mind.

"Yes," Philo continued gently, "the unaware, controlled human is disgusting, as you say. But it is not disgusting in the *way* you say. You don't realize how significant it is cosmically. That is the 'no' part.

The anger surged inside. My head suddenly became saturated with contradictory thoughts. I rejected Philo, then I rejected myself for not rejecting him earlier, mocking him in my mind, and then mocking me for mocking him—on and on, back and forth.

Philo just watched me, an almost half-smile playing at the corner of his mouth. His watching, a beacon of clarity in my confusion, helped me to watch myself. And as I watched with single-pointed focus, the defensive resistance would always calm down. It was, after all, just an automatic mental mechanism, possibly the first ever functioning machine.

"You see, John, there is a larger perspective available here," Philo said as if a sudden, raging internal flash-storm had not just happened. "You humans are on an epic adventure of consciousness. Humanity has created the individual. Paradoxically, the individual is a cultural construct, which is itself collective. This is your invention, your contribution. You are currently exploring the contours of the separate and highly individualized consciousness operating out of a cultural software package. You have created something that is, cosmically speaking, a great gift and opportunity, but it has come at a great cost. The cost is the very exact thing you just finished ranting about—the propensity to illusion and the seeming ease at which the solitary individual can be influenced, shaped, manipulated, and controlled. In a word, the 'individual' can be constructed, but not necessarily by the individuals themselves or even with their input. In other words, John, the thing that troubles you is a misuse of the essence of the gift of humanity.

"I don't see the connection between the superb individuals you talk about and the pathetic, fully deluded individuals I see today."

"Consider this. To create a cut-off, solitary and thus reflective individual, you must first cut the psyche's awareness off from the whole, including the whole of the cosmos, the whole of nature, and the whole of humanity. But cutting off from the whole is what creates the conditions for fear. The cut off individual begins to fear for his personal safety and the security of his property. This fear-based urge to protect self and property from the predations of others leads to an urge to *control* them. Paradoxically, the fear of hurt or loss of self and property also leads, as your Thomas Hobbes presciently noted, to a willingness to be controlled by others."

"That's really bad."

"Yes, John, it is bad, but it is also good. It is bad in that fear, especially chronic, unrecognized, and largely free-floating fear, is what drives so many of those you call deluded. This *is* bad. It decays well-being and it undermines happiness. It is a great burden to bear, which is why most people do not take the effort to identify and heal their fears but rather stuff them somewhere below the level of their ordinary awareness. There, hidden, the unhealed fear works like a toxic poison, progressively damaging the psyche and, by extension, the society. Fear lubricates the urge to manipulate and control. The more fearful people are, the less flexible and aware they are and the less intelligence they can access in the moment. As we say on my planet, everything a person really wants is on the other side of fear."

"So what could possibly be good about fear?"

"That's exactly the thing, John. Fear itself is not good. But a consciousness that is prone to fear, especially the sort of unacknowledged, free-floating fear I am mentioning, opens a reflective being to all kinds of transformative experiences he or she would not normally have. Indeed, since fear can only be pacified by the accepting love that stems from a sense of oneness, of an essential belongingness to something larger, both cosmically and socially, the human propensity to fear ultimately leads individuals to a greater awareness of oneness and love."

My mind was spinning. It wasn't hard to understand what Philo was saying. It was all the ramifications and implications, opening and unfolding before me as I sat trying to absorb and assimilate it all—this is what had me spinning.

I had not noticed in all of this that the Barn was getting ready to close. I said to Philo, "I can't wait another week. We are right in the middle of this. Please."

"That's the spirit, John," he replied, smiling warmly. "Others might be repelled by what I am saying, but you can't get enough of it. How about tomorrow?"

"Thank you," I said with honest and deeply felt gratitude.

CHAPTER 56

THE JOURNEY BACK
TO WHERE WE BEGAN

The next day came quicker than I expected. Suddenly I was approaching Philo again. My mind had not stopped spinning, however. In particular, I was stuck on the thing Philo said about the 'good' part of fear, about how dealing with fear would lead the individual to a greater awareness and experience of oneness and love. It wasn't that I did not understand the point. I understood it well enough. It was that the point bothered me. *All* this fear, leading to *all* this suffering, producing *all* these lives full of pain, sorrow, and deprivation—and all of it being caused by fear. From a cosmic point of view, why all the painful trouble? Why not just start with and stick with oneness and love? Maybe we need more Buddhists and Hippies to be sages and teachers.

Philo could see immediately my consternation. Even before I could explain, he said, "Stuck on the need for fear, I see, the notion that some good can come out of all this pain and horror you see."

"How can you see that?" I snapped back, fearful he was reading my mind. I did not like the idea of anyone, let alone him, reading my mind. I mean, I sometimes thought he was little more than an alien dipshit. I didn't want him reading that in my mind!

Philo chuckled pleasantly. "Actually, John, I can't see that. I *anticipated* it. It was what you were wrestling with when we ended last night. As you walked up, you looked troubled. It was my quite reasonable guess that you were wrestling with the same issue you were wresting with when you left last night."

Philo often turned out like that—namely, that things he said that seemed 'occult' or 'alien' were actually just intelligent and rational observations. I said to him, "You are entirely correct. So, please, if you will, illuminate me about this idea of the huge, dispiriting, and unnecessary suffering I see everywhere is really a good thing."

"Again, John, it is decidedly not a good thing. It isn't even, cosmically speaking, a planned thing. But it is what it is, and I am giving voice to that. Think about it this way. Let's say a person is internally blocked. I don't mean conceptually. They are constipated. They take a laxative which helps them completely eliminate what is stuck in their bowels and which otherwise would have remained stuck. In the same way constipation leads a person to take a laxative, being internally blocked can lead a person to expand awareness. You could say that a fearful mind is a constipated mind."

"Nice image, but why get constipated in the first place. Wouldn't it be better just to have clean bowels?"

"Yes and no."

"Not that again. Let's come back to that. Let me redirect my question. If constipation is fear, then what is the laxative?"

"Now there is a question that gets right into the down and dirty," Philo said smiling. It is a lot like the Buddhist image of the beautiful lily growing out of the ugly mud pond, only here the mud is actually dark brown, gooey human poop. The lily—or laxative, depending on your preferred imagery—is deep inner awareness or mindfulness. It is what you exercised last night when you were feeling flushed with flashes of anger. Now this magnificent capacity to attain a clean observational distance from inner mud is what used to be called detachment. Unfortunately that word is now taken in a different way. Properly understood, one does not 'detach' from one's feelings, however unclean and muddy they are. To detach from one's feelings is to become imprisoned in them. Let's say it is to mentally constipate oneself. What one detaches from is not one's awareness of one's feelings but one's automatic and constipated response to them. You could say one needs to be aware of the inner mud, but not project it."

I interrupted. "Philo, this does not seem like a good deal. The individual becomes afraid and thus deluded. That makes him able to be manipulated, controlled by forces that degrade and corrupt his personal well-being, leading him to act—or fail to act—in ways that degrade the social order, thus creating widespread suffering, poverty, insecurity, and misery. Things get bad. Then, in the pits of this toilet, a few individuals discover deep love, a love that is more powerful and creative than fear. It doesn't add up. If love is a sort of toilet paper, why not just equip the toilet with it?"

Philo laughed merrily. "I love this poetic way of speaking, using images and symbols rather than mere empirical data. I've noticed that the more educated you Earthlings become, the *less* you talk this way."

"Are you denigrating my education?" I demanded.

Philo laughed again, even more rollicking. "I am not denigrating your education. I am denigrating the current idea of education on your planet. In many ways, becoming educated these days is a matter of learning not to see. 'Seek and do not find' might be a good motto for it."

"We can talk about the corruption of education another time. I am concerned about this bad deal. The universe gives all of us suffering and some of us a lifetime of intense, unrelenting disappointment and suffering, and in return, you say, some few blessed individuals discover love and oneness. I don't like it."

"Well you certainly do not put it in a particularly attractive way." He started chuckling again. "Good one. Love as toilet paper. I'll have to remember that one."

"Philo," I said sharply, it does not add up."

"But it does," he replied pleasantly. "The discovery of deep love, of a love deeper and more powerful than fear, as you so nicely put it. This is cosmically significant. It is the pearl of great price, the blossom of evolution."

"But it so unfair."

"Yes, to see suffering spread so thickly everywhere is certainly not appealing. One must do everything one can. What did your Jesus say about this? Even though you will always have the poor with you, woe to the one through whom they are made poor. Still, your dismay and dissatisfaction is quite valid. It comes from an individual, one with considerable compassion, caring, and love, looking out at other individuals who are suffering and in misery."

"As opposed to what?"

"As opposed to looking out not as an individual but as a species, and looking not at individuals but at your species. This is a time, John, to begin to *trust* your species. Your species is evolving, and you are part of it. From that point of view, it is all worth it. All of it."

"But it seems so unfair, Philo."

"I suppose in many ways it is. One thing that might soften your feeling is to realize that fear is not at the bottom of all of this. Fear is not the deepest level of mud."

"What is?"

"Greed. Looking at your species, what originally denigrated the primordial love and oneness was not the individual as such. But individuals soon became greedy. They started thinking, 'this is mine and not yours.' Then they started to fear that the other would steal what is their own. Thus was fear born. Your world—its politics, its religion, almost all of its morality and much of its art—is the invention and creation of fear."

"I'm really trying to get this, Philo, and it is flashing in and out. But the fear, sorrow, anguish, and suffering I see everywhere, most of it unnecessary, is making it difficult."

"As it should be. But, John, to come to see, understand, and practice love, not as a strong desire, an abstract concept, or a pleasing feeling, but as a creative force, something that fills you and moves you, that becomes a Tao—it is cosmic in its significance. It is nothing less than evolution's finest moment as well as its culminating achievement."

"It seems like bad design to me, Philo. I mean, why not just begin with the love?"

Philo sat back thoughtfully. "Ah, the seduction of paradise. You are asking why did we not just stay in this paradise? In other words, what is the advantage of this suffering over that bliss?"

"Exactly!"

"Well, apart from the fact that there is a snake in every paradise, where is the adventure, the thrill of discovery, the opportunity for psychic evolution and growth by staying in a five-star heaven forever. A fully fed and completely satisfied hog is still a hog, and if the hog is an angel in heaven, then heaven is little more than a top-of-the-line pig pen. We have religious myths and legends on my planet that indicate that souls wanted to incarnate in the material realm."

"For what possible reason?"

"The colors are brighter, the sounds more intense, the food tastier," Philo said laughing. "Ok, I'm having some fun. Think about it this way. Let's look at your music. Last night that final thing you played ended on a rich, complex, unstable chord, a major seventh with an added ninth and thirteenth. It floated nicely above everything, wrapping up your performance."

I raised my eyebrow, impressed. Philo had an amazing insight into all sorts of things, but especially music. He continued.

"But you can't just play that chord. By itself it doesn't work. It is unsettled, even disharmonious. What you did was spontaneously create a composition in which that chord was the culminating statement. You did this by setting up a harmonic momentum. By introducing varying degrees of dissonance to tease the consonance, and then resolving the dissonance with the consonance, you created a tonal adventure, a musical journey. The journey was intense, and the last chord closes the adventure with a pint of fine ale in front of a roaring fireplace in a friendly pub. It is one thing to walk in to a pub and order an ale, but it is an entirely different thing to do so at the close of a harrowing adventure. You can't start your journey with that sense of satisfied accomplishment. You have to earn it, to accomplish it. This is what your species is doing."

"But what's the point if we end up where we began?"

I noticed Philo was bug-eyeing me again. I was comfortable with this. It no longer creeped me out when he did so. Even though a person who was watching us would say we were arguing, it was not that I was trying to prove him wrong. It was more that he could see something I could not, and I was questioning him to be able to catch a glimpse of it myself.

Finally Philo said, "We are making real progress here, John. But I see I might need to back up some and fill in some cosmic history for you. I think you have another gig in three days. How about if we meet after your next gig?"

"Agreed."

CHAPTER 57

A MOST GLORIOUS
PLANET EARTH

The gig was a disaster. The music was quite good, scintillating even. And the venue was very well attended. In fact, more people had been coming to my gigs recently, and they were listening more intently than ever before. It was almost as if Philo had turned them on to what I was doing. They seemed to be appreciating the tonal adventures, as Philo put it, that I was creating. It was what I had hoped for and worked to accomplish for many long years, but now that it was starting to happen, all I could think of is how it was keeping me from talking with Philo.

I had spotted Philo well hidden in the back during my last set, but as soon as I finished playing, I was swamped by well-meaning listeners who wanted to talk about what I was playing. At any other time and in any other universe, I would have been delighted, but tonight it kept me from Philo.

Before he left I did manage to catch a moment to arrange to meet the next morning at the Ragged Edge Coffee House.

As I walked to the Ragged Edge the next morning, I was reflecting on how important these conversations had become for me. I still did not have the 'key,' and the stories he was telling me were getting weirder and weirder. It had already long since reached the point where I could not share what we were talking about with my academic colleagues and keep a straight face. It was like I was now living in two worlds.

Still, I have always had the ability to enter into the 'spirit' of a discourse, engaging in a teleological suspension of disbelief. It was no more difficult for me to talk to Muslims about the idea of God than it was to talk to atheists about the same topic. I understood deeply that in order to connect and converse with another, I had to enter into their world. I could challenge bits of it, but only by speaking from the promontory of other bits of it. It was a lot like playing music. If I was, say, playing Gypsy Jazz, I didn't just play. I could be creative, daring, and new, but only in the context of the sensibility and patterns of that tradition.

Philosophy and thinking were not different.

Now while the disbelief I was suspending in talking to Philo was mounting up, forming formidable piles even, I was nevertheless gripped. I didn't have all the answers I wanted, but I felt fully engaged by the process of inquiry we were involved in. It felt like I was being instructed in a secret history of the world, being illuminated by the deeper reality of the truth of how things stand.

Certainly that is what my conversation with Philo this particular morning felt like. I had barely sat down before Philo jumped right into it. Because we had not been able to speak the night before, it almost seemed as if he felt he was behind schedule, so to speak, and needed to hurry to catch up.

"I've been thinking," Philo said as I pulled my chair out, "that you need to take a more expansive view of your magnificent planet."

"Meaning what?" I asked, genuinely puzzled by what he was getting at.

"Meaning you have to try to be less provincial," he said.

He said this flatly, as if he was telling me I needed to try the bagels. Even so, I felt stung by the remark. Being detached, I was able to watch my reaction to the sting. I could see the sting was directly related to my aspiration to be cosmopolitan and sophisticated, not a provincial bumpkin. I could also see myself automatically mobilizing for defense and counter attack, preparing to attack the notion I was provincial and defend the idea I was cosmopolitan. However, as I maintained single pointed focus and watched all of this non-reactively, the sting faded, the sense of alarm subsided, and the automatic urge to fight dissipated.

My attention then gently moved outwards and I noticed Philo looking at me all bug-eyed. I don't know how much of what had just happened inside of me he could sense, but he seemed immensely satisfied. He continued.

"To help you with this, let me invite you to imagine the planet Earth from the point of view of alien visitors. What do you imagine the aliens see as they approach Earth after a long and completely boring journey arriving?"

"That's easy," I said. "I imagine they will see a most beautiful piece of real estate. They will note it is chock full of valuable resources. They will be smacking their greedy alien lips." I felt very sophisticated making this observation.

Philo smiled at me with warmth and acceptance. "Excellent," he said, full of approval. "Most excellent, in fact." I beamed, feeling validated. He continued, "That, John, is as good a statement of the provincial attitude as I will probably ever hear."

I felt crushed, put down, mocked. Anger flashed in me. "How is that provincial?" I stammered.

"Well, let's think about it. How might the CEO of a coal company or a Wall Street hedge fund manager answer if we asked him to anticipate what the aliens might see?" He continued without waiting for an answer. "They would give some version of the same answer, an answer based on their projection of an overriding interest in profit."

He was right. I felt suddenly a bit silly, a bit CEOish. Reversing myself, I said, "Perhaps the great treasure of Earth is not the minerals in its ground but the depth, complexity, and beauty of the humans and the cultures they create."

Philo laughed with genuine glee. "You could be a politician, John. That's a great Earth talking point, one that will get you elected—on Earth!"

His reaction seemed strange and made me uncertain of myself. "But I am right, am I not? The treasure of Earth is in the psyche and not in the ground."

"Oh, entirely," Philo responded. "But in your second, corrected answer, you have become even more provincial."

I must have looked hurt because Philo continued, addressing what I was thinking but had not said. "So let's make sure we are using the word provincial in the same way. You are thinking of a provincial attitude as a small attitude, a merely local one. It is not a particularly enlightened attitude. As George Bernard Shaw had Marc Anthony say in his play, *Anthony and Cleopatra*, about someone who was judging Egypt by the standards of Rome, 'Pardon him, Theodotus, for he is a barbarian. He thinks that the customs of his tribe are the customs of the world.'"

"Yes," I replied, "which is why my second answer, which is more expansive and less materialistic, is thereby less provincial."

"Nicely put. But when I say something is provincial I am not evaluating. I am simply identifying. To have a provincial opinion is simply to have an Earth opinion. Your second opinion, which I agree is more expansive and less materialistic, is also more of an Earth opinion because it is even *more* provincial."

I felt miffed. "I guess being an Earthling, I do tend to see things in an *earthy* way," I replied with an edge. "But let me turn this around," I said, feeling a sudden inspiration. Let me ask you, a philosopher from another planet and therefore one who is well-suited by temperament, training, and origin to take an alien point of view, what an alien will see upon approaching Earth after a long and boring trip to get here?"

"Fair enough," Philo replied good-naturedly. "Here is what an alien will see. Earth is beautiful, a blue/green jewel hanging in the sky. Yes on that. Earth is also valuable. It is chock full of rare, natural treasures and resources—which so many Earthlings take for granted—that would fetch a fortune on the intergalactic market. Double yes on that. And also there is profit to be made from it all, lots of profit. In that aspect, Earth is like a great piece of massively undervalued real estate. Triple and quadruple yes on that."

"That is the point I was trying to make in my first guess."

"Yes, and you did make it. But this is not the point I am making. The alien will see these things, and the lower level aliens, the very ones who will flood your planet the second the embargo is lifted, will be like that. Alien carpetbaggers, if you will. That is what they will see. They will be like robbers who break into a museum and steal classical Greek statues to use as target practice, reasoning that the arms are broken off anyway."

"What is your point?"

"My point is that different aliens will see different things. Slave traders will see a source of great slave stock, bankers will see loot, sex addicts will see opportunity, on and on it goes. But none of that is why Earth is the most important spot in the entire universe right now and why Earthlings are so feared."

This was shocking. Philo had been getting more and more 'out there,' but here he was leaving me stranded on the ground. He continued.

"Earth is unique. I don't just mean it is different. In all of the universe, there is nothing like it. It represents the promise and possibility of something totally new, something unprecedented."

"Then why are you calling me provincial?"

"John, to fail to see this is provincial, the very heart and soul of provincial."

I was gripped. My mind was trying to run away and to explode at the same time. "Please continue," I said.

"You could think of your planet as a sort of intergalactic crossroads. I don't mean this geographically, as if intergalactic traders crossed paths here. I mean this in terms of energy. Earth is a place where radically different and even opposing energies all have a toehold, a home. It is the place where contrasting and conflicting energies and potentialities meet, mix, and merge. They also take to battle."

"This is what I have been saying, that the bad energy is winning."

"This is not what I am saying, John. I am saying something quite different. What ends up coming out of the boiling stew of contrast and difference will shape the future of the entire universe, either dooming existence to an interminable Dark Age or opening up all of existence to a Bright New Dawn. In this, your planet is the battlefield for the future of the entire cosmos. If Earth fails, the entire universe will be imperiled. Conversely, if Earth succeeds, even in the smallest measure, the entire universe will benefit. An inspiring new age will dawn. The stakes could not be higher."

It was too much to take in. I could understand what Philo was saying in a science fiction and space battle sort of way. It was a fun and frothy idea, but it did not have any emotional depth for me. It was like the last scene of the Star Wars movie where Luke, Leah, and Hans received medals for their heroic defense of the rebellion. Hoorah and all that, and then the lights come on in the theatre. That is where I felt I now was, sitting in the theatre with the lights on, the illusion having faded.

Philo noted this change in my expression and suggested we meet again the next morning. I agreed, somewhat thankful to get away. This was too much. It was making me doubt him again.

CHAPTER 58

EACH EARTHLING
IS A PLANET EARTH

As I approached the coffee shop the next morning, I wasn't sure how I felt. As gripped as I had been, I hadn't even thought about our last conversation in the twenty or so hours since it ended. It was just too 'out there' for me to get a handle on. I couldn't even say I disagreed. It was more like hearing a joke one did not understand. One does not disagree with the joke. One simply ignores it. In fact, it was only because I was on my way to talk to Philo that I recalled it.

I still didn't get it.

Philo was sitting calmly when I arrived, seemingly unflustered. I tried to explain my state and he just waved it away. He then initiated the next phase of our conversation.

"I think I recall saying, John, that your planet is the essential and crucial battlefield for the future. And I'm not referring to the necessary struggle to keep it from being bought and sold on the open market. It is so much deeper than that."

"Deeper than I am capable of reaching?" I asked, wanting him to explain.

Philo looked at me blankly. "Obviously," he said. And then after a brief moment in which I, feeling diminished, did not respond, he added, "And not entirely unexpected." I was not sure whether he was putting me down or expressing disappointment in me. I didn't say anything and he continued.

"Now, John, here is the crux of the issue. If the many conflicting energies swirling about on your planet can meet, mingle, mutually accept and tolerate, and co-exist not only peacefully but ebulliently, then there will be an explosion of cosmic light from your planet. This light will effect everything, everywhere, and not just on your planet. What makes this important is that it will be a *different* sort of light, an *unprecedented* sort of light."

He paused to give me a chance to interact. I was beginning to grasp and feel some of the magnificence of this vision. It seemed very flattering not only to me personally, but to everything about humanity and our planet. It made us all cosmically important, just as we are! But it also seemed like a fairy tale, one not only with no grounding in solid reality, but one with no bearing on it. It had no message that I could see. To me it sounded like saying that if pigs could fly, then perhaps we could train them to deliver mail. Perhaps. But no one is going to start training a pig in the expectation that it will start to fly any time soon.

"Well?" Philo said. He was looking at me, expecting a response.

"It is a noble vision," I said, hurrying together some words. "It sounds good but it is a little idealistic. I suppose if we could get all the different parties, nationalities, and interest groups on our planet to get along, things would be nicer here, and I can see how that would be an inspiration to others similarly divided."

Philo looked disappointed, if not crushed. He took a deep breath and continued.

"It is not that sort of thing at all," he said pointedly. "The many different energies I am talking about are not the agendas and conflicting desires of different social groups. Those energies and the conflicts between them exist, to be sure, but they are derivative. What I am trying to illuminate for you is that these energies in all their raw conflict and mutual antagonism exist within the depths of each human being. The state of the world is thus but a pale reflection of the inner presence and activity of these energies; the world is derivative of them, in fact. I am talking psyche here, not politics. The point is that each of you is a little planet Earth, internally conflicted and troubled with the different inner parts alternating between bullying and being bullied by the other parts. The result is that most of you are in a state of permanent war with yourselves. The harmonization of this conflicting, warring energy is a psychological accomplishment, not a political one."

I sat there even more stunned. What he was saying seemed absolutely ridiculous. To say each of us is a little planet Earth sounds like a fable of high ridiculousness. But it also seemed insightful, even possessing great profundity. I felt deeply conflicted and troubled. My mind was racing but could find nowhere to rest. Finally I uttered in a weak, totally unconvincing voice, "This seems interesting."

Philo looked eager to engage and to continue but also frustrated by my wooden response. "Interesting, you say," he said, looking disappointed.

I rallied, perking up with some new energy. "Interesting, yes. Interesting in the sense that it is mind blowing. It shakes everything up. Right now I am all shook up."

"Holy smoke and sakes alive," Philo said, slyly smiling. "This is interesting, yes—more interesting than you can imagine. Let me just say this here. The fact that each of you is a little planet Earth energy-wise is *also* why your entire planet, energy wise, is a sort of big human being. Your political systems and economic arrangements—they too are a sort of big human being. How so? This way. The energy dynamics of both the political system and the individual human being are exactly the same. The energy blockages, the ways of unblocking, the tendency to falsehood, the use of ideals to cover sordid realities—it is exactly the same in both psyche and state. And right now humanity's 'personal relationship' with its institutions and social practices is deeply unhealthy and dysfunctional. It is like being married to a philanderer who lies shamelessly."

"Like Plato said," I jumped in, feeling pleased to be such a good schoolboy. "You know, the way Plato said the state is a psyche writ large and a person a sort of miniature state with different classes and all."

I expected Philo to look pleased but instead he looked mildly disappointed. I immediately thought I must have done something wrong. What? Maybe it was that I had just spoken to impress and deflect and not to advance inquiry. Should I feel chastened? Did I do something wrong? My confusion in this regard just showed how out of it I was.

"Yes, John," Philo said not at all unkindly, "the energy process of healing and progress is precisely the same in both high politics and in individual therapy—the energy identity of the psyche and the state, as you put it. There is much to explore here, and not the least being what Plato had to say on this, but I want to move on. I am trying to illuminate for you some essential aspects of the situation both humanity and your planet are currently immersed in."

"Is that why you could not just give me the 'key' we talked about earlier and which I asked you for? It wasn't that you didn't want to. You wanted to, but you knew I needed more background before you could do so?"

Philo seemed to physically relax when I said this. "You never cease to amaze, John," he said with a beaming smile.

"So can you give me the key now?"

"We are getting close. There is a delightful Earth saying that applies here—'infinite patience brings immediate rewards.' This is not something to rush. How about if we let this sink in and I'll be sure to show up at your next gig so we can talk some more?"

"Fine with me," I replied. "But I'm not sure what it is I am letting sink in. You said each human is a little planet Earth and that if we humans can get our shit together, the whole universe will benefit. I can let that sink in as much as it wants. It isn't the sinking in part that seems difficult. It is the 'believing this to be true' part that I am having difficulty with."

Philo looked at me with deep acceptance. Confused as I was and even bordering on hostile to him, I felt completely safe in the warm embrace of his gaze. This time he was not reading me but loving me.

"So what do I do until then?"

Philo smiled a smile that would rival Middle Eastern sunshine. "That is the great part, John. You don't have to do anything. Everything that needs to happen already is happening. All you need to do is hang on for the ride."

"It doesn't feel that way at all. There must be something I can do?"

Philo looked thoughtful. "I think maybe there is," he said finally. There are many sorts of governments in the world that perform many different functions. There are also many different ideologies that shape, however inadequately, the many different functions of government. Given that, here is what you can do: try to figure out which type of government operates in your psyche to govern the many conflicting parts of the complex creature that you are."

It didn't make a lot of sense, but it was enough to enable me to say goodbye and leave without any lingering bad feeling.

CHAPTER 59

I DISTANCE AND DIMINISH PHILO

Even before I met Philo, I'd been attempting to practice single-pointed inner awareness or mindfulness. In practical terms this meant struggling to be aware-as-from-a-distance of whatever I might be feeling at any time. Correlated with this was the need for courage—the courage to admit and accept what I was actually feeling, no matter how petty or ignoble it might be.

Of course, Philo had helped me in this aspiration immeasurably. In fact, my tepid attempts to become mindful took fire after we started talking. I could not have reached the relatively high level of mindfulness I have now attained were it not for his sustained help and support.

Ironically, it was my accomplishment in this regard—that is, my expanded ability to notice and acknowledge my feelings—that made it impossible for me to ignore the fact that something had changed and I no longer trusted Philo implicitly. Maybe it was him calling me 'provincial' and advising that I try to be less so. That hurt. It also didn't seem true. Me, a provincial? It really bothered me to hear him say this.

So strong was my negative reaction to being called a provincial that it impacted my feelings towards Philo, so much so that my next meeting with him had started to feel more like a chore or social duty than the magnificent and important opportunity it had seemed up until last week. To show the magnitude of this change in my attitude, if Philo had asked me to postpone our next meeting, I would not only have agreed to do so, but I would have been glad about it.

But the show must go on, of course. Still, something was different. I noticed it as soon as I started playing. My playing seemed a little off. It was not that I was making mistakes but that my playing was uninspired. Whether this was a cause or an effect of my diminished enthusiasm for my conversations with Philo I don't know, but the sudden lack of fire and inspiration was noticeable to me.

Now when one has been playing for a long while and is still practicing and continuing to learn, a unique phenomenon begins to unfold. After one has been playing for a while, getting better on one's instrument is not like digging a ditch, where the more you dig, the bigger the ditch gets. Instead, one continues to dig the ditch, but it stays the same size until, suddenly, it gets bigger all at once. In other words, as one practices, the improvement is discontinuous. For the longest time there is no discernible improvement until— suddenly and as if by serendipity—there is an improvement!

In other words, as one advances and becomes more experienced, the improvements gradually become less dramatic, and the long, fallow periods between improvements become longer.

For whatever reason, many long-time players have stopped practicing. If they continue to practice, as I have, what gradually happens is that the horizon of one's best continues to creep up, but in widely spaced, discontinuous and gradual increments. There are fewer breakthroughs, and they are less noticeable when they occur. What is noticeable, however, is a dramatic improvement in the base-line level of one's worst. As strange as it may seem, practicing helps one's worst to keep getting better, which does not necessarily entail that one's best is getting better.

There is nothing mysterious about this. The worst improves because, over time, one will pick up enough tricks and fallback formulas to keep the worst from dropping below a certain level. As a result, even when one is not at one's best and not thrusting into the higher levels, the music does not collapse but stays well above a relatively highly drawn line of one's worst.

This is how it was this night. I just didn't have it. I wasn't flying high. I was making no discoveries. Instead, I was falling back on tricks, formulas, and discoveries made long ago and regularized into my playing. Listening in the audience, it would have been hard to detect the falling off. The music would be solid and competent, just not spiking into the ethereal, marching into the novel, and flying into the unknown.

Towards the end of this somewhat unsatisfying gig, I saw Philo. He looked the way he always did, mildly oblivious and cleverly obscured. For the first time since we had met, however, I felt disinterested in him. I wondered if he was also losing interest in me. Was he starting to see me as just a stupid, provincial fool of an Earthling?

There were fewer people around as I finished, which is how it usually is when one does not soar and fly. I really think people pick these things up even if they do not consciously identify them. Professional entertainers are usually really good at faking inspiration and excitement, much the way an experienced sex worker can fake complete sexual satisfaction with a client. Indeed, the ability to fake high-flying inspiration and not high-flying itself is increasingly what *defines* a professional today. But beneath all the fakery there is a core reality than cannot be faked. And there are some people who cannot be faked.

As I prepared to approach his table, I began to feel a bit of anticipation about this very thing. Although Philo was brilliant at noting my flying highlights, would he notice my flatland playing tonight? Would he himself even continue to be interested in me or would he fake it? I resolved to watch very carefully to find out. I would even bug-eye him if I needed to.

I put my guitar down and approached his table.

As I approached he turned his head languidly and looked at me, blankly it seemed. I took the initiative. As I reached his table I said, trying to be normal, "Here is Mr. Philo Man, one whose origins are unclear but whose words are clearly shocking and outrageous."

Other than generally feeling on the outs with Philo, I did not mean anything heavy or hostile when I said this. I have since considered and reconsidered what I said, trying to hear it as Philo might have heard it. I may not have been intentionally sending a specific message, but I certainly was communicating my inner state to him whether I wanted to or not. I remember being struck by Philo's expression. The look on his face indicated confusion, and his features pulled slightly together, signaling an attempt to make sense of my greeting. Without thinking, I added an explanation as I pulled out my chair.

"I am obviously intrigued by what you say, Philo, but I also feel that what you say is crazy. So crazy, in fact, that I wonder if I am crazy just to listen." I didn't say this as an insult or confrontationally. I meant it merely as an observation. I thought I was being mindful.

Philo looked at me sharply for an instant then broke into a relaxed smile. "Oh, the twists and turnings of the provincial mind," he said.

That bothered me. I had the immediate image of someone looking at a puppy hopelessly chasing its own tail and saying with amusement, "Oh, the twists and turnings of the puppy's mind."

I felt insulted.

"Why call me provincial?" I replied with an edge to my tone. "I mean, most of the things you are saying are off-the-wall and crazy outrageous, but when I express just a little bit of my recognition of the fact of this, you insult me, calling me a provincial."

Philo laughed without malice. "John," he said in a balanced tone, "when I call you provincial I am not insulting you. I thought we clarified this already. I am classifying and describing, not insulting."

For some reason, this irked me. It came across to me like a schoolteacher correcting a wayward pupil. Instead of mollifying me, it bothered me. "So you are classifying me," I said, feeling out of sorts. "Maybe the organ grinder's monkey does not want to be classified. Maybe he just wants to be talked to."

Philo was looking confused again. My reaction clearly was not what he was expecting, and he seemed to be trying to make sense of it. Once again, I blustered on, offering an explanation before Philo could say anything.

"Philo," I said, "anyone in my shoes would doubt, even mock mercilessly the things you say, and they would do so a lot more readily than I do. I may be gullible, but with you I have been super gullible on steroids. Compared to most other people I am . . ."

"Slightly less provincial," Philo interrupted. That silenced me like a sudden and unexpected slap to the face. I was stunned. He did it! He insulted me just as I was complaining to him about the way he insulted me!

There were a few tense moments during which we bug-eyed each other. I don't know what he saw, but for all appearances, all I saw was that he was carrying on as he had always done. Then he took a breath and continued as if nothing had happened.

"Remember the definition of provincial in this context," he said, sounding like he was lecturing. "To be provincial as I am using the term is to look at things in the manner of a typical Earthling. Certainly you are less typical than most other Earthlings, but that is because you are a philosopher and have a bit of a cosmic perspective, the view from the mountaintop, so to speak. In this case, however, it is as if you are cultivating a view from outer space, which is even more cosmic. Even before we met, you had been nurturing and cultivating this perspective. When I describe you as provincial, therefore, I am simply acknowledging that you are still tied to Earth. There is nothing wrong with that, of course, but if I have an agenda, it is that I want you to jump higher, to be even more cosmic."

Philo said this in a completely clean and chatty manner, as if nothing had changed. For me, however, what he said was pompous and enraging, so much so that hearing it poisoned everything he had ever said to me.

Given what subsequently happened in the next few days, I have reviewed these moments over and over again, consulting my hastily scribbled notes for clues. It took a while, but I finally came to see and then later came to admit that I had a hostile attitude. It was like I was possessed by the attitude.

Again, given what subsequently happened, I have reflected long and hard on that attitude. I've asked myself how it happened. How was I able to cancel out all of the insights and palpable personal help I received from Philo, turning him into an enemy? I have sorrowed over that and lamented it, but clearly it happened. How?

Part of it, I am sad to say, is the very help Philo gave me. He used to say that every light casts a shadow, and the greater the light, the greater the shadow. What happened here, I think, happened in the shadow of the light Philo had provided for me. Clearly I had become significantly more internally aware and mindful as a result of having these conversations with Philo. Often, and with great delight, I would discover tricks of my mind and deeply embedded mechanisms of automatic response. The discoveries were thrilling. And inspiring. And confidence building.

And there was the problem. I was so thrilled, inspired, and full of confidence that I became prideful. And as we Earthlings have known from at least the time of the ancient Greeks, pride always precedes the fall.

What happened then was that Philo triggered me, which he had done consistently through our conversations. We both understood that a triggered reaction is a great revealer of inner blocks, filters, and automatic cognitive mechanisms. This time, however, I was full of pride, and so instead of becoming internally attentive in order to try to catch out the psychic architecture of my automatic response, I believed the trigger. I got furious at Philo.

Looking back, I can't believe I did this. Of course, I knew and had repeatedly experienced that having a negative reaction is an indication that some inner block, pattern, filter, or automatic defense has been activated. As Philo said repeatedly, it's not that we *just* get angry or upset or insulted. It is always in terms of some inner assumption or automatic framing that we generate our negative response. The negativity then distracts our awareness completely away from our inner functioning and towards the perceived external threat, thereby cloaking the automatic functioning of the now activated inner deflecting mechanisms. The negative response, then, is an indication that one or more of these hidden mechanisms are operational. The trick then is to see them. One has to look very carefully.

Having caught a glimpse of one of these automatic deflecting responses in operation is significant for a number of reasons. First, one now knows where it is to be found, its hiding place exposed, so it will be easier to find it again in the future. Second, these things are designed to work *below* the level of ordinary awareness, so noticing one indicates one has successfully extended one's awareness beyond and below the ordinary level. And third, because these things function automatically, becoming aware of them will weaken their automaticity and provide one with the option of circumventing or cancelling the reaction.

I did this with Philo over and over, but not this time. Why not? I think the reason why I did not is because, based on my earlier successes, I was confident in the range of my new awareness. This very confidence and pride of achievement functioned to make it easier for me to forget. In this way I became automatic.

I didn't know it at the time, but things between us were about to turn in a surprising, dramatic, and completely ill-fated way. It is to that change I now direct my focus.

CHAPTER 60

PHILO FIGHTS BACK

To return to our fateful conversation . . . .
I had expressed extreme displeasure over the fact that Philo had called me provincial and had advised me to aspire to be less so. I was in the act of pointing out that I was much more open and trusting of him and what he was saying than most people would be. "Compared to them I am—"

Philo interrupted at that point to say, "—slightly less provincial." I was stunned. He was telling me that compared to the typical low awareness, ethnocentric Earthling, I was "slightly less provincial."

Hearing him say this really angered me. I felt rage. It didn't help that he had gone on to add, without seeming ruffled in the slightest, speaking as if he was describing how many cars were in the parking lot, that I had somewhat successfully nurtured and cultivated what he was calling a 'cosmic perspective.' He was acknowledging that and now encouraging me to take it further.

He reminded me that in this context being provincial meant thinking and acting like a typical historically patterned, culturally shaped Earthling of the time and place. "It is to harmonize with and even dissolve entirely into the established patterns of the day," he said. "Of course, everyone does that to some extent. The difference is between the people who dissolve so completely into the patterns that they have no spot from which to stand back and look at the whole. A classic case of not seeing the forest for the trees."

"But you, John," he continued, "being a philosopher are less typical than most in that you have a bit of a cosmic perspective. This has led you to cultivate and nurture the view from the mountaintop. I gather, in fact, that you are not the carefully-analyze-every-detail sort of specialized philosopher who dominates the profession in your increasingly specialized world. Instead, you are the big picture type of philosopher that your planet desperately needs but which is currently in short supply."

He was right about the type of philosopher I was. In fact, people have often sneeringly said my philosophical reflections were more poetry than science. I would try to correct that perception, but it just went on. It only stopped when I started to thank people for that observation, accepting the remark as a high compliment. I would say I was honored to be placed on the side of poetry. This is why I was flattered by Philo's observation that I was not a typical philosopher. He was acknowledging this with approval.

But I also felt surging, fiery anger. It felt primal. It gave rise to an overpowering impulse to defend humanity from this wrathful attack. The words, 'I will defend my fellow Earthlings from this alien attack on their character,' kept sounding in my mind. The words soon became my resolve. In my mind's eye I could see in the sky an unfurling banner with those words emblazoned in bold letters. Suddenly all the tender feelings for humanity and all the burning anger at insensitive, critical aliens for mocking humanity seemed to coalesce into a fireball and explode.

I said to Philo with a tone of barely contained outrage, "I resent your attacks on humanity, Philo, and I intend to defend humanity from your attacks on their character." I was almost panting.

Philo looked stunned. He wouldn't have looked any different if I had just turned into a toy airplane and flown three circles around the room. "Incredible," he uttered in a voice of amazement, shaking his head in disbelief.

"So like a true provincial I want to defend my people. Is that it? Or is it that I am a provincial because I am prepared to defend my people?" I was on a raging rant. "Why don't you sue me in cosmic court instead of wasting my time with your tedious putdowns of my fellow Earthlings! Humanity is not as clueless as you think, Mr. Big Spaceman. We have some really great things going for us. I think it might serve you well if you opened your eyes a bit to some of the wonders and goodness of humanity instead of just sitting around criticizing all the time."

I was breathing hard. Most would call it panting.

Philo had a strange, mesmerized look on his face. It was like he genuinely could not believe what he was seeing and hearing. He was literally dumbfounded. I tried to bug-eye him but I was too upset to see anything. It did look like he flashed anger and then absorbed it, transmuting the energy of it, but I can't say for sure. I did see him take a couple of deliberate, deep breaths. Maybe he was calming himself, maybe he was only pretending to, or maybe something entirely different—something alien—was going on inside of him. I don't know. All I know is that he looked directly at me with his patented half smile and said, though this time with more edge in his voice, "Amazing."

"I'm being provincial, right. So sue me," I sneered.

Still smiling, though looking ever so slightly forced, Philo replied, more calmly this time, "For an Earthling to act like an Earthling and to tap into, however inappropriately, the primal urge to protect his own kind, this is not something to sue one for. I just wish I could capture your reaction here in a frame and offer it to you as an operational definition of provinciality."

I found myself frothing in so much anger that even though I could hear and understand what he was saying, I could not connect his words with any meaning. Instead of understanding all I had was anger. I didn't say anything and Philo continued.

"But none of that is what amazes me, John."

"So what does?" I snapped back, ready to mock and fight

anything he might say.

He stared at me and I felt a surge of fear, so angry did he seem. He then delivered the most impassioned statement I think I have ever heard from anyone, human or alien!

"So here I am," he said, "an alien philosopher visiting your planet. It is a highly illegal action to do so, one that, if punished, would end my life as I know it. Now why would I take that risk?" He glared at me and I felt his intensity burning holes into my face.

"I take that risk because I love Earth and its people. I grew up listening to black market recordings of Earth music, particularly rock, blues, and jazz. But it wasn't just the hits. In fact, what were most prized were the rare recordings of 'garage bands.' Some of your teenage recordings, John, were prominent among the rare gems. The Dagenites—your teenage band!—is at the top of the heap. The song *I'm Gone Slide* is especially popular. Of course, taped jam sessions, recordings of ordinary clubs and raw demos are also highly prized."

"I've come to every one of your gigs since I've been here, listening in rapture. I've been patiently trying to explain to you through your thick provincial crust how unique and unprecedented in the entire universe your planet and humanity are. I described it to you as a 'cosmic crossroads,' a place where contrasting energies, aspirations, and lifestyles meet, mix, clash, and coalesce. It is a place of deep contrast and extreme ferment. The end result will be something that will function as a herald for the entire inhabited universe, either a portent for an interminable dark age or a harbinger of a bright new dawn. And should the new dawn emerge, it will not just bring forth light, as magnificent as that is, but a new sort of light, something not yet seen in all of existence. This light will change existence! Do you remember any of this, John?"

He was staring at me with fierce intensity. I can't say I observed this, but I think he was panting. It was not only the angriest I had seen him, but the only time I had seen him angry. I managed to squeak out a mousy 'yes' to his question.

"So you remember this, do you? Yet you express not just anger, but a holy, righteous anger at what you perceive as my slight to Earth and its people, and you rise up to defend your planet and your people from my harsh and unforgiving words!"

I didn't know what to say.

"You wouldn't know this, but the movers and shakers of the entire intergalactic order are terrified of the new possibilities that Earthlings and Earth civilization can bring into existence. To them, ensconced in greed and fear, humanity is a threat. They see Earth not as a property but as what your own leaders would call a terrorist organization. Something having the potential to destroy intergalactic civilization as currently constituted."

"I'm sure our weapons could never stand up to yours," I said, conciliating.

"I'm not talking about weapons, you provincial idiot!" Philo snapped back. I felt slashed, like something really sharp had cut deeply into me. It doesn't hurt at first but then the pain opens, expands, and swallows you.

"I'm talking about energy," he said forcefully. "I'm talking about love—not love as a feeling or a desire, but love as a fundamental, constitutive cosmic force, a force deeper and more primal than gravity."

"That's a lot to take in, Philo," I said, feeling hurt, chastened, intimidated, and blank.

"So keep working at it," he said sharply. He then stood up. "I will see you the day after tomorrow in the coffee shop at noon. If you are not there, then I'm not sure when I will see you again."

He said this in a straight, unemotional tone. It wasn't a mean tone, but it didn't do anything to make me feel good. He then turned abruptly and walked straight out.

I was stunned.

All I could think of was whether our next meeting was going to be our last meeting. I didn't know what had just happened. I didn't even remember very well what I had been so angry about. I felt a little apprehensive, almost guilty.

But mostly I just felt crushed.

CHAPTER 61

I BALANCE MYSELF AND COME BACK

I walked to the meeting with Philo feeling repentant, confused, and conflicted. I was thoroughly remorseful for my attitude and behavior. I kept saying to myself, 'This isn't me.' But of course, as much as I deplored my outburst, there was no getting around the fact that I was the one who had erupted. Even so, I also had a strong sense of having been hijacked. It wasn't that I was trying to pass off responsibility. It was that in looking back on my angry outburst, it felt more like it had happened to me than that it was anything I had done. It was as if my state of being and seat of control had been hijacked.

In short, even though I regretted what I had done and took responsibility for it, I also felt like what I had done had been done to me.

I remembered that Philo had once spoken about this exact thing. He said it was sometimes the case that the trigger of a certain automatic defensive response would be hidden even more deeply in the psyche where it could function as a sort of last gasp, failsafe response. It was rarely triggered, but when it was, it would take the form of a totally uncharacteristic explosion of extreme anger. This concentrated outburst of anger functioned to deflect attention away from whatever the focus had been by being so ragingly over the top that it would itself become the focus.

Philo said that even those who had worked to extend their awareness deep enough to be able to identify the triggers of their automatic responses—even then, a person could be unaware of their automatic defensive response. The upshot of this was that when the automatic response did finally get triggered, a person afterwards would often feel a sense of having been hijacked.

He used that word.

It made me feel a little better about myself to consider this. I was hijacked. It was that simple. Of course, what I was hijacked by was not alien or even external. It was by me. So to excuse myself on that basis seemed disingenuous. It is like someone accused of criminal assault defending himself by saying it was his hands that had done the punching, not him.

So in spite of feeling hijacked, I would begin to feel bad about myself. Then I would try to convince myself that I was not entirely wrong to have exploded in anger. No! Philo had really pissed me off—repeatedly! Shouldn't he harbor some blame? And since he got really angry himself, how enlightened is that?

Back and forth my monkey mind scurried.

I was walking to the coffee shop thinking how appropriate it was that we would be meeting somewhere called the Ragged Edge when I suddenly remembered something Philo had once said that put my mind to rest. It had happened right after Philo had first told me he was from another planet. I was asking him questions about what it was like on his planet. Looking back, I can see that I did not take entirely seriously his claim. It was more like he had told me about this fantastic video game he was playing that would take you to another planet and so I asked him questions about the planet. I took the video game seriously, but I didn't believe it was real.

In other words, I allowed his claim to rest in the realm of fiction from whence it had sprung.

But I remember having asked him how people on his planet comprehended bursts of anger and the irrational, often hurtful things that people say when angry. I remember he had been somewhat dismissive of my questions about his planet. It wasn't that he wouldn't respond to them. It was more that he didn't take them all that seriously. His answers were brief and frequently dismissive. He obviously had no interest in talking about things back home, as it were. But I remember that when I asked him this one question, he responded very differently, taking my question seriously and responding in detail.

This is how the question had come up. A couple sitting at a table across the room from us had apparently been having an argument. It had reached a boiling point and the man had raised his voice. I could not hear what he said, but his tone of viciousness and animosity was clear and disturbing. The woman had then stood up and said in a chilling tone something I could hear clearly. She said, "You sick bastard. I never, ever want to see your repulsive face or hear your revolting voice ever again!" With that, she turned and left, head held high and rigid. I was looking in that direction and the guy glanced at me, the expression on his face a bizarre mixture of embarrassment and rage. I remember he looked at me in a way suggesting he wanted to say, "What am I supposed to do? The woman is mean and crazy."

The room was silent for a few moments. Then conversation began to pick up, the guy stood up and left, and normalcy slowly re-emerged. There was a sort of a feeling of altered space, however, where this outburst had occurred.

Philo had watched the entire episode as well, of course, but had not said anything. I asked him whether such a thing would ever happen on his planet. He chuckled to himself and said that indeed it would. Such things happen, he explained, anytime a culture supports differentiation from the group and individuals think of themselves as equal. "Sergeants rarely express open vicious anger at Majors," he said, "but they will do so towards their wives, children, and house pets."

"That's a steep cost to pay for individualism," I said.

"To the contrary," he said, "it is a bargain. The emergence of the individual, not the solitary individual but the responsible individual, the self-legislating ethical individual—this is the blossom of cultural evolution, the point of it all. Even cultures that utterly suppress the individual cannot foil the individual's emergence. In that case, the culture starts to act like a sort of super-sized individual, only now without the good sense and moderating influence of others.

He continued. "This is what has happened to your country, John. On your planet your country acts like a sociopathic individual, one that is a bully with material interests and no compassion for its victims. But actual Americans, even the ones who implement and operate the system of global bullying are, by and large, not sociopaths and do not lack compassion. As many people around the planet say, 'Love Americans, hate America.'"

At the time I was more interested in individual psychology on his planet than group psychology on mine, so I asked how people on his planet would process and understand what we had just seen happen. "If those two were married, would that outburst mean the end of the relationship?" I asked.

"Why would the relationship end over that?" he inquired back, seeming genuinely puzzled.

"The couple expressed hate to each other, and in a public place," I replied, surprised he did not see the significance. "It indicates something is deeply wrong in the relationship."

He looked at me, seeming a bit surprised and taking in what I had just said. Then he said, "Well, right there is a difference between your planet and mine."

"How so?" I asked, genuinely interested. "I mean, the mutual nastiness we witnessed was so intense that for the couple it had to be powerfully significant. How could it be different on your planet?"

"Well," he answered in a relaxed way, "I can think of two big points of difference between how Earthlings would assess and understand the couple's public spat and the way we would comprehend it back home."

"Please explain," I asked, very interested.

"By all means," he responded heartily. "The first difference is the way you Earthlings assume that the way to get to the good is to eliminate the bad. Your schools provide a perfect example of this assumption. Take instruction in writing. You ask students to write something, and then you mercilessly criticize what they have written, both in terms of *what* they say and *how* they say it. Students hate it, of course, but the teachers do not generally criticize hatefully. They do so as a service to the student."

"This is good, right?" I asked.

"Yes, the teacher's attitude is good. I am not focusing on that but rather on something deeper—namely, the assumption that the way to produce something good is to identify and criticize what is bad about it. This assumption is very deep in your cultural programming."

He paused to look at me and then continued. "Someone once asked Michelangelo how he was able to sculpt 'living' masterpieces. He replied that he just took a large block of marble and scraped away everything that does not belong to the finished work. And that, John, is the way you humans are culturally programmed to approach moral and intellectual improvement—that is, you scrape away what is not fully moral or intellectually respectable. Scrape, scrape, scrape. It is the idea that when all the bad parts are scraped away, what will be left is good in every way."

"But that's how it is done," I remember saying, not fully grasping how else to go about making improvements. "How do you do it on your planet?"

Philo smiled and shook his head slightly. "It is so different on my planet, it is hard to describe. You see, it isn't just that we *do* things differently; it is that we *think about* things differently. I could tell you what we do, but it wouldn't make all that much sense."

I was not satisfied by Philo's response and wanted to know more, so I asked, "Let's use that argument over there as an example. That was a dramatic event for each of those two people. It may be the last time they are together or they might work together on what the issue was, but it is something that has to be dealt with. So how would it be dealt with on your planet?"

"Good question, John," Philo replied pleased. "You identify a fault-line difference between your cultural programming and mine. On my planet it would not be dealt with at all."

"What?" I exclaimed, shocked. "A couple fights in public, one stomping out after savaging the other, having probably been savaged herself, and you aliens would ignore it?"

"Not ignore it, just not elevate it. To us, the anger episode would mean—nothing. And even if it did mean something, it would not be what you Earthlings would generally take it to mean, as the revelation of something nasty and dark lurking inside. We would not characteristically take it to mean anything like that. To us it would mean nothing more than that under the right conditions we could lose our centered awareness, especially when we are dealing with primal issues like love, commitment, finances, and family difficulties. Regarding the couple we saw, we would think that the primacy of the issue they had been discussing had led them to leave their 'watching' awareness. It was as if they had been hijacked by their inner fear. They then temporarily stop being themselves and become instead the panicked voice of their fear."

"But it has to be dealt with," I protested, not seeing an alternative.

"Really?" Philo replied, arching his eyebrows. "Look at what happens when you 'deal with it,' as you say. A couple has a nasty spat so they deal with it. Meaning what? They talk about it. And what happens? Where they had a nasty spat about something, now they have another nasty spat about who was primarily responsible for the nasty spat. In other words, they deal with it by having a nasty spat about the nasty spat. It could even happen that after having a nasty spat about the nasty spat, they then have another nasty spat about *that* nasty spat. In other words, talking about a nasty spat usually does not resolve it. That is because it can't be resolved. The conflict is only a seeming conflict. Properly understood, it is only a clash between ego programs. The two people, when both are present, do not have the conflict. There may be differences and even disagreement, but it does not take that explosive form."

"I'm not quite seeing this," I said.

"Think about it this way," Philo said. If one member of a couple has the flu and can't hold food down, the other would not take the vomiting as a personal statement. He or she would instead clean the mess and try to make the person feel better. He or she would not feel a need to argue with them or even break up with them because of their upset stomach. And when the person gets over the sickness and feels better, there would be no need to revisit the fever and deal with it."

Nothing to deal with after a nasty spat! I understood but was astounded. "Ok, so what would an enlightened couple do?" I asked.

"That is exactly what an enlightened couple would do," he replied. "They do not give the outburst meaning and significance it does not possess. What is said in such a state is not what a person really thinks. It is what fear, anger, hate, and ego frustration use the body to say when the person, having lost the clarity of his or her self-awareness, is no longer there. Instead, the body then becomes the voice of fear, anger, hate, and ego frustration. It isn't the person speaking any longer but a complex of those fearful, angry, hateful, frustrated voices vomiting out. It doesn't mean anything more than that."

Our conversation then moved on to other things, but recalling that episode as I was walking to meet Philo the day after our nasty spat made me feel a whole lot better. I was thinking that when I saw him in just a few minutes my attitude was going to be normal, as if nothing had happened yesterday. I had a nasty ego response and lost my seat, nothing more than that. Other than that, it had no meaning and was best ignored. There wasn't even any vomit to clean up.

Stepping up on the front porch of the Ragged Edge, I felt better. For the first time in days, I once again really felt eager to see Philo. I also felt it would be easy for me to ignore his angry response as well. We will just go back to our conversation as if nothing had happened. And, as Philo had explained back then, when properly understood, nothing had happened.

But Philo was not there.

I waited for an hour and he did not show up.

CHAPTER 62

PHILO IS GONE AND THINGS GET WEIRD

I was forlorn. What happened? Was Philo still mad at me? Had he left the planet in disgust? Had his anger at me led him to be careless and get noticed and arrested . . . by aliens? Was all of this just a big practical joke after all so that, once I got angry the way a normal person would, the joke lost footing?

Then there was that strange sense I had from time to time that our conversations were being filmed. Maybe they were. That would be bad. Maybe his disappearance had something to do with that?

Thinking about these possibilities—and especially the last one—I was getting increasingly upset and fearful. In addition to wondering what I might have done either to have driven Philo away or to have gotten him in trouble, I also started wondering what I might have said in the course of these conversations that could be used to ridicule me? Would my words display me as a gullible fool? Should I be embarrassed?

My mind was turning all of this over and over, but with no new data coming in, I was not figuring anything out. Instead, I was only making myself distraught and increasingly anxious. It bothered me that I couldn't recall anything I had said or done involving Philo that I regretted. It bothered me even more that, given a second chance, I would probably have said or done the same thing. I was in the dark. Even my anger outburst, which I now deeply regretted, was not of sufficient intensity to shame me in most social circles, not to mention that I was defending humanity after all. And as Philo himself had so clearly said in that earlier conversation I recalled on my way here, on his planet the significance of such an outburst would be calculated at zero.

Then again, maybe Philo's own outburst at me had so profoundly shamed him that he felt he had to run away. Maybe this is an alien thing. Maybe aliens don't get angry. Perhaps he had been here so long that he was starting to go native, and so it was a severe wake up call for him when he got angry. If so, then perhaps in the interest of his own health of mind he had immediately left for home. Perhaps aliens don't feel a need to say goodbye to provincials.

What if Philo had gotten sick and didn't have any of the medicine he needed? Maybe he is suffering right now in some cheap motel room? Maybe a car hit him or he got beaten up? Maybe he is dead!

My mind was racing in a most troubled manner, leaping from one calamitous scenario to another. I didn't know anything definite, but that didn't stop me from compulsively speculating. As I did so, I didn't know whether to be furious at Philo or worried for him. I didn't know whether to be mad at him or sad for him. I was really out of sorts.

Philo had never missed an appointment before. Not once. There were times he had not shown up when I hoped he would, but every time he had said he would be there, he was. Every time. Knowing this, I was having trouble just accepting the simple fact he had not shown up let alone understanding why he had not. I kept looking in the corners, thinking he might be there after all. When I didn't see him, I tried to convince myself that he was just a little late or that— silly me—I had gotten the time wrong. Maybe I was supposed to meet him earlier and he thought I had failed to show?

My mind was alternating between feeling tender concern for him and then bitter anger towards him. I would go from feeling guilty for my own part in the spat to feeling resentful at him for the easily preventable sorrow he was now making me go through.

Yet as troubled and unsettled as I was, beneath all of this

turbulence was a lurking fear that I had brought this all about myself, that whatever was happening was the result of the fire of inappropriate anger I had directed at Philo.

The fire of my desperation grew beyond my ability to contain it. I didn't know what to do. All this time spent talking with someone who said he was an alien and I had no idea where he went when we parted. Maybe he beamed back to his planet and only beamed down for our talks? Did he stay here between our talks? Where? Did he talk to anyone else in the way he talked to me? I had seen him talk to a few people when we were together. He always seemed appropriate: polite, correct—and instantly forgettable.

After more than an hour of waiting and worrying myself into stormy confusion, I left the Ragged Edge in a daze. I tried going home but I didn't want to be there. I tried playing guitar but I didn't want to do so. I even tried my meditation but I couldn't get into it. Finally, I just started walking around town, but not exactly aimlessly. I was looking into every place he might be. I didn't really expect to find him, but at least the walking occupied me.

Around and around and back and forth I walked. Hours passed. I was tired and hungry but I didn't want to rest or eat. It was just starting to get dark and I was beginning to feel an overwhelming sense of desolation. I was trying to convince myself to walk home and grab a bite to eat when, passing the Parrot, I noticed something in the periphery of my vision.

Glancing through the locked gate that looked down the wide alley that is to the right of the Parrot, I saw two people talking on the back street. They were at least 100 yards distant, far enough away and sufficiently obscured that I could not see them very well and could not shout out to them. But even under these conditions, it struck me that they both looked a bit like Philo. What I mean by that is they were both somehow equally non-descript and difficult to describe. They looked similar to each other, but not like twins. It wasn't that you would mistake one for the other. It was more like they were dressed similarly in a way that suggested they were from the same place.

Maybe that place was another planet—Philo's planet!

Maybe that *was* Philo!

I edged closer to the locked gate and scrutinized them from a distance with narrowed eyes, trying better to see. They were too far away to determine anything definite, but it almost looked like one of them could be Philo.

I stared desperately in mounting hope. The one I thought looked most like Philo seemed agitated in a most un-Philo like way. He was gesticulating in a manner that suggested he disagreed with the other one. The dynamic between them suggested that the other one was in charge, though of course I did not know that and was only interpreting what I was seeing. I urgently wanted this person to be Philo but, looking from that distance, I could not be sure.

If it was Philo, however, it was clear he was not in a good mental place. I should have been leaping for joy thinking this might be Philo, but what I saw was only making me more upset. Maybe he was being arrested? Whoever he was and whatever was happening, it was clear that he was not happy. It was disorienting to see this. Other than the mutual outburst the day before, I had never seen Philo even mildly upset. However, this person I was staring at in desperation seemed to be totally distraught, more so even than Philo had been yesterday.

As I stared, this person did seem increasingly to look a bit like Philo. Desperate as I was, that vague similarity was enough for me to persuade myself that it was indeed Philo. But if it was Philo, why did he seem to be so exceedingly troubled. It was as if he was dissenting from something terrible he had just been told. Of course, that was an interpretation on my part, but it did look that way. They were talking animatedly and it did not seem like a pleasant conversation.

The Philo character was doing most of the talking at this moment and he distinctly seemed to be protesting or disagreeing. Clearly it was not an amiable conversation of the sort I associated with Philo, yesterday notwithstanding.

They could not see me and I could not reach them, standing as I was peering through the locked fence gate. To reach them I would have to leave my observation point on the other side of the locked gate and enter the front door of the Parrot. Then I would have to walk through the bar section to a side door which opened out to the middle of the locked alley, taking me half of the way to where they were, from which point I could approach them.

That was the only way for me to get to them, but I was reluctant to let them out of my sight.

Suddenly and without much thought or even having made a conscious decision, I turned to my left and, leaving them out of my sight, walked to and entered the front door of the Parrot to gain access to the side alley. I was hurrying as fast as I could, even rudely rushing when someone I knew tried to talk to me, moving to stand directly in front of me and blocking my way. I made excuses as politely as I could and sidestepped him. It was rude, but that looked like Philo outside. The bar area of the restaurant was crowded and I had to painstakingly maneuver my way to the side door that opened onto the outside alley. It took longer than I wanted—agonizingly longer.

When I did finally get through, the person I thought might be Philo was gone.

The other guy was there, however, shuffling some papers into a kind of folder or briefcase, preparing to leave. I rushed towards him, calling out desperately, "Where is Philo?"

I would say he looked at me as if I was a ghost, but it was so much more dramatic than that. It was more like he was involved in some highly illegal activity and I was a plainclothes cop busting him.

He looked at me with shocked panic playing on his features. In fact, he looked so desperate that I felt a flash of fear. I was pretty upset and turbulent in my own mind, but just then he seemed even more so by a wide margin.

"Where is Philo?" I demanded again as I reached him, this time even more urgently.

He looked at me and took a breath. He was giving me that bug-eye look I was well accustomed to with Philo. A look like that coming from someone like him in a circumstance like this normally would have freaked me out. This time, however, his bug-eye stare actually calmed me somewhat because it reminded me of Philo. He only stared for a few brief moments but it seemed much longer of course. I could see him gathering himself. Finally he said, and not kindly, "You should not be talking to me."

"I have to!" I almost yelled.

He took a long time to respond, still bug-eyeing me. He was not pleased. "You are out of order," he finally said. His words had the sting of cold command. "We can all talk tomorrow at departure."

"No," I protested. "Now!" I was too upset and didn't have time to ponder what he meant by departure, but his mention of that certainly added to my turmoil.

He glanced around nervously. "You must stop. You cannot talk to me here," he said.

"Where then?" I demanded.

He glanced around again and then looked back at me. He seemed wary and on high alert. He checked what looked like a cell phone. He could have been reading a text message, but I don't know. He did seem to soften ever so slightly, however, saying, "We can't be seen leaving together. I will turn and leave. Give me a moment and then you can follow me." Then, eyes narrowing and adopting a tone of high authority, he added, "Do not look like you are following me or even that you know me."

"I'm not letting you out of my sight," I replied with firm conviction.

He seemed to be calculating. He looked at his phone again. "Fine," he said. "I am leaving now, but do not acknowledge me in any way. Follow at a safe distance, but try to hide the fact you are following." He stared at me with unsettling intensity for a second, and then said, "And please stop acting. It is no longer the time for that."

With that he turned and left, heading not back towards the side door I had come out of but in the opposite direction, away from the alley altogether. I followed, trying my best to be non-descript myself.

I would not have thought it possible, but this whole weird situation had just gotten a whole lot weirder. What was that he had just said about me acting? This was too creepy and weird to make sense of. Me, acting? What was he saying? Did he think I was just pretending to want to find Philo?

CHAPTER 63

THINGS TAKE A DRAMATIC TURN
FOR THE WORSE!

The guy only walked a short while to the back of a number of large buildings that fronted the square. The backs of these buildings sprawled out into the alley in many different blocks, shapes, and angles, creating a number of obscured and darkened entrances. There were many doors, but none of them were meant for public use. None of them seemed to be in regular use, either. Most of them looked locked but none of them seemed particularly secure.

The guy walked directly to a particular door. Not surprisingly, it was partially hidden and somewhat hard to see, sort of like Philo himself. It opened easily to his touch, however. I was close behind him but far enough away that the door could have closed before I got there, so I prepared to run the last distance. If it had closed, I would not have known which building it gave access to because the buildings were a jumble, protruding unevenly into the back alley, overlapping and connecting, creating a maze of mixed entrances.

Without glancing back at me, the guy walked through the door, which remained open behind him. I continued my pace and walked in after him.

Before I could reach to close the door behind me, it gently closed on its own accord. From the outside the door looked old and battered, hardly something that could withstand a hardy kick from someone wearing boots. As I walked in, however, I could see the door was actually a high-tech barrier. It looked like it could withstand a military blast and seemed to be made of some mysterious high-tech substance.

The room itself was about the size of a typical bedroom. It was a perfect square about twenty feet long and wide with a high ceiling. It felt like a box. I noted that it did not have any windows, and the walls, floor, and ceiling were all a sort of flat, military gray. It was obvious that no effort at all had been made to make the room appealing in terms of either aesthetics or comfort. The room looked like it had recently been cleaned out. Unplugged wires dangled from the walls at various points, and stark, sturdy military style tables stood where the wires extended from the wall. It was obvious that equipment had been plugged in and had only been recently removed. A few simple chairs were spread around the room and there was one larger chair with cushioning. It was not a recliner, but unlike the other starkly functional metal chairs, this one was clearly designed for comfort.

There were no pictures on the walls or anything that suggested people spent time there. The room was cleaned out. It put me on edge just being there. It almost seemed like it was a detachable cube posing as a room. The walls, gray and flat as they were, seemed somehow strong and secure. It felt like we were completely sealed off in this room. Maybe my body could sense this was a dead space and that the walls blocked all radio waves and cell phone signals.

Whatever it was, it was dead silent in the room. It had the feeling of being deep in a cave—or worse, of being in a sealed tomb.

The light in the room was sufficient for reading, but it was a harsh, gray sort of light. There were no actual light fixtures I could see, making the room feel even more unsettling to me than the situation would warrant. The light seemed to just be there, as if the whole room, including floor and ceiling, was a sort of luminous computer screen.

To me, having only been seconds inside, the room had the

feeling of a prison or of a control room in a submarine. Whatever it was, it was designed for work, not for play or relaxation. If I was on edge before, I was actively worried now.

But the most striking thing in the room was this guy. He had sat in the comfortable chair and seemed to relax completely. The effect was striking. From tense and angular, both mentally and physically, he became completely calm and relaxed. He motioned to me to take a seat. So dramatic was this change in him that I looked to double check whether he was the same person I had spoken to in the back alley. Of course, I had not taken my eyes off him, so it had to be the same person.

I sat in the chair he indicated. He was stretched out in his chair, luxuriating in this bleak and unfriendly space. He looked like he felt completely secure, unlike before in the alley where he looked like someone in the midst of battle with bullets whizzing closely by.

He smiled at me with genuine warmth and asked how he might be able to accommodate me. "I want to see Philo," I said, trying to sound less urgent than before. He chuckled when I said that.

"Normally I would ask you whether you were production or technical, but it is pretty obvious that you are production. And good, too. Kudos to you and the entire team."

"I just want to see Philo," I replied, totally confused by what he was saying but ignoring it.

He stared blankly at me. Finally, still seeming completely calm and relaxed, he replied, "Again, you have my acknowledgement. Very, very nicely done. Good acting. Totally believable. I've never been production myself. I hate going out there no matter where we are, but this here is one of the worst. It was only because of the emergency that I was out there before. But in spite of what you may have heard about me, I really do appreciate you production people. I really do. I mean, where would technical be without you folks, the frilly pretenders." He laughed to himself.

It was like he was talking another language. I had no idea what he was talking about, but I was so confused and upset that I was not able to formulate a thought. He looked completely relaxed.

"You must know, of course," he continued, "that I should turn you in for this breach." He looked at me pointedly. It seemed pretty clear that to be turned in was something very bad and I was supposed to be alarmed, but I was just too scrambled to react. He seemed to be waiting for a response and it looked like he took my not saying anything as a response of confidence on my part.

"You must be one of the important ones, an indispensable, or you would be on your knees begging me to keep quiet," he concluded. He took a breath and seemed to calm down "But don't worry," he continued, "I can understand why you production guys, especially one of you indispensables, would be upset. Hell, even I am a little shaken. But you guys. Hey, you have my total sympathy, you really do. But as talented as you are, you have to stop this smart monkey routine. I know it takes a long time to get it down, but the show is ended. The curtain has closed. You can relax now. We are completely safe in here. Nothing can get us here."

"But I need to see Philo," I said urgently, completely failing to comprehend him. His reaction startled me.

"Stop," he said with the impact and clout of authority. "I'm cutting you a lot of slack here, but if you don't stop, I will report you. Believe me, you do not want that. It doesn't matter anymore how good you are at this or how much time you spent perfecting your impressive mastery of the local culture. It is over. Your skill set no longer matters." His voice had the impact of authority. This was a person with command authority and lots of experience using it.

"Can I see him just one time, just for a minute?"

"Not possible. Don't ask again."

"But I have questions."

He laughed a brief, humorless laugh. "Don't we all. This has been sudden and urgent for all us, but the emphasis now is on urgent. At this point all that matters is executing a completely clean extraction. Anything less will create even greater problems than we already have."

"Can I talk to anyone?"

He looked at me softly. It was as if he had sympathy for me. "I don't suppose there are many production people left. You are one of the native plants, obviously. I can understand your plight. I know you have been trained and drilled never to let your cover down, but this is a safe room. In here, it is not even like we are here. We are isolated from them in every way. Even if they knew we were here, they could not get in. They could not even determine if we were here. And if we had to, we could self-extricate, though that of course would only be a last resort."

He paused to give me a chance to respond. I was trying to grasp the import of what he was saying, even though it didn't make a lot of sense to me. I understood his words; I just didn't have any grasp of their context, which was too weird and different to make any sense. Mostly, though, I was thinking about Philo.

He continued, interrupting my thoughts. "Listen, I know you normally always keep up the act, even in a safe space, but things have changed. The plants should have all been pulled. I am pulling you now. You can stop."

I just sat, completely and entirely stupefied. I had no idea what was happening or what he was talking about, but it was clear that he knew Philo and was in contact with him. All of a sudden I found myself talking—not thinking, just babbling.

"It was me, I know," I said, babbling nervously. "I don't know what he told you, but my outburst yesterday wasn't anything. It didn't mean anything. I have to let Philo know."

He didn't say anything. His eyes got wide and he seemed amazed.

I continued on, more confused than ever. "Philo is mad at me," I blurted out, more as a question than a statement.

He didn't say anything and I could not read anything on his face other than a sort of admiration. It was as if I had started an impressive, Olympic level gymnastic routine.

I continued feeling more and more out of touch, "The whole thing yesterday was nothing. Just a mutual ego reaction, best forgotten and not analyzed."

He still did not react, certainly not in any way I could tell. Philo always seemed to be talking to me with his posture and expressions. Even when he didn't say anything, I felt he was communicating. This guy was the opposite. He was like a blank wall. It was as if he was watching a movie or some sort of performance.

All I could focus on was my argument with Philo. I desperately needed Philo to know I realized it was all my fault. Hoping to explain, I spoke in a frenzy, unable to contain myself, "I think I understand the whole thing, really. Philo is right. I am provincial. I am a typical Earthling. Typical."

I paused and noted he was taking it all in. "But here is the thing," I added, feeling frantic, "Philo is also typical! He isn't a typical Earthling, of course. He is a typical alien." I thought I noted a flash of alarm on his face when I mentioned alien, but I was too wound up to stop. "Philo and I are just typical, that's all. We both are."

As soon as I finished, his face came alive. Amusement slid into his features and then the amusement grew into a smile and the smile into a chuckle. The transformation was stunning. It was like a child who was feeling sad because he had been told he could not go to the park, and then the words were added, 'because you are going to the movies.' The sadness does not as much go away as it morphs into joy and excitement. The morphing is quick but amazing to see. Adults keep the morphing better hidden, but with children it is rather obvious. His face was like that. Suddenly he was amused. In fact, he started to laugh and even pretended to applaud.

"What's so funny?" I asked, feeling put down. "This is my insight I am sharing with you."

"I love your insight. Totally brilliant. Impressive. And delivered with consummate skill."

"Then why laugh at it?" I asked somewhat petulantly, feeling hurt.

"Your delivery is brilliant, completely impressive in every way," he said, "but your insight is lacking in just one tiny detail. I am a technical nerd to mention it but, hey, that is what I do." I was uncomprehending. He was talking in a cheery tone.

"But, but, but . . . ." I sputtered, trying to formulate a thought.

"If you will allow me my one small nitpicking comment, without taking away any of the brilliance of your demonstration." He paused briefly to look at me before continuing. "I am part of technical, after all, and contrary to what you production people think, we do appreciate what you do. Production and technical are a team. But your brilliant demonstration is wrong in one tiny detail. Brilliantly acted, I will give you that, but on a content level, this one detail is wrong."

What is that?" I asked, not comprehending.

"Well, I have to say," he said, chuckling and obviously enjoying himself, "that your insight about the two of you is not only wrong, but it is clearly and obviously wrong. The fact that you can't see that is . . . well . . . it is sort of funny." He was laughing with abandon, greatly amused by something.

"It is wrong?" I spluttered. I felt more of a sense of surprise than anything else. "I am an Earthling and Philo is an alien. That is wrong?"

"No, that isn't what I'm talking about at all," he said, glancing to his side. It is the 'typical' part that is wrong, so wrong as to be funny."

"I don't understand."

"Listen," he said, in a sharper tone suggesting the joking was coming to an end. "Philo could be fairly and accurately described in many revealing ways, but being 'typical' is not one of them."

I didn't say anything and he continued. "C'mon, you must know this. Philo is in the public eye a lot. He gets called many things every day by lots of people, and very few of comments are flattering. But nobody would ever, ever call him typical."

"What word would you use to describe him then?"

It was one of those intuitive questions that Philo used to love. The guy thought about it for a second and then said, "It isn't easy to think of a single word, but if pressed I guess the word I would use is the local word, 'hippy.' It isn't perfect but I like the way it fits."

I just sat there so dumbfounded as to be speechless. This was too weird. I could be tripping for all I knew. Maybe I was. Maybe this was part of an extended practical joke! I wanted to say something but nothing came out. It seemed like some long moments passed silently. Finally the guy spoke up.

"Listen, thanks for the demonstration. You are good. I'm very impressed. If I wanted to know what it would be like to sit and talk with one of those primitives, I would know. Thanks to your talent and your craft, I have had the experience." He shook his head in amazement. "It is like it really happened. Kudos to production." He paused and seemed to be feeling sympathetic. "I can only imagine how difficult it must be to be so amazingly good at what you do, to have trained and practiced so long, and then to have no chance for recognition for your impressive accomplishment. I remember when I first started in this work, someone from production, gifted like you, told me being a plant is a lot like being a spy. That is, when you are really, really good at what you do, nobody even suspects that you are doing it."

I had this sudden image. It was as if in talking to me he was telling a young Michael Jordan that as good as he had become at basketball, there was not going to be any basketball on his next assignment. That is, he seemed to be feeling bad for me.

He said, "If this were not a total pull out—and when have you ever heard of a *total* pull out after such success—you would have a rosy future. If nothing else, you would have a great future training the next generation of plants. I mean, you have totally mastered this emoting thing. I could easily take you as one of the talking primates out there, even now. No wonder you don't want to stop."

He paused and shifted from sympathy back to boss mode. "But just because I appreciate a good show doesn't mean that others do as well. In fact, a good general rule is that the higher up you go on the command and authority ladder, the less appreciation you will find. I am an exception. But it is time for you to stop and return to normal. No one is watching any more. It has all ended. The plug has been pulled."

"What are you asking me to do?"

"I want you to be a good boy and implement the highest priority withdrawal protocol."

"I don't understand."

"Listen," he said in a sharp and commanding tone, marking an abrupt change of mood. "This is not funny anymore. Get real immediately. But for my indulgence here, you would already be in big trouble. You are flying in asteroid infected space."

Just then his cell phone made a sound. It wasn't a pleasant sound but more like an alien honk. It was impossible to ignore. He took it out and I could see that it probably was not a cell phone, certainly not like any that I had ever seen. He was looking at something on it. I assumed it was text of some sort because he seemed to be reading. He also seemed to be getting alarmed. He looked up at me with what looked like panic flashing across his features.

"There has been a change," he said in a strangely wooden tone, less commanding than before but still dripping with authority. He was reading what he was saying to me. "You have many valid questions," he read, "and they will all be answered." His tone was wooden. It was as if *he* was obeying orders.

I didn't say anything. My ability to make sense of this had long since disappeared. He continued to read, not even trying to disguise it. "Someone will meet you tomorrow at this time. He will be sitting at the table partially under the stairs at the Garryowen pub, the one you mentioned to Philo. Do not say anything about this meeting or about Philo to anyone or the meeting will be cancelled. Do you understand?"

He looked up at me with a blank, military expression.

"Will Philo be there?"

"He will not." He did not read this. He walked to the door and opened it, indicating it was time for me to leave.

"I want to see Philo," I said. "I need to see Philo. How can I do so? Can you help me?"

"Listen," he said coldly, "you cannot." I had just stepped through the door. "But look on the bright side. At least you get to do your act a little longer."

"Why can't I see Philo?" I pleaded.

"Philo has been terminated."

He said this coldly and without any emotion.

And then the door clicked efficiently shut behind me.

CHAPTER 64

THE NEW GUY ISN'T VERY NICE

I could not have imagined that things could get worse, but the sudden news of Philo's death utterly unhinged me. I cried all the way home. What had just happened in that room was completely bizarre, but the stunning revelation of Philo's death, which must have happened while I was in that strange room with that strange guy, completely trumped every other consideration. I could think of nothing else.

That night and the day of waiting passed strangely. I was grieving, exceedingly upset, and totally unable to do anything, of course. My suffering was made all the worse because in addition to grieving for Philo, I also felt a bedeviling sense of responsibility for his death. I kept thinking that whatever had led to his death had to be my fault in some way. I didn't know how my behavior and his death were connected, but that did not keep me from having a lurking feeling that they were related and that I somehow inadvertently triggered something that had led directly to his death.

I also speculated that perhaps Philo knew my outburst would trigger something calamitous, and that is why he got so upset himself. That is, perhaps he knew my behavior was running the risk of prompting a dire blowback, and so his subsequent anger, which at the time had struck me as completely out of character for him, was the result of that. Perhaps he was trying to save himself by stopping me!

But then why would he have agreed to meet me the next day? Assuming he wasn't flat out lying to me, which doesn't fit my experience of him at all, he must have expected to still be alive. As best as I could recall, his abrupt departure struck me at the time as a bit uncalled for, but I accepted it as an opportunity for the two of us to calm down.

But also, wholly apart from these guilt-driven speculations of mine, this entire situation was so weird that in spite of feeling shocked grief, I was finding it difficult to relate to it all emotionally. There was no community here. No one I knew had any knowledge of Philo, so I had no one I could talk to about this. Also, the whole series of conversations were just floating in my memory like an ungrounded fantasy. Indeed, there were moments where the entire episode, from the thrill of our first meeting to the shock of his death—all of this just seemed to float a little above reality, like a blurred but complete memory of a movie seen long ago. In fact, the state of my mind was such that if I did not have my notes, I might have questioned whether any of this had actually happened.

Then strong feelings of loss and grief would flood back in, trumping all of my thoughts with mute pain and insistent grief.

I was cycling through so many different and even contradictory thoughts and feelings, all of which were manifesting with the walloping impact of great intensity, that I had difficulty sometimes even identifying what I was feeling. I was feeling so many things, and they were all tugging at each other. And, of course, topping it all off and abiding through this emotional turbulence were the three pillars of misery—a sense of loss, a sense of guilt, and a sense of fear.

And if that were not enough, hovering above all of that was the emotional impact of the dreary realization that I would never see Philo again. My sense of loss over not seeing him any more served as the skeleton of the entire body of my suffering. My recent flare-up aside, I liked Philo a lot and missed him more than I might have thought I would. He was my friend and partner in philosophy. He had helped me tremendously and I am today a more evolved, more aware person than I was when I first met him. Under his influence I had developed my awareness and intuitive sensitivity and cultivated a grounded confidence in my instincts that extended their range and impact. Simply put, thanks entirely to him, I had evolved my being.

And relative to how he had helped me to evolve my being, it wasn't that he gave me steps to follow and told me what to do or even that he gave me esoteric information that wowed me. It was that he consistently validated and reinforced my deeper instincts, making it easier for me to identify them and lean into them. He gave me confidence, but not by delivering pep talks and telling me I could do it. He wasn't trying to make me feel good. He gave me confidence by gently validating and supporting those insights and aspirations of mine that were leading me to evolve, which at the time were only partially identified by me and expressed tentatively at best. In the process I had developed and nurtured capacities and abilities I had not previously suspected but which now I could not help but acknowledge.

Even in my grief-stricken state in which these new abilities were covered over in grief and functionally inoperative, I was fully aware that I had benefitted from Philo's tutelage.

I kept remembering insightful things he had said. As soon as I got home I had consulted my notes, more for grounding and validation that the conversations had really happened than to find anything in particular.

But I did find this one nugget. He had once observed that even though most Americans valued confidence and tried to cultivate it, very few of those seeking to be able to act confidently understood what confidence really was. "They try to be confident without knowing what confidence is," he had said.

As usual, I did not understand his point, so he brought my attention to the word itself. He pointed out that the two Latin-derived components of the compound word 'confidence'—*con* and *fides*—actually clarify what, properly understood, it really means to be and act with confidence. In Latin 'con' is a preposition that means 'with.' Conjoined with 'fides,' which means 'trust' or 'faith,' the combination suggest that doing something confidently means doing it with trust in oneself and faith one will be able to accomplish it. It does not mean adopting a certain attitude or becoming willful and pushy, dismissing objections.

Recalling this, I rummaged through my notes and found what he had said. His exact words were, "To act with confidence means to act with deep, spontaneous trust. Such a thing is rare because it involves a highly evolved state of mind."

I had forgotten the next part, but he had gone on to add, "Now here is a thing about your caged up Zoo culture. You cheapen the presence and activity of proper confidence by thinking of it as an attitude one can adopt. This is a shockingly shallow understanding of what acting confidently means. To be confident is to act out of an advanced state of consciousness, not just to adopt an attitude. It is to implicitly and deeply trust one's self, whether to sing, to dance, to self examine, or to speak in front of reporters. You can't just *be* confident any more than you can just *be* a piano player. Confidence is not about performance but about presence, the living presence of the real you. It is something that has to be nurtured and developed, and while it is possible to fool others, it is not the sort of thing that can be faked. And its appearance, even after long and patient practice and training, is quite a significant accomplishment."

I started crying reading this. Clearly I was now much more confident as a result of the time I had spent with Philo. But that recognition, which caused great pain when I considered he was now gone and I would never see him again, also led me to feel totally stupid that I did not take better advantage of the time we spent together.

In addition to my grief and despair there was also the nutty puzzle of what was now happening. Was Philo *really* an alien? How about the boss guy in his safe room? There was nothing definitive to prove it either way. For example, was that guy identifying me as 'production' proof of something authentically alien? No! If this were a massive ruse, then that would merely be part of the ruse—and a most simple one at that.

How about the times I had a bizarre and somewhat paranoid feeling that our conversations were being taped. Why would I have that feeling? Perhaps it was because they *were* being taped and I could somehow tell on a subliminal level. And so would this prove the alien hypothesis? Again, no. While aliens may exist and might even tape conversations, the fact that a conversation has been recorded does not in itself prove that aliens did it. Whether or not aliens exist and tape conversations, I know for certain that human beings exist and do tape conversations.

But why would humans want to tape Philo and me? Maybe they were trying to demonstrate how gullible and easily deluded people are, including especially highly educated people. Perhaps I was prime exhibit number one.

What about that secret alien room? Did that room prove alien existence? Again, it did not. It was just an empty room, albeit set up brilliantly to suggest evacuation. Nothing particularly alien about that. It certainly did look like it had just been emptied out, but that of course is the easiest possible way to decorate something to suggest an alien presence. True, the dangling wires seemed strange and their connections appeared different from anything I had seen before. But what did I know about connections? Faking me on something like that would be quite easy, especially since I am not a techie myself and am unfamiliar with the state of the art in such things.

In my mind all of these considerations kept leading to the other dark regret I was struggling with. I mean, other than what Philo and I talked about—and almost none of it was about him personally—I knew almost nothing about him. How could we have talked so long and so productively and yet I knew nothing about him? I kept imagining being on Oprah to talk about my time with Philo. In my vision, that kept replaying in my mind as I felt this regret, the show would start with some polite opening applause. Then the mood would change dramatically as person after person in the audience would stand and ask with mounting anger, "But didn't you ask him this obvious thing . . . or that one . . . or this other obvious thing?" I see them all astounded at the fact I did not, collectively expressing dismay, disbelief, disappointment, and then fury. My vision would end with legions of them standing up to shout at me, sharp edges of anger in their voices, "How could you not ask him any of these things?"

But it is more than that. I didn't know any personal things about Philo the person. But I also didn't know any of the impersonal things. I didn't know how he moved about. I didn't know where he went when he left. I didn't even know if he went anywhere. For all I knew, he might have beamed back to his planet when he departed from me. Or he might have hibernated. Or it might be—and this was always a recurring fear of mine—that this was the mother of all practical jokes.

The point is that I knew so little it was embarrassing. I felt humiliated! How could I have carried on these conversations on the assumption that he was an alien from another planet without at least asking about *some* of these things? It made me look like—and I certainly now felt like—a gullible village idiot. Being confident is all good and fine, but being an idiot is a dire failing!

And then, to cycle back to the present, there was the fact that this strange guy in the so-called safe room knew about the table under the stairs—or at least whoever it was who messaged him knew. That is weird! No, it is revealing! Someone obviously did know, so the question was, 'How did that person know?' It was not the sort of thing that was likely to have been mentioned. And even if the person had been eavesdropping on our conversation in the safe room, how did he know about the table under the stairs? Then I had a sudden thought—perhaps it was Philo who messaged him? Could it be Philo is alive and was talking to that person? Or could it be he was trying to talk to me in code, the reference to that table under the stairs being something that only he and I would know about? If so, then maybe it will be Philo who is going to meet me at the table?

Thinking helped me to feel better, but since it was only speculation, I could not accept my thoughts as true. Since the message sender obviously *did* know about the table, whether it was Philo or someone else, the fact of that knowing tells me there are other facts to be discovered here. It was another piece of a puzzle that so far has made absolutely no sense at all. This is because none of the pieces seemed to fit together.

And then there was the Hippy thing. Philo a hippy? A hippy and not a philosopher? Not a spoiled brat . . . or a brave intergalactic traveler . . . or a criminal planet hopper? Not any of this but a hippy! That was weird. I mean, if these guys really were alien, they clearly are not dummies when it comes to Earth culture. Philo himself was certainly very savvy. He might have been a bit strange, but he passed in public as one of us—nondescript and plain, but essentially normal.

Also, there was Philo's behavior towards the end when he had been undergoing dramatic mood and attitude changes. What did that mean, and what did it indicate? Again, like all of the other evidence, it could mean almost anything. It was a fill-in-the-blank situation. Through the greater part of the conversations lasting months and right up until the last few weeks, Philo had been emotionally even. In the last few weeks, however, he had alternated bi-polar fashion between a sort of depressed anxiety and a manic relief. What did that bi-polar shifting back and forth mean? Did it indicate that something was going wrong in alien reality, something that was freaking him out as it was happening and which ultimately resulted in his death? Perhaps. But maybe he was acting. Maybe this was part of the set-up, part of the ruse.

However I looked at it, whichever part I picked to examine, whatever I thought about it, no matter how I analyzed it, everything always came back to 'maybe.' There was nothing definitive. Lots of strong indications, to be sure, but none of them were definitive. All of them could be taken differently. Maybe aliens. Maybe not.

And now, after an evening, night, and day of grieving, here I was stepping up the front stairs into Garryowen for the promised meeting. Even as I walked into the bar, I was feeling a little stupid. I mean, what possible reason would I have to think that anybody alien—or anybody at all—would be here? I had a faint hope that Philo would be here, but not enough of a hope that I was not still tearing up at reminders of him. Maybe the guy yesterday was just cleverly putting me off, faking a text message? But why would he do that? He could have just kicked me out, so why this ruse? Maybe he was setting me up for the ultimate display of gullibility, my real grieving over a non-existent alien's not real demise.

I was feeling shame and disappointment over my own apparent limitless gullibility when I saw someone sitting at the table under the stairs. It was not Philo, but he certainly had that non-descript look!

CHAPTER 65

HE IS MEAN AND INSULTING TO ME

I walked up silently and began to pull out a chair. As I was doing so, I could see clearly that it was not the guy I had spoken to yesterday, though he certainly looked a lot like him in an unspecific, non-descript way.

Normally I would not have walked uninvited to sit at a table a stranger was already occupying, even after the invitation yesterday. After all, I wasn't sure the invitation was authentic, not to mention that this guy might just be a normal customer who did not have any striking features, either in dress or physical features, and who just happened to be sitting there with absolutely nothing to do with any of this. But I did not feel that sense of quick panic that comes when one suddenly realizes one might be making a social mistake. Without thinking or considering the situation, I instinctively acted as if he was here to talk to me. I guess you could say I was confident— in Philo's sense of the term—that I was acting appropriately.

Whatever doubt there may have been was dispelled when he spoke first.

"I know you have a lot of questions. Believe me, I *know* that. I can even anticipate your questions. Here is the thing. This is a crisis situation and we have limited time, so we need to be efficient with it. I am going to make a statement. My statement will answer a lot of your questions. I want you to listen without interrupting. I won't repeat it. When I am done, you can ask me a few questions. I won't have much time, so be very thoughtful with your questions. In fact, I would strongly counsel you that since our time is so limited, you need to be very wise with your questions. I strongly recommend that you avoid the 'who-gives-a-shit' philosophy type of questions you are always going to. Do you understand?"

My mind was spinning again. He was insulting me, but to what end? Why even come here if he is going to be so uncivil. Still spinning, I blurted out, "But Philo was a philosopher." I had intended to ask him about the funeral arrangements, but he had taken charge and this is what I said in response.

He gave me a mocking look, smirking down at me from a perch higher than mine. "Yes, I suppose Philo *is* a philosopher," he said airily, inexplicably emphasizing the present tense of the verb. "But then again, so are you. And so am I. And so is everyone! After all, anyone can look up at the stars and pontificate. But can we bank on it? Does it pay the bills? Do the crops get harvested because of it? Does it extend the light of what we know and thus illuminate the dark caverns of what we do not know?"

"But you are giving voice to a vulgar and shallow understanding of philosophy," I protested.

"And you," he said, interrupting me, "have just started to waste time on the very bullshit I am trying to caution you against. Now be a good boy and listen to my statement and then you can ask what you will."

He said this unemotionally. It was as if he was telling his servants what he wanted them to do. There was no emotional charge, just the assumption of direction and the assertion of control. "I will begin now," he said.

At that moment, just as he was starting his statement, it sank in that it was not Philo that had sent the message about the table. My mood had lifted ever so slightly seeing this guy sitting at the table, but now it started to plunge again into the depths of mute pain as I started to wonder how he knew about this table under the stairs. I had only discussed the table with Philo privately, so how did he know about it? Without actually intending to, I found myself blurting out, "So how did you know about this table under the stairs?"

He looked at me blankly for a few seconds. "I am going to ignore that question," he finally said. After another menacing pause he added, "I do this on your behalf. We are wasting time even now. You will soon see that the question is not important. Just trust me on that. Now, would you like to squander any more of your time by interrupting me with pointless questions?"

"No," I answered meekly.

He stared me down with a dismissive glare and then continued. "Referencing your conversations with Philo, he had been trying to explain to you that the miniscule numbers of the intergalactic elite, the ones who shape the social and political topology of the cosmos, are *afraid* of humanity. They see Earth as a potential revolutionary hotbed, a flash point that could explode and change the entire universe."

This sounded completely off to me. Even given the real existence of an intergalactic context, I could not see this at all. An intergalactic civilization with space travel scared of us humans? How ridiculous. I mean, if there are aliens and they can fly all the way to Earth when we don't even know they exist, then it is pretty obvious that their bombs are going to be bigger than our bombs. It is as simple as that. Before I could say anything, however, he continued.

"Philo was having some trouble getting you to see this. You kept referencing how 'screwed up,' as you put it, things were on Earth. Over and over you would point to pollution, growing inequality, loss of privacy, legalized state murder, rampant and growing police brutality, massive food insecurity, the ongoing material deprivation of billions of people around the globe, the loss of an independent media, the ever widening corruption of culture and concomitant decline of standards in all of your institutions, not just in schools.

On and on you would go. It got tedious. Obviously you just weren't getting it."

"I still don't."

He looked at me in the most condescending way possible. It was as if I was a potentially irksome flea and he was deciding whether it was worth the effort to swat me. He shook his head lightly from side to side while scrunching his lips, suggesting it was taking a lot on his part just to bother to talk to me. I thought he might just call it quits right then and there. But he took a breath and, with a hint of stoic weariness, continued, "Your objections were not factually incorrect. You were not wrong in your descriptions. Your questions and concerns needed to be acknowledged and addressed. Truly, how *does* a new cosmic light, something that literally transforms the universe, come out of the mess that is humanity?"

"Exactly," I said, feeling validated.

"It doesn't, obviously," he said flatly. "That should be obvious. There is not much that could come out of such a sorry swamp of a cesspool." He said this with a blank expression.

"I'm lost," I said. "This is the point at which I lose it."

"I know," he replied, "and if you will stop interrupting me, I will explain it to you." He seemed really disappointed in me. "It is decidedly and definitively *not* all those bad things you continually pointed out that constitute the magnificence of humanity. Yet again and again and again you would point them out, as if you were announcing something epic in its importance. At first it was good to get those things on the table. You could even say that was your anticipated function at first. But it soon got tedious. Everyone watching had long since gotten the point that it is not the things you kept complaining about that held the potential to alter the universe—everyone, that is, except you. So at some point your continuing to blather about those things was just a waste of valuable airtime. It was like a comedian telling the same funny joke over and over. The joke starts off as hilarious, but pretty soon the joke is not funny anymore and the comedian gets yanked."

"I don't accept that," I interrupted. "Philo and I were two philosophers carrying on a leisurely series of conversations. Why this attack on the free and relaxed spirit of our talks?"

He stopped me short with a cutting look. I felt slashed. After pausing (as if to let me bleed?) he continued. "Let's try it one more time just for old time's sake." He said this with a sort of viciousness. "All those bad things about Earth culture you mention over and over are perversions. They are perversions of humanity and they are corruptions of culture. Instead of going on in such a provincial way about it, let the truth of that sink in. They are *perversions*. Instead of continuing to try to convince Fox News, you need to stop. You needed to stop with Philo so the show could move on."

He glared at me. I couldn't focus on what he was saying very well because of his bullying forcefulness. He was over the top. His uncharitable impatience was not philosophical in the slightest. I missed Philo. Plus, how did he know all of this stuff he was saying about me? How did he know what I said to Philo? And what is this reference to airtime and viewers? It was a poor metaphor if you ask me. And who was this guy?

"What *will* change the universe, John," he continued, "is what is beneath those perversions. It is what those things are perversions of! Think about it. A perversion means something is being perverted. The perverted thing is not the thing; it is the thing that has been perverted. And Philo was doing his best to help you to see that the thing being perverted is humanity, and that beneath the perversions is something amazing, something that holds the capacity to change the universe."

"But so many humans are stupid and selfish," I said, much like I would with Philo.

He looked like I had slapped him—in public.

He took a breath, seeming to need to calm himself. Then he seemed to change his approach. Adopting a slightly less hostile posture but still dripping with condescension, he continued. "I want you to grasp this, but like others tell me, there is only so much you can get a primitive to see. I feel like a person trying to get a goldfish to grasp that he is swimming in a fishbowl. I shouldn't feel such disappointment when the goldfish fails to see." Then, brightening ever so slightly, he added, "But we keep trying."

"Thanks," I said, feeling stupid for saying so.

"Consider exhibit number one, your typical human being." He said this in a dry, clinical tone, as if he were a physician describing a broken bone. "Your typical human being labors under some deep restrictions, most of which he or she is utterly unaware of. First, she is not anything like who she thinks she is. Her culture provides her with a number of distorted thought pictures—everything from her being nothing but a smart, sexed up animal to being that animal with a completely detachable soul that, depending on what the animal does, will survive Earth life to be tortured for all of eternity by a God of perfect love as a punishment for letting the animal host act like one."

He paused for effect. I did not say anything.

"Second," he continued, "the world is not at all like what this human thinks it is, even when she is schooled in the latest and most advanced of the hard sciences. Almost all humans take one of the two signature human creations, science and religion, as reality itself, thus diminishing the capacity of either to illuminate. Neither science nor religion is reality, of course. They are pictures of reality—maps as some of you put it. But taking the map for the territory, which almost all of you always do, means that almost all humans live embedded in fantasy pictures."

He looked threateningly at me and added, "Do not interrupt." After a brief pause he resumed, "Third, even though humans do not know reality directly but can only picture it, whether through their senses or the ingenious mechanical devices they create, they have to live and act as if they do know reality. This is stressful. And finally, circumstances are changing all around humanity faster than they can cognize and certainly faster than they can keep up with. This, too, is stressful and it is what leads so many of you to hunker down in the past, whether it is your petty personal past or that of your culture."

Just then our waitress showed up.

CHAPTER 66

BACK TO HUMANITY'S CAGE

The distraction of the arrival of the waitress came at the perfect time. It only took a few moments to clarify our order, but I noticed that this new guy, whose name I didn't even know, was wooden with her. I had seen Philo interact with people while we were sitting together. He was always smooth—good enough not to stand out, but not so good that he did stand out. This guy was different. Even when he talked he was like a statue. He was so wooden that he could easily be remembered as such. Clearly he was no Philo.

The waitress left, none the wiser about us, and he returned to our conversation.

"So we were right in the middle of my pointing out the objective circumstances of humanity, how both humanity and the universe are different than what you humans think and pretend it is. I was doing this to counter your own tediously repeated claim that humanity is stupid and selfish when, in a beautiful touch of irony, we were interrupted in accordance with this primitive Earth system of servitude, making someone serve us for a pittance. It is primitive. Nothing against the dear girl, but how blind, sick, and distorted a culture has to be to institute such a practice. In spite of her best and most highly motivated 'service,' I wager good odds that she is still struggling economically."

He was right about our waitress of course, but I didn't know what to say regarding his 'defense' of humanity. It sounded more like a savage attack on humanity to me, closer to what I had been saying all along than the opposite he seemed to think it was. But I had

391

trouble saying anything because, as I was listening to him overwhelm me, I kept missing Philo.

Philo would take things in small steps and bite-sized lumps, letting me assimilate each part. This guy is the opposite. He lays it all out at once, so much so that I could not assimilate what he was saying. Instead of feeling illuminated as I did with Philo, I felt stunned and stupefied listening to him. And even though he said he was defending humanity, I felt put down and insulted. The result was that I did not have anything to say about what he was saying. Instead, I kept thinking how I had so often complained to Philo about what I perceived at the time as his ridiculously slow pace.

But on top of all that, I thought that, if anything, what he was saying totally supported my point about humanity's failings. Before I could say that, however, he continued.

"Here I am, blathering on pointlessly just like you. You must be corrupting me, making me native." He looked at me with a hint of a sparkle in his eyes. It was not much of a sparkle, coming as it did on the backend of an insult, but it was our closest moment yet.

He returned to what I was saying when our server had showed up. "So before we were interrupted, you were giving voice to the prevalent idea among you humans that humanity is by nature selfish. Of course, except for those few at the top, who are indeed openly, brazenly, and successfully selfish, garnering to themselves as much of what is available as they can, most of you humans are only selfish in small, restricted ways, usually at the expense of those closest to you, those it is the easiest for you to take advantage of without consequences."

I was doing my best to listen to his statement and not interrupt.

"In fact," he continued analytically, "I find it nothing short of fiendish the way you humans can say that it is human nature to be selfish and then claim yourself to be an exception to that natural quality on the basis of one's personal morality."

392

He fixed a stare on me and said, "This is really devilish, so try to follow along here." I nodded warily.

"Note that you humans will rarely make your claim to personal superiority on the grounds that you are above nature and thus are *not* selfish. Instead, you accept that you *are* selfish because, as you have been culturally constructed to assume, humanity is by nature selfish and you, after all, are only natural. So you do not generally deny what you think of as your nature. Instead, you establish your conceit on the basis that your morality makes you better than those other naturally selfish bums, especially those at the top, who lack your morality. This is ingenious in a wicked sort of way. It enables you to give yourself moral credit at the specific moment you are acting in a way your morality specifically condemns. That, my friend, is a human quality that stands out not only for its brazen hypocrisy but also for its incredibly clever disguise. But I need not linger."

"I can see this myself, and have even complained about it," I replied. "You act like I am wrong to find fault with humanity and that you are disagreeing with me about it, but everything you say just repeats what I am saying. Like you, I see hypocrisy and selfishness all around. But unlike you, I have trouble believing in heroic human goodness rising up out of this cesspool of selfishness and hypocrisy to save the universe. I want to believe it, but where is the evidence of the goodness?"

The guy looked disgusted at me. Shaking his head in sorrow, he replied, "I hear you mouth these words and I feel sad to note this expression of your deep programming." He sighed, fully accepting the sad fact as he had stated it. "As I am trying to explain," he continued wearily, "there is something beneath all these carefully constructed perversions. Let's try a different approach. Let me ask you, can you imagine a better world?"

It took a second before I realized he was waiting for an answer.

"Yes," I said hurriedly.

"Then, please, at my request, actually imagine such a world. I'm asking you to take a few moments and actually *imagine* that better world."

It was a very strange request. However, one of the things I had learned from Philo—and he had often asked me to imagine things—is that to imagine something is not just to think about it. And it isn't primarily to picture it, though that is what most people do. It is to use all of one's senses actually to put oneself into all of the sensory and cognitive modalities of the imagined scenario. It is to feel the air, to smell the breeze, to look at the buildings, to feel the vibe on the streets, to note the mood of the people. It is a comprehensive mental experience involving many modalities. Philo had said that if one did this fully multi-modally, it would be like completing a crossword puzzle—that is, when one got enough of the letters filled in, one could suddenly start to fill in words one did not even recognize. So I took the time to imagine a world of people living on purpose, people who knew they were part of a supportive whole—even as they endeavored and felt encouraged to individuate on their own terms. It felt good imagining this. I filled in lots of details.

"That's good," the guy said, almost seeming pleased "I can see for myself how good it feels for you."

"Sort of like masturbation," I said.

A strained silence followed, as if I had interrupted the Pope to insult him. Then he started chuckling, but not in merriment. "You can be such a provincial Earth fool," he said. I just demonstrated to you the power that can change the universe, the very power that led the intergalactic elite of yore to fear you and put you in your sorry cages. And in the context of that revelation you liken the cosmic magnificence of your potential to masturbation."

"I guess I missed the demonstration," I replied, ignoring his attitude and insult.

"You are the demonstration," he said sharply, raising his voice. Then he leaned back wearily and, after a brief moment of silence, said, "Imagine that," smiling to himself as if he made just made a clever private joke.

He was being rude and insulting, but something in me tingled regarding what he was saying. Pretty clearly, any human can imagine something different than what is. We can imagine pigs that fly, airplanes that swim, and fish that oink. In our imaginations we are not bound to 'what is.'

But this is still not the cosmic power of imagination that the Romantics embraced and advocated. Instead, it is the impoverished understanding of imagination first articulated by John Locke. He famously described imagination as the power to take what we experience—oinking pigs, flying airplanes, and swimming fishes—and then recombine the qualities of what we can already picture. So we can imagine pigs that fly, airplanes that swim, and fish that oink but not, Locke assured us, anything that has not already been revealed to our senses. In this limited view, imagination can only rearrange our sensory experiences. It can't give us a new experience, one that transcends our senses.

This is pretty much the dominant view these days. The minor view, associated especially with the Plato, certain strands of Medieval thought, and Romanticism, harmonized with what Philo had been emphasizing to me and what this guy was now saying—namely, that imagination is more than simply the capacity to recombine what we have already experienced, merely involving the remixing of previously sensed qualities. Contrary to this is the notion of the Romantics that imagination is a strong and penetrating power that can extend our sensibility to where our senses are not able to go. That is, we can expand our actual knowledge by means of our imagination.

I still did not say anything, however.

"Now that we have clearly established your ability to imagine," he continued, "I want you to imagine something else."

He had said this with a pompous tone. He seemed to know what Philo knew, but his attitude was totally different. I was really missing Philo, and not just for his kindness and patience.

"So imagine for me the following world. It is a world populated by a creature that is quite unlike anything else in existence. When this creature showed up suddenly and unexpectedly on a backwater planet, the masters of civilized outer space, correctly noting the creature's awesome potential, reacted like the Titans did when they first observed the splendid powers of the Olympians. That is, the rulers did not take delight in the potential capacities of this new creature; instead, they felt threatened by the potential future impact of those very capacities. They thus began to fear the creatures as potential future rivals. Taking counsel, they decided to imprison this creature of great potential to prevent it from ever reaching that potential. Cleverly, they made cages that seemed so entirely natural that being imprisoned in them would seem entirely natural, just like having a nose or a foot. So all the creatures were caged. Some of the creatures complained, but to the greater number of them, those complaints were ridiculous. To the majority, it sounded like these few were complaining about having arms instead of wings and toes instead of propellers. They mocked the few who complained about their cages, and it became established in human culture that complaining about what was called the human condition was a sign of immaturity and a lack of seriousness."

"It sounds pretty accurate," I said.

"No interruption," he snapped back. "Now these early creatures, knowing only their cages, then developed religious rationalizations regarding the cage. Most creatures were taught that the cage—that is to say, the human condition—is a punishment by God and that, if they were fully obedient to the zookeeper, they would be rewarded when they died by being released. Others were taught that the cage is nothing more than an illusion and that they would ultimately find freedom by being obedient boys and girls who cultivated acceptance and even contentment about being confined to the cage. 'God is just,' such people learned to say."

He stared menacingly at me for a moment. Since I did not say anything, he continued. "Of course, the tough-minded rejected these religious rationalizations. For their part, they said everyone lives, rots, and dies in the cage. That is just the way it is. There is no liberation, not even in death! Others who are not as tough—and this is the most recent rationalization—puff up with smiles and claim there is actually not a cage at all and that we only feel imprisoned because we fantasize about how things could be instead of living in reality. In other words, once again, the cage is not really a cage. It is just the way things are."

He looked disgusted. "So many rationalizations and so many people fighting with each other from inside their cages about which rationalization is the 'truth.' It's a sorry mess, really." He looked directly at me. "Can you imagine that," he said, but it was not a question.

I still did not say anything, but he did not seem to be expecting me to. "Now what a lot of us were hoping you would finally ask Philo is something of a technical point. You see, you were told that humanity had been confined to a cage throughout most of its existence with no record of anyone ever not being in one. You seemed to accept that. You were also informed that humanity is shaped and saturated by a culture that tells them constantly that the cage is natural and, in fact, isn't even a cage. It is just the way things were, like clouds in the sky. You seemed to accept that as well. So the technical point we were hoping you would inquire about is how, given such massive cultural indoctrination, your species could ever come to grasp that they were in a cage in the first place?" He paused to let that sink in, staring at me the whole time. When I didn't say anything, he added forcefully, "This is an exceedingly important point."

I felt slapped. "They can't," I said weakly, "if that is all they have ever known."

"But they can. You just did it! Don't be so blind. Pay attention."

This guy was tedious to the max, but it seemed like he might be on to something. I was trying to get it.

"So let's continue," he said. "If one needs empirical evidence of the existence of this cage before being able to admit to its existence, then one will always be confined in the cage. Always. Any attempt to call attention to the cage would be received like someone pointing to his own arm as evidence that a cosmic rope is keeping him tied up. That is, it would make absolutely no sense and the assertion of it would be taken as evidence of mental dysfunction."

I asked, "So what is humanity to do to free itself?"

He looked exasperated. "Are you listening? Do you understand your own language? I am going to say to you again, this is where imagination comes in! *Someone* has to be able to walk out of the cage and then turn and look and see it. But since no one can actually do so, someone has to *imagine* doing so. Again, the power of imagination is the cosmos altering power that so threatened the elite rulers back then that they responded by putting humanity in cages in the first place. As crazy as it might seem to you, all of the power and capacity to consciously change and evolve the world is contained in the simple two letter word, 'if.' This tiny word betokens the miraculous power of the counter-factual. So it turns out that the thing that got you humans imprisoned in the first place is the thing that is your liberation. If only you could see this. If only you could have *imagined* it and understood Philo when he tried repeatedly to explain it to you."

He stopped and fixed me with a stare. "Even now, I wish you could understand what I am saying."

"I think I see it now," I said. "Imagination is liberation."

"I'm on a deeper level!" he barked back at me. "I accept you don't have much of an idea of what I mean when I say anything is possible with the human. What you will immediately think of is a human agent with amazing powers, sort of like one of your imaginary superheroes."

A thought finally came to me. "But surely humans are not the only creatures with the ability to imagine. Certainly Philo had it. And for all I know, you might as well!" I said this as a dig against him. It was not much, but I was being overwhelmed and it was the best I could do.

"That is true," he replied with a hint of a smile. I had the feeling he got my dig and appreciated it somewhat. "But no one in all of known existence has the power and capacity of imagination that humans do. I remember you were freaked out when Philo told you about the purchase of Earth. Yes, there is a fortune in minerals here. But let's talk about the most valuable treasure. It's not minerals. They are certainly valuable, but they are not the most valuable thing on your planet. That honor goes to human art. The art you humans make is unparalleled in the entire universe. It is the closest thing to the creative power that imagined reality into existence that has ever been recorded.

"So imagination really is liberation," I repeated, feeling clever.

"Stop playing with this. Try to feel the scope and gravity of what I am saying. I am talking about the future of the entire universe!"

I was chastened, but I had no idea what he was trying to get me to see.

"The human gift of imagination is not a matter of an individual with an agenda. I am not talking about knights and cowboys using their imaginations to make plans to capture castles and rob banks.

The access to larger openings provided by imagination can allow a human, more so than any other species or creature in the universe, to recognize, open to, and align with the deepest energy flow of existence itself."

"This is very deep," I said, trying to be conciliatory.

"You are an idiot," he shot back. "I can't get into theology right now, but it is by means of imagination that the human can become the agent of that cosmic force religious humans call 'God' and scientific ones call 'evolution.' This force is not a toga-clad guy sitting somewhere in the sky and rooting for the Cowboys in football and your country in foreign affairs, and it is not a blind force working through the competition of the fittest to survive. To summon it up in a phrase, this cosmic force is the ground layer of being. I won't say any more than that, but the point is that the human can align with it more perfectly than any other species—and not only that, they can do so by many more magnitudes of precision than other species. Humanity is thus capable of becoming agents of the universe itself, tools of the very forces that brought the universe into existence in the first place."

I must have looked really uncomprehending because he shifted focus. "So blah-blah all you want about the cage, the only thing that matters at this point is liberation from it."

"How is that done?" I asked.

He smiled ever so slightly, "That is your first real question, and it is not a wasted one."

"Are we back to talking about the 'key?'" I asked.

He gave me a look that would cut through steel. "We have never once stopped talking about it," he said, and none too kindly.

"Then let's get on with it," I said, doing my best to sound none too kindly myself.

CHAPTER 67

THE NEW GUY LEVELS WITH ME, SORTA

A t that point the tone of our conversation changed. He stopped being so vicious and started to seem to try to help me. In fact at that very moment I caught him looking at me sort of like a game show host who was poised to ask the contestant the question worth a million dollars.

"You are able to imagine that humanity is trapped in cages," he said with a smile. "That is good. It is a significant and completely essential requirement. Most humans cannot. You can also imagine, as you did earlier, what life out of the cage might be like. That is also good. But the question then comes up that if you, and indeed many others, are able to imagine the existence of the cage and life outside of it, why are you all still caged up?"

I was thrilled to hear him say this. That question of why we are still caged *does* come up. It had come up repeatedly in my conversations with Philo, but he never seemed to be willing to answer it directly. We were always just getting to it. But this guy was totally right: that is the only question that matters at this point. I felt vindicated hearing him say this and significantly more open to what he might say next as a result.

He continued. "Now this seems like a puzzle but it is not. The cage makers are very sophisticated. And the cage is very much what you would call high-tech, though of course it is high-tech in a psychological way rather than in a mechanical way. Part of what makes the cage so effective is that it functions in the depths of the mind, well below the level of ordinary awareness, to limit the range and cognitive possibilities of imagination."

"But I can imagine anything," I said. "I can even imagine you picking up some minimal manners and acting a little less horribly."

He laughed good naturedly at that. "Point well taken," he said, "but your example is not accepted." He chuckled again, this time more to himself. "The thing is, you see, that this psychically engineered limitation of imagination is not in the area of what you can imagine. You are right to say you can imagine anything. You certainly can. I would even wager that you could imagine a person in my shoes, dealing as he is with the hopes of the entire universe and facing the possibility of a most dire setback, might act brusquely and with minimal manners in certain circumstances. In a desperate life and death situation, any sensible patient should be willing to overlook the rough bedside manner of the harried, over-booked surgeon who was trying save him. But moving on . . . ."

I nodded at his clever rejoinder.

"No, John," he continued. "The limitation on imagination is not in the area of *what* you can imagine. It is in the area of *how* you imagine things. You have been set up and programmed to think of imagination and art as 'fancy,' as something someone is just making up. Sadly, you no longer have a sense that imagination, properly understood, cultivated, and developed, is a non-empirical way of accessing a larger reality. Note carefully that among humanity of all types, if a person says he has thought deeply about a thing, his words will have more power than if he said that he had sat down and imagined how things would turn out."

Hearing this stunning claim—that imagination is a non-empirical way of accessing a larger reality—I would not say my own mind immediately balked. It did however seem to go blank. I felt like a young child in Iowa being told about the ocean for the first time. "But wouldn't any larger, non-empirical reality we merely imagined just be something we imagined? I mean, I can imagine a forest full of unicorns." This seemed like a sensible question to me.

He looked at me, but not unkindly. "Thank you for that perfect live demonstration of how imagination is limited. What you just demonstrated is the *limitation* of imagination, not the *power* of it. You imagined something not real to prove the point that imagination does not tell us about reality. That is a bit like someone drinking muddy water to demonstrate that coffee does not taste good!"

I sat uncomprehending.

"But enough of this," he continued, only now with an air of frustration. Unlike Philo, he obviously had no interest in exploring the side angles of his points. "Imagination," he went on, "is not a matter of looking, measuring, and counting. Nothing can be tied down with certainty in imagination. There are no certainties. In any imagined scenario the hazards of illusion, wishful thinking, and sheer pigheaded error stain every window, weaken every bridge, and wash out every road. Yet, in spite of this the possibility for far-seeing, expanded vision remains."

"That is beautifully put," I said, expecting him to slam me for distracting. Instead he smiled kindly.

"So it is," he said, looking up and to the right, as if he was noting the beauty of his words for the first time. He gathered himself and continued.

"It is a most dire and troubling development in Earth culture that you have come to think of art more as entertainment than as a revelation of truth. Art is now packaged, presented, and sold to you as entertainment. You *expect* to be entertained by art, and if you are not—well, it has now been established and accepted among you that it is a valid criticism of a work of art to say, 'I don't like it' or 'I didn't enjoy it.' How pathetic! Imagine if a mathematician rejected a bold new proof on the grounds that he did not like some of the numbers that were used in it or that he did not personally enjoy following the proof."

He seemed to catch himself and make an internal correction, continuing in a more pleasant tone, "No, don't bother imagining that. Let's continue instead."

I was beginning to warm to him. A little bit of niceness on his part went a long way with me. One of my mother's sayings floated through my awareness, that you can catch more flies with honey than with vinegar.

This guy was acting nicer now, but he still wasn't Philo. I missed Philo.

He continued. "Art now functions to make staying in the cage more pleasant and tolerable. And to a large degree it has been commercialized, turned into a product. It is now fully acceptable for people to use imagination to acquire things for themselves, cars and boats and stuff. Little wonder, then, that imagination no longer functions primarily as a liberator, breaking chains and shattering cages. People now look to it for entertainment, not liberation."

"How did this happen?" I asked, trying to sound anguished.

He dismissed my question. "Not important. Again, the only thing that matters is leaving the cage."

"But if we need imagination and art, and people think of art as entertainment, which they do, then what can we do?"

He looked disappointed again. "You don't need to 'do' anything. Look to your younger generations. They are increasingly different than the older generations. The older ones criticize them, but as far as getting inspiration from art, the younger ones are better. Even having grown up in a completely commercialized culture that has commodified everything for them, they are taking art and music and imagination way more seriously than the older generations. Video games especially, which many of you older ones complain about for taking away imagination, are really exercises in application of extreme imagination. It may not be utopian imagination at work, but what happens in the game is definitely not limited to the way the world is. What is imaginatively implemented in these games is generally far worse than ordinary, daily reality—and that is the point! Not that bad things are imagined—that is a sad perversion of the power of imagination—but that *different* things are imagined."

I was having trouble seeing video games as proving much of anything about the power of imagination. He saw this and clarified.

"Let's say imagination is a power to act outside of passively accepted confinements or, as you humans call it today, a box. I am giving an example here, not a definition. Let's further say a person has this power and uses it to make things ugly. The application of the power is small, but the power itself is not. It is like your unicorn example. You imagined a unicorn. It doesn't take much power of imagination to think up a unicorn. There you used your power in a small way. But you could also use your power of imagination in a large way. You could imagine a just world. You could imagine a world in which people came before profits. You could imagine a world in which sustainability mattered."

This was making sense to me, but before I could say anything he continued.

"What you have to grasp here," he said ominously, "is that the widespread misuse of imagination, using art to entertain rather than to liberate or reveal, does not tell us anything about the full range and scope of the power of it. Imagination, properly understood and expressed, is a power of the mind that is not tied to what is. The way this power is used by humans right now is pitifully small. But the power is there."

This was so different from how I normally thought about things that it was hard to assimilate. But it did make sense. This is probably why older people don't generally excel at video games. It isn't just that older people can't work the controller. It is that they can't imagine powerfully enough to take the imagined narrative seriously enough to stay engaged.

"How did all of this happen?" I asked.

"Again, not important. How do we end it? That is the only question that matters at this point." He said this with an air of complete finality.

"That's why Philo came here, isn't it, to help to liberate humanity?"

"Not at all," he replied. "It was a professional move on his part. And a brilliant professional move it was. He almost pulled it off. But what was behind this bold career endeavor of his was a genuine love of Earth music. In that sense, you could say he came for the music. In a larger sense, he also came out of his great love and appreciation for all things human."

I was suddenly sorrowing over his allusion to his death, the point about him almost pulling it off.

Noting a change in my demeanor, the guy tried to placate me. "You have probably noted that I don't share his enthusiasms, not all of them anyway. Never the less, we both understand the importance of humanity in the larger scheme of things. But being here changed him—from aesthete to revolutionary. He boldly took up the cause of humanity. He has a special affection for humanity—and for you, too, John. I guess you could say he wanted to be Earth's Lafayette, you know, the cultured outsider who risks all on your behalf. In fact, he got so into it that he was terminated."

I felt stabbed with agony. This reminder of Philo's death was just too painful. "Philo was terminated," I muttered, repeating the sad words. I felt tears rising up like a surfer on a massive wave of pain. It was like that brief moment when you have cut yourself deeply but before the pain hits and the blood gushes. Then the pain hits. I began to cry softly. "Who did it? This is terrible. We have to find them." Great waves of grief began to wash over me.

The guy looked at me like I was completely crazy and undergoing a psychotic episode. "What are you talking about?" he asked, genuinely puzzled.

"The *termination* of Philo, his murder!"

He looked shocked. "Philo wasn't murdered," he said. His show was cancelled. And it was terminated right when his ratings were peaking. I guess having the number one show in all of inhabited space cancelled right before the biggest episode of the season—I can see how that could feel like a murder."

"His show?" I mumbled, feeling deeply lost. "What show?"

The guy looked at me in mounting shock. His eyes suddenly looked like two flying saucers. "You don't know?" he exclaimed, not asking me but rather expressing his complete astonishment. He looked like someone who had just seen his mother turn into parakeet. He seemed to be trying to gather himself.

"Philo is not dead?" I asked, feeling greatly relieved.

"No, he is not. We have to move on," he said abruptly. His whole manner had changed. It was as if he was about to offer to sell me drugs when he just realized I was a Narc.

"So why are *you* here?" I asked, my mind still racing. "I assume you are taking great legal risks being here, just like Philo. Why take the risk for a species you do not seem to be able to look at for more than a moment without turning up your nose?"

"It is not simply for you or even for humanity," he said hurriedly. "The risks I take are taken on behalf of all sentient beings in all of the galaxies. It just so happens that the fate of all these beings is inextricably tied up with the fate of humanity."

"So what do we do now? What should I do?" I was still trying to process the revelation that our conversations were being recorded and that it was part of a show. He had even mentioned that it was the top-rated show!

"That is your second good question, and your last question too, I am sorry to say. I have very little time remaining. Here is what you can do. Turn your culture into a video game."

He was talking quickly, like a salesperson listing the advantages of the product by rote, knowing that you probably would not buy it. His voice had a singsong quality to it. I could tell he was already preparing to leave. It also seemed to me that he was trying to process the revelation that I did not know my conversations with Philo were being broadcast as a show.

"What I mean by that," he continued, "is to begin to 'play' your culture. Be *in* it but not *of* it. Above all, though, enter into it, fully enter into it. Enjoy the beer the way you and Philo did. Enjoy the music. Fight for your rights and the rights of those you do not know. But in the midst of your immersion, be able, in imagination, to flash out, to rise above."

"I've been doing that," I said, still wondering about the show. What show?

"Yes you have been doing that, and quite well, too. Keep it up. That is what you can do. Again, distance yourself from your culture even as you are immersed in it. Constantly remind yourself that the cage, like your food, your education, and your aspirations—all these are aspects of your culture. So you never actually leave your culture. You just imaginatively distance yourself from it—again, even as you are fully immersed. Trust me. Just do it. It is the way. It is what you can do."

He didn't give me a chance to say anything but glanced around quickly. It was obvious he was starting to make his exit and was going to leave very shortly.

"But what about the key?" I protested.

"What key?" he asked distracted.

"The key to the cage! I can't believe I have to remind you. That is what we have been talking about. And what about Philo? I can't tell you how thrilled I am he is not dead. When can I see him?"

He was glancing around desperately and started to stand up. "Look, I have extended my time already," he said, his eyes darting towards the door. "Here is the best I can do. Go back to the safe room tomorrow at this time. I will try to be there. Keep an eye on the parking lot outside. That is the best I can do."

"Can Philo come?"

He had already stood up. He looked down at me and said, "No. His fate is yet to be determined. You have to forget all of this. Now! Believe me, for your own safety you must forget all of it. I will do my best to be there tomorrow. No promises." He stepped away from the table, leaving me to pay the bill.

"But what about the key?"

He turned, a look of disgust on his face. "There is no key. The key idea is an image, a metaphor. Just like the cage idea is a metaphor. Imagination is the real key. In the same way you humans now *imagine* your cage, calling it not a cage but instead 'nature' or 'reality' or 'the way of the world,' so in the same way must you now *imagine* your release."

And with that pitiful clarification, he was gone.

CHAPTER 68

PHILO IS INDEED TERMINATED

I was really glad Philo had not been murdered. But as far as his show having been suddenly terminated—what was that about? What show? And then, after all of this, to have someone who knew all about Philo tell me straight up that there is no actual key and that in order to become free of my cage all I have to do is to begin to imagine being free—what is that about?

None of this made a whole lot of sense. For my part, I was exhaustively frustrated, with my analytical mind spinning in repetitive circles trying to make sense of all of this. I kept compulsively spinning out theories—maybe the show was this, maybe it was that.

My current guess was that it was some sort of intergalactic travel show. I kept thinking that if video cameras had been available in the cowboy days of the Wild West, we would have lots of film of shootouts and bar fights. Maybe Earth is a sort of intergalactic Wild West and Philo brought a camera crew and production team here to film the action. But then what about me? How did I fit in? Talking to me could hardly hold the excitement of a Wild West shootout.

So just why did he film me for his show? And what was I being filmed as? To show how stupid Earthlings were? Apparently lots of aliens out there already thought that. Certainly the two different members of the crew I had spoken to in the last couple of days did. And why did he not try to enlist me in on whatever he was doing? And if there was a show, and a hugely popular one at that, why was it cancelled—and right before what would have been the most watched episode of all time? And what about the legal risks he took coming here? How could he have a most popular hit show and yet need to be so secretive, all the while worried about being exposed to his own people? Was that all acting and fake?

My mind simply could not make sense of the limited evidence that was available to it. I could make sense of this little part and I could make sense of that other little part, but I couldn't make sense of all of it together. The different parts didn't fit.

And then there was the upsetting fact Philo was gone and our conversations, by all appearances, had permanently ended. I was glad he was alive, of course, but the prospect of never seeing him again was still horrible to consider. I could easily enough tell myself that all things come to an end, it only being a matter of when, but this ending did not fit. I've been at concerts where I have thought that the timing was right when the performers finally walked off the stage and ended their performance. The audience was pleased and not at all disappointed there were no more encores. But losing Philo did not seem like this at all. It was more like the band had walked off in the middle of their set!

Indeed, even granting that Philo had not been killed, the sudden termination of this long and productive series of conversations with him felt like a death. It was not only that I was I left wanting more— more conversations, more interaction with Philo, more personal growth and mastery, more of everything—but also that this ending just did not feel right.

I am also surprised at how out of sorts I had been at what turned out to be the time of the end. The end is the most important time of any show. This is where the knockout illumination needs to be, the mega-insight, the culminating understanding! This is where I would finally put it all together, epitomizing the adventure of the liberation of humanity from its cages, when I and perhaps others would step boldly forward into something new. But to hear at the end of this adventure of liberation of humanity from its cages that that there is no key to the cages—this is not a good ending in any possible galaxy. And not only that, but also to be told at the literal end of the show by someone in obvious authority that in order to find release from our cages we humans should work on imagining we are free— this is a letdown!

Now one of the most powerful influences Philo had on me was to encourage me to reassess the cognitive significance of feelings as well as their overall importance in the scheme of things. This was not entirely new for me. I had long before learned how important feelings are. Indeed, part of the shadow side of the illuminating movement of thought associated with the European Enlightenment period of the 17th and 18th centuries is an eviscerated understanding of the place of feelings in a fully rational life. In the worldview of the new science, reality is nothing more than what physics studies. Our feelings are accordingly downgraded to the status of mere personal responses to the objective states of affairs that physics studies. As such, they lack cognitive significance and instead only flavor and color our personal perceptions of real things, telling us nothing about those real things themselves. Only the hard sciences, and especially physics, do that.

But long before meeting Philo I had learned that our feelings quite often give us important information. Even understood in this eviscerated way, as the subjective reactions of our self-in-the-world, our feelings tell us about ourselves and, for that very reason, make the attention to and study of our feeling life worthwhile. Such studious attention can reveal our hidden blocks, our secret desires, and the contours of our deepest programming. This is significant information.

Having come to understand the importance of feelings in this sense many years before I met Philo, I had plenty of practice attending to and observing my own feelings and those of others quite seriously. I had discovered that as a result of becoming sensitive to what others were feeling, I was able to communicate with them much more effectively. In this context of sensitivity, those I was communicating with generally much appreciated my understanding of their feelings. In fact, Philo and I had both instinctively relied on this empathic ability we shared as part of our work together, and I think it was my ability to do so that made our talks so productive in the first place.

But Philo also disputed the restriction of feelings to merely subjective responses. He accepted feelings as fully legitimate tools of cognition. He said that when cleansed, combined with imagination, and understood properly in context, our feelings could actually provide a sort of knowledge of the external world, revealing things about the external world that would otherwise be closed to our eyes and ears and the instruments that extend them. He even claimed that by working skillfully and patiently with our feelings we could gain a sort of access to worlds beyond our world. The idea is that when cleansed, our feelings can penetrate the realm of the higher mysteries of existence better than our instruments can. As he often put it, the universe is larger, deeper, and more enchanted than we realize.

It shocked me to hear this from him, but he was not simply asserting that the cognitive worth of our feelings is on a level with physics. He was saying that, properly cleansed and attended to, our human capacity to feel could surpass physics—and by many magnitudes.

Of course, the sort of comprehension that imagination-working-with-feelings can provide is highly interpretive. It is always and necessarily fuzzy, lacking clarity, and rarely even close to anything that smacks of certainty. With feelings it is a matter of trust—and even trust is a matter of feeling.

So given that the verifiable, empirical evidence I had available to me was strictly limited and that the few points of fact I did possess did not add up to much, I thought that I might be able to use my imagination-working-with-feelings to gain new insight—even, as Philo would put it, to gain new knowledge. It would be to put Philo's teaching to a practical test.

In that spirit, how I might be feeling right now is potentially important information. In this chaotic situation I find myself in, perhaps I could use my imagination to provide me with revelations. The question of focus then becomes how I am feeling right now?

That is the problem. I don't know! The problem is not that I don't feel anything . . . or that I feel something but don't know what it is I feel. The problem is the opposite. It is that I feel so many things that I can't pick any one feeling to work with. Not only that, but my feelings are all over the place. For every strong feeling I have, I have another one that contradicts it. And all of these many different strong feelings are flying around in me like so many angry birds fluttering in my head.

I can enter into any of these fluttering birds and have the intense feelings that characterize that particular bird. An entire world and reality emerges. For example, in the Proud Bird I am proud and pleased that I was sufficiently open in the first place to be able to have these conversations with someone claiming to be from another planet. In the Shame Bird, however, I feel stupid that I was so open to accepting unknowns that I did not push to learn more about Philo. In the Angry Bird flitting off to the right, I am furious at Philo for leading me on. In the Sorrow Bird, I suffer Philo's sudden absence and I lament that I never pressured him to give me a ride in a spaceship.

So if you had asked me how I was feeling heading to this meeting at the safe room on the basis of the hope that the new guy would be there, I would not have known how to answer. Which feeling would I give voice to, and on what basis would I choose that particular one?

I also did not have much expectancy that the new guy would be there. When it became clear to him at the end of our long conversation that I did not know a show was being filmed, he had obviously freaked out. He seemed flabbergasted that I did not know Philo had a show. What show?

Then a powerful thought hit me.

What if the show *was* our conversations?

This thought totally stunned me. It was like being slapped suddenly. There was a moment of shocked silence . . . and then a flurry of nervous questions immediately started to besiege me. What had I said? Did it make sense? Would it be considered wise? Did I embarrass Earth? Should Humanity be ashamed? What did I wear? How did I look on the show? Was my guitar playing as inspiring as I remembered? How was the sound quality? On Earth one is hard pressed to get a good sound on a live TV broadcast. How was the audio quality in a broadcast to outer space?

Then I suddenly stopped all this mental chatter as if I was being pulled over by a cop. Siren and flashing lights! Stop! Turn the radio off! The cop would saunter up and ask me what self-respecting alien could possibly find an entire series of conversations with me interesting, let alone forming the substance of the highest rated show currently in outer space? How could me playing guitar and then talking to Philo—how could this be interesting enough not only to merit having a show, but to have a show that was rated as the most popular?

I felt intimidated even to consider it.

And so my mind raced continually in circles like these. I didn't even try my distancing meditation.

Suddenly it was not too early to go to the meeting. I had decided to go early, not expecting the new guy to show up. I kept replaying those last few moments of our meeting in my mind. When he learned I did not know about the show, something snapped and it seemed like he could not get out of there fast enough. Still, I thought that by nosing around, I might be able to see something. And there always was the possibility that he would show up after all. Maybe even Philo would show.

It had all come to this. Now was the time for me to go and find out once and for all—or not find out anything at all. I kept thinking that it can't end like this. I kept hoping it would not end like this.

But there was nothing to do now but try . . . .

CHAPTER 69

IT ENDS AT THE LAUNDROMAT

It had been early afternoon, just past 1:00, when I met the mean guy the day before at the table under the stairs. As he was leaving he said he would try to be at the safe room at around the same time the next day. I couldn't wait that long, so as soon as he left I went immediately to the safe room to check to see if anyone was there.

I rode my bicycle and kept going back to check every couple of hours for the rest of that afternoon and well into the evening. The next morning I checked first thing. I rode my bike around and around, trying to look normal, keeping an eye out for anyone who might come or leave. Unfortunately, there was no one there.

I had come back at 12:30. Still no one.

It was now almost 2:00, a full hour later than he'd said he would be there. No activity.

I was deciding whether to leave. On the one hand, I wanted to be here in case someone stopped by, which I thought someone might do, even without expecting to see me. If someone did so, I did not think they would stay long, so I wanted to be sure not to miss them. But on top of that, if I left now it would mean I had accepted that the conversations were officially over. It meant that I would never learn what had happened, who Philo was, and what this show was that was cancelled.

This last item—the existence and cancelling of the show—had raised in me a painful curiosity. What was this show? It seemed like it had to be something to do with us talking. If so, was it meant to make me look like a fool? Perhaps it was meant to mock humanity, with me being exhibit A? Maybe it was a 'two mocks with one show' sort of thing, mocking both me and humanity?

Conversely, maybe the show was meant to show how worthwhile humanity is? This was certainly in harmony with what Philo was saying. He talked a lot about the mysterious worth of humanity, even going so far as to claim that humanity was the hope of the future for the entire universe! If this was what the show was about, I wondered if it succeeded. Maybe it did not succeed? But the show was apparently incredibly successful. Was the show cancelled, then, *because* it was succeeding?

Alternatively, did the cancellation have anything to do with the buyout of the planet? Was the show supporting or opposing the buyout? Presumably the show opposed the buyout. But I had spent a lot of time denigrating humanity and the state of human culture. Maybe this was serving the cause of the buyout. But that would make Philo a complete liar, a cosmic scoundrel, an enemy. This just did not feel right.

Then again, did the show even have anything to do with me? Perhaps talking to me was a diversion from the filming of Philo's show? Maybe that is what he was doing all this time, just hanging with me between episodes. Maybe the show was an alien version of a travel show.

I didn't know anything, and my leaving the safe house, no longer riding around looking for someone who was not there and almost certainly would not come, would mean that I would never know.

I desperately wanted answers to these and many other equally pressing questions.

On the other hand, as intense as my desire for answers was, I was tired of riding around in the back alley area where the safe house was. It was boring, especially since I didn't ride far from the area for fear of missing some sort of quick, pop-in-/pop-out visitor. And adding to the incentive to leave, I also had absolutely no expectation that Philo, the new guy, or anyone else from another planet would show up. So while riding around did forestall my anxiety about finally lowering the curtain on this long-running adventure, it did not seem likely that the curtain would be staying up for much longer anyway, no matter what I did. I could only ride around for so long.

I had just decided to take one more spin around when I saw someone. He had that non-descript look and had just come out of the door of the safe room carrying a box. He was walking to a non-descript car in the parking lot right next to the safe house. The car was an old Ford, I think.

I felt excited. The fact he was so completely forgettable and ordinary looking and kept his head down—this only added to the excitement. Judging from Philo and the other two aliens I had seen, this non-descript look was their go-to disguise.

I kept thinking 'this could be it' as I rode into the parking lot and up to the guy. He saw me when I was still about twenty feet away. He looked startled, way more so than he should be. If I had been a cop, I would have questioned him on that basis alone, my suspicions having been raised by how startled he was. It was a guilty sort of startle.

I straddled my bike in front of his car, feeling rapidly rising hope and excitement.

"Hi," I said, trying to sound unthreatening and undemanding. He was frozen, standing at the trunk while straining to hold the box. The way he handled the box seemed to suggest that whatever was inside was either heavy or valuable or both. He was obviously taking special care to keep it balanced while fiddling to open the trunk.

He looked alarmed, even frightened when he looked at me. He didn't say anything. Before the silence drew out too long, I spoke again.

"I was expecting to meet someone here about this time," I said. He looked blankly at me, his face not registering anything. I then had one of my sudden intuitive flashes. "I was expecting to meet someone about the show," I added.

That did the trick.

His eyes narrowed and he glared at me for a few long seconds before jerking his gaze off of me to take a nervous panoramic look all around. He looked shaken.

"Maybe you could help me?" I added.

"Didn't you get the memo?" he asked, none too kindly.

"I guess not," I said. He didn't seem to recognize me. Of course, there was no reason he would—unless he had seen the alleged show, which for all I knew either may not have existed or may not have involved me. I was hoping to get some information, so I acted like a low-risk flunky who just needed a little help.

"Idiots," he stammered. "I hate everything about this production, starting with this forsaken place and ending with the pitiful excuse for professionalism regarding the termination and departure." He paused, thinking. "That includes you," he said menacingly. But instead of questioning me to find out who I was, he returned to his complaining. "Like I told everyone before we came here, if it is a bad idea to begin with, it is going to be an even worse idea to end with. And going to a primitive planet to film is not going to add any glamour to an already bad idea."

Then he got a suspicious look on his face. "Are you production or technical?" he asked.

"Production," I said.

"Then what are you talking to me for?" he asked angrily.

I did not say anything because it felt more like he was criticizing me than questioning me.

"Oh, don't worry," he said after a moment in a more conciliatory tone. "It doesn't matter anymore anyway. Protocol has been busted so many times on this show already that I don't even know if they are even counting any more. This whole thing has been and obviously still is"—he glared right at me when he said this—"one long sorry joke. You production people are the punch line of this joke, and I don't mean the kind of joke that makes you laugh."

Seeing his anger, I decided to go for broke. "I was hoping to see Philo," I said.

I could tell immediately that mentioning Philo was a mistake. His face narrowed into concern and then fear, and he glanced nervously around again. "Hey, easy now," he said. "Protocol may be busted, but it's not anything goes. We still have to wrap up and get out of here." He glared at me. I must have looked suitably chastened because his look once again softened.

"This has been hard on all of us," he continued. "But don't worry. Even though I should, I won't be reporting you. We've got enough to worry about now that the termination is official. Let's just get off this gloomy globe and go home." He smiled at me ever so slightly and carefully began to position himself and the box in order to be able to open the trunk safely.

I wasn't sure whether to mention Philo again. Judging from his reaction, it seemed like a bad idea.

"Did you see any of the shows?" I asked.

"Me?" he snorted. "I don't watch that junk. Then he turned to look at me, a sort of demented half-smile on his face. "Here is what I say. If I want to watch a monkey, I will go to the zoo." He started laughing, as if he had said something hilarious. "That's what I told my friends back home and that's what I'm going to tell them when I get back from this forsaken zoo of a planet."

"Any idea why it was terminated?"

"That's the question of the day, isn't it?" he replied. "Don't they tell you production guys anything? Just yesterday someone else in production asked me the same thing. I told him that as far as I was concerned, they never should have done this show in the first place. I told him the question is not why they finally cancelled the stupid show but why it took them so long to do so in the first place!"

He said this triumphantly, as if he knew more than everyone else. In doing so he reminded me of so many Americans I talk to who think they understand everything and that everyone else is stupid.

"Try that one on for size," he said, almost as if he was taunting me.

"Why do *you* think the show was terminated?" I asked.

"How would I know? I never even watched the stupid thing."

"What is your best guess?"

"I'm not much for guessing," he said. "But if you were pushing me and I had to say something, I would say that that damn talking machine—I'm not going to risk saying his name—made the monkeys look too good. Why did they let him do that? Why even waste time with these stupid primitives? Who cares what they think or do or discover?" He shook his head in despair at all those who did not share his understanding. "Sometimes people making decisions can be too damn clever for their own good."

He had gotten the trunk open and was carefully placing the box in it. "This office is now officially closed. In fact, there can't be many of us left on this zoo. I heard some troopers were here, but I haven't seen them. I can't wait to get this ugly disguise off." He looked at me a little more kindly. "It won't be long now for either of us," he said, including me in the upcoming exodus. He moved around to the car door.

"You know where to report? Need a ride?"

"Nah," I said, making an effort to sound nonchalant. "I'm fine. I just thought you might know something about the termination. You're right," I added, "they don't tell us anything."

"Why would they?" he scoffed. "You production guys are always a danger to go native. Take you, for example. I hate this disguise, but you look like you could have been born and bred in it. Even the monkeys would accept you as a monkey." He then looked sharply at me. "You better watch out you don't start thinking like one. I hear if you wear the disguise long enough, the monkey ladies start to look real good." He laughed at what struck him as his own fine wit and great humor. Then he suddenly looked concerned. "Any of you guys get busted?" he asked.

"Not that I know of," I replied.

He shook his head in sorrow. "I guess it is only Mr. Talk-all-day. I wouldn't' want to be in his shoes right now."

That was Philo he was talking about, I was sure. "What do you think will happen to him?"

"Who knows? He can always say he didn't know. He will probably claim he was just being a show host, doing his job. He has quite a following, you know. I never got it myself. His other shows may have been stupid, but they weren't like this. This was something different. I think he might be in real trouble, but what do I know."

"What sort of trouble?"

He laughed without humor. "Are you just pretending to be stupid or are you doing a brilliant monkey imitation? You're not going native are you?"

I laughed a few chuckles trying to humor him. "Not me."

"You want to hear something completely unbelievable. I heard that this show was the highest rated ever when it was terminated! Can you believe that? What is happening to us? Talk about the decline in standards. My father would have been ashamed."

I shook my head in feigned dismay, as if the popularity of this mysterious show, whatever it was, was the most damning possible indictment against intergalactic civilization.

"This place may be a pit, but things are going downhill fast back home. I even heard that the final episode, the one they terminated, would have been the most watched show ever in all of history. Can you believe that! What is going on? This stupid, sorry excuse for a show gets scheduled, and then, contrary to everyone's expectation, it not only becomes popular but actually becomes the most popular show on the entire intergalactic network. Then, hours before the final episode, the one that would have set viewer records as the most watched show ever, they cancel. It doesn't make sense. It is like spending all your money on a lottery ticket with almost no chance to win, and then when you do win, you throw the ticket away."

"It doesn't add up," I added, hoping to egg him on.

"But the people who watched the show," he said, his lips twisting to an expression of revulsion. "Why don't they just go to a zoo?" He laughed again, thinking he had said something funny.

"Maybe they liked his guest?" I said, hoping to prod him for more information.

"Well, I did hear the primitive he talked to was pretty clever. Played some of that awful noise they call music here as well. Imagine being that guy. Here he is, a top intergalactic star. He could clean up. He could get hired anywhere. People would pay big bucks to hear him talk and make that dreadful noise. He could have anything he wanted, living at the absolute peak of luxury." He started chuckling again. "But the best part is that he knows nothing about this and will not be able to cash in. Not for anything."

He looked around nervously again and closed the trunk. "I hear he is pretty much a nobody here. How about that, one of the richest people in the universe, but poor on his own planet and not able to cash in on any of his fame or fortune."

I shook my head, feigning shock but not saying anything. He continued, "But who cares about him. What gets me is that this was the highest rated show. What is that about?"

"What do you think?"

He chuckled and shook his head. "That's way above my pay grade. Just more evidence of corruption, that's what I say." He opened the door. "You sure you don't need a ride?"

"No, I'm good."

"Maybe. But right now you don't look so good. In fact, you look downright ugly. Ugly like a monkey." He laughed a rollicking laugh at his wit as he took his seat. He put the car in gear and pulled forward a few feet and then stopped right next to me, winding down the window to say, "Be sure you make your departure. I heard they aren't waiting."

"Thanks. I will."

"I just hope they don't get nasty with us," he said reflectively. "Hell, I was just doing my job. I hate these animals as much as anyone."

And with that he drove off.

It was the last I heard.

For more information, visit: www.johnbardi.com

www.ingramcontent.com/pod-product-compliance
Lightning Source LLC
Chambersburg PA
CBHW071219250626

47163CB00001B/44